NEYUKI

根雪

also by M. Harmon Wilkinson

Under Shōko's Bed

NEYUKI

根雪

M. Harmon Wilkinson

Content Warning

This novel depicts emotional, physical, and sexual abuse and violence as well as suicide.

Cover Design by Laura Duffy
Interior Design by Marny K. Parkin

Published by M. Harmon Wilkinson
www.mharmonwilkinson.com

ISBN 978-1-954362-04-8 (Hardcover)
ISBN 978-1-954362-05-5 (Paperback)
ISBN 978-1-954362-06-2 (Ebook)
ISBN 978-1-954362-07-9 (Audiobook)

For Wallis, Maurine, Clifton, and Vera:
patient, inspiring,
and valiant in the face of frostbite

Japanese
Content and Pronunciation

Translations of all Japanese words and phrases are given in a glossary after the main text. Units of measure (metric or US customary) depend on the point of view. English place-names are used if they are common (e.g., "Tokyo" rather than the Romanized Japanese "Tōkyō").

Basic Japanese pronunciation is relatively simple. There are five vowel sounds: *a*—f*a*ther, *i*—*ea*t, *u*—m*oo*n, *e*—b*e*d, *o*—al*o*ne. A line over a vowel merely lengthens the time it is held (e.g., the *ō* in Jirō is held about twice as long as the *o* in Chieko). The Japanese *r* has no English equivalent but is somewhere between *d* and *r*. It is similar to a Spanish *r* but without the trill. Finally, all syllables receive the same emphasis (i.e., no accented syllables).

Dialogue of characters speaking Japanese here occasionally includes the word "Sir." One would rarely use such a term in Japanese, but it expresses the same feeling as humble and honorific verb forms in the Japanese language that have no English equivalent, as well as other sometimes subtle differences in word choice that reflect the speaker's rank or position relative to the listener.

Named Characters

The Grames Family

William "Will"	Associate Professor of Marketing
Laurie	Wife of Will Grames
Sarah	Age 12
Rebekah "Becka"	Age 7
Rachel	Age 4

Japan Graduate University of International Studies (JGU) Faculty/Staff

Baig, Syed	Assistant Professor of IT
Charles, Daniel "Danny"	Assistant Professor of English
Cook, Anson	Assistant Professor of Finance
Ikenami, Kiyoshi	Professor of Accounting
Itō, Makoto	Manager, IT Services
King, Stephen "Steve"	Associate Professor of IT
Malik, Teddy	Professor of IT
Matsuyama, Chieko	Assistant to Dean Yoshida
Peregrine, David	Professor of Law
Satō, Shinichi	President of JGU

Watanabe, Jirō   Assistant Professor of Accounting

Yoshida, Junichirō   Dean of JGU

Yuriko   Assistant to President Satō

JGU Students

Brian   Student from Canada

Nguyen, Huong (VietKitten)   Student from Vietnam

Nguyen, Trinh (VietGoddess)   Student from Vietnam

Police

Hasegawa, Yūji   Detective

Kurimoto, Yoshie   Translator and IT Specialist

Ogawa   Forensic Specialist

Others

Cook, Miho   Wife of Anson Cook

FairladyZ2006 (Z06)   Subscriber

Ikenami, Yōko   Wife of Kiyoshi Ikenami

King, Rumi   Wife of Steve King

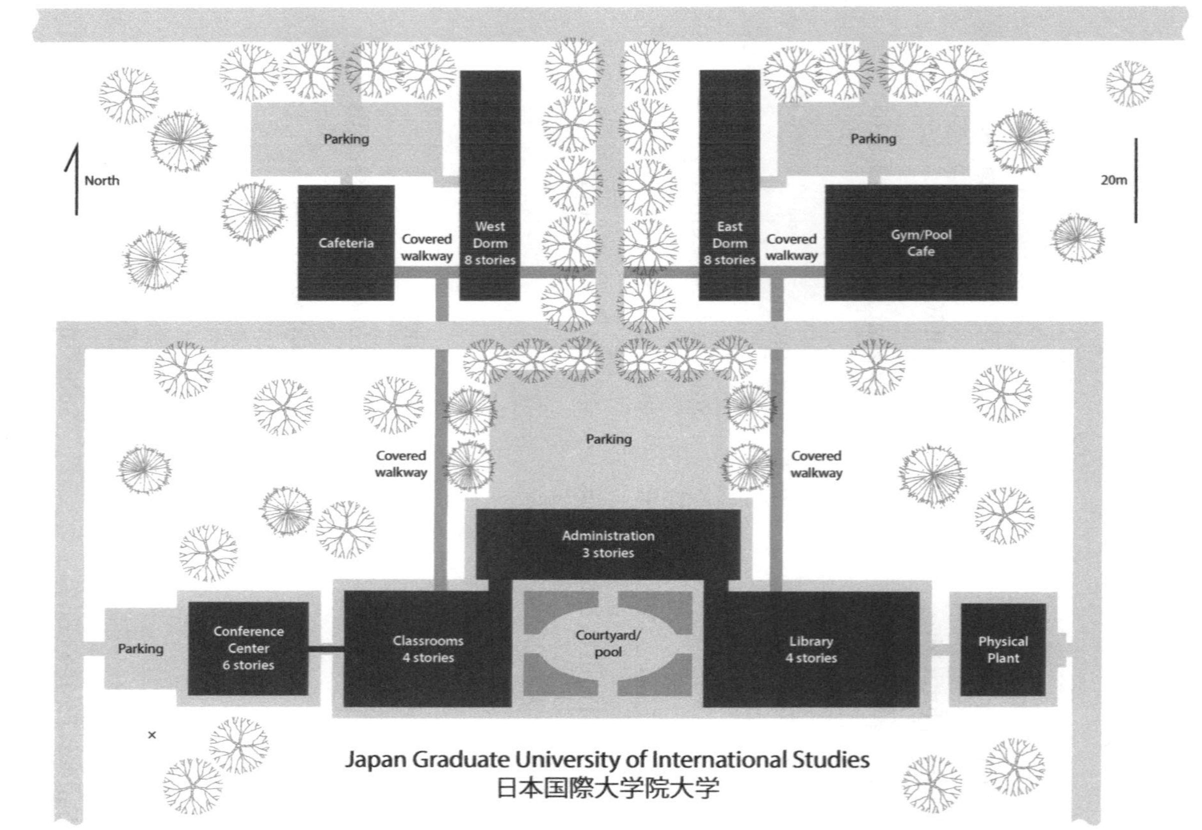

North
Parking
Parking
20m
Cafeteria
Covered
walkway
West
Dorm
8 stories
East
Dorm
8 stories
Covered
walkway
Gym/Pool
Cafe
Parking
Covered
walkway
Covered
walkway
Administration
3 stories
Parking
Conference
Center
6 stories
Classrooms
4 stories
Courtyard/
pool
Library
4 stories
Physical
Plant
Japan Graduate University of International Studies
日本国際大学院大学

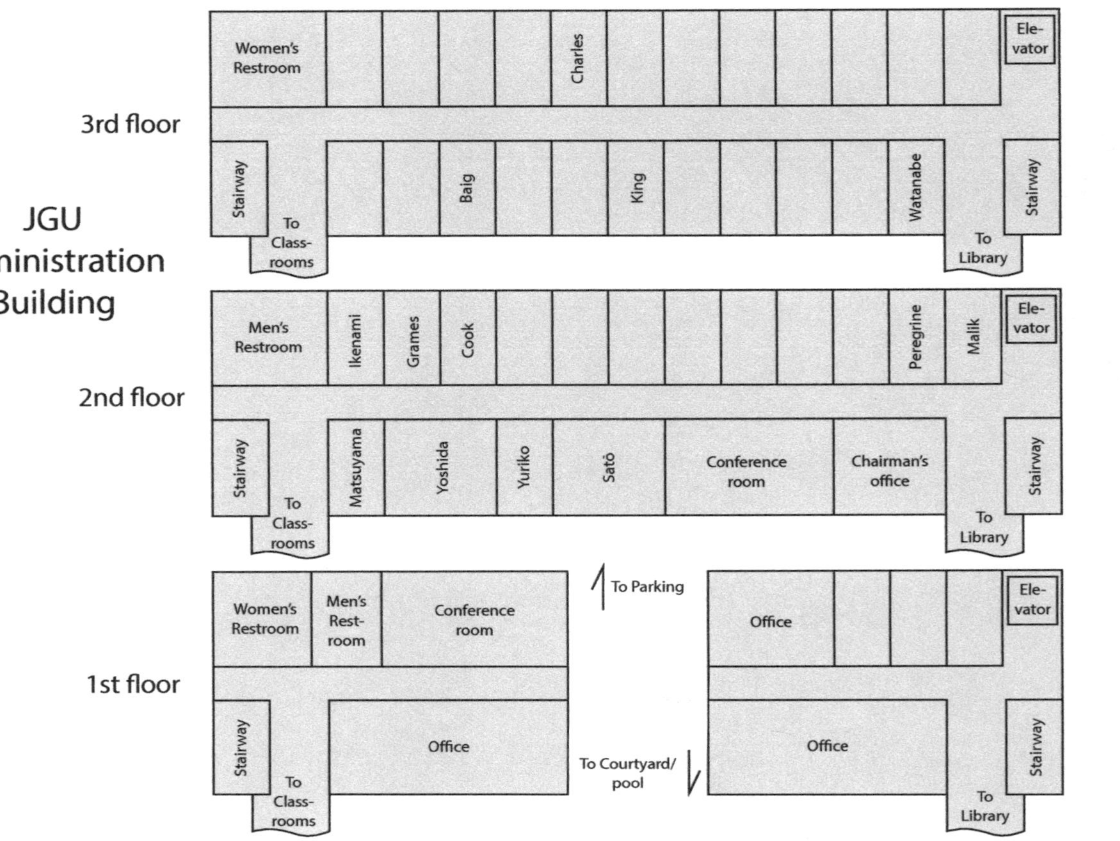

JGU
Administration
Building

3rd floor

Women's Restroom
Charles
Elevator
Stairway
Baig
King
Watanabe
To Classrooms
To Library
Stairway

2nd floor

Men's Restroom
Ikenami
Grames
Cook
Peregrine
Malik
Elevator
Stairway
Matsuyama
Yoshida
Yuriko
Satō
Conference room
Chairman's office
To Classrooms
To Library
Stairway

1st floor

Women's Restroom
Men's Restroom
Conference room
Office
Elevator
To Parking
Stairway
To Classrooms
Office
To Courtyard/ pool
Office
To Library
Stairway

Prologue: Due Diligence
前説：企業精査

Wednesday, 23 December 2009

1

CHRISTMAS WAS TWO DAYS AWAY, AND PROF. WILL Grames's students should've thought of him as Santa Claus. After all, if they did the work, even badly, he passed them, despite this being graduate school. He never actually told them that, though. And Will, tall, fit, and clean-shaven, was hardly the image of Santa. That was set in stone by Haddon "Sunny" Sundblom, who painted Santa Claus, commonly with a Coke, for thirty-three years starting in 1931 for his sponsor, Coca-Cola. It's said Santa wears a red and white suit today because those are the colors Sundblom used, Coca-Cola's colors. Will had hundreds of such stories, but the students would get none today.

Will strode down the starkly unadorned hallway toward his classroom as dull morning light streamed through a great wall of glass. Would his students see him today as the Grim Reaper, bearer of the final exam they were dreading? Will was a decent guy, though. He treated the students as he'd like to be treated, genially and with respect and a little leniency. He loved his wife and kids and showed it. He even did platelet donations every week before they moved to Japan. So why did the echoing footsteps on the well worn but polished linoleum sound like a mausoleum?

Will passed Prof. Kiyoshi Ikenami, and he addressed his senior colleague with a pleasant smile. *"Konnichi wa."*

In response, the man did not so much as acknowledge Will's existence. Will hadn't gotten the greeting wrong; Ikenami was simply cantankerous and rude to almost everyone, especially foreigners. Will was used to his slights—although blithely taking no offense was also Will's way of returning it. It was disconcerting in a university this small. With only three dozen faculty, few of them senior, Ikenami's frostiness chilled the friendly atmosphere the university had promised. At least Ikenami, Professor of Accounting, was not someone Will, Associate Professor of Marketing, had to work with daily.

The last of the students took their seats when Will entered the classroom, which smelled of chalk. Although the university had long intended to switch to whiteboards, it never happened. Will didn't mind. He'd never cared for the odor of whiteboard markers. There was a long row of windows on one wall. A large oak tree, naked of leaves, hosted a murder of crows—an ill omen for the exam?

Will greeted the thirteen students warmly, then said, "There are only six essay questions. I don't need long answers, just good ones. You have ninety minutes, fifteen minutes a question. A good, concise answer should take five. Also, there are no computations required, so no price elasticities to calculate. Remember I'll be grading your ideas, not your English."

Will handed out the exams, then quietly answered questions. As the students knuckled down to write, Will realized he'd brought nothing to do. He flipped his phone open, wishing he could call his wife, Laurie, and pass some of the time with her. That wouldn't distract the students at all, would it?

He snapped the phone closed. As if startled by it, the birds took flight—all but one. Will eyed the lone crow glaring stubbornly at him. It suited the monochromatic scene: the meadow grasses drained of color, the bare tree limbs, and the sky heavy with lowering clouds.

Was it a mistake to move to Japan for a job at a school that might not survive? Rumors said a spring shutdown was coming. He'd dragged his family along with the promise of a three-year adventure. Laurie never complained, but that could just be her pioneer spirit. And even if the school kept limping along, what if his research didn't pan out? He wouldn't be able to get back to a decent school in the US. They could end up stuck here.

No, be positive, he told himself. Everything'll be fine.

He blew a deep breath out slowly as his attention returned to the students. Some professors might read a book, but he felt a duty to at least appear vigilant. Still, Will was beyond bored. He even looked for anagrams in the course's name. ("Cratering pigsty" and "gyrating triceps" were the best he came up with.) At length, he noticed his beady-eyed spectator again. Had it been there this whole time?

I guess even the birds are at loose ends. Are Japanese and American crows the same? I could check if I had my computer.

Will looked at his watch: four minutes left. No one had finished early, a bad sign. Still, they'd be all right; they'd done the work.

The students turned in their exams. A few offered Will thanks or well wishes, but most looked drained and dour. He'd tried to make the exam easy, but somehow, he always missed the mark. Anyway, it was over. Will gathered the papers, wished them a fun New Year's break, then turned off the lights and headed for his office.

He passed Ikenami in the hallway again. Will merely bowed his head this time, still a polite gesture. Ikenami ignored him. Why did he flout everything his mother must've drilled into him about politeness? He'd driven away multiple junior accounting professors. With the university this weak, it wasn't as if there was an endless supply.

Will tossed the exams onto his desk. He wanted to go home, but a diligent professor would grade them. He checked his watch: 12:16 p.m. It would only take a couple of hours.

There was a knock on Will's door, and he called out, "*Dōzo.*"

David Peregrine, Will's closest friend on the faculty, opened the door. "Hey, what's up?"

"Just finished my Pricing exam. They did not look pleased."

"Exams are almost done. Then it'll be the break, and all will be forgotten."

"Now there's grading. I hate that."

"Shouldn't take long. Come get lunch first," said David.

"I think I'll burn through this and head home early. Still planning on dinner at our place tonight?"

"Been looking forward to it all week."

2

T HE SUNSET WAS HAZY AND LEADEN, BUT IT WAS TOO COLD for anyone to be outside paying attention, so Will doubted anyone was disappointed by it. As dusk fell, he was in the *genkan* refilling the tank for the kitchen's kerosene heater.

Laurie joined him in the entryway. "Don't you hate how early the sun sets?"

Will shrugged. "What I really mind is that only two rooms in the house are heated and we have to sleep with electric blankets. I mind cracks in the walls you can see daylight through. I'm surprised we can't feel the breeze inside. For me, the long nights are simply part of winter. I know it's hard on you. We could get a sun lamp to fight off Seasonal Affective Disorder."

"No, I always get through it. And we knew what we were getting when we signed a lease this cheap. But I am looking forward to spring sunshine. We just passed the solstice. The days are getting longer."

"Yeah, but it's a sine wave. In the troughs, things change so gradually it's hard to notice."

"That mathematical brain of yours."

He shrugged again.

"What time's David coming over?"

"I told him six thirty. He'll be punctual. It's Japan, after all."

"He's American like us, though," said Laurie. "Hey, what do we do about ski boots for the girls for Christmas?"

"Cards under the tree? We can take them shopping in the afternoon."

"That's so odd, shopping on Christmas day."

"Simply another day here," said Will.

"Seems like there ought to be more joy."

~

AFTER DINNER, AS LAURIE GOT THE GIRLS SETTLED WITH blankets to watch television in the living room, Will and David talked in the warm kitchen.

"Wait, you're going on vacation *with someone*?" asked Will. "Have I met this someone?"

"If you had, I'd be all the less likely to tell you."

"Why? What girlfriend did I ever scare off?"

"None, but you've never had a chance, so any non-frightening streak is inconsequential."

Laurie came in. "What are you two talking about?"

"David has a girlfriend, but he won't say who."

Laurie rolled her eyes. "What are you, eight years old or something? Is this a 'serious' girlfriend or merely a 'having fun' girlfriend?"

David smiled. "She's a 'having serious fun' girlfriend."

"They're going off on vacation together."

"Where to?" asked Laurie.

"See, Will? That's a normal question. Can't you just live with the mystery?"

"So, where?" asked Laurie again.

"Skiing at Myōkōkōgen."

"They have snow?"

"Enough for the resort to open. Even if the skiing isn't very good, the *onsen* will be the stuff of memories. I love hot springs."

Will wondered aloud, "Do you think it'll snow here by Christmas?"

Laurie sat. "It waited till New Year's last winter. I'd like to ski before winter term starts."

"One big storm would do it," said Will.

"The girls want the snow, I bet," said David.

Will winced. "I'm not looking forward to shoveling three feet of it. It was that much almost every time last year."

"What else are you doing over the break?" asked Laurie. "It's almost three weeks."

David looked uncertain. "Projects around the house have been waiting."

Will poured himself another cup of juice. "I won't be seeing you around the university?"

"Not if I can help it. It just sucks the life out of you. It wasn't this way even last year. The place might not have been vibrant, but at least it had upside potential."

"Makes me wonder if I'd still have come."

"You mean if you'd done your due diligence before you signed on?"

Will raised an eyebrow at David's little dig. "I can't believe how many sponsoring companies headed for the hills since the founder died. It's only been what, six months?"

Laurie looked worried. "You think you'll have jobs next year?"

"Oh, sure," said Will with no conviction. "But I'm not optimistic about getting my contract renewed."

David scowled. "You have a better chance than me."

"How come?" asked Laurie.

"Will's in marketing, a core subject. How many business programs keep a law professor on the faculty? As they slim down, I'll be the first one they cut loose. Just when I finally learned to say the Japanese name of the university, Nihon Kokusai Daigakuin Daigaku."

Laurie chuckled. "Japan Graduate University of International Studies is an awfully long name for such a tiny school."

Will smiled. "JGU fits it all right. Anyway, some sponsors are still with us. We may pull this out."

"If the dean can find us companies where we can do executive teaching. But the president is so jealous, he hobbles him at every turn," said David.

Laurie knitted her brow. "Why do you need a dean and a president?"

"The university was supposed to grow to several schools," David said. "Each would have a dean, and the president would oversee the entire university. But things never got that far, and now they never will."

3

STORY TIME WAS FINISHED, THE GIRLS WERE TUCKED IN, and Will and Laurie were dealing with a conundrum. "No, Rachel, Santa isn't Jesus," Will patiently told their four-year-old daughter.

"Then how does he know what I want? Are Santa and Jesus friends, so Jesus tells him?"

Will knelt on her *futon.* "Santa knows because we tell him."

Rachel's eyes opened wide. "You know Santa?"

"Well, not personally. We write him letters for you."

"What do you say to him?"

He brushed the hair off of her face. "We say thank you for the wonderful toys, and we ask for more stuff."

"Does he ever say no?"

Laurie was suppressing a smile, but Will was serious. "Only if you're bad."

"How does he know that?"

"We have to tell him."

"Please don't tell him I ate the little purple grandma's cookies."

Will glanced at Laurie and asked Rachel, "Instead of taking them to her?"

"She wasn't home."

"Ah. Are you sorry?"

"Uh-huh."

"Okay, we'll tell Santa." Will double-checked that Rachel's electric blanket was on and tucked her in a little more snugly.

"How old is Santa? Becka says he's so old he's gonna die soon. Maybe even before Christmas."

Laurie frowned. Will said, "He is very old, but he's feeling fine. Don't you worry about him."

"I don't want him to die."

"He won't."

"Should I pray for him?"

Will nodded. "Sure. Pray about anything that worries you."

"'Kay."

"Go to sleep now."

"I didn't say my prayers yet."

"Okay, Mommy will help you."

"I like it when you help me."

"How come?"

"Mommy prays too long."

Laurie frowned again. Will said, "She'll keep it short tonight."

"'Kay."

He kissed Rachel good night and headed downstairs to the kitchen. Laurie soon joined him. She shivered as she entered the warm room, and Will stood to give her a hug. He said, "I'm a little concerned that Rachel lied about those cookies for the neighbor."

"Really? I knew she ate them. I pressed her a few times. I was sure she'd crack. Lies always come out in the end. What about you, though?"

"What do you mean?"

"Talking about writing Santa letters, all sincere."

"Santa lies aren't real lies."

She shrugged. "Maybe not."

"You've told Santa tales yourself."

"She still couldn't tell Santa and Jesus apart. Good heavens, Will."

"She's four. She remembered her prayers. Let her be a kid. We won't have her like this for long, so innocent. Or Sarah and Becka."

"I need to have a chat with Becka. Can you believe she told Rachel Santa's about to die?"

"Poor Santa. He's been so old for so long."

Laurie smiled. "Hale and hearty. Never sick a day in his life."

"Yeah, but how much of that might be the elves coping for him? The reindeer could be covering, too, and Santa can't really find his way around anymore."

"Reindeer are that clued in?"

"That Rudolph's an opportunistic sort. Would stop at nothing to stay in front."

Laurie smiled. "People aren't exactly who they seem to be on the outside, are they?"

"Reindeer either, I guess."

Friday, Christmas Day, 2009

4

Laurie and Will were taking a frigid evening walk. She sighed. "I talked to Mom online this morning. She told me her brother nearly died of an opioid overdose."

Will stopped walking. "How do people get themselves in so deep? I always thought he had it together."

"Except for this. He's in rehab now."

"I hope he kicks it."

"I'm glad we realize how dangerous they are. That'd never happen to us."

"Don't count your blessings before they hatch."

"That's chickens, and you're cute."

Will smiled.

"Nothing like that would ever happen here in Nagano-ken. It's as if there's no crime, no meanness, no cause to think you'll ever be sad. It's a bucolic little town, isn't it?"

Will gave a wry smile. "That sounds awful, somehow. I mean, it has the word 'colic' right in it."

"You have a truly twisted view of the world."

"I try. Maybe I'll get lucky."

She was quiet for a few seconds. "You meant that double entendre, didn't you?"

He shrugged.

She laughed. "Come on, if you're going to proposition me, at least own it."

"Okay, I meant nothing sexual, but once you brought it up, I was on board."

"If we try before bedtime, you can bet we'll be interrupted."

"Why can't kids let their parents fondle each other in peace?"

"We should just take a drive," said Laurie.

"Ooh, we haven't done it in the car in years. Why do you suppose that is?"

"Uncomfortable?"

"If you're in anything short of a teenage state of arousal." Will turned back toward the house. "Of course, now we have kids and drive a minivan. Changes how things can be done."

"You want to pretend you're a teenager?"

"Leave our three kids at home and go lose twenty years? Do I get to have no idea what I'm doing?"

Laurie laughed. "Only if I do too."

"Keys are in my pocket. What could go wrong?"

"I'll tell the kids we're off to the store. After all, if we don't know what we're doing, this won't take long."

Will started the van as Laurie disappeared into the house.

She returned a few minutes later, Rachel in tow. Laurie buckled their youngest child into her car seat and joined Will in the front.

"Change of plans?" asked Will, trying not to sound resentful. At the same time, guilt pressed on him at his reaction to spending this time with his little one.

Laurie looked apologetic. "She really wanted to go to the store."

THEY WERE HALFWAY TO THE SUPERMARKET, DRIVING PAST long-harvested rice fields, when they topped a gentle rise and saw a police car waiting. Will was barely speeding, but Laurie was rattled by his reaction. "Oh no no no." He braked hard.

"What? You're okay. It's only a police car. You weren't going that fast."

"I don't have to be speeding. They could pull me over just because they feel like it."

"Could, but they're not going to."

Will slowed more as they approached the police car. Laurie furrowed her brow. "You don't need to slow down so much. Everything's fine."

Will stared at the black-and-white car, hands white-knuckled on the steering wheel. Laurie noticed he wasn't breathing. "Hey, take a breath. You look like you're panicking."

Will forced himself to inhale, but it looked shallow.

"You realize it's an irrational fear. We've talked about this."

"It doesn't matter whether it's rational; it's not going away," said Will breathlessly.

"Those warnings about Japanese police from your dad when you were a kid?"

"Most likely."

Rachel asked, "Is Daddy okay?"

They passed the car, and the officer seemed to give them no notice.

"Yes, kiddo, Daddy's fine." Laurie quietly asked, "Right?"

"Yeah." Will shook one hand and then the other, still struggling to breathe.

"Do we need to switch and me drive?"

"Damn," said Will under his breath, his hands still strangling the wheel.

"Pull over. Let me drive."

Will blew out his breath, ragged and slow. "No, I'm okay."

Laurie put her hand on his leg and whispered, "No, Will, if seeing the cops does this to you, you're not."

"Okay, you're right. Maybe you should drive."

I

Bounded Rationality
限定合理性

Sunday, 10 January 2010

5

WINTER TERM WOULD START TUESDAY, AS MONDAY WAS A holiday to honor the birthday of the university's late founder. Will wanted to be ready, so he went in on Sunday to make sure his syllabus and first lecture were in order. He also hoped to make a little progress on a research project that had mostly languished over the New Year's break, just like everything else. It hadn't snowed, so he and Laurie hadn't been able to take the girls skiing with their new boots. He wondered where the time had gone.

Will stepped out for a walk around the courtyard between the three buildings at the center of JGU. The short trip to get a cup of coffee would be a good chance to stretch his legs. As he walked into the stairwell, he saw Professor Ikenami lumbering up toward him, and offered a simple, "*Konnichi wa.*" Ikenami didn't respond, but as he was taking up most of the space on the stairs, Will waited for him to complete his climb. Ikenami reached the second-floor landing but continued to stand in Will's way, catching his breath.

At length, Ikenami said, "You got email. I chair Cook's review and you are on committee. Review is done. We do not renew contract."

JGU had no tenure system for faculty. Everyone was on contract, generally for three years. It took Will a moment to realize what the man had said. As he was about to respond, Ikenami turned toward the opening to the stairwell.

Will could have let it pass. Ikenami lacked the authority to decide on Prof. Anson Cook's contract renewal. Besides, Anson was the best rookie JGU had ever hired. But Will, who so often chose discretion, took a rash step into Ikenami's path. "You know that's for the dean and president to decide. We only advise. We owe Anson an objective review."

His point made, Will was ready to head downstairs. But before he could move, Ikenami elbowed him hard in the chest to push past.

Will staggered back. Anger flashed across his face. His hand closed into a fist.

Ikenami shrank back in alarm, arms over his face.

As he stepped back to dodge a punch Will would never have thrown, his foot strayed over the landing's edge.

Ikenami teetered, eyes wide and arms flailing in great circles like a cartoon character. But Will didn't smile, for terror gripped Ikenami's face as he began to fall.

Gravity had him.

Ikenami bounced and rolled like a great sack of potatoes down the stairs.

Will stood frozen, staring at Ikenami laid out awkwardly on the landing between the first and second floors.

He recovered his wits and was about to run down to help, but Ikenami sat up and glared at him, looking ready to charge up the stairs and attack.

Peeved as Will was, he wasn't about to trade blows, so he abandoned the stairway and hurried into the connected classroom building.

He stopped midway down the hallway and looked back. Ikenami was seething at him from the top of the stairs but did not look injured, so Will walked on as Ikenami spewed threats that echoed down the hallway.

To walk it off, Will took an especially long stroll that ended with a leisurely coffee at the university café. He hoped that when he got back to his office, Ikenami would be gone, but his door was ajar. Odd.

Guilty and chagrined but still irked, Will slipped into his own office.

~

TRY AS HE MIGHT, WILL ACCOMPLISHED LITTLE FOR THE NEXT four hours. His mind kept going back to the quarrel. Being tired was part of it. So was his usual unease at the start of a new academic term, two days away. Still, he felt guilty.

Ikenami, what a blowhard. He was the self-styled rock of JGU's academic reputation. He had provided data for a paper that turned into a major hit. Someone at the University of Michigan did all the work, but the letter *I* came first alphabetically among the minor contributors, so Ikenami ended up as the second author. The notoriety had made him insufferable.

Now Ikenami wanted to lord it over Anson and not renew his contract. Worse than unfair, it was probably xenophobic. Why was someone who despised foreigners working at an international university?

An apology, though . . .

Damn his conscience, but if he had to eat crow, it was time to get it over with and be able to work undistracted.

Will walked out into the hallway. Ikenami's office was next door—and his door was still ajar; unusual, because the doors had automatic closers and only stayed cracked if you purposely stopped them from latching. Will knocked.

There was no reply. He knocked again. Still no response.

He nudged the door open with a polite, "*Gomen kudasai*"—only to find Ikenami collapsed on the floor.

Will immediately knelt by Ikenami and put his fingers to the man's neck. No pulse. He pressed his ear to Ikenami's chest. No heartbeat.

Dead? From what, a slow brain bleed?

Should Will do chest compressions and call for an ambulance?

He held his trembling fingers to Ikenami's neck again.

That fall *killed* him?

Will stood and looked at the body, his hands balled into fists, as white-knuckled as they'd been on the steering wheel when he saw the cops two weeks ago. Chest compressions would make no difference.

Neither would an ambulance. The man's eyes were wide open, staring up at the lights, pupils dilated. His skin was cyanotic and cool. Ikenami was dead.

And Will's life was over.

WILL PINCHED THE DEADBOLT KNOB, TRYING TO STEADY HIS fingers. He turned it and felt it slide to. With the world locked out, he switched off Ikenami's lights and leaned his head against the wall of the frigid office. He listened. No footsteps, no voices, no sound at all.

I should call someone.

He slipped his hand into his pocket for his phone.

No, I should run.

As Will turned back toward Ikenami's corpse, a sodium lamp shining through the window from the parking lot made him squint.

He imagined a police car driving up the long, narrow road into the university, red lights flashing. They'd escort him to the car, and when that door slammed shut, he'd be finished. He'd confess. When it mattered, he always did the right thing.

So why was JGU's prize accounting professor cooling on the linoleum?

Will pounded the wall with his fist.

Prison . . . for murder . . .

Will's father had been a consular official in Tokyo when Will was young. He warned Will as a teenager to never risk arrest. The horror stories of foreigners accused of minor crimes had left Will terrified of the Japanese police ever since. The conviction rate is ninety-nine percent. They could hold him for weeks, maybe months, interrogating him without a lawyer, grinding him down until he confessed. He'd never read of a crime in Japan where the suspect didn't confess.

He imagined Laurie as a single mother, struggling to get back into urban planning, raising their girls alone . . .

Will stared at the rotund body splayed out before the desk like a frog awaiting dissection. Although compelled to check again for a pulse, he didn't. He could hardly bring Ikenami back to life by pressing on his neck one more time. Ikenami was still wearing his coat, as if he climbed back up the stairs, walked up the hall, entered his office, clicked on the lights, and toppled over like a big, puffy domino.

I just came to apologize! It was his own fault he fell. I never touched him.

So what, they'll only charge me with involuntary manslaughter?

Again, decency and common sense urged him to dial 110.

Or was it 119? Which brought the police and which an ambulance?

It was a corpse. Either would do.

And after that? The police would delve into everything to explain Ikenami's bruises. There were none on his face, but there must have been huge ones on his body. Fresh bruises would point to violence, violence to murder, and if anyone heard the altercation, they'd point the police to Will.

I have a PhD from Columbia. I can solve a simple problem like this.

Although he tried to escape into the cool, rational, academic part of his brain, yet another vision of police cars was all he could muster. He pressed his palms to his temples.

He could leave and forget it. But Ikenami had shouted his parting invective down the hall after Will. "How dare you attack me! You will regret this, Grames! You will pay!" Just because no one was gawking in the hallway did not mean no one heard.

Someone recounts the argument, the bruises are evidence, and I disappear.

The cold logician in Will finally offered: unless Ikenami went home and died there.

Died at home, bruises all over his body?

Unless . . . there was no body.

Will looked at Ikenami. How . . . ?

No! That's heinous!

To dispose of the remains would be pure evil, yes, but to move them . . .

What? Impure evil?

Maybe. But if they found Ikenami someplace else, no conclusive evidence would link the fall to his death. It couldn't have been serious if Ikenami was well enough to drive away.

Why didn't he get there?

Because he didn't go home. He went . . . to that new Italian restaurant.

Why didn't he get there?

Will pondered, hoping for something, anything, but nothing came.

He didn't, that's all.

A medical examiner could determine when he expired. He'd stick a probe in Ikenami's liver like a meat thermometer and calculate the time of death in his head. That would place Ikenami here, not in town hours later.

Unless the body reached ambient temperature.

In January, it wouldn't decompose. If they discovered it, not tonight, but tomorrow or the next day, they'd never know when he passed.

Will almost smiled at his cunning—

No, it's not smart, it's perverse.

But it's better than prison.

He stared, paralyzed, for a long minute.

To hide all that mass . . .

He shut his eyes but still saw the corpse in negative on his eyelids.

His heart was pounding.

Will unlocked the door and stepped into the hall to breathe. Again, he fought the impulse to run. A JGU student caught with marijuana last year had been kept in jail, incommunicado, for twenty-three days before they deported him. That was nothing compared to this.

Moving the body hurts no one. Ikenami ends up no more dead. It merely hides how he died.

As Will's thoughts congealed around hiding the body—just for a day—and dumping it in town tomorrow night, he felt evil in his gut: malignant, cold, and alien.

He checked his watch: 8:44 p.m. If he was going to do this, it had to be now. Returning home after ten, eleven at the latest, would raise questions.

Will stepped back into Ikenami's unlit office.

What about an alibi? I have nothing!

Without a definitive time of death, he wouldn't need a specific alibi.

Will realized he was playing a game in his head: "I'm so smart I can solve anything." His predicament was too terrifying to acknowledge, rationality hiding just out of sight—until the avalanche of reality eventually thundered down and buried him.

How rational is anyone, though? Herbert Simon won a Nobel Prize for "bounded rationality."

Will imagined Simon dragging Ikenami's remains through the halls of Carnegie-Mellon's business school.

But while what passed for rationality tonight called for hiding Ikenami in the cold for one day until he could move him into town, he had no place to hide Ikenami's car. That needed to go to town—now. The body could wait.

6

WILL KEPT AN EYE OUT AS HE REACHED TRATTORIA NAPoli. He circled the block twice looking for passersby before parking by a large, unlit vacant lot, perfect for dumping the body tomorrow night. Will was certain no one saw him leave the university. He had brushed himself off before he got into the car and pulled his stocking cap down low so as not to leave stray hairs. The cheap cotton gloves he kept in his car precluded fingerprints. He was even careful not to touch the outside of the door handle and held the steering wheel and gear shift by the posts, hoping not to smudge Ikenami's prints. It was Ikenami's car, with Ikenami's bag, as Ikenami would have left it. If Will escaped unseen, nothing would tie him to the car.

He glanced around once more to check whether anyone might spy him from a window. He got out of the car, locked it with the key, fearing the keyring remote might flash the lights or sound the horn—and froze. Did Ikenami lock it? It wasn't locked when he got in. Little details could ruin everything!

In this small town, lots of cars stayed unlocked. Chieko Matsuyama, the dean's assistant, always left her key in the ignition.

Will unlocked it.

Her car was too old to steal.

I have to move!

He relocked the car, then walked for a block before he ran. Will had worn jogging pants today, so it didn't look odd for him to be running, but he kept to backstreets as he headed toward the river. He was aware of every sound. There were few, as the whole town, even the gas stations, closed an hour ago. Restaurants and bars and the lone convenience store were still open, but most were on the other side of the railway station. He covered the six blocks to the river without seeing a soul.

The bridge was the riskiest segment of his return. The river was not large, but they built the levees for a hundred-year storm. Will had to traverse seventy illuminated yards. Even from a distance, people would know he was a foreigner simply by how he moved. Anyone connected to the university would recognize him instantly.

Will listened as he scanned the road for headlights. Utter stillness. With still-gloved fingers, he took Ikenami's mobile phone from his pocket. It had troubled him when he found it in Ikenami's coat. If discovered with the body, unanswered calls might help establish when he died. But why would it be switched off? For all Will knew, the phone company recorded that. Off for a full day and back on might also raise suspicions. So Will had decided to "lose" it on the bridge. Unanswered calls to a lost phone would be as normal as Will could get.

Crouched in the dark, Will calculated: seventy yards . . . seventeen seconds . . . plus five for the phone . . .

He recognized he was stalling. He rose, checked the road once more, and ran.

Not to look suspicious, he kept his gait quick but relaxed.

As he neared the deepest spot in the river, he slowed for a moment and dropped the phone. The battery cover popped off, and he left it where it lay. He perched the phone by a railing post.

No sooner had Will straightened up than he heard a vehicle behind him.

He took off running, then looked back. It was not yet on the steep approach to the bridge.

He glanced again. It was moving fast.

Another desperate glance—he would never make it across before the car had him in its headlights.

The urge to sprint the final thirty yards was nearly uncontrollable, but nothing would look stranger.

He ran on, dreading the moment when his long twin shadows would appear in the headlights' glare, waiting for a student to pull up and ask whether he wanted a ride, waiting . . .

He looked back again.

The vehicle had turned before the bridge approach.

A near miss. How many more would there be? His chances of cheating them all would approach zero as the odds piled up.

Still, as he left the bridge and disappeared onto a backstreet and then into fields, his path was set: deceit, fear, and guilt.

So he ran through the January night, unlit by the waning crescent moon hidden behind the thick cloud cover. The air was cold on his skin, and all was silent but his own breathing and the soft pounding of his shoes on the dirt.

BACK IN HIS OFFICE, WILL CHECKED HIS PHONE, LEFT THERE for fear the phone company kept geo-tracking logs. Laurie hadn't called. There would be no evidence of his absence. He collapsed in his chair with relief.

It was fifteen minutes before Will could take the few steps to Ikenami's office. He entered using the key and looked anew at that icy stare. Lying to himself that he was shivering from the cold, he thought about where to put the body. There were unheated, rarely entered rooms, but he didn't have their keys. He needed someplace nearby, unlit, with easy parking for tomorrow night, when he would move the body into town. An enormous meadow spread behind the university, the size of a dozen football fields. This time of year, its western end was thick with *susuki,* pampas grass that grew tall, stiff, and higher than Will's head. It was far from the dormitories, shielded from sight by the classroom building and the university's Conference Center, and bordered by a small parking lot.

Getting the body to the field . . .

Although much shorter than Will, Ikenami outweighed him by at least forty pounds.

I need wheels.

There was a waist-high cart that faculty and staff used to move loads of books, papers, and such. Will often saw it by the elevator. He looked around Ikenami's office and saw a throw blanket on a small sofa by the wall.

Will sighed aloud and winced again at the corpse on the cold floor.

I have to do this.

He retrieved the cart and positioned it by the body, locking the wheels. As he folded Ikenami's arms on his chest to turn him over, it surprised him to see the crystal on Ikenami's wristwatch broken. Not just cracked—it was shattered. The watch stopped at 4:09. He fell at 3:56 p.m. Will knew because he had checked his own watch, afraid everyone might have overheard, until he remembered it was Sunday and few were about.

4:09 p.m.

So what? Besides, it's only when he collapsed. There's no knowing when his heart stopped.

Unable to believe the coldness of what he was about to do, Will stopped and took a deep breath. He felt sick to his stomach, but steeled himself and began again. Shards of the watch crystal surely littered the floor and were embedded in Will's shoes—but that problem had to wait. The immediate complication was what the police might think if Ikenami turned up with a broken watch but no bits of crystal nearby. Best simply to leave it in the desk. After all, Ikenami was at school today. And who notices wristwatches, anyway?

After putting the watch away, Will rolled Ikenami onto his stomach. He struggled to lift the body. It was like moving a cow. He heaved with all his strength and got Ikenami off the floor. Will firmed his grip and lifted him into the air—but turning toward the cart, he lost his balance and the corpse hit the cart with a loud clang. Will held his breath and listened . . . but heard nothing.

Letting himself breathe again, Will was at the point of arranging Ikenami on the cart when he noticed his hands shaking. They looked just as his grandfather's had when he placed the doctoral hood around Will's neck at graduation. He clasped his hands together. He took deep breaths and tried to settle himself as the muscles in his right arm flexed involuntarily over and over. Would the nervous tic attract attention? He was always tense at the start of a new term, and this was not the first twitch anyone might have seen.

Ikenami was face down, his head and shoulders hanging off the front of the cart and most of the length of his legs extending off the back. Will removed Ikenami's necktie, then reached under his waist and slipped off his belt. He tied the necktie around the cart's top shelf and Ikenami's chest, then tucked the dead man's hands under his waist. He bent Ikenami's legs so his feet were tight against his buttocks and secured them there with the belt. Two empty boxes on the cart's lower shelf would make it look like Will was moving things from his office. With the blanket thrown over the body, affecting a relaxed air, he ventured into the hallway.

Will took the elevator to the first floor, and after checking whether the coast was clear, he pushed Ikenami's trussed corpse into the night. He traversed the brightly lit parking lot scattered with cars. Three offices on the front of the building had lights burning, all behind closed blinds.

In the middle of the lot, Will took a second look at the windows. Only two lights! The person who belonged to that light that had turned off only had to make it down from the third floor. Will probably didn't even have a minute. He scanned for cover, but there was no car large enough to shield him. His only chance was to run for it—with the cart. As he sped up, the cart made a terrible racket on the rough asphalt— could people really hear it, or was it just Will's heightened perception? Regardless, Will pushed even faster, using his own weight to keep the cart steady as best he could.

The curb at the far edge was only fifteen yards away now. Will glanced back but saw no one. Ten yards. Another glance. He pulled back hard as the curb approached but still hit it too fast. The top-heavy cart bucked wildly. He pulled down on it with his full weight. The belt and necktie held, although Ikenami's arms both came loose and flopped down, his hands visible below the blanket. Will lifted the cart's front wheels onto the sidewalk, all the while focused on the other end of the lot, where at any moment—

It was one of the senior faculty. The cart was in plain sight, but he couldn't help that. Will dropped behind it and peeked around. The professor walked to the nearest car and got in, oblivious. Will's heart was racing. The vehicle started. Will waited, watching—and the car didn't move.

Don't warm it up. Just leave!

Will watched, helpless, his arm flexing again and again, as the professor sat there, and then another office went dark. Not again! But he couldn't move yet.

The headlights came on.

Yes! Now go!

Will stood as the car disappeared, and he lifted the back wheels over the curb. He rolled the cart, Ikenami's arms still hanging loose, around the side of the building into the shadows. He peeked into the lot. The second professor was walking this way! Will waited, pressed against the building, as her footsteps got closer and closer. She could see Will if she looked! Finally, she stopped, unlocked a car, and got in. She started it and lit the scene red with her taillights. Thankfully, she didn't warm the engine; she just turned on her headlights and drove off.

Will checked the lone remaining office light. It was still lit.

The path from here was safer. He skirted the classroom building and the Conference Center. He had to traverse its empty parking lot, where the cart stood out. But then he had a stroke of luck: it started raining softly. That would focus anyone outside on getting indoors, not on Will.

The cart clanging at every pebble and pavement crack was nerve-wracking, and Will started humming "Somewhere Over the Rainbow" to calm himself. As he looked to the buildings, scanning them for activity, he realized the song had changed to "Ding-Dong! The Witch is Dead." He grimaced at his own subconscious.

At the edge of the parking lot, Will untied Ikenami and strained to hoist the body onto his back. Carrying it firefighter-style gave Will the leverage he needed, but it was all he could do to steady the weight. He took a step, but staggered and almost fell. He tried a smaller step, and another. It was fifteen yards to the *susuki,* and Will damned himself with every step. Once into the tall, stiff vegetation, he trudged a zig-zag path, as the *susuki* flattened with each step. Seven yards in, he dropped Ikenami. It took forever to put his belt and necktie back on. Then Will laid him out flat on his back, as he'd been in the office, as he would lay him out in the vacant lot tomorrow night. Rigor mortis would set in by then, but how long would that last? If the corpse was still stiff, it would be harder to move with its arms and legs outstretched. By now, though, blood would have pooled in the underside of his limbs and torso, and Will feared any other position would betray that someone had moved him.

In his office again, Will went to his phone. He'd missed a call from Laurie at 10:14 p.m., five minutes ago.

"*Moshi-moshi,*" came Laurie's thickly accented Japanese.

"Hiya."

"Oh, hey, I called just now."

"Bathroom break. I'm tired. Time to head home."

"Did you do everything you needed to?"

Will hesitated. "Enough for tonight."

"Good, it's late and cold, and I need you to keep me warm."

Will donned his coat. It felt odd over his damp clothes. What dozen things should he do tonight? Closing his door, he saw he still had the gloves on, so he took them off. He would dispose of them on the way home. Then he remembered Ikenami's keys in his pocket. He put them in a desk drawer. He'd put them back in Ikenami's pocket tomorrow night.

Will caught himself stealing down the stairway. It might be better to talk to someone on his way out. That would look more innocent. So he whistled "Take Five" as he emerged from the stairwell in case anyone was about.

He was just heading toward the parking lot when a familiar voice called from the courtyard behind him, "Hi, Grames-*sensei*!"

Will turned and saw two first-year MBA students from Vietnam. "The Nguyen sisters!"

They smiled. They had the same last name but were not related, merely mother-tongue intimates in a foreign land. "You work so late?" asked Trinh, the taller one.

"The term's starting. You ready for my class Wednesday?"

"Everyone says it is so hard," said Huong, looking forlorn.

Trinh asked, "Tomorrow is university holiday, yes?"

"Founder's Day. He'd be ninety-eight, but he died recently."

Huong looked puzzled. "Why is Ikenami-*sensei* class tomorrow?"

"It meets tomorrow?" Will fought the vision of struggling through the *susuki*. His arm ached. Did they notice it twitching?

Huong still looked puzzled. "It is strange, only Ikenami-*sensei*'s class—"

"No, tomorrow we have Japanese class too," interrupted Trinh.

Will blew his breath out. "Professor Ikenami's class . . . I don't know. Language class scheduling's always different, so it's no surprise they'd start early, even on a university holiday."

Huong said something to Trinh in Vietnamese, then told Will, "I must go. Goodbye," and trotted away.

Trinh looked embarrassed. "She . . . has to call home." She glanced back at her friend before asking, "You will be in Japanese class again?"

Will had missed that the discussion about tomorrow morning's language classes applied to him, but he was taking Japanese with the students, and tomorrow needed to be normal. "Yup, I'll be there."

Trinh, about to go, stopped short. "You swim tomorrow?"

"Uh . . . yeah, if the pool's open."

Trinh smiled. "See you tomorrow."

Will smiled, too, despite his wish that tomorrow would never come.

7

"*T*ADAIMA!" WILL CALLED OUT AS HE ENTERED THE HOUSE.
"*O-kaeri-nasai!*" Laurie called back.

Will took off his shoes in the *genkan* and slipped through sliding *shōji* doors into the hall and more *shōji* into the living room. Laurie lowered her book and gave him a sunny smile from within her bundle of blankets on the sofa. "Hey, hard worker," she said.

"Reading?"

"Kawabata."

"I thought you finished everything in translation."

"I ordered this online, *Palm-of-the-Hand Stories.* Really short ones."

Will nodded. "You know it's all right to run the heater."

"It's cozy enough if you wrap the blankets right. Have you eaten?"

Will had no appetite, but the more normal he acted, the better. "Go on to bed. I'll get something."

"Okay," she said, but returned to her book without moving.

Before going to the kitchen, Will detoured upstairs. He stood in Sarah's doorway, half expecting to see her breath steaming up out of her quilts. She would be a teenager next month. He watched Rebekah, seven, and Rachel, four, even longer.

In the kitchen, Will got a sleeping pill, heated curry rice in the microwave, and tried not to think. If he concentrated on his spoon, the world might fall into place.

It didn't.

What an idiot, to let an argument spin out of control—even arguing at all.

"Did you fall asleep in there?" Laurie called, and Will woke from his musing to see the food gone.

He slid open the *shōji.* "I was more tired than I thought."

"I turned the electric blanket on, so the *futon* should be toasty."

Will turned to go.

"Hey, you forgot me."

"Oh, sorry."

"Unwrap me?"

Will sat and pulled apart the blankets. He wondered why Laurie was blushing. Moving the last blanket, he found she was naked inside her little cocoon.

She covered herself and smiled. "Like I said, hey, hard worker."

Will feigned interest. "We should've ditched central heating years ago."

II

Moral Hazard
モラル・ハザード

Monday, 11 January 2010

8

L AST NIGHT, LAURIE HAD BRIEFLY KEPT HELL AT BAY, BUT even before she was breathing peacefully, Will's demons had returned. He finally dropped off in a wee hour and slept fitfully, his dreams disturbingly vivid. In the morning, an earthquake woke him. It was Japan; things often rattled. Will closed his eyes and tried to go back to sleep.

Soon he was roused again, this time by wood creaking under great stress. He heard a monstrous thud on the roof, then quiet. The sound, perfectly familiar, yet forgotten since last winter, was no earthquake. It was snow. The blanket on the steep roof, probably a foot thick, was sliding down as a single enormous block, ponderous and wet. Each time the snow slipped, it dropped as a roof-size mass onto the rows of thick ceramic roof tiles below. It sounded like a pile driver. The block picked up speed, and the cadence quickened. Pounding engulfed the house— then a second's ominous silence—before tons of snow slammed into the ground and the entire house jumped as if startled from a deep sleep.

Will sprang from the *futon,* slid open the *shōji* screen and the foggy window—and watched a billion gigantic flakes drifting placidly down through profoundly still air. The rice field behind the house was already knee deep in snow. It must have been falling since midnight.

That rain! I should have realized.

Will dropped back on the *futon*. In a *susuki* thicket, under a layer of deepening snow, waited the remains of a dead accounting professor—and Will had put him there. He wanted to scream.

Will rubbed his forehead. No, focus on the problem at hand.

Nature had solved Will's immediate problem: the corpse was hidden. But the weight of the snow would also flatten the brittle *susuki*. When the snow melted, the body would be obvious.

It wouldn't melt before tonight, though.

He felt the smothering snow as if it were him in the field instead of Ikenami.

Will headed downstairs in a trance. As he stepped off the stairs, Rachel yelled, "*Ohayō!*" She ran at him and leapt high. Will snapped from his stupor just in time to snatch her in midair, toss her nearly to the ceiling, catch her again, and hug her tight.

"It's snowing, Daddy! It started oliver-sudden in the night!"

Will pressed his face to his four-year-old's, her grin and laughing eyes distilling the joy of life into a space the size of a tea saucer.

Rachel squirmed. "Daddy!"

Will was holding her too tight, so he pushed a finger into her ribs, and she burst into laughter and wriggled more vigorously. He put her down and watched her shiver and run off giggling to the kitchen, the only room they heated in the morning.

I held her as if I'd never see her again.

He'd never tried to weave a fabric of lies that wouldn't fray and tear under scrutiny. Nor had he ignored his sympathy for a missing man's family. What he had done was beyond the pale. He stared at the kitchen door. While the kids might not notice if he acted oddly, Laurie would. Yet he could never tell her. Laurie's moral compass was too true. She could never live with the guilt.

Will's toes were freezing.

This is ridiculous; I can enter my own kitchen.

He donned a mask of normality and stepped into the kitchen. He would simply hide his mood in the morning rush of getting kids off to school and grownups to their Japanese classes at the university.

As Will showered after breakfast, he massaged his sore arm. He wouldn't have this twitch if he'd done the right thing.

I'll fix it tonight, he told himself for the dozenth time.

Even if the weather cooperated and covered the body with snow after he moved it into town, Ikenami would have dirt and vegetation stuck to his back. Will had to remove all that evidence. How? No answer came in the shower, none while steam rose from his skin as he dried himself, and none as he slipped on a well-worn, long-sleeved T-shirt. On the back was a big tree frog wearing sunglasses, ironically unperturbed.

WILL TRIED TO LOOK NONCHALANT WHILE HE AND THE GIRLS waited by the *genkan* as Laurie located everyone's tall rubber boots. They were a necessity in the Japanese Alps, where locals measure snow in meters and slush is often ankle deep. Will warmed up the van as Laurie walked the girls to their bus stop. Becka peeled off with a wave and walked to her elementary school a block away. Rachel got a hug before Laurie left her with Sarah, the oldest, to wait for the kindergarten bus that conveniently came before Sarah's middle-school one.

The university was only five minutes away. As Will silently drove, Laurie said, "I'm glad you're not going fast. It's so hard to see."

Will didn't respond.

That was her only comment, except to muse, "It's so pretty, the world gone wholly white."

Tall ginkgoes along the university's entry road, gray-black skeletons only yesterday, now held their breath and strained to keep piles of snow balanced on every twig. Streetlights wore enormous balls of snow like knit hats. Laurie said, "It looks so soft, like someone tucked the campus in for a nap."

Will managed a wan smile. He couldn't tell her the snow felt more like a shroud, or the sky, close and featureless, like death.

They parked. Will waited while Laurie stood up the wipers, as too much snow sliding down the windshield might mangle them. Then they walked through the muted gray that seemed to follow them inside the dim corridors.

The hallways were unlit because JGU was scrimping to save every yen. Tuition from the university's mere 320 students could never cover its expenses. When Japan's economic bubble burst in the early 1990s, the extravagance of the university's founding withered as budgets, once flush with corporate donations, dwindled. JGU's founder, a financier of incomparable influence, retired long before the economy soured. Only those companies with the greatest obligation to him continued their support. Now that he was dead, even they were defecting.

Laurie hurried up the stairs to her Beginning Japanese class on the second floor. Will paused short of the room where his Intermediate class met. He was happy that the university had let him take Japanese classes to brush up on the language he had learned as a youth.

His classmate's voices flooded out of the room. None had been enrolled in Will's fall term courses, so in Japanese class he'd been just another student. It hadn't stopped them from calling him "*sensei,*" but Will stood firmly on the "friend" side of the faculty-student divide. This morning, he couldn't have felt more distant.

He checked his watch: 7:58 a.m. He paused and imagined himself as one of those innocuous, silent flakes, falling and melding into a sea of white. No notice, no guilt.

As he entered the classroom, the professor called the students to order. Everyone took their seats. All but two were from fall term, so they were familiar with the professor's routine. She explained her expectations in clearly enunciated Japanese. Will's eyes were drawn to the window. Everything appeared so dull and bright at the same time. It was strange how rain clouds looked dark, but snow clouds looked light.

She asked them to introduce themselves, a familiar drill. Brian, a first-year MBA student from Canada, went first.

It was 8:14. Class let out at nine. It seemed to be snowing harder, though it might have been the changing morning light. Will wanted to check the weather. He could have done that before class. How many crucial mistakes had he made? If it snowed like this all day—

Everyone was laughing, so Will smiled. Brian sat.

A day's snow in the mountain valleys of Nagano-ken might measure three feet. It happened last year half a dozen times. At one point it got to be over ten feet deep. It could go on for days, or it could stop, the sun could come out, and it could melt. The temperature was barely below freezing. He needed a weather forecast.

No, he needed to listen. He missed one of the new students' names—missed everything she said, apparently; she was taking her seat again. Next was one from Scotland in Developmental Economics. He looked about twelve.

Could he leave Ikenami there until spring? He'd have all winter to devise a plan. Perhaps he could dig him out in the lull after winter term. Final exams weren't until April. Last year the field melted in—

Trinh was regarding him with . . . worry? She was next, but a simple introduction wouldn't faze her. Wait, had he spaced out through another one? 8:28. Trinh slipped out of her desk and stood. All the male students stared—at him? Oh, Trinh was looking at him. He smiled. She had said something about him. Now she was saying how much she values her friends and being true to them. She smiled at him again and bowed to everyone.

Next came the other new student. She and the first one Will had missed were exchange students from Hong Kong in the Master of Public Administration program.

The snow might keep the remains covered until April, but he couldn't count on it. Digging the body out would be tricky. With the *susuki* all mashed down and no deep snow, there would be nothing in the field to give him cover.

The new student was sitting down. Wait, what was her name? Damn.

Will was next. He took a deep breath, put on a calm face, then stood and bowed. He said in Japanese, "My name is William Grames. I'm American, born in Willcox, Arizona, one of four children. I have two older brothers and a younger sister. I lived in Japan a long time ago when I was a child. I came back as an associate professor of marketing a year and a half ago from Champaign, Illinois, with my wife and three daughters. All the first-year MBA and MPA students will have to face me in class starting Wednesday. I intend to be as merciless as the Japanese Language Program faculty."

Laughter.

He ended with a polite, "*Yoroshiku o-negai-shimasu,*" and sat.

Trinh smiled at him. 8:36. Next came a second-year MPA student from Uzbekistan hoping to work with nongovernmental organizations. Last year, he aced Will's class. Some eyes were beginning to glaze over. He sure liked to talk.

A short, dour woman from South Korea was next. She spoke softly.

Moving the body tonight would be best. He'd just tell Laurie he had to work late again. Fitting Ikenami, in full rigor, into the minivan would be awkward. And there was still the problem of dirt on his back.

The soft-spoken woman was sitting already. Last came another first-year MBA. She was Singaporean Chinese.

The professor was looking askance at Will. Even if she hadn't noticed his arm twitching, he must look distracted. People might remember that once they realized Ikenami was missing. Will focused on the student from Singapore, but all he caught were her polite closing words.

His watch showed 8:47. The professor wanted to talk about snow, question-answer format, newcomers asking, second-year students—and Will—answering. How much does it snow? How deep does it get? It was Will's turn next, so he managed to listen. Why do they tie up trees and make shelters over bushes? Will answered with authority: tens of meters of heavy, wet snow would fall over the course of the winter and compress to ice. It would crush anything unprotected. He sat back and tried to look normal but imagined the winter's snow reducing Ikenami to hamburger—although perhaps not if he was frozen solid. Will shivered.

Time was nearly up, so the professor made a parting comment in Japanese. "Usually, by this time of year, we have a snowfall so heavy it does not melt before the next snow. We don't see the ground again until spring. We call that first snow that lasts all winter '*neyuki.*'" She wrote the *kanji* on the board: 根—root, 雪—snow. "I think this will be it!"

9

Laurie was waiting outside Will's office. "How was class?"

"Like last term," answered Will curtly as he unlocked his door. "Plus two exchange students."

"We have three."

Laurie closed the door, grabbed Will, and held him tight as she looked up at him. He stared over her head out the window.

"Hey, what's with you today?" she asked.

"The new term, I guess. I never feel ready."

"You have the whole first-year class, right?"

"Marketing Management. Gotta be big and bad."

"Couldn't be if you tried." She kissed him. "You need any help?"

Will shook his head.

"Okay, see you tonight." She looked deeper into his eyes, then with another quick kiss, she disappeared.

Will switched on the radiator below the window. Watching Laurie clear the snow from the van, he wanted to go with her. He wanted to collect the kids from school, drive to Narita Airport, and abandon Japan forever.

Will jumped at a loud knock on the door. He called out, "*Dōzo.*"

It was Jirō Watanabe, a young accounting professor who had been a doctoral student at the University of Illinois while Will was on the faculty there. He'd had trouble finding an academic position. It was no surprise. Despite a sponginess that evoked the Pillsbury Doughboy, he lacked the jolly demeanor. Will could not remember ever having a normal interaction with him. He moved in erratic, squirrel-like bursts, and his eyes were always open wide as if in perpetual alarm. Will wondered if they were painful.

Watanabe opened the door only far enough to lean in his head and one shoulder. At Watanabe's stare, Will shivered, but covered it with a smile. "Don't you hate these heaters? Roasting or freezing, nothing in between."

Watanabe blinked nervously, as he always did, before blurting out, "Hi." He stared at Will for a few seconds before he said, "Uh, good morning, Grames-*sensei.*"

Will opened his mouth to respond, but Watanabe continued, "I'm looking for—" He stopped, apparently realizing Will was about to speak, but went on again before Will could say anything. "Oh, obvious. Looking, I mean, not who. I mean . . ."

"Looking?"

Blink. Stare. "Bad heaters, yes. Anyway, I haven't seen Ikenami-*sensei.*"

Nor will you ever.

Watanabe lurched on. "The next office. But you know that." Blink, blink. "Have you? Seen him, I mean?"

Long sleeves hid the goose bumps on Will's arms. "No, I just got in."

"Oh." Blink, blink. Stare. Blink.

"Is he usually in by now? I pay little attention."

"I don't know."

"If I see him, I'll let you know."

"Thanks." Watanabe vanished like a vaudevillian on a hook.

As the door was about to latch, he stuck his head back in, stared at Will again, and said, "It's not me."

"Who's not you?"

"That needs to see him." Stare. "It's Malik. I mean, Malik-*sensei.*"

"Okay," said Will.

Watanabe disappeared again. As the door closed, Will wondered whether some caring psychiatrist could help the man—

As if Watanabe is the one who needs treatment?

Half an hour later, Will was still staring into the bright gray sky outside his window. What he'd done was mad. What he was considering was criminal.

No, what I've already done is criminal.

Regardless, he had to see it through.

Time to stop fretting and do something.

He couldn't work, so he looked up "crow" on the internet and discovered that Japanese crows are indeed a different species than

American crows. The Japanese ones are bigger and have much larger beaks.

Will looked out the window. No crows today.

If only his biggest problem was still the risk of getting stuck at this school if his research didn't pan out. He never should have come to Japan. It was idiotic to drag his family to a foreign country.

No, the idiotic thing was moving that body. He wanted to check on it. Was it visible? Had someone already seen it? Would police soon arrive?

He still needed to do something, though. It was only a few steps to Dean Yoshida's office, across from Ikenami's. As Will crossed the hall, he could see Chieko, the dean's assistant, on the phone. She signaled for him to come in. She was always warm, helpful, and conveniently across the hall, so he took whatever questions or problems arose to her first. She, in turn, used Will as her first source for any question about English, America, or most things foreign.

Soon Chieko was saying goodbye, bowing to the phone—everybody did, including Will. She turned her smile full bright on him. "Hello, Grames-*sensei*. Can you believe the snow? I had to use shovel to find my car."

"It's safe to drive that little thing in the snow?"

"Don't make fun of my car!"

"What are you doing here? It's a university holiday."

"Yes, but Ikenami-*sensei* scheduled class so some staffs must come too."

Damn! "Professor Watanabe came knocking on my door—"

"What for?" she interrupted, looking as if she had bitten into something spoiled.

"He asked whether Professor Ikenami was in."

"I have not seen him."

"If you do, please tell him Watanabe's looking for him."

She opened her eyes wide, stared at Will, and blinked.

"You are so bad," said Will.

She smiled. "Yes, I tell him."

Back at his desk, Will gazed at the ceiling. He had talked to someone about Ikenami without flinching, but it didn't stop the churning in his gut. He wanted to see the field. Last night, he'd checked it from the Conference Center's second floor and the body seemed concealed, although in the darkness he couldn't really tell.

Will cast about for something to distract himself, but the urge to see the thicket in daylight eclipsed every thought. Yet looking would do nothing to solve the problem of moving Ikenami and placing him so he looked as if he had collapsed and died near his car in town.

As Will sat and stewed, an idea from last night percolated through: Ikenami could simply vanish.

Disposing of a body . . .

How?

He cringed. The whole idea was so wrong.

He sat up, woke his computer, and opened a weather website. The forecast called for snow all day and much of the week. His finger tapped on the keyboard.

Difficult, yes, but not impossible. There must be a way.

He had read a Japanese novel where women cut up corpses and disposed of them in trash bags—but in Tokyo, not a tiny town like this. It also described how difficult the dismembering was. Even if Will could somehow stomach it, he had nowhere to do it. It would be simpler to just dump Ikenami in a landfill, if the town had one.

No, the very idea of disposing of the body is fiendish!

I should look at the field from the Conference Center.

He had no reason to be there.

Then again, neither did anyone else, so no one would see him.

Will spent the entire walk scolding himself for the risk, but the opulent Conference Center was indeed deserted. They had built the six-story building with visions of executive education programs, just one of the many dreams for JGU that had never come to pass. It now stood like a ghost at the western end of the huddle of university buildings. Will had never understood why no one used it. Its second floor had a commons area that looked out through a long, curved wall of glass toward high foothills that jutted into the valley south of the university.

Approaching the window and the ocean of white that stretched into the distance, Will looked far to the right. The snow, almost two feet high, had flattened the *susuki,* just as he had expected. Last night's thicket looked like everything else: soft, flat, white.

"Hi, *Sensei.*"

Will jumped at the sound of Trinh's voice.

"Sorry I surprise you."

"No, I just didn't hear you come in. I came to see the snow. This is my favorite space in the entire school."

Trinh walked over, stood close to Will, and looked outside. "I come here to think or study. The big windows are nice. I wish I can have a place like this for my room."

"Someday when you're rich."

"Rich is a pleasant dream. So many other dreams, too."

"I have a lot of dreams for the future, too. Too many, I think sometimes."

"My mother tells me you cannot have too many dreams."

Will looked at Trinh, serene as the niveous scene outside and, as anyone would have said, easily more beautiful. "She's wise."

Trinh smiled up at him. "She's pretty too."

Will smiled back. "I know."

"You have seen her?" She laughed.

"No, just . . ."

Standing so close, it occurred to Will what rumors would fly if anyone saw them together in a darkened, deserted scenic lookout—and his real trouble snapped into sickening perspective. "I should get back to work."

WILL AND TRINH LEFT THE CONFERENCE CENTER'S SECOND floor via a skyway that connected to the second floor of the classroom building, one of three buildings that were the core of the university. On the north was the three-story administration building. On the east was a four-story library, and on the west, the four-story classroom building. The library and classroom building looked out onto a bricked courtyard through glass-walled atria that rose the whole height of the buildings. A shallow pool took up almost all the courtyard space. It had a large oblong island in the middle, accessible by a wide bridge from each side, where people could sit and study, although the courtyard could get awfully noisy. The pool was empty, except on special occasions, because the university could not afford to run the pumps. Now the recently empty pool and its island were full of two feet of snow.

As Will and Trinh entered the classroom building, Trinh said she was going to the library, so they walked together. As they neared Ikenami's door in silence, Will forced his attention to Trinh to squelch the memory of Ikenami dead on the floor. As he glanced down at Trinh's face, she looked back expectantly, but he was too distracted to say anything. On the far side of Will's office, Anson's door was open, so Will pointed and said, "I'll say hi to Professor Cook."

Will watched Trinh walk away before approaching the young finance professor's door. "Hi, Anson. Enough snow for you?"

Anson grinned. "Are you kidding? There's no such thing."

"Oh yeah, you ski."

"You, too, if I remember."

"It's fun, but you're a real skier, like since you were two."

"Three, maybe."

"Salt Lake City, right? How do you like the snow here?"

"It's awful. Like skiing on oatmeal." Anson laughed. "I ski anyway."

"Let's go sometime. You can give me a lesson."

"This week, before classes get busy?"

He should have known Anson would agree. "Yeah. We'll set it up."

Will stepped into his office and the glue of his tenuous facade dissolved. Right now, he had no wish to spend a day with the friend who had precipitated Ikenami's demise.

ALONE IN HIS OFFICE, WILL WAS ACCOSTED AGAIN BY THE memory of Ikenami's face, inanimate, like a wax figure, dead not by a blow or even a push, but a mere fist clenched in anger. Without that fist—with a single moment of calm—Ikenami would be alive. The fall must have killed him. Bleeding in his brain could have given him enough time to make it to his office before he collapsed on the floor and died.

I killed him as surely as if I'd beaten in his skull.

But getting rid of the body . . .

He could burn the body. Or he could haul the corpse into the mountains where it would decompose or be eaten by animals. The forests were so dense they might never find the bones. Then again, if birds circled, the authorities could find it immediately. He could bury it. He merely had to drive up a mountain road—now choked with snow.

Will was leaning on his office door, eyes closed, cursing both himself and this twist of fate, when he felt a fist pound on the outside of the door. He barely had time to step away before Steve King came bursting in. King, who bristled at the name Stephen (it didn't matter; everyone called him by his last name), was associate professor of IT. He came from working-class roots in New Jersey, and though he left twenty-five years ago, he still had the accent. Smile too big, laugh too hearty, always cocksure; he had put Will off from the day they met.

"All ready for the new term?" asked King with a grin.

"Yes, I'm pretty much set."

King looked around the office.

Will cast about for something to say. "How about you? All set to go?"

"Of course," replied King.

Will knew the polite thing would be to invite King to sit, but then he might stay. They stood, ill at ease, until Will said, "I guess we're both on the review committee for Anson's contract renewal."

"Yeah, kind of a bother, if you ask me. Anyway, that's why I came by. I wanted to find out the schedule, but 'The Emperor' isn't in."

Last week, Will might have smiled at the students' nickname for Ikenami, but he stayed on topic. "Watanabe was looking for him earlier."

"You got a nice view. Is it quieter on this side?"

"Quiet enough."

"They ought to get rid of that stupid pool that's always sitting there empty. Fill it with dirt and plant some trees and shit. That'd quiet things down."

Will gave him a nod. "Might help."

"You don't know when we're gonna meet about Cook's thing?"

"Not a clue."

King nodded, said, "Okay," and walked out.

Will rounded his desk, collapsed in his chair, and pondered the snow yet again. He sensed it piling up on him, his mind creaking under the weight.

He checked the time. JGU's swimming pool would be open in ten minutes, so he grabbed his swim bag and headed that way. As an afterthought, he realized he should do a normal, unsuspicious thing and tell Chieko that King was looking for Ikenami too. As he approached the open doorway, King was already talking to her. "Of course I can wait, but shouldn't he be here by now? He has class today, right?"

King had his back to the doorway. Chieko saw Will in the hallway—recognition flickered across her face—but she kept her eyes on King. "He never miss a class. I am sure he will come soon. Is there a problem?"

"No, just call me when he gets in."

"I do not track when he comes in."

"Whatever. Thanks."

As King was leaving, Chieko made a face, and when Will stepped into the office, she said in a hushed voice, "He is so rude!"

"He didn't sound that rude to—"

"No, before. He said I should know about Ikenami-*sensei*. It is not my job to watch when people come and go. Also, I do not open faculty office for him. Ikenami-*sensei* can be alone if he wants."

Will's arm flexed again. It ached awfully.

"I am assistant for Dean Yoshida, not for associate deans Ikenami and Malik."

Will answered, "Yes, but King is practicing to be a full professor, when it'll be his job to be rude."

Chieko dismissed it with a wave of her hand. "He will never be full professor. What about you? Will you be rude when we promote you?"

"You're going to promote me?"

She smiled. "What can I do for you?"

"I was going to tell you that King is looking for Ikenami. Also, is the swimming pool open today?"

"Yes, all facilities are open."

"Thanks." Will bowed as he left. He looked forward to losing himself in the water—

I could sink the body!

The river's too shallow, but the reservoir behind Naganawashiro Dam . . .

The dam was forty feet high. If he weighted the remains so rotting pieces didn't break off and float, it would silt over, lost until they rebuilt the dam decades from now.

Lost . . . just like any trace of the man Will used to be.

10

WILL GLIDED THROUGH THE STILL WATER, HIS HANDS carving long, graceful *S*'s under the surface. The physical exertion afforded his mind a modicum of peace. He swam alone, tiny splashes echoing through the cave-like basement of the gymnasium building. It was an adequate lap pool, twenty-five meters long and four lanes wide. There were rumors it cost too much to heat and would be closed. Usage now was restricted to three hours Monday-Wednesday-Friday and five on Saturday. Still, Will rarely had to share a lane with more than one person.

Since late August, when the new students arrived, the person he shared with most often was Trinh. It shouldn't have mattered—swimming is a silent, solitary sport—but Trinh always made conversation. At first it was awkward: he was a professor, and she was—stunning. Awkward or not, though, Will had no say in who shared his lane. He was generally the first to arrive and others would take the slower lanes, none bold enough to impose on the professor. Then Trinh would show up, smiling brightly, and jump in next to him. Still, the first time, exchanging greetings, making small talk, sensing the stare of every eye, including the underwater ones—Will was so nonplussed that he left early. But then they were enrolled in the same Japanese class. It gave them something to talk about. Besides, Will appreciated fast lane partners, and after Will, Trinh was the fastest in the pool. It wasn't long before they were friends. She got to know Laurie, too, and soon Trinh was offering to babysit. The girls adored her.

Seeing Trinh standing in the next lane, Will stopped and lifted his goggles onto his forehead. "You're not playing in the snow?"

She grinned. "I played early this morning already. Second-years say so much snow here, but I could not imagine. It is a shock to see."

"Wait until it's two meters deep."

"That is above my head!"

"That's above *my* head."

She laughed and Will smiled momentarily—until he thought of what lay under the snow. Trinh seemed to notice the pall. "*Sensei,* are you all right today?"

Will mustered a smile. "A little tired."

She looked at him pensively. "Yes, maybe I feel like you."

"Then we should swim!"

11

Although Chieko Matsuyama had no responsibility to keep track of Ikenami, King's visit had left her acutely aware of each footstep in the hallway. As noon arrived without Ikenami, instead of joining friends in the staff lounge, she ate at her desk with the door open. At one p.m., she used her master key to check Ikenami's office. Then she headed to the large, tiered room on the first floor of the classroom building where the required first-year business courses met. She knew by the din that Ikenami wasn't there, so she waited in the hall. Soon a pair of Japanese students, de facto representatives, emerged to ask what was going on.

Chieko called the Programs Office and presently the manager arrived. They conferred as the two students listened. Chieko would call his home and the manager would announce that today's class was canceled. Chieko returned to her desk, ready to leverage her position in the dean's office into as much chagrin for Ikenami as possible.

But his absence took his wife by surprise. "He's not at the university?"

"No, what time did he leave home this morning?"

"He didn't. Or I should say he was supposed to return from his mother's last night but never did. I assumed he was held up, arrived this morning, and went straight to the office."

"No, he has not come in yet."

"Do you think I should call his mobile phone?"

"That's up to you, but I will call it now, if you don't mind."

"Not at all. Please do."

Moments later, Chieko was ringing Ikenami's phone. He probably missed the last Shinkansen out of Tokyo last night and was sitting impatiently on a train approaching Nagano at that moment. Which would also explain why he was not answering: it is bad manners to talk on the phone in a train.

She was about to hang up when a boy whispered, "*Moshi-moshi?*"

"Ikenami-*sensei*?" asked Chieko.

Silence.

"Professor Ikenami?" she asked.

"Uh, sorry Mom, I forgot to turn the phone off," came the child's voice, no longer whispering.

Chieko's voice came more soberly. "Who is this? Is this Professor Ikenami's phone?"

She caught a shrill voice in the background before a woman sternly said into the phone, "*Moshi-moshi.* Is this Hiroyuki's mother?"

"No, my name is Matsuyama, and I am calling from Japan Graduate University of International Studies. I believe the phone the boy has belongs to one of our faculty."

"I see," said the woman. "Then it seems we have a matter for the police."

Chieko heard a collective gasp in the background followed by the stifled clamor of an entire class exploding into whispers. She said, "Yes, I would appreciate it if you turned in the phone. May I ask where you're located?"

The woman answered, "Three kilometers from the university, the primary school."

"Oh, I see. May I ask when the boy found the phone?"

The class fell deathly silent as the teacher repeated the question in a tone that surely left the poor child quaking. There was unintelligible mumbling before the teacher responded to Chieko, "Last night about nine on the big bridge over the river. It's scuffed and the battery cover is missing. I hope the owner is all right."

Chieko said, "As do I. Thank you for the information, and please contact the police."

Chieko informed the Program Office, then called the dean but got his voice mail and had to leave a message. Next, reluctantly, she phoned Prof. Teddy Malik, the other associate dean, appointed primarily by seniority. He seemed to exist in his own peculiar fog. He was a minute behind in any conversation, and his wording was so vague that Chieko had a hard time following him. She kept her explanation short and direct. "Ikenami-*sensei* missed class, and a child discovered his phone on the bridge in town last night."

Malik was quiet for a few moments before he said, "Oh, you should, you know, maybe call someone, or if you, kind of, you know, call the police maybe, I think."

"The child's school will call the police already."

Malik said, "No, I mean about Ikenami-*sensei* being missing."

"I think we can call others first. He will be embarrassed if he has to talk to police about being late."

"Oh, I suppose so. Okay. Let me know, if you, when, anyway, what you find out."

Chieko gazed down through the courtyard at the students clustered in the wide, glassed-in corridor outside Ikenami's classroom; then at the falling snow, crystals clumped together into great white flakes the size of carnation petals. With grave foreboding, she dialed Ikenami's wife.

12

WILL TARRIED LONGER THAN USUAL AT THE POOL, ENOUGH that Trinh had to hurry to class and left him still swimming.

Alone in the water, visions of the body—and how to get rid of it—finally crowded his mind. He had never seen the reservoir in winter, but he imagined the road into the mountains would be clear that far. If it wasn't, he could wear snowshoes and pull the body on one of the kids' sleds. Like a dream, he saw Ikenami on a blue plastic sheet, the kind they sell in every home center. He watched hands, his own, truss the corpse in the tarp and tie it closed, finishing with a concrete block at each corner.

Nausea forced Will from the pool, but standing under the shower's warm spray, the reservoir kept intruding. How would he get Ikenami into deep water? By the time he grabbed his towel, he had a basic plan. It was beyond desperate and macabre, but it would likely work.

~

As Will returned to his office, students were still milling outside Ikenami's classroom. His absence would start a chain of worries and phone calls that would bring the police. They would question everyone who had ever argued with Ikenami. They would concentrate on just a few, though, so if Will passed the initial screening, that might be the end. Killing someone everyone hated might be relatively safe.

He walked toward his office with a touch of confidence—and revulsion. There were many people with actual reasons to despise Ikenami. Will had none. In fact, his friend David, a likely prime suspect, was walking toward him with a smile and a wave. "Hi, Will. How were your holidays?"

"Besides a trip to see the *onsen* monkeys, we had a quiet Christmas here."

"Oh yeah? Did you get a good look at them?"

"Yeah, there are monkeys all around, sitting in the steaming water, warm, all content, looking like little old men, gazing your way as if they couldn't care less. The kids loved it."

"Did you hop in with them?"

Will winced. "Oh, David, that's disgusting. There are feces floating in the water, for heaven's sake."

David laughed even as Will imagined Ikenami floating facedown surrounded by monkeys heedlessly soaking.

David asked, "Hey, join me for lunch? I'm heading to the café."

"Sure."

David was a University of California—Berkeley-trained lawyer hired five years ago when Dean Yoshida decided business students should be exposed to the law. David had no Japanese ties, so why he left a lucrative law practice in Seattle for the backcountry of Japan was a mystery.

The café was just a dozen tables and a minuscule kitchen that took up one corner of the gymnasium building, but it was tall and airy, with a great wall of windows that faced the heart of campus and the mountains to the south. It was always occupied, despite serving mostly frozen fare heated in a microwave oven. Will and David took a table near the windows.

Brian from Will's Japanese class stopped at their table. "Hi, professors. Did you hear Ikenami-*sensei* didn't show for class? The staff didn't know."

David reacted with surprise. "That's not like him."

Brian shrugged. "Anyway, we're going skiing. Want to join us?"

David shook his head, and Will said softly, "Not today."

They watched him go, and David said, "Ikenami harps on us to be here every day, and he's AWOL for his first class? What's the story there? And after insisting on starting on a university holiday."

"Why did Yoshida let him schedule class today?"

"Trying to keep Ikenami on his side in his fight with Satō?"

Will nodded. The failings of JGU president Shinichi Satō and university politics did not hold Will's interest like they would've yesterday.

David said, "Oh, guess who's making the rounds of faculty offices shopping a cap on overseas scholarships."

"Must be Ikenami."

"Preaching the school's mission is to give Japanese an international educational experience, not to squander resources on foreigners."

"Foreigners as atmosphere?"

"I prefer a zoo animal analogy."

"What kind of cap was he proposing?" asked Will.

"Fifty percent, and he's still pushing it, unless he's gone for good."

Will rubbed his arm.

"Hey, you okay?"

"Yeah. I get nervous twitches before every term. Hurts though. Anyway, we've tried recruiting more Japanese students. You know why Ikenami was so willing to bet the farm cutting off foreign scholarships?"

"Why?" asked David with a smile.

"It's not his farm. It's a moral hazard problem: he decides the risk level, but he's not the one who'll be unemployed if JGU goes bust."

Will turned to the window, but saw Laurie raising their girls without a father—all from one moment of weakness, now compounded as Will bet all their futures on a maniacal plan, as if he alone stood to lose.

While they ate, Will wondered who the police would question first. David made no secret of his disdain for Ikenami. Will got splashed with Ikenami's wrath mainly by standing too close to David—and yesterday, by standing up for Anson. Could David end up in trouble as a prime suspect? No, he was too facile with the law. They'd never pin this on him.

"Will? I swear, you're in space today. I was saying you don't suppose he died or something."

Will looked at his food, afraid he'd blanched, but he covered with mock seriousness. "Impossible. Then God has to deal with his meddling."

"Wait, meaning if there's a heaven, Ikenami goes there?"

"Okay, so Satan has to handle him. If neither can put up with him, he lives forever."

David laughed. "That reminds me of something I heard last night. It's by a Japanese monk named Shinran from eight hundred years ago—"

"Since when do you study Buddhism?"

"I memorized the Japanese: *Zennin naomote ōjō o togu iwan ya akunin o ya.*"

"Which means?"

"Even a virtuous person can attain salvation; how much more so an evil one."

Will knitted his eyebrows. "Which means?"

David shrugged. "I'm not sure. We didn't get that far."

"We?"

"Oh, did you hear Ikenami's latest thing? He wants to be on the IT committee. He brought it up after finals and Yoshida told him to save it for January."

"How do you hear these things?"

David shrugged again.

"Why was he interested in IT?"

David gave him an odd look.

"What?" asked Will.

"You keep using the past tense for Ikenami. It's . . . eerie, and kind of morbid." David smiled. "Prescience? We can hope!"

"*I'm* being morbid?"

They paid for lunch and walked back toward their offices. On the administration building's second floor, Malik's office was first, followed by David's. Anson, Will, and Ikenami were at the other end of the building, so Will said farewell and continued on. He was putting his key in the door when Chieko stepped out of her office, followed by a woman Will had never seen. Chieko caught his eye and began her introductions. "Grames-*sensei*, this is Mrs. Ikenami."

13

I NSIDE HIS OFFICE, WILL LEANED AGAINST THE DOOR. He should have left Ikenami where he fell. They would have found him by now. The police would have come, Will could have answered their questions, even recounted Ikenami's fall. Or not. Ikenami's wife would not have looked at Will, lost in worry, asking whether he'd seen her husband. He would not have lied, saying he merely saw him come in yesterday. What if the body didn't melt out of the snow in town until spring? How much torment must a wife endure before she calls herself a widow, until the remains appear, mangled by the snow, unrecognizable? Only a monster could inflict such heartache.

A note slipped under a door could say Ikenami lay frozen in the *susuki*. They'd have no reason to suspect Will—unless he'd left evidence.

But Ikenami in a field meant murder. He just told the widow he saw Ikenami yesterday. Once the medical examiner determined a fall caused his death, even without witnesses to what happened on the stairs, the last person to see him alive would be a suspect.

Will tried to think it all through, but his arm hurt so badly he couldn't concentrate. Images of police kept appearing: hours of questioning, detectives screaming as they caught him lying. Interspersed in the torture, he saw Rachel's face as she leapt into his arms this morning. He pressed his palms to his eyes to stop the tears, but they ran down his arms. He would not dispose of the body. Thoughts of the reservoir were gone. There was no choice but to move it, though, and to stay silent, even after they discovered Ikenami, probably in the spring.

THE DAY WAS DRAGGING ON FOREVER. WILL NEEDED THE DARK to retrieve the body and get it into town. These hours were interminable.

There was a soft knock on Will's door and David slipped into the office. "I had a visitor," he said as he sat.

"Who?"

"Matsuyama and Ikenami's wife. She doesn't know where he is. I wondered whether they suspect me—sticky, since I have no alibi—but then they went next door to Malik's office. Have they knocked on your door yet?"

"I ran into them as we were coming back from lunch."

"How weird is this? I'm beginning to think something might be up. Have you heard anything?"

"No. I saw him here late yesterday afternoon."

"He'll show up at home tonight."

Will, unsure what to say, looked down.

David shrugged. "Or tomorrow it'll be the police knocking."

14

I T TOOK CHIEKO TWO HOURS TO VISIT FACULTY OFFICES with Ikenami's wife, but despite the meager information they gleaned, she had needed help, and Chieko felt the time was well spent. They parted with deep bows at the main entrance after promising to keep each other informed.

Back at her desk, a note surprised Chieko. President Satō wanted to see her. She assumed he wanted the dean, so she called Satō's assistant, Yuriko.

"No, he wants you."

"About what?"

"He didn't say, but he keeps asking where you are. He's all worked up."

Chieko hurried to Satō's office. Yuriko, a friend of Chieko's, gave her a sympathetic look, then knocked on Satō's door and announced her.

Chieko entered the office, said, "Excuse me," and bowed deeply. Satō glanced up sternly and motioned for her to approach, but then returned to his reading. She stood at attention for the next two minutes.

Without looking up, Satō asked, "Why wasn't I informed immediately?"

"Of what, sir?"

His eyes shot to her face. "Don't yank me around! You called Yoshida. You called Ikenami's wife. When were you going to get around to telling me that our most important professor is missing?"

Dean Yoshida is more important by far, Your Worthlessness. "I had nothing to report."

"All afternoon and you know nothing?"

"Only that he came by here yesterday and no one has seen him since."

"Where's Yoshida?"

"I believe he is in Hakone with his wife."

"He doesn't think he should attend the start of a new term?"

Who are you to say anything, Mr. One-Day-a-Week? You make ten times what I do, and you don't even qualify as a part-timer. "It is a university holiday, our founder's ninety-eighth birthday."

Satō's eyes narrowed and his voice was strained and high, "I know whose birthday it is. I knew our founder. He was my mentor, my friend! You can't—you—you could make me lose face by being uninformed on such a vital matter!"

She looked over his head in silence.

"Anything about Professor Ikenami, you will inform me at once."

"Understood."

"You will apprise me before anyone else."

Dream on. "Understood, sir."

Satō glared at her. "That's all. Get out."

She bowed deeply. "Excuse me." At the door, she bowed deeply once again and repeated, "Excuse me."

Yuriko watched, eyebrows raised, as Chieko closed the door. Chieko looked back, tears of rage welling up in her eyes.

Her friend whispered, "What did he say?"

Chieko stepped close and said in a low growl, "He might lose face by not knowing such an important matter."

"What's this about?"

"I didn't call him to say Ikenami-*sensei* is missing."

"So?"

"I guess he misses him."

They both chuckled, breaking the tension.

"To whom does he lose face?" asked Yuriko. "No one talks to him."

Chieko shook her head in disgust.

Yuriko asked, "Is there anything I can do?"

"Warn me if he's about to blow." Chieko turned to go but stopped short and looked back. "Do you have . . . a bad feeling about this?"

"How he treated you? It's deplorable."

"No, about Ikenami-*sensei*."

Yuriko thought about it and nodded, looking distressed.

"It's awful, but I feel like he's not coming back." Chieko's own words shocked her, even as she went on. "I think something dreadful happened. I'm afraid he's dead."

15

T HE SCENE OUTSIDE WILL'S WINDOW REMAINED THICK with snow as the background faded from gray to nothingness. Now the flakes glowed pinkish orange in great spheres around the parking lot's lights.

Will stood and stretched. He still didn't know how to clean Ikenami's back so a forensic investigator might believe he had collapsed in the snow.

What if Will dumped him off the bridge into the river instead? He'd be such a mess when they found him that no trace evidence would matter. It also fit with his phone being found there. He could dig Ikenami out of the snow, lay him on a blue tarp, and drag it out of the field and right into the back of the van. Once on the bridge, it would take less than a minute to dump him into the river.

First I have to put Ikenami's keys back in his pocket.

He was surely mad.

WILL TRIED TO APPEAR CALM WHEN LAURIE CAME TO RETRIEVE him for dinner, but he was quiet and preoccupied. Still, he called out, *"Tadaima!"* as he opened the front door.

"O-kaeri-nasai!" came the girls' chorus from the kitchen.

Will opened the kitchen door and found Sarah and Becka doing homework while Rachel played delightedly with a bowl of goop.

"Whatcha got there, kiddo?"

Rachel's reply was all matter-of-fact. "A polymer. See? It doesn't stick to my hands. Mommy made it for me."

Will raised an eyebrow at Laurie, who responded, "It's just borax and laundry starch. What, she should be watching TV?"

"No, polymers are fine. I better go shovel. Don't blow up the house while I'm gone."

Sarah laughed. "Okay, we'll wait till you get back."

On his way out, Will grabbed cotton gloves, old running shoes he could throw out, and a blue plastic tarp, still in its original wrapper, that they had bought last summer. He stowed it all in the rear of the minivan.

Will got the hefty scoop shovel they used for deep snow and worked around the front door. He pushed the scoop under the snow-pack with his foot, pulled the handle back, and broke off a massive three-foot-deep block. He dragged the shovel to a street-side grate, opened it, and dumped the snow into a culvert that brought water rushing past the house year-round.

There was sweat dripping down Will's temples by the time Laurie called him to come eat. He stopped and craned his neck, looking straight up. Somewhere there were clouds, but all he saw were flakes appearing out of nothingness far above him. Do acts appear out of nothingness, stupid, mindless acts that make no sense, that ruin happiness and hope, that leave people broken—or dead?

16

L AURIE LOOKED DISAPPOINTED WHEN WILL SAID HE NEEDED to return to the office, but all she said was, "Don't stay too late."

At least his, "I'll be back as soon as I can," was truthful.

He planned to work until ten, when he would call Laurie, tell her he had another hour of work to do, and suggest she go to bed. Then he would dig Ikenami out, move the van to the Conference Center lot, and get the body into the back. A short drive to the bridge, a quick toss, and he could drive away as if nothing had happened.

As if.

Anyway, he'd be home by eleven.

Will somehow managed to work while he waited, preparing both of next week's lectures before his concentration collapsed. He looked at his watch: 9:42 p.m. He could call Laurie early.

WILL WORE AN OLD FLEECE JACKET, LIGHT GRAY TO BLEND IN with the snow, and a gray stocking cap pulled low around his face. It was chilly on his way to the field, but the jacket would be warm enough once he started digging. His feet were cold in the old shoes he was planning to throw away. The new snow, so silent as it fell, crunched jarringly on the pavement as he crossed the Conference Center parking lot, plowed earlier that evening. No one was near, and the snowy air would muffle any sound. Still, the noise was like a rake on his tired, raw mind.

He walked to where he guessed he stopped the cart last night. He marveled that it had only been one day. Looking across the snow, now over three feet deep, he imagined last night's field, visualizing the *susuki,* remembering where he dropped Ikenami's corpse.

Will lifted his leg high and kicked into the wall of snow. He pushed off with his other leg, lost his balance, and fell forward. He righted himself, took another couple of steps, and then realized he could place the shovel flat on the snow to brace himself. It speeded his traverse, but it still took him five minutes to get to the spot he had picked out—or at least what he thought was the spot. It was hard to tell.

Digging would be the proof. Crouching low to make himself harder to see, he sank the shovel deep and threw a block of snow as big as a beach ball off to the side. The shovel made slicing sounds as he carved through the settled snow, working his way down. It took longer than he had imagined. He had to enlarge the hole to keep snow from toppling into it, and he eventually had a hole three feet in diameter. Will extended it steadily lower until he reached—*susuki.*

Ikenami had to be close. Will dug to his right. He was sweating and longed to take off his cap, but stray hairs might drop into the snow and remain as evidence. Being able to dig from a position on solid ground was easier on his back, so the second hole went faster. Within a few minutes he hit flattened *susuki* again.

Maybe to the left. It was already 10:19. He didn't think the holes were taking that long. Although he'd started a few minutes early, he was swiftly exhausting the time he'd allotted not only for finding the body, but dumping it and getting home. He picked up the pace, but when he finished the next hole, it was 10:24 and he'd found no trace of Ikenami.

Will looked up at the Conference Center and saw lights on the top floor. The top two floors were hotel-style rooms. President Satō had co-opted one for himself, although he spent most of his time in Tokyo. Will hadn't realized Ikenami was within easy view of Satō's windows. Now he stared apprehensively at the light, but the curtains were drawn.

Will turned back. He had to dig again, fast.

First, I should reorient myself.

He retraced his path to the parking lot, took off his snow-crusted cap, and opened his jacket. He rested, looking over the field again, calming himself. Eyes closed, he imagined it without snow. He retraced last night's steps in his mind. Eyes open again, it was difficult to translate the image from his memory into what he saw now. Still, it looked like he needed to dig about six feet farther out. He zipped up his jacket, donned his cap, and lurched back through the snow.

His arm throbbed. He hoped the next hole would do it. At the same time, he hoped it would be empty. The thought of seeing Ikenami's frozen remains so revolted him that he had to force it from his mind for fear of being sick to his stomach. If he couldn't find the body, he wouldn't drag it on a tarp, like a gigantic frozen starfish, to the van. He wouldn't wrestle it to the railing of the bridge. He wouldn't be haunted forever by the sight of it dropping into the river nor the sound of the splash as it hit.

Ikenami was not six feet farther out.

He dug to the right again: 10:42. A hole to the left took only five minutes: 10:47. He'd expected to be driving home.

Farther yet to the right?

17

PRESIDENT SATŌ WAS WAITING FOR A CALL FROM THE CEO of Yamato Heavy Industries, who was also the chairman of JGU's board of trustees. (He adamantly refused the title of "chairperson.") The man unnerved Satō. He had taken over Yamato Heavy at thirty-six after his father died. Through ruthless competition, he had kept it one of the strongest industrial conglomerates in Japan, despite the long economic malaise. He had not favored Satō's hiring, although Satō, an old protege of the founder's, was the founder's choice and there was no refusing him. Then a few months after Satō started, the founder died, leaving Satō with no power except that afforded by loyalty to the founder's memory. Poor handling of Ikenami's disappearance might mean the end of the lucrative position that would build him a retirement house overlooking Lake Biwa, far from his shrewish wife in Tokyo.

Satō parted the curtains and gazed at the thick white air. Putting this miserable, minuscule university in the backwoods of Nagano-ken, far from Tokyo or Osaka, was shortsighted. And the snow they thought was so picturesque, that they showcased in JGU's brochures, only accentuated its isolation.

To the chairman's credit, he recognized the place was sputtering. Rumors said he was seeking a larger, stronger university as a partner. They would surely eliminate either the president or the dean. Although the chairman and Dean Yoshida were not close friends, they were graduates of the same university, and Yoshida was the senior. It gave the two of them a permanent senior-junior bond. For the one and a half years since Satō became president of JGU, the chairman had answered each of Satō's complaints, every implicit request to put Yoshida in his place, with such consistency that Satō knew the words by heart. "Yoshida is the one person keeping you afloat. If he leaves . . ." At least the chairman had yet to finish the threat.

Satō took hold of the metal rods attached to the curtains and was about to pull them open wide when the phone rang. He scurried to answer before the second ring. "*Moshi-moshi.* This is Satō."

He heard the chairman's gruff voice. "I'm told you have an urgent matter."

"Yes, thank you for returning my call, and I'm sorry to make you call so late. We have an unfortunate situation here. One of the faculty has—"

"Ikenami-*san.*"

"Oh, you've already heard."

Silence.

"The police are now involved," said Satō.

"They should not be?"

"No. I mean no, they should be. But . . . I'm concerned about what this might mean for . . ."

"For what? Just say it," said the chairman.

"The search for a partner school."

"Has the board decided on a search?"

Satō was apprehensive. "Not that I'm aware."

"So . . . ?"

So Satō had been cozying up to senior faculty, hoping for allies in his never-ending squabbles with Yoshida. So besides the idiot Malik, Ikenami was the only one with whom he'd made the slightest headway.

Satō closed his eyes tight and pinched the bridge of his nose with his free hand. "So . . . I guess that's all. I will keep you apprised of the—"

"Just contact my assistant. Goodbye."

"Good—" Satō heard the click before he could finish.

18

IN THE PARKING LOT ONCE AGAIN, WILL TOOK OFF HIS dripping-wet cap and stretched his aching back. He massaged his arm, now so painful he could hardly move it. He had spent the whole day worrying how to dispose of Ikenami and not a moment's thought on how to find him? What next? Farther out into the field? Farther to the right? The left? He had no idea. The only thing to do was dig.

By 11:27, he'd lost count of the holes, and there was no trace.

He stopped and listened. All was stillness except for faraway laughter. The top floors of the two tall dormitories were visible from Ikenami's field merely as lights. Would students venture to the other side of the university to play? Probably.

He had to find that body—now!

Will's holes covered a circle eight yards in diameter. There were still spots where a body could fit, but only if positioned perfectly, with no protruding finger or shoe or corner of a coat. Ikenami might be one hole away or fifty. At least the chances of being seen dumping the body were falling as it grew later.

No chance of being seen at all if I never find him.

Will worked through the Ikenami-size spots within the circle, but simply lost ten more minutes.

Again, he tried looking the area over from the parking lot, but his memory was fried.

He poked with his shovel around the perimeter of his digging area, and he hit—

A large lump of matted *susuki*.

Next came a tree stump.

The other side of the digging area had two more lumps of *susuki* and now it was 11:55 and he was dripping sweat and he ached and he was a fool and he was going to prison for the rest of his life. Crouched in the cold, Will realized he was digging not just for Ikenami's corpse, but for his family. Oddly, in reverse, each empty hole was for himself, because from the moment he struck Ikenami, with his chain of actions that would follow, the Will he had been would forever be lost. So, longing for Laurie and his girls and the guiltless life he could now only mourn, Will sat in the snow and sobbed.

19

WILL SLID THE DOOR OPEN QUIETLY. IT ONLY TOOK A MINute to put away his unused corpse-moving supplies before he locked the door, closed his eyes, and tried to slow his pounding heart.

Opening the *shōji* into the hall, Will was surprised to see the kitchen light on. When he opened the door, he was greeted by Laurie's smiling face and the warm aroma of cinnamon.

When she saw him, she asked, "What happened to you?"

"The van got stuck, and I had to dig it out. It took forever."

"You okay?"

"Fine. Well, tired and sweaty and a mess, but okay."

Laurie hugged him. "Aw, I'm sorry. The van okay?"

"Not a scratch."

She kissed him. "Want a sticky bun? First batch is done, and the second comes out in," she looked at the oven, "two minutes."

Will sat.

"I called you earlier, but you didn't answer."

"The phone was on silent in my coat pocket. Sorry." The lie flowed so easily that Will wanted to crawl under the table in shame.

Laurie told him about her day, but Will caught mere snatches as the night's grim pall descended on him again. It stunned him that he felt more guilt over a lie to Laurie than over digging for a frozen corpse in the snow so he could dump it in a river. He could end Ikenami's wife's torment with one short sentence: "He's dead because of me."

Man of character that he was, Will stoically sat at his kitchen table with his loving wife and complimented her sticky buns, fresh from the oven.

20

THE WEBMASTER TURNED OVER—AGAIN. IT WAS LATE, BUT sleep was hard to find these days. Was the room too warm?

He got up and turned down the thermostat. He looked through the snow at the university's glow in the distance.

How long will it take Trinh to come forward?

She was heading down the stairs, almost to the landing between the second and third floors, so she was above Will and Ikenami. They were on the second floor when the altercation happened, so he doubted either of them saw her. Just at the entrance to the third-floor landing above her, he was certain no one, not even Trinh, saw him. He wasn't sure she comprehended Will's argument with Ikenami, but she did its end, drawing back with a muffled gasp as Ikenami fell.

The police would come around soon enough, but she might clam up, intimidated. She had plenty of friends, though. She would tell someone soon, if she had not already. As the search heated up, someone was bound to talk. No one keeps another's secrets.

III

Word of Mouth
流布

Tuesday, 12 January 2010

21

WILL GAZED OUT THE BEDROOM WINDOW AT A MORNING muted gray by heavy clouds. He took in the white expanse that lay before the mountain's base a quarter mile away, still as a snapshot. It was rice fields the day before yesterday, neat rows of stubble from the fall harvest. Snow here came with almost no wind, no drifts. He could still make out the shapes of the fields that rose in terraces toward the mountain, the narrow berms between them echoed in soft bas-relief in the otherwise smooth mantle of snow.

There was likely a new foot, but it looked little deeper. It was compacting—it would even without the weight of new snow—so the depth was hard to judge. A lone gash cut across the fields, a road to a small ski resort, its lifts and runs partly visible in the distance. Will couldn't see the roadbed, only the break in the snow. Last night, he should have used a pole to feel through the snow, like an avalanche rescuer. The more the snow compacted, the harder probing for Ikenami would be. At least the new snowfall would turn the gaping scars he had opened in the field behind the Conference Center into mere soft depressions—he hoped.

Will watched the silent scene for movement. He saw no cars, no people, no birds or wisps of smoke. The only motion was his own breath—proof of life—as he waited, wondering, just like Ikenami's widow.

22

M om, are we Christians?" asked Becka, still working on her breakfast.

"Of course! Whatever would make you ask that?"

"Our teacher was talking about religions in different places and how most people in America are Christians, and then she asked if we were."

"What did you tell her?"

"I said, 'Yeah, I think so,' but in Japanese."

"You were right."

"How come we don't go to church anymore?"

"Because we don't understand anything they say, dear."

"I do."

Laurie had not thought the family was missing anything in terms of godliness, but after drying her hands, she gave Becka a hug. "Maybe we should start going to church, then."

23

M akoto Itō pulled his four-wheel-drive SUV into the Conference Center parking lot. It was early enough that he had his pick of spots by the building, but he chose one facing the field. The forecast called for sun in the afternoon, and the southern exposure would clear his windshield. He gazed toward the hills to the south covered in snow, well over a meter. At least the students were enjoying it. From his high vantage point, he could see a large area where they must have played last night.

Itō made his way through the Conference Center and around the courtyard to the library, where he managed JGU's small IT Services staff, tucked away in the basement. He switched on the hall lights. Someone would extinguish them soon, but he preferred to start his day without feeling as if he was navigating a tomb. For three years he'd been suggesting they move the office to an unused room on the top floor, sunlit, with a panoramic view of the valley. There would be minor costs, so no one listened.

He let himself into the office, dimly lit by a line of windows high on the wall. They were adequate in the summer but covered with closely spaced wooden slats in the winter, lest the snow shatter them. Filtered through billions of ice crystals, what light shone through lit the room an eerie blue.

Itō savored the stillness. His group occupied a single room, so this was his only opportunity to work alone. He needed to analyze site traffic. Since he reworked the web pages before fall term, overall internet traffic was up markedly, and he wanted to know what was driving it.

24

Detective Hasegawa reviewed his notes as Officer Kurimoto, an English translator and IT specialist, sat at attention, her cap in her lap. She was only in her third year with the force, but Hasegawa had no partner of late, and he needed an English speaker. Experience was inconsequential. Hasegawa might have been able to handle the broad questioning of English speakers, but he worried about missing critical nuances.

Another, shorter officer entered the room and slumped down in the chair next to Kurimoto. Hasegawa looked at his watch: 7:58 a.m. "You're late," he said, without looking up.

"No, sir," said the young man, "I have two minutes."

Hasegawa trained his eyes on Officer Ogawa, a forensics specialist. At Hasegawa's glare, Ogawa rose in his chair and matched Kurimoto's posture. Hasegawa had not worked with Ogawa, either, and he would have preferred someone older—experience in forensics mattered—but Ogawa was next on the duty roster.

Hasegawa returned to his notes. "You've been briefed?"

"Only the location, international university, an hour's drive toward the mountains," answered Kurimoto.

"No local detective in a small town like that, so it's prefectural head-quarters' responsibility, and it's fallen on us. A professor is missing,

Kiyoshi Ikenami. He was to return home Sunday after spending a week visiting his mother. A primary school student found his mobile phone on the town's central bridge that evening. Lucky he found it with all the snow they've gotten. That's the phone you were looking at this morning."

Ogawa said, "Yes, sir. There are a few partial prints. I'd like to fingerprint the child and anyone who's handled it. I can get the missing guy's prints from his home today."

Hasegawa looked into Ogawa's eyes. "His name is Ikenami."

"Yes, sir. I will ask Ikenami's wife for permission to take fingerprint samples from their home today."

Kurimoto asked, "With the phone on the bridge, you think he jumped?"

Ogawa relaxed again. "Pretty ineffective way to kill himself. How high's the bridge, six or eight meters? He'd probably wash up downstream with a broken leg and die of hypothermia."

Hasegawa stared at Ogawa again. "It's fifteen meters and there's been a suicide from that very spot."

Ogawa stiffened again and folded his hands in his lap.

The detective continued. "The phone was also where someone might put it if he was trying to make it look like suicide."

Kurimoto asked, "You suspect someone murdered him?"

"Perhaps, or Ikenami could have planted it if he wanted to disappear. It's most likely he didn't feel like going home, but his wife," Hasegawa checked his notes, "Yōko, says this is completely out of character. Last night, she submitted an official search request. We'll treat it as a potential murder or suicide until we find evidence to suggest otherwise."

"Understood."

"The wife was surprised he didn't return home, but assumed he'd stayed Sunday night in Tokyo. He didn't show for class yesterday. University calls his mobile phone, kid answers, he's missing."

"When was he last seen?"

"Sunday afternoon or evening at the university, by another professor . . . Gureimuzu . . . something like that. So far, that's all we've got. We'll ask Yōko-*san* whether she wanted him dead while you collect prints from the house." He looked again at Ogawa.

"Prints. Yes, sir."

"Whether · she · wanted · him · dead."

Ogawa looked bewildered.

"You're collecting prints from all over the house. All ten fingers take a lot of examination. While you're at it, you're noticing any signs someone might've murdered him at home. Meanwhile, we keep his wife busy with a long interview about their marriage and his habits and whether he had a girlfriend and on and on till you're finished."

"I turn the place inside out for evidence she murdered him."

"You search thoroughly but discreetly for anything not in keeping with a simple disappearance."

"Thorough but discreet. Yes, sir."

Hasegawa looked at Kurimoto, who smiled back in sympathy, and told her, "I'll interview the wife. You help him."

Kurimoto bowed crisply.

"After the wife, we visit the university. The faculty and students hail from around the world, and they teach in English, so many won't speak Japanese. Can you handle all the accents?"

Kurimoto answered, "I will do my best. I dealt with an incident there last year. I don't anticipate any problems."

"Good. Anything else?"

Neither made any response.

Hasegawa checked his watch again: 8:02. "Let's find him. We go."

25

I HEARD HE KILLED HIMSELF," SAID ONE OF THE STUDENTS gathered in the hall after Japanese class.

"Someone said he hung himself in his office. The body's still there."

Will heard Huong behind him say, "No, police think it was murder."

Huong was in Laurie's Japanese class, so if Huong was out, Laurie must be, too, and heading for his office. Will was surprised at Trinh looking sternly in his direction, until he realized she meant it for Huong.

Trinh sighed in apparent exasperation. "No one talks to family or police. No one knows nothing."

Brian looked at her reprovingly. "Anything. No one knows *anything*."

"Except Brian. He knows everything," said Huong.

Another student joined in. "We can tell a new rumor and check how long before someone tells it back to us. Say he left to join far right . . . arm . . . ?"

"Wing," said Brian.

"Joined a far right-wing . . . or what is the word? Sounds like 'fashion'?"

"Fascist?"

"Yes, tell everyone he joined a fascist group."

Will frowned and turned to leave.

After Will's exit, Trinh told the group, "See you in class later."

Huong smirked and said in Vietnamese, "Hurry or he'll get away."

Trinh narrowed her eyes in return, but Huong just smiled as she launched into another Ikenami rumor.

Trinh caught Will at the top of the stairs. "*Sensei,* do you hear anything about Ikenami-*sensei*?"

"No. I saw him on Sunday. I've heard nothing since, except he's missing."

As they walked up the hall, Will's eyes were glued to the Conference Center skyway. Trinh looked that way. "You go to the Conference Center?"

"No, to the office."

Trinh said, "I saw him Sunday too. Maybe close to same time as you."

Will stopped. "You saw him?"

"He did not look happy." She hoped that would be enough for him to understand. She didn't want to embarrass him by coming right out and saying she witnessed the argument and Ikenami's tumble down the stairs.

Will was quiet before he gave a wry half-smile. "Did he ever look happy?"

Trinh smiled back. "Maybe not."

Will started walking again, and Trinh said, "I think he was angry."

"What about?"

"Hi," Laurie called from down the hall.

Will stopped and looked at Trinh for an answer, but she waved at Laurie.

"I was waiting for you at the office," said Laurie as she approached.

"My class wondered whether Ikenami snuck off to a fascist group."

Laurie frowned. "At least he wouldn't have to change his politics. My class was all rumors, too, mostly him dead, and all three scenarios: natural causes, murder, and suicide."

"What did you offer?"

Laurie looked askance at Will and asked Trinh, "What do you hear?"

"So many same rumors, all very grime."

"Grim," said Will, with a reassuring smile. "Grime is dirt."

Trinh tried not to be chagrinned. Improving her English was one of her reasons for being here. It wouldn't do to react badly when friends helped. She should leave Will to his wife, though, so Trinh bowed. "See you later."

Laurie smiled and Will said, "See you," as Trinh left.

LAURIE HUGGED WILL'S ARM AS THEY WALKED UP THE HALL. They were turning into the administration building when she said, "Sexy shirt today."

"This?"

"No, silly, hers."

"Oh. Yeah, I suppose."

When they reached Will's door, Laurie said, "You know she likes you."

"Who, Trinh?"

She laughed. "Said like someone who's well aware."

"You think it's a problem?"

She thought for a second. "No, not Trinh."

"Good. I'm not sure she does, but I don't want things to get . . . weird."

Laurie chuckled. "Probably just a crush on a cute professor with good Japanese."

Will unlocked his door.

"If she shows up at the pool in a suit any skimpier, though," she poked Will hard, "I'm stepping in."

26

LAURIE HUNG AROUND UNTIL TEN, TALKING TO WILL AND studying *kanji.* As he watched her blow him a kiss and drive away, the sun emerged from the clouds. Laurie had said the weather would clear up, but Will had hoped for clouds into the afternoon. A full day's sunshine could reduce the snow by half, and the thinnest spots from last night's dig might melt through completely. How close had he come? As the sun thawed the edges of the holes, would a shoulder or shoe emerge?

Again, he fought the urge to look. If some telltale bit was showing, there was nothing Will could do about it in daylight. Besides, nothing would be more incriminating than showing interest in the field where Ikenami's frozen head might be protruding from the edge of what the police would recognize as an obvious search area.

Will looked again at tomorrow's lecture slides. He tried to think of examples to use, but his mind kept replaying what he'd have to tell the police.

I need a pole for searching. If I bought a piece of bamboo—

He had to stop. He had no excuse for buying a bamboo pole.

Why not come forward now with some reasonable explanation?

Like what?

No, it would have to be an anonymous note. A few simple words and Ikenami's family would know. It would bring terrible grief, but that was coming anyway.

No matter how they located the corpse, the police would assume it was murder, and as the last one to see Ikenami, Will would be a prime suspect. They would interrogate him, he would crack, and it would destroy Laurie and the girls. He had to find the body and dump it in the river. The choice was between hurting Ikenami's family or his own.

It's what anyone would do, he told himself.

He did need a pole. Last night's snowfall was compacting, melting.

Will stared at his computer until he gave up, put on his headphones, and started a chill jazz playlist. Before long, he stopped hearing the music, alone, afraid, ashamed, as the trees dripped in the sunshine.

It was nearing noon when Will slipped off the head-phones. He *had* to see.

He rubbed his arm as he walked. He tried to act as if he was going no place in particular. More than acting calm, he needed to *be* calm, but he did not know how. He was strung tight on a good day, but any day now could be his last before arrest, trial, and prison. As much as his arm ached, he was thankful the nervous tic was hiding inside his sleeve and wasn't a shoulder shrug or eye blink. Still, if his arm got much worse, the pain would bring the tic so far into consciousness that his brain would choose another spot to fidget in relative privacy from itself—but in full view of other people.

Once inside the Conference Center, Will went to the windows. It was a beautiful view, every surface blanketed in thick white beneath a cloudless azure sky. The sun reflected brilliantly off the field, sparkling in bright colors like diamonds, but Will focused on the surface, not the color. He had worried that last night's digging would show as an odd scar in a smooth field of white, like a big scoop missing from a fresh tub of ice cream. Instead, he saw a field crisscrossed and trampled by students who had played chase, fashioned *kura* snow huts and snow-men, and pelted each other with snowballs for the last two days. They were probably still tossing snow by the dormitories. Will's digging was just another disturbed spot, now crossed by half a dozen sets of tracks, not only his trail to and from the parking lot.

Will was surprised to find his search area was closer to the parking lot and half as big as it had looked from the ground. He guessed he needed to dig two shovel-lengths south and one east of last night's edge.

If the snow lasts the day . . .

It was down to waist deep, a foot less than this morning.

He would have to dig tonight.

How deep by dusk? Two feet? Less?

Will gazed out at the snow, trying to calm himself, but finally, cursing his arm and the snow and Ikenami and his own idiocy, he turned to go.

WILL WAS SURPRISED TO FIND LAURIE WITH HIS HEADPHONES on when he got back to his office, and it took him a second to remember why she was there. "Lunchtime already? Where today?"

Laurie smiled at him, head bobbing to the music. "Cool jazz, man."

Will donned his coat and boots. He stood to go, and she quit playing beatnik, hurried to the door, and grabbed his hand. Small as it was, the gesture had him feeling almost hopeful.

When they got to the van, Laurie drove—and headed for one of the university's less used southern exits, straight past Ikenami's field.

27

THE SECURITY GUARD STOPPED BEFORE AN OPEN DOOR, bowed deeply to the three police officers he was escorting, and walked away without a word. People often lost the gift of speech when Hasegawa showed his badge, but having two uniformed officers in tow must have made an especially deep impression.

Hasegawa's watch showed 12:13 p.m. He noticed they were directly across from Ikenami's office. Someone had taped a piece of paper to his door with "Do Not Enter" in both Japanese and English.

In the open office was a woman in a well-fitting, black, department-store suit. She wore a Fendi scarf around her neck, a big bow on the side, flight-attendant fashion. Her hair was short, almost boyish, but it fit her face nicely. When she saw them, she stood and stepped around her desk. She was short and trim, about thirty-five, although the length of her skirt suggested she might be younger. Except for the scarf, she was sensibly frugal right down to her shoes, but she wore it well. She put her hands in front of her and bowed deeply.

Hasegawa bowed and said, "My name is Hasegawa. I'm the detective in charge of the Ikenami case."

"Thank you for coming. My name is Chieko Matsuyama."

Hasegawa introduced Kurimoto and Ogawa, followed by more bows.

"President Satō is on campus today. I can show you to his office."

"In due time. Ikenami-*san*—Yōko Ikenami—suggested we talk with you first, that you would best be able to help us begin our investigation."

"I don't know why she said that. I'm not authorized to represent—"

"More than an official contact, we need to know the terrain."

She bowed again. "I'll do anything I can."

"Thank you. To begin with, would you be so kind as to open the professor's office? Officer Ogawa will carry out a forensic examination."

She hurried to comply, and as she unlocked Ikenami's door, Hasegawa asked, "Has anyone been in the office since he disappeared?"

"A janitor would have emptied the trash, but yesterday was a university holiday. I opened the office for his wife after he missed class. I don't think she touched anything. She just stood and looked worried. After that, I posted this sign and instructed the security guard not to let anyone in."

Ogawa set down his bag in the hallway and was putting on white fabric gloves when Hasegawa showed Chieko back into her office.

Hasegawa indicated her chair. "Please sit. Make yourself comfortable."

"Thank you. Please be seated yourselves." She motioned to chairs along the wall, and Hasegawa and Kurimoto sat. "May I bring you coffee or tea?"

"No, please don't bother."

"It's no bother."

"Please sit. Let's talk."

Chieko sat. Hasegawa waited silently, and soon Chieko asked, "What do you think happened?"

Hasegawa sat back in the chair, eyes down, and showed a worried face. "I don't have the slightest idea." He raised his gaze to her face. "You probably know more than we do at this point."

"I know nothing."

"Rumors spread fast in a little community. You've heard things."

She looked at him blankly.

Hasegawa smiled knowingly. "There's no need to be circumspect. Things that circulate, ridiculous as they seem, can have a seed of truth. We need those bits of history and rumor as starting points, the edge pieces of a puzzle. I'd bet you know more of those pieces than anyone."

She looked taken aback, so Hasegawa softened his voice. "I meant that you're right across the hall with your door open all day. You know when he comes and goes. You see who visits."

"Yes, that's true."

"You'd hear if there was an argument."

"I never heard one."

"Never?"

"With students, sometimes. But none this year. I don't think there were any last year either."

"How about arguments with non-students?"

"Not in his office."

"Where?"

"For example, in faculty meetings."

"Arguments?"

"Yes."

"With whom?"

"Everyone." Chieko shook her head and frowned.

Hasegawa smiled again as he leaned forward. "He's difficult?"

"No, worse."

"I take it he has enemies."

"People who don't like him—your notebook's not big enough."

Hasegawa chuckled.

"But I can't think of anyone who might have done him harm."

"The harm part is for me to worry about. Let's start with the last person who saw him. He's a foreigner?"

"Yes, Grames-*sensei*. Many of the faculty are foreigners."

"As one might expect here. He gets along with Ikenami-*san*?"

"As well as anyone does, I guess."

"Have you ever seen them argue?"

"Argue . . . no."

Hasegawa waited.

"Ikenami-*sensei* screamed at him for playing music in his office."

"That must've been uncomfortable."

"It was awful. The music wasn't loud. I hadn't heard it with my door open. And it was jazz, not rock music."

"That must have upset Grames-*san*."

"He was put out, perhaps, but not too upset, I think. He apologized and turned it off. Now if he listens to music, he uses headphones."

"A restrained response."

"Yes, Grames-*sensei* is easy to get along with."

"He's a friend of yours?"

She shifted her weight in the chair. "Yes."

Again, Hasegawa waited.

"He helps me when I have English questions."

"How long has he been here?"

"This is his second year, so sixteen months, I guess."

"He likes it here?"

"Yes, he lived in Japan as a child. He speaks Japanese well and feels at home here."

"Ikenami-*san* made his life difficult?"

"Oh no, I don't think so. In fact, I'm sure. He would've told me."

"You're that close?"

She hesitated and glanced over at the female officer before she answered, "Yes, I guess we are. He and his wife are both good friends."

"Perhaps you could introduce us."

"Gladly."

"First," he checked the time: 12:21, "we should talk to the president."

It was a short walk down the hall to President Satō's office, where they found him standing at his assistant's desk. He was a man of medium height and slight build. His billowy white hair was overdue for a cut. His suit might have looked good on him when he bought it twenty years ago, but it was too big now and made him seem withered. The well-worn Seiko on his wrist did not surprise Hasegawa.

Satō spun around. "The guard told me you had arrived on campus." He scowled at Chieko. "They came to the dean's office? Why? He isn't even here today. You should have brought them here."

She bowed and left without a word.

"Come in, come in." He ushered them into the inner office, and after presenting them each with a business card, invited them to sit on a large sofa. He took a soft chair. "This is most distressing. Ikenami-*san* is our prize professor. Do you have any idea what might have happened?"

"I'm afraid not."

"That's awful. What can we do?"

"Cooperation is all we need. I'm sure we can find him."

"I hope so. We all hope so."

"May we ask you a few questions?"

"Of course."

Hasegawa opened his notebook. "When did you last see Ikenami-*san*?"

"Oh, I can't remember. Let me ask my secretary."

"If it's been that long, we don't need a precise date."

"Oh, all right. It was about a month ago."

"Thank you. Is there someone who might have harmed him?"

"No, he was well liked."

"He had no enemies?"

"None."

"No one he fought with?"

"Certainly not."

"Tensions? University politics?"

"Oh, I suppose we have politics. What university doesn't? But they are not . . ." He shifted in his chair. "If I may speak confidentially . . ."

"Always."

"The dean, Yoshida, is the primary source of political squabbles. He is always pushing his own grandiose ideas. He and Ikenami-*san* do not get on well. I don't know about recently, but Yoshida . . . he's a rather brazen self-promoter and I think he may be jealous of Ikenami-*san*'s stature."

"You think he might have harmed Ikenami-*san*?"

Satō looked surprised. "Harm? Oh no, I wasn't accusing him."

"Is there anyone else?"

He considered it. "Perhaps Peregrine-*san*. A foreigner—a *true* foreigner—who does not understand or appreciate Japan or its culture. He is one of Yoshida's closest allies. He takes the lead in attacking Ikenami-*san* so Yoshida can stay above the fray."

"Were they fighting recently?"

"Perhaps not."

"Could you tell us whether Ikenami-*san* seemed depressed lately?"

"No, he is a rock. I have never seen him depressed."

"Are the two of you close?"

"Yes, we are good friends."

"He confides in you."

"Yes, we talk about all kinds of things."

"You would know whether he was depressed?"

"I can assure he has not been."

"Or in a difficult position financially?"

Satō paused. "I wouldn't think so."

"Or having an affair?"

Satō's face darkened and his voice took on a scolding edge. "I hope you won't ask those questions when you talk with others."

Hasegawa stared into the old man's eyes, stone-faced, but Satō said nothing more. Hasegawa said, "You did not answer my question. Is it possible he was having an affair?"

"No."

"You would have known?"

"Not necessarily, but perhaps."

"You spend time together outside the university?"

"Yes."

"How much time, more or less?"

"Not so much."

"The last time you did something together was . . . ?"

"We had dinner . . . some time ago."

"When? This fall?"

"Perhaps . . . in the spring."

"I see." Hasegawa was almost finished, so he took his time making notes. Satō looked restless, so Hasegawa wrote slower.

"How long do you expect your investigation to take?" asked Satō.

"That's hard to say."

"We will cooperate fully—that goes without saying—but it is a small campus. I would imagine you could complete your interviews quickly, possibly today."

"Today?"

"Or however long it takes, of course. Just so you find him."

Back in Chieko's doorway at 12:43, Hasegawa asked her, "Could you introduce us to Grames-*san* now?"

She led them across the hall, but no one answered her knock.

"He could be out for lunch," she said.

They stepped back into Chieko's office and took their seats.

"The president and Ikenami-*san* are close friends?"

"They are?"

"That surprises you?"

"I just . . . I didn't think he had any close friends."

"The president or Ikenami-*san*?"

"Either." She smiled. "The president isn't on campus enough to have much of a feel for happenings here."

"How about the dean?"

She nodded. "He does. He'll be back tonight."

"Perhaps we could meet with him first thing tomorrow morning."

"I'll see to it."

"You were saying earlier that Ikenami-*san* has . . . perhaps not enemies, but people he doesn't get along with."

"Many."

"We'll talk to them—perhaps all of them—but for now . . ." He paused, leaned forward, and used a soft voice, "Of the many who . . . have difficulty with him, who has the most?"

He watched Chieko sit back, one arm across her waist and the other hand on her chin as she looked down. Her finger tapped on her lips. When she looked up at Hasegawa, he thought he detected a twinkle in her eye. "Do you speak English?"

28

THE SUNSHINE REFLECTING OFF THE RECEDING SNOW WAS giving Will a headache, so his eyes were closed as they approached the parking lot after lunch. It also saved him from having to see that detestable field.

"The cops are finally here," said Laurie.

Will sat up. He needed one more day without prying eyes! And a pole. And some clouds.

"You okay?" asked Laurie.

"Just hoping they don't find anything."

"You don't want them to find him?"

"No, of course I do, just not *here*. JGU's got enough trouble as it is."

"You going to be okay talking to them if they come by?"

Will tried to loosen his hands as he stared at the police car. He knew they'd come. He'd even supposed it would be today. There was no need to be apprehensive.

"You okay now?"

"Yeah."

Laurie pulled into a parking space and turned off the van.

"You're coming in?" asked Will.

"Okay, I know it's morbid, but I want to see what's going on."

No, Laurie, that's the last thing you want to see.

AS WILL AND LAURIE CAME OUT OF THE STAIRWELL, HOLDING hands, Watanabe was outside Ikenami's office. The door was closed.

Laurie moved closer to Will as they approached, and Will said, "Hi, Jirō. What's up?"

"Cop's inside."

Will and Laurie stopped. Will asked, "What are they doing?"

"Just one. He kept looking at me. Then he closed the door."

"Ah." Will watched Watanabe shift his weight from one foot to the other, back and forth. "What was he doing before that?"

"Sweeping the floor."

Will still had the shoes he wore that night. They surely had shards of the watch crystal in the soles.

"Ouch." Laurie winced as she yanked her hand away from Will's. He realized he'd squeezed both his hands into fists.

"Grames-*sensei*," Chieko called out from her desk. Everyone turned, but she stared at Will, so he left Laurie in the hall. Chieko waited until Will was at her desk before she whispered, "Make him go away."

"How?" whispered Will.

"I don't know, but he is too creepy. The officer looked bothered."

Will nodded and turned to go, when Chieko said in a normal voice, "Oh, and the police want to talk to you."

Will froze for a second, but then forced a smile at Chieko before he stepped into the hall. Laurie was about to say something, but Will pursed his lips. She took the signal and went to stand at Will's door.

Will hid his hands, where his tension showed so clearly, in his pockets and gave Watanabe a concerned look. "Jirō, you seem . . . worried."

Watanabe's eyes widened. "No. Yes. I mean, yes, we should worry. I've heard things."

"Oh? Like what?"

"Like he was murdered."

"C'mon, you know that's people talking based on nothing," replied Will, trying to make his tone comforting, not dismissive.

"I heard the police were involved, and here they are."

"Yes, Professor Ikenami is missing, the police are here, and that's worrisome. That's no reason to believe rumors. I've heard suicide rumors too."

Watanabe glared at him. "That's not true!"

"I didn't believe it. I was merely showing how untrustworthy rumors are." Will softened his voice. "Jirō, we're all concerned, but waiting here will only worry you more."

"I need to talk to them."

"With the door closed, it looks like he's not ready to talk just yet."

Watanabe glanced up the hall. "There's others."

"Other police?"

He nodded as he scowled up the hall. "They're talking to Peregrine."

"You say, 'Peregrine,' as if you're upset at him."

"What if he killed Ikenami-*sensei*? He's obviously a suspect."

"Because the police are talking to him?"

Watanabe clenched his jaw.

Will tried to be soothing. "First, no one said he's dead, let alone murdered. You know after David, they're coming to talk to me. Am I a suspect?"

Watanabe looked surprised.

"The way you're acting, they'll talk to you too."

"Of course. They should. Maybe I can help."

"We all want to help. Everyone wants him found. Have you eaten?"

"No."

"Go get lunch. When the police talk to me, I'll tell them you're eager to meet with them."

Watanabe shifted his weight and blinked a few more times before he turned with a jerk and walked toward the stairwell.

Will looked in at Chieko, who smiled and applauded silently.

As he approached his office, Laurie said, "He looked like he was ready to jump out of his skin. He never made eye contact that entire time."

"He always looks like that." Will unlocked the door.

"Poor guy." Laurie followed him into the office.

Will sat on the corner of his desk. "You want more of this?"

"You have to admit it is entertaining, in a freakish sort of way."

"Glad you're having a good time."

"Oh, don't be such a Boy Scout. You can't tell me you don't have even a tiny hope he's gone for good."

No, I cannot.

29

DAVID LOOKED CONCERNED AS HE ADDRESSED KURIMOTO. "I hope nothing has happened to him."

Kurimoto said, "I translate. Please address Detective Hasegawa."

"Okay."

David was in his mid to late forties, tall, trim, and good looking, in a craggy sort of way. He also seemed far too relaxed, but Hasegawa wasn't sure whether it was innocence or practiced calm. The man was a lawyer, after all—despite being dressed as if to go fishing. The cool exterior could have been an American thing. Nagano prefecture was rural compared to Tokyo, so Hasegawa's dealings with foreigners had been limited. The Americans in Nagano were mostly tourists or kids straight from college working in high school English classes, but he had found them to be almost universally smug.

Hasegawa answered, through Kurimoto, "Yes, I hope so too."

Hasegawa expected some reaction, but David returned his gaze impassively. It was a full ten seconds before David said, "I'm happy to cooperate however I can. Did you have questions?"

"When was the last time you saw Ikenami-*san*?"

"Before I left for the holidays." David glanced at the calendar on his wall. "Probably December twenty-fourth."

Hasegawa gave him a chance to say more, but all he got was David's stare. "You did not see him on Sunday?"

"I did some shopping in the morning but was otherwise home all day."

"Can you think of anybody who might wish Ikenami-*san* harm?"

"Wish or act?"

"Either, please."

"Half the people at the university probably wish he would disappear. He's roundly despised by the foreign students. It also includes faculty who've been forced out, notably the last four accounting professors we fired—all foreigners who left Japan, I believe. I only knew one. The rest came and went before I arrived. The staff have trouble with him too. I'm not sure about his family. All that said, I don't know anyone who would do him harm."

"Do you wish he was gone?"

"Yes."

"Why?"

"He's one of our top three or four faculty members in terms of name recognition, so if we lose him, the school's reputation will drop, but only temporarily. He's not irreplaceable, and in the end, he's bad for the school. It makes no sense for an international university to employ a professor who hates foreigners. He's hurt student morale, and he's a constant source of trouble to the faculty."

"Trouble for you?"

"He has no significant impact on my life. He merely makes the university a less pleasant place to work."

"Ikenami-*san* shouted at you in a faculty meeting?"

"He's shouted at many people in faculty meetings. I'm proud to have been the object of some of his rants. It's a sign I'm trying to do something positive for the school."

"Have you heard about any threats?"

"Yes, he makes noises about ridding JGU of one person or another."

"I meant threats to him."

David looked down as he thought. "No." He thought for another second and added, "It's odd. You'd think someone with that many enemies would have generated a few threats."

Hasegawa was still writing, so it was a few seconds before he asked, "Have there been any new or odd rumors about Ikenami-*san*?"

"I heard he wanted to be on the IT committee."

"Why was that?"

"I don't know."

"Is that a major responsibility?"

"Not especially."

"What does the committee do?"

"I've never served on it, so I can't give you details. I suggest asking the IT manager, Itō-*san*."

Hasegawa looked through his notes and checked his watch: 1:34 p.m. "Thank you. Perhaps we will talk again."

David nodded and stood as Hasegawa got up to leave. Kurimoto opened the door and stepped into the hall, but Hasegawa turned back and asked in English, "Do you think Ikenami-*san* will come back?"

"I hope so. For his family's sake, though, not for ours."

30

WILL WATCHED LAURIE TURN TO THE DOOR AS FOOTSTEPS approached and stopped. Someone knocked. She looked at Will as he called out, "*Dōzo.*"

In walked a police officer and a man in a suit. The uniformed woman spoke. "Good afternoon, my name is Kurimoto. I am translating for Detective Hasegawa of the Nagano Prefectural Headquarters of the National Police Agency."

Will and Laurie stood, and as the officers bowed, they bowed back.

"My name is Grames, Will Grames. This is my wife, Laurie."

"Pleased to meet you, I'm sure," said Kurimoto.

Through Kurimoto, Hasegawa said, "Your colleague Ikenami-*san* has disappeared. May I ask a few questions?"

"Certainly. Please make yourselves comfortable." Will motioned to the two chairs facing his desk. Laurie moved and stood behind Will.

"I heard you saw Ikenami-*san* here on Sunday."

"Yes, in the afternoon, about four."

"Can you remember the exact time?"

"Just before four. Let's say three fifty-five."

"Was he in good spirits?"

"He may have been tired. Coming up the stairs, he was out of breath. He was kind of cranky, but that's not unusual."

"What is 'cranky'?" asked Kurimoto, before translating Will's answer.

"Cranky . . ." Will thought briefly. "*Ki-muzukashii? Fukigen?*"

"*A! Nihongo umai desu ne!*" said Hasegawa in praise of Will's Japanese.

Will waved off the compliment. "*Iya, sō de mo arimasen.*"

"How did you learn Japanese?"

"I lived in Japan when I was younger. My father was a diplomat. He thought it would be best for the children to experience Japan, so he put us in local schools. I started in fifth grade and went all the way through middle school."

"Your father is a wise man."

Wise enough never to get into a fix like this.

"Ikenami-*san* was cranky about what?"

"He does not want to renew the contract of a young professor."

"His name?"

"Anson Cook. Next door."

"Ikenami-*san* told you this?"

"Yes. I'm on the renewal committee with him. I told him we need to wait. We don't decide; we only make a recommendation."

"He agreed?"

"No, he was angry and stormed away."

Hasegawa spoke to Kurimoto in Japanese. "Storm? Like rain?"

Will answered for her, "Yes. A storm is angry weather, lots of wind. He walked away like angry weather."

Hasegawa replied directly, in English, "Oh, English phrase is so interesting." He smiled at Will again, looked at Laurie, then rose in his seat as if he was uncomfortable and looked down at Will's lap.

Will realized what Hasegawa was doing just in time to relax his hands. He had not realized he was wringing them.

Hasegawa settled himself again. "Ikenami-*san* simply walked away?"

"Not happily, but yes. Anson is one of our best, and Professor Ikenami had no right to treat him that way."

Hasegawa was silent.

"Then I walked over to the café, got a cup of coffee, talked with some students." Will glanced up at Laurie. "That's why I was having trouble getting to sleep, the coffee." Will stopped.

What a stupid thing to say.

"And when you came back—"

Hasegawa's phone rang. He stepped into the hallway but opened the door far enough that the automatic closer stuck in its open position. He was talking before he noticed. Will looked away, but caught all the Japanese.

"*Moshi-moshi.* This is Hasegawa." "Found? Where?"

Oh no, not the body!

"Yes, we'll be there in five minutes."

It couldn't be the body, but they already found the phone, so what?

"Car," whispered Hasegawa to Kurimoto in Japanese as he stepped back into the office.

Kurimoto stood. "We must go now. We will speak again soon."

Will stood. "I'll be here."

As they were stepping into the hall, Hasegawa said something to Kurimoto and she asked, "What time did Ikenami-*san* leave?"

"I didn't hear him go. I wasn't paying attention. His lights were off when I went home. That was . . ." He looked up at Laurie.

"Ten twenty?" she guessed.

"Thank you." Kurimoto bowed and closed the door.

Will sat. Laurie rested her hands on his shoulders as he stared at the door. "You didn't tell me you argued."

"It wasn't a big deal."

"Or that you might have been the last to see him."

He took a second before he said, "Well, if he left, somebody, some-place, must've seen him."

What if the police wind up thinking that? They won't find anyone else. They'll conclude that Ikenami never left campus.

"You okay?"

"Yeah, sure."

Laurie perched on the edge of his desk, facing him. "You don't look okay. I should take you home."

Take me out of the country!

Laurie looked out the window. Following her gaze, Will saw the police car pulling out of the parking lot.

There was a soft knock on the door. It opened and David stuck his head in. "The plot thickens!" he said with a smile before he stepped in and eased the door closed.

Laurie asked, "Did they talk to you? Oh, and Happy New Year."

"Happy New Year to you too. And without Ikenami, it might be!"

Laurie took a chair. "You don't have to be so gleeful."

David sat in the other one. "Hey, I hope nothing happened to him," he said, before he smiled and added, "but if something did, *c'est la vie!*"

Will forced a smile. "Watanabe says they talked to you and you're a suspect."

"Am I? I'm moving up in the world. Yeah, I may have been the first one of the faculty. They had to come by eventually; better to get it over with. Besides, if I'm a suspect, I can stitch together an alibi."

Laurie asked, "What did they ask you?"

"When I saw him last, who might have wished him harm, what about me, did I wish him harm, what have I heard, stuff like that."

Laurie got serious. "Have you heard anything?"

"That's your best question? Not, 'Did you want the bastard dead?'"

"I wouldn't call him that, but fine, did you?"

"Been planning it for months!"

"You're terrible."

David chuckled. "No, I've heard nothing, or nothing credible, anyway. I've heard the same things you probably have: he committed *seppuku* in his office; he ran off to join a fascist cabal; stuff like that. The rumors about him being murdered could be true, but no one's talking suspects. My name is likely making the rounds as we speak. Anyway, I told them about Ikenami being interested in the IT committee. That's still the weirdest recent thing. I told them to follow up with Itō. I hope I got the guy's name right."

Will nodded.

"As exciting as this is, he'll turn up. It's probably just another nervous breakdown."

Laurie gave David a bewildered look.

"I never told you?" asked Will.

She shook her head. "No."

David leaned forward. "The first year I was here, Ikenami was teaching the same course he missed yesterday, and he kept getting questions from some cocky Indian kid. After a few weeks of it, the kid asked another of his questions and Ikenami lost it. He was taking a drink of tea or something and threw the plastic bottle at the kid and screamed at him. He ranted on about how backward India is, how it would never change because its government is corrupt, its society medieval, its population immoral and uneducated, and education wouldn't help because they're mentally inferior—"

"Good heavens!" said Laurie.

"Yeah! Then he stormed out. The class was in an uproar—and more than the Indian students, the Japanese, because they felt it reflected on them. They complained en masse to Yoshida."

"What happened?"

"It took a couple of days before Ikenami agreed to apologize, and by then it involved the entire school. Yoshida apologized on behalf of the university, deep bows and all, which you know is a *very* big deal, a tremendous loss of face. Yoshida must have been ready to kill Ikenami. Then Ikenami's apology—well, saying it was half-hearted would be giving it half a heart more than Ikenami gave it."

Laurie shook her head.

"Anyway, they had to blame it on something, so they said he was exhausted from overwork. He spent a few days in the hospital."

Laurie shook her head. "Wow."

"You saw him the day before yesterday. Did he look okay?"

"Bombastic as always," said Will. "He didn't say hello. He just told me he'd decided Anson's contract won't be renewed."

David raised an eyebrow. "I thought Anson was doing well."

"Better than that. It'll be a miracle if someone doesn't steal him."

"When we hired him, I remember Ikenami saying that getting a new PhD of Anson's caliber was a stroke of impossible luck," said David. "It's the only time Ikenami didn't push to keep a search going, hoping to find someone Japanese. Didn't Anson have an offer from some top school in the US?"

Will nodded. "Two, I heard. Haven't you ever wondered why he came here?"

"Not really. People do odd things. I did."

"C'mon, David, this is the greatest love story in the school's history. You really haven't heard?"

"No."

Laurie sat up. "Let me tell. I adore this story."

David laughed. "Can I take a rain check? I have a student coming by in two minutes."

31

WILL FOUND HIMSELF ALONE FOR THE FIRST TIME SINCE Laurie picked him up for lunch. What had been four feet of snow this morning was now approaching two. He wanted to check the field.

But he needed to stay here.

It occurred to him the snow had melted enough that he could use something around the house, like a ski pole, in tonight's search.

If Ikenami doesn't melt out . . .

He should check whether Chieko had news.

Chieko was on the phone, but Will poked his head into her doorway, and she waved for him to come in and sit.

She was talking to someone in Japanese, but Will understood enough. "Yes, it would not surprise me if they talked with the managers." She listened again. "They didn't say when they'd be back." After a brief pause, she bowed to the phone. "Thank you. Goodbye."

Chieko sighed, looking exasperated. "Everyone asks, 'What happened to him?' 'Is it a crime?' Someone asks, 'Was he kidnapped?'—as if someone would kidnap Ikenami-*sensei*! What is '*hijōshiki*' in English?"

"Absurd, irrational."

"Why are they irrational in the situation like this?"

Because I freaked out at the thought of the police and panicked. Everyone else's reason? "I haven't the slightest idea."

"Me too," she said. Then she motioned for Will to be still. She looked at the hallway and called out, "*Hai, nanika go-yō desu ka?* May I help you?"

Will heard someone take a hesitant step toward the door before Professor Malik appeared. He was the only full professor in IT, and the lone associate dean now that Ikenami was dead. He'd been at JGU for ten years. Before that his background was fuzzy, although Will knew he was from Malaysia and his family had money. He'd even heard Malik was descended from the royal family of one of the old kingdoms. But all Malik talked about was Swiss boarding school or his college years. All his schooling, including his PhD, was in continental Europe, but somehow, he ended up with UK citizenship—rumor had it by paying a British woman to marry him. Will was unsure whether he was still married. Malik lived like a bachelor not far from campus. He'd been a regular visitor during Will's first weeks, introducing him to the school and offering bits of advice and warning. As Malik maligned various faculty and staff, Will apparently did not show enough enthusiasm, and Malik drifted away.

Now Malik stepped into the doorway looking surprised. "Me? No. Or maybe. Is Yoshida-*sensei* coming back today? I think, you know, we ought to maybe have a special faculty meeting today or . . ."

"He comes back tonight."

Malik looked at Will with surprise and back at Chieko. "He doesn't know about Ikenami-*sensei*?"

Will saw Chieko bristle at Malik's implicit criticism of Yoshida, but her voice betrayed nothing. "He knows and will be back tonight."

"Anyway, have the police found anything?"

"I don't think they will tell me."

Malik nodded and looked at Will again.

Chieko said, "The police talk with faculty. Were you here Sunday?"

Malik took a step into the office. "No."

"Will you be here tomorrow?"

"Yes, I will be here, or in and out, sort of here, mostly, all day, I believe. When are you scheduled, Will?"

As Chieko answered for Will, he saw the faintest hint of a smile. "They talked with him today and are not interested in him anymore."

Malik nodded and asked Will, "What are they asking about?"

Chieko answered again. "They want to know who argues with Ikenami-*sensei*. Grames-*sensei* is next door, so he can hear and tell to the police."

Malik looked apprehensive. "We didn't argue."

Chieko looked away, as if avoiding having to contradict Malik, but Will could still discern the smile in her eyes.

Will played along. "I only mentioned what I'd heard, but I wasn't sure of voices, so . . ." He looked down at his hands.

"I never argued with Ikenami-*sensei*. Who said we argued?"

Malik looked distressed, and Chieko's conspiratorial look disappeared. "I think you do not have to worry so much."

"Oh, I wasn't, you know, worried, but sort of, I don't know, it's been stressful. It's so disturbing, I think. Don't you? That's a reason, you know, I wish the dean was—anyway, I'm available whenever."

"Thank you," said Chieko, and she bowed as Malik walked out. She whispered to Will, "Why is he so upset? Why should dean run back here? Can dean find Ikenami-*sensei*? Malik-*sensei* is so critical."

"He doesn't bother me much."

Chieko whispered, "He is associate dean so I must talk to him, but I do not like how he talks. He never says something clear, so I do not trust him. I wish he would leave JGU, but he has been here so long. What do you call person who does murder again and again?"

"Serial killer."

"Cereal, like corn flakes?"

Will spelled it, and she wrote it down.

She smiled. "If JGU has serial killer, I vote he kills Malik next."

HALF AN HOUR LATER, THE POLICE STILL HAD NOT RETURNED, so the knock on Will's door was not Hasegawa with more questions. "*Dōzo.*"

Trinh opened the door. "I'm sorry I disturb you."

Will stood. "Not at all. Have a seat."

He walked around and sat on the front edge of the desk. "What's up?"

"I heard something, and I worried, so I came here."

"Another rumor?"

She nodded. "I heard you and Ikenami-*sensei* were arguing."

Will's pulse quickened.

Someone heard—or saw? This can't be a coincidence.

He sat in the other chair. "We argued very little, although we did on Sunday. I wonder whether someone overheard."

Trinh looked worried. "Maybe."

"We were in the stairwell, so someone could have."

"Only there?"

"Yes. It only lasted a minute."

"The rumor is something else, shouting in his office with fighting."

"No way. Brief words in the stairwell was all." Before he dropped dead.

Trinh stood tentatively. "I should let you work."

Will stood. "Okay." Trinh didn't move, so Will said, "Don't worry about me. You can worry about Ikenami-*sensei*, but I'm fine."

Trinh stepped closer and put her hand on Will's arm, so he put his hand on hers. "Really, don't worry." She did not move her hand, so Will lowered it, and after a second, squeezed it and let it go.

"If I hear rumor again, I will say it is not true."

Will stepped to the door. "It won't help. We'll talk about word of mouth this term in class, and I'll tell everyone it's impossible to stop. Trinh, if you argue, people will only wonder why. Better to let it go."

She gave him a resigned look and whispered, "See you later."

Will sat at his desk. Was this rumor merely the altercation on the stairs blown out of proportion, or something else, someone focusing attention on him? Either way, soon everyone would hear it—including the police.

32

Hasegawa watched Ogawa process Ikenami's car, but finally convinced it offered no immediate clues, he and Kurimoto split up and, together with local officers, canvassed the area for witnesses. They covered three blocks in every direction, but no one had seen a thing. Ogawa had finished by then, so the three officers returned to the university.

Ogawa went back to Ikenami's office. Hasegawa, rather than following up with Will, wanted to talk to the subject of Will's argument with Ikenami. At 4:22 p.m., he knocked on Anson's door.

"Come in."

Kurimoto introduced herself and Hasegawa, and Anson invited them to take a seat. As his colleague explained that she would translate, Hasegawa looked the young man over. He was tall even for a foreigner, a little on the thin side, but he looked strong. He was dressed in cotton twill slacks and a white shirt, no tie, and medium-quality loafers. His skin was as fair as Hasegawa had ever seen, and his thick, straight hair, so blond it was almost white, was short and looked freshly cut. He looked . . . clean, disconcertingly so, as if there ought to be light glinting off his face. How had he gotten to be a professor, even at a junior level, so quickly? He looked younger than Kurimoto, although with foreigners, ages were hard to judge.

"Yes, I heard he's missing. Do you think something happened to him?"

"We're trying to find out. When did you see him last?"

"In December, I guess. When the term ended."

"You didn't see him on campus on Sunday?"

"No, I was at church in Nagano-shi on Sunday morning. We didn't get back until mid-afternoon."

"We?"

"My wife and baby and me. We spent the rest of the day at home."

Anson sat quietly, hands folded in his lap, as Hasegawa made notes. "You worked closely with Ikenami-*san*?"

"Me? No."

"He was not your supervisor?"

"No, he teaches accounting and I'm in finance."

"We were told he is the chair of your contract committee."

"Oh? I guess that makes sense. There's no full professor in finance."

"We heard he wanted not to renew your contract."

That knocked him back in his chair—before the translation came. The kid obviously spoke Japanese. His hands gripped the chair's arms, and after a few moments he said, "I didn't know that."

"Do you know why he opposed renewing your contract?" asked Hasegawa, still using Kurimoto for translation.

"No, why?"

"I am asking you."

Anson bowed his head for a long time—worried or conflicted, it was hard to tell—before he returned his gaze to Hasegawa. He didn't speak right away. He simply looked into Hasegawa's eyes. Eventually, he spoke. "I've known for a long time he didn't like me. I've gotten emails from him on university matters, but I don't think he's spoken to me in over a year. He's pretty gruff with everyone, but with me . . . I think it's personal."

"What is this personal feeling?"

Anson looked away. "He's never come out and said it." Hasegawa watched. Anson looked him in the eye again for a long minute. "It's because of my wife."

33

WILL ANSWERED THE PHONE. "*Moshi-moshi.*"

"Hi." It was Laurie. "You sound exhausted."

Will leaned back and closed his eyes. "Hi." Talk. I want to hear your voice. Talk all day long.

"You ready to come home?"

Yes. The light was fading, and the snow had indeed melted down to two feet. "What time is it?"

"Not even four thirty, but you looked tired today. How about I pick you up early?"

"Sounds great."

"Good. I'm downstairs."

Will looked out the window. Laurie was waving from the van. He waved back. "I'll be right—"

There was a knock on the door.

"*Dōzo.*"

It was David again. He was quiet when he saw Will on the phone.

"David's here and he looks like he has news. Come on up."

David shook his head. "No news."

"It's okay, Laurie's already off the phone. What's up?"

"They're talking to Anson now."

"I saw the car out there half an hour ago."

"They've been talking longer than that."

Laurie breathlessly slipped into the room a minute later. "What news?"

David said, "Anson's having a long talk with the police."

Laurie looked at him in surprise.

"A lot longer than mine, anyway."

"You think he's caught up in this somehow?"

Will frowned. "Impossible. David maybe, but not Anson."

"Thanks a lot."

"What if Ikenami was blocking his contract renewal?" Laurie sounded worried.

Will shook his head. "Yoshida would do anything to keep Anson. Yoshida's the only one who's started his career with as many publications as Anson, and Yoshida was at Wharton, not this backwater. To accomplish what Anson has is phenomenal. Ikenami's opinion is moot."

"Especially if his disappearance isn't temporary," added David.

Will frowned.

David glanced at Laurie, then at Will. "What's that look? I keep getting the vibe that his disappearance has something to do with you."

Will didn't move. He would have looked at Laurie, but she was radiating anxiety, so he stared at David before he looked away and rubbed his arm. "You saw his wife yesterday. No matter what we think of him, this is hurting people. Matsuyama-*san* says he never misses class. Something's up."

"You think it's time I put together my alibi?" asked David with a smile, as if trying to lighten the mood.

Will stayed somber. "I might have been the last one to see him."

Laurie asked, "So?"

"Isn't the last person to see someone always a suspect?"

"Is that all this is about?" asked David. "For the police to stay interested in you, you'd need a motive. There's no monetary gain. I don't think Ikenami was impacting your career, or threatening to block a promotion."

Laurie glanced over at Will. "We're not telling people, but we're hoping to leave after this contract, and with the papers Will has in the publication pipeline, he's well on his way. All he needs is his current research to work out so he can have working papers by then. So we're hoping promotion isn't an issue, and neither is contract renewal."

David frowned. "Not what I wanted to hear, but I'm happy for you."

Laurie said, "What happens if they can't find him?"

"You know how unusual it is for someone to disappear? I'm guessing he keeled over with a heart attack as it started to snow."

"Buried."

"Even if this doesn't melt, they'll find him. They'll start searching places he frequented or wherever they found his car."

Will asked, "Search how?"

David thought. "With poles like avalanche rescue teams?"

Like minds.

Laurie looked contemplative. "Or dogs. That's what I'd use."

Dogs.

Will glanced out at the rapidly darkening sky.

Damn.

34

CHIEKO WAS DONNING HER COAT WHEN SOMEONE KNOCKED on the open door.

"Officer, I thought you might be gone for the day."

Hasegawa stayed in the hallway reviewing his notes as Kurimoto said, "No, we had leads in town. Did Ikenami-*san* frequent any restaurants?"

"I think his wife packed lunches."

"Did he ever visit an Italian restaurant in the center of town, near this side of the station?"

Hasegawa said, "Trattoria Napoli."

"I don't know, but it's been popular since it opened last summer."

"What do you make of his vanishing without a trace?"

Chieko took a small step back. "It's disturbing."

"Yes, extraordinarily so."

Chieko nodded and handed Kurimoto a sheet of paper. "I thought it might help you to know which faculty will be on campus tomorrow."

"Oh, how thoughtful. Could you also tell us where to find Itō-*san*, the IT manager?"

"His office is in the library's basement. Also, Professor Watanabe seems eager to speak to you."

"Why is that?"

"He didn't say, but he wanted you to know."

"Have we seen him?"

"The nervous-looking man who was watching Officer Ogawa today."

"Ah, yes. Is he here now?"

As Chieko called his office, Hasegawa looked at his watch. "There's no answer," she said.

Hasegawa nodded. "We'll talk to him tomorrow. Which way is the library?"

Chieko pointed to her right. "Go to the end of the hall, turn right, and you're there."

"So compact," said Kurimoto.

Chieko smiled as she picked up her purse to leave. "Extraordinarily so."

∽

ITŌ WAS AN AVERAGE LOOKING MAN IN HIS EARLY THIRTIES who, Hasegawa guessed, had never shopped outside the local discount stores. His shirt was fraying at the collar and cuffs and he'd worn his pants smooth at the knees. He wore no wristwatch (young computer types seldom seemed to), and his shoes were not real leather. He was clean, however stingy his budget and threadbare his fashion sense. When Hasegawa suggested they talk in private, Itō showed them into a chilly room that housed the university's servers and invited them to take a seat at a large table. Watching Itō shiver now, Hasegawa wondered whether he regretted the location.

"You knew Ikenami-*san* was asking to join the IT committee?" asked Hasegawa.

"No, I hadn't heard that."

"Why did he want to be on the committee?"

"I don't know."

"Who is on this committee?"

"The managers of the Programs Office and Student Office, and from the faculty, the three IT professors and the new English professor."

"And you."

Itō nodded.

"What are the committee's responsibilities?"

"Prepare and oversee the IT budget, consult with the president on major spending, make sure that IT staff and infrastructure meet the university community's needs, decide what face JGU shows with its web pages, things like that."

"Have there been any controversial decisions?"

"Some say we should close the PC labs now that students all have their own."

"I see." Hasegawa waited.

Itō added, "People worry about money, of course."

"Oh?"

"IT changes—fast—and replacing and upgrading systems is expensive. Money's tight, so those decisions are always controversial. Everyone wants a fast, stable, secure system, but no one wants to pay for it."

"Perhaps there are clues about Ikenami-*san*'s interest in IT in his email. We'd like to see his recent correspondence."

Itō pushed his jaw forward and looked down.

"Is that a problem?"

"It's just . . . I've never been asked for access to an email account. I don't know whether you need a warrant."

Kurimoto said, "It's a university account, so he has no expectation of privacy. You control it, so you can grant access."

Itō shifted his weight. "I should probably talk with President Satō."

Hasegawa checked his watch: 5:19 p.m. "No problem. Call him. Now."

Itō stood. "Yes, I'll . . . be right back."

When the door closed, Kurimoto said, "He's stalling."

"Could be privacy concerns. From what people have told us about Ikenami, I can imagine this fellow fearing him."

"We have Ikenami's laptop from the car, so we'll have all his email anyway, as soon as we get past the password."

"If we're lucky, there's the chance of emails disappearing from the university systems between now and then, little telltale discrepancies."

"Would someone be that stupid?"

Hasegawa shrugged. "Most people know nothing about IT."

Itō returned. "The president was unavailable."

Hasegawa stood. "What do you plan to do?"

"It is not my place to open private correspondence to third parties. I'll keep trying to contact the president. If I get permission tonight, I'll put all the email into a file and send it to you."

Hasegawa held Itō's gaze as he stepped around the table and got right into Itō's face. "You seriously want to make us wait?"

Itō didn't move his feet, but Hasegawa could see him leaning away.

Itō bit his lip and glanced over at Kurimoto. "Or . . . I suppose . . . if he had no expectation of privacy . . ."

35

Come," whined Huong. The looks from the other students in the library embarrassed Trinh. At least it was in Vietnamese, so no one understood.

Trinh put a finger to her lips. "People are studying."

"Come with me!" Huong whispered.

"I already ate."

"You didn't relax or play or have a drink."

"We have class tomorrow."

"So what?" Huong pulled the book out of Trinh's hands, looked at the cover and laughed. "Marketing class hasn't started and you're studying already? You have it worse than I thought."

Trinh grabbed the book back.

"Don't worry, I see how he looks at you. He's got it too."

"He doesn't look at—"

"Everybody looks at you, Trinh, including your special professor. When are you going to—"

"Never."

"I hate you. Just because your parents named you 'Chastity' doesn't mean you have to live like a nun. When you finally do something with him, you won't even tell me. For all I know, you already did."

Trinh scowled at her.

"You did!"

"You know better than that. I never will, not with anybody."

"So you keep saying, but why not?"

"Because in a place this small, everyone knows everything. I don't want a drink. When you drink you act like a bar girl. Isn't it enough that guys treat us that way because we're Vietnamese? You have to validate their prejudice? It puts a stigma on every woman from a poor country."

"Don't be so repressed. It's not a job. We won't be ruining our careers. This is *school*—in a foreign country! Besides, we're not poor, we're hot."

"We're serious students trying to get good jobs."

"You're serious so you can impress your professor."

"You'll never let me read, will you?"

Huong shook her head as she tugged on Trinh's sleeve.

"Fine, one beer."

Trinh had worried that Huong would turn one beer into six. Now, as Trinh nursed her first, Huong was on her third. Brian was leading at four, while the young-looking student from Scotland lagged with orange juice.

"Is there class tomorrow, or can we drink all night?" asked Brian.

"Drink!" said Huong, and she leaned against Brian, who put his arm around her.

Trinh had seen Huong hang on Brian once before back in September. Huong woke the next morning in Brian's bed and spent the next two hours sobbing to Trinh, pleading never to let her do it again. Now Trinh pulled on Huong's arm. "We have classes tomorrow, and Japanese class is at eight. So we say good night now."

"You put me to bed now, big sister?"

"Yes, time for bed, baby sister."

Brian said, "Aw, I can take baby sister. You go ahead."

Huong gave Trinh a look of pretend surprise.

Trinh's voice lost its cheeriness. "Brian, you do not call her that."

Just then, the café door opened, and Huong sat up. Trinh turned around and saw why: it was Daniel Charles, the new English professor from Australia. He'd been hired mid-year to replace a professor who quit with almost no notice last summer. Blond, tan, and barely older than most of the students, rumor had it he'd covered his office walls with surfing posters.

He approached their table with a smile, looked at everyone, and then focused on Trinh. Every guy she talked to today had stared at her shirt—she had even caught Will glancing—and the new professor was no exception. Finally, he focused on her face. "May I join you?"

"Yes, professor," said Trinh with no enthusiasm.

"Call me Danny."

Trinh smiled politely, Huong giggled, and as Danny got a chair, Brian whispered to his Scottish friend, "Guy's got nothing but first names, like he's royalty."

Huong moved her chair to make room for Danny, and as he took a seat, he called out, "Asahi Dry," to the server across the room and winked. He looked around the table. "All first-years?"

Everyone nodded, and they did a quick round of introductions.

Danny smiled at them all before he looked at Trinh. "I don't have any of you in English class."

"We tested out and the guys are native speakers."

"I bet the blokes could use some work on their accents."

Huong tittered, and Danny asked her, "No snow in Vietnam?"

"No, first time for me. It is so pretty. Does it snow in Australia?"

Brian smiled mischievously. "No, bad for the koalas."

Huong smiled at Danny. "They're so cute."

Trinh could see it was time to go. "Come, baby sister. Time for bed."

"Yes, it's a school night," said Danny.

Huong frowned, but Trinh stood and collected her bag and her friend. "Good night, blokes."

Danny grinned. "Good evening, ladies."

36

SARAH SLIPPED INTO THE LIVING ROOM AND GRABBED A blanket. "Can we watch Japanese TV?"

Will asked, "Are you done with your homework?"

"Yup."

"How's your sister doing?"

"Almost done too." She smiled. "Only Mom has homework left."

Will went to check on Laurie and met Becka coming through the kitchen door. He closed it behind himself to stop the shock of cold air from the hallway, although even with doors closed the drafty old rooms held heat like a beggar's rags.

Will sat by Rachel, who was coloring. "How's Mom doing?"

"I'm not watching her. I'm busy with this."

"Your sisters are watching something in Japanese. *Mi ni iku?*"

"*Kōkōsei dorama nanka iya.*"

Laurie looked up, and Will said, "High school drama."

"I know. All the girls are watching it," Laurie said. "Do you have to go back and work anymore tonight?"

"I don't want to." It was true. He wanted to stay home—forever.

"Why don't you get some rest? I don't like you out late in the snow."

With another day of sunshine, Ikenami would melt out. Will had no choice but to move him tonight. "Roads are dry after today's sun."

"Not since it started snowing again an hour ago. It's supposed to snow all night and could be forever."

It would be perfect for moving the body—the snow would hide his digging—but Will loathed the thought. Besides, with a foot of new snow by the time he could dig, the ski pole wouldn't suffice for the search.

Laurie told Rachel, "Why don't you go watch TV with your sisters?"

Rachel tried using her sad look, but Laurie lifted her off the chair and ushered her out of the room. Laurie sat next to Will and took his hands in hers. "What's going on? This is more than start-of-the-term tension."

"It is?"

"Something's bothering you, and you're not telling me."

Ikenami's dead. It was my fault. The police will find out and put me in prison. I'll never see you and the girls again. So I have to go and move the body, as much as I hate it. "No, everything's fine. I should go."

"Will, I know the Ikenami thing has you spooked. When you saw the police, it was like you thought they were there for you. You've got to suppress your cop phobia or it's going to be trouble. I know you must feel bad about arguing with him on Sunday, but you need to calm down or they'll think you're connected to this. I don't want you going back and running into them tired like you are now."

"I'll be fine."

"Why don't I give you a sleeping pill and send you to bed?"

Oh, Laurie, why not give me the whole bottle?

LAURIE LAY IN THE *FUTON* NEXT TO WILL, WHO WAS FINALLY sound asleep, and found herself thinking about Trinh, of all people. The image of Trinh after Japanese class had intruded more than once today, along with Will's, "Who, Trinh?" Not that Laurie was losing him, but a body like Trinh's couldn't help but stir any man who wasn't dead. And Trinh's skintight shirt—she knows how to use what she's been blessed with. It was particularly true in the pool, where Trinh wore a two-piece swimsuit. It was a lap suit, not a bikini, but it still accentuated her figure to a scandalous degree, especially the "Adidas" printed across her bottom. At least her hair—full, hip-length, black, gorgeous—was hidden in a swim cap. Still, in the times they had swum together, Laurie had never seen her approach the pool without at least one guy stopping and pretending to adjust his goggles. She had even seen someone swim headfirst into the wall as Trinh stood in the next lane.

Yet what was there to grouse about? Trinh was sweet. The girls loved her.

Laurie had worn plenty of provocative things when she was that age.

That age . . .

As much as she'd enjoyed it, she had no desire to go back. The girls were worth the price, and her body wasn't so different, considering.

She'd worked to keep this shape, refusing to let childbearing take the toll it had on her mom. After each of the girls, Laurie had sweated and starved and willed herself back into her original size. But her mom had five. There was no telling what two more would've done to Laurie. Getting in shape after Rachel was hard.

I shouldn't have been so vain. I shouldn't have hounded myself over how I looked.

How could she not, though, when Will looked like he did? She wanted to be a couple, to fit. Now she did. And she had three girls—pretty darn good ones—and with a little more churchgoing, she'd be keeping her vow to raise them into the finest women they could become. Fulfilling that might even balance the guilt over the mediocre job she felt she was doing so far.

And the fit mattered.

She'd been neglecting the pool. She needed to start swimming again.

She sighed and turned over.

It has nothing to do with Trinh. Or her little two-piece.

37

The room went dark as Trinh locked her door, but then she lit the lamp by the bed and turned it down low. Although she would never admit it, she liked the Webmaster to watch. She teased too: turning down the bed, setting the alarm, pulling a brush through her long, thick, silken hair, stroke after stroke, pretending not to notice what it did to him.

She pulled off her socks and dropped them on the bed.

He urged her on with his eyes, but she returned to brushing her hair. Finally, she secured it in a thick, ebony ponytail with an elastic band.

She looked in his direction—he smiled—and she stood.

Trinh pulled her T-shirt off differently than Japanese girls did. A Japanese girl would slip her arms out of her sleeves into her shirt before pushing it up and off. Trinh just grabbed the bottom of her shirt, arms crossed, and pulled it inside out as it slipped over her head. He sat transfixed as she peeled it up in stages, revealing ever more of her soft brown skin. Today's shirt was tight. It caught when she tried to pull it over her curves. Her hips undulated as she worked to free herself, and without realizing, he leaned forward.

Free at last, she picked up her socks, tossed them into the hamper with her shirt, and turned to face him. His pulse quickened. Her fingers grasped the waistband of her tight black pants as she drew in her flat stomach, and with a flick of the wrist the button popped open. She pushed them down to her knees, her ankles, and stepped out.

She looked almost shy as she turned away, unhooked her bra, and dropped it on the bed. He loved that about her: she showed no conceit, even though everywhere she went, men watched. They tracked her with their eyes, lust craning their necks, as she sashayed through any room. She was ready. She revealed it in how she moved, not only tonight, for him, in the secrecy of her room, but everywhere. The Webmaster knew from the first time he saw her. She was flipping her hair over her shoulder, swaying her hips for balance as she pulled her bags off the bus that ferried new students from the train station. Not that she wasn't the demure, innocent girl she appeared or believed herself to be, but there were parts of herself that, while she had yet to embrace them, were growing stronger, urges she would surrender to so completely that—

She pulled flannel Hello Kitty pajamas from the dresser. He laughed. Still demure.

IV

Marketing:
Creating Customer Value
マーケティング：消費者価値の創造

Wednesday, 13 January 2010

38

"Y OU SEEM MORE RESTED THIS MORNING," SAID LAURIE, AS
Will turned the corner into the university.

If only rest could solve this.

"If you're swimming today, I may join you."

"I'd like that," said Will.

He drove through the great rows of ginkgo trees that framed the administration building and its tall clock tower. Behind the trees on either side were the university's two eight-story dormitories. Through a dusting of tranquilly descending snow, the buildings looked gray, despite a coat of white paint last year. Many had complained it was a waste of money. Now all Will could think of were whited sepulchers.

Laurie sighed as they pulled in. "The police aren't here, but that doesn't mean Ikenami isn't still missing."

He needed to stay missing. Would things calm down enough tonight to move the body? Had he missed his final opportunity last night?

How many interviews remained for the police today? Will might have the whole evening to find and move Ikenami. Then Will imagined the frozen corpse plopping into the river. He squeezed the steering wheel tighter as he thought of Ikenami's wife and children, their torment—

"You getting out?" asked Laurie, apparently for the second time.

A lull fell as Will entered Japanese class. Every student turned his way, but only Trinh made eye contact. She held his gaze, looking pained, as the professor started class.

39

You think it was suicide?" asked Hasegawa as Kurimoto drove across the bridge in the middle of town.

Light rain in the city of Nagano had changed to snow as they neared the mountains, so Kurimoto kept her eyes on the road and drove on.

"That was a question."

Still, she did not reply.

Hasegawa did not look at her. His voice, while still authoritative, was softer. "I realize you're young and people rarely ask your opinion, but working with me, you will speak up. Especially with a weird case like this. We need ideas. That's fundamental to good police work. You will talk, and you will not wait for me to ask. Understood?"

"Yes, sir." She drove on for a while before she timidly said, "I guess I am thinking suicide."

"Why?"

"It's just . . . I don't see anyone having a motive for murder."

"The lack of a body all but rules it out. I have never seen a suicide with no body."

"Yes sir, but who, his wife?"

Hasegawa looked out the side window, as if addressing the snow. "Not inconceivable, but I've worked a couple of cases where women killed their husbands. She's not the type."

"A murderer at JGU may be harder to believe than suicide."

"Some odd people there."

She smiled. "In my limited experience, sir, everyone is odd."

Hasegawa chuckled.

"They hardly seem like murderers. There's no motive."

Hasegawa closed his eyes and leaned his head back. "It's not a jealous lover or husband. Who would have an affair with a guy like that?"

It was Kurimoto's turn to chuckle.

"Anyway, I guess that leads us back to suicide."

"Unless he ran away," said Kurimoto.

"There would've been signs. No one told us he was acting erratically."

Kurimoto was quiet for a minute before she asked, "What about the broken watch that Ogawa found? That could be a clue."

"Or merely a broken watch."

"I read his report about the car. Ikenami must have been the last driver, right? There were only his prints on the steering wheel, and lots of them. Anyone else driving would have wiped them out. His were the only prints on the door handle. His office showed no signs of being a crime scene, either."

"He left his office, drove into town, and vanished."

She was briefly silent. "What about a stranger, a robbery gone bad? Or, he's young for it, but he's diabetic, so I can believe him parking, getting out of the car, and dropping dead of a heart attack. A quiet town like this, no one notices the body before the snow covers it."

"Except for his phone on the bridge."

"He's robbed on the bridge, killed, and dumped over the side."

"Who robs people on bridges? Too open."

"He's on the bridge, has a heart attack, pulls out his phone to call for help, but it's too late. He drops the phone as he topples over the railing."

"The odds of that?" Hasegawa suppressed a smile. It impressed him that someone this young could keep from wilting as he incinerated her ideas one by one.

"Robber-killer plants the phone on the bridge to throw us off."

"Highly unlikely, but possible."

"We're back to suicide."

"As weird as it seems."

"If he is lying dead under the snow somewhere, how do we find him?"

Hasegawa said, "Ogawa will be here this afternoon with a canine searcher."

"Maybe we should alert the towns downstream to keep a lookout for a corpse in the river, especially in places it might get hung up."

Hasegawa looked over at her, one eyebrow raised. "If you think so, have Ogawa get it started."

Kurimoto was smiling as she parked the car. She turned it off and looked at Hasegawa. "Dean Yoshida is first?"

Hasegawa checked his watch: 8:32 a.m. "Yes. After Yoshida, we can ask his assistant who's on the IT committee. In these interviews, whether it's English or Japanese, if you have a question, ask—not in the middle of a line of questioning—but you're not just a translator."

Kurimoto nodded smartly. "Understood."

JUNICHIRŌ YOSHIDA WAS AN IMPOSING FIGURE: BROAD-shouldered, tall, and smartly dressed in a bespoke suit. To Hasegawa, Yoshida's size was an accident of birth, and his dress was merely a sign of money—if anything, a negative indicator of character. Yoshida's demeanor, though, impressed the veteran detective. He was out of place in this tiny university. He belonged where things happened, a top university or boardroom.

After Chieko brought coffee, Hasegawa leaned forward and spoke. "I'm sorry to say the situation is grim. No one has seen Ikenami-*san* for over sixty hours. If he was hurt—say, had a heart attack and collapsed—hope is essentially gone. Of course, someone could have killed him in a robbery or any number of other possibilities, all disheartening."

Yoshida shook his head. "It's hard to believe a violent crime occurred in a little town like this."

"We must look at the family. That's just his wife and children."

"Then we're speaking of murder, correct? I cannot imagine Yōko doing such a thing. The children either. Actually, I got a call last night from the son. They admitted Yōko to the hospital. She's worried herself to exhaustion, thinking she may have driven him to suicide."

"I'm sorry we must consider that. Had he shown signs of depression?"

"No, but he's never been a cheerful, convivial sort. He could have been depressed without people sensing it."

"Was he under unusual stress recently?"

"Not that I'm aware."

"Money problems?"

"Unlikely. He's as tight as they come. He affords himself a few luxuries, I guess. The man always wears nice shoes, for example. But when you check his accounts, don't be surprised if they're stuffed with money."

"Was he . . . involved with anyone?"

"An affair? Hard to imagine. But we're hardly confidants, so I wouldn't know."

Kurimoto went on. "Have there been threats against him here at the university? Any physical altercations or serious arguments?"

"No. Ikenami's full of bluster, willing to steamroll people. He can be insulting and mean. I suspect he's covering feelings of inferiority. Some things he's said make me wonder if he was bullied as a kid and never got over it. Physically, trust me, he's a weakling—truly a mouse—he'd run if anyone raised a hand to him."

Hasegawa asked, "Did anyone have a vendetta?"

"Some faculty members who have left deeply resented him, but they took jobs overseas."

Hasegawa glanced over at Kurimoto. She leaned forward and asked, "We heard he was hoping to be dean, but they hired you instead."

"True, but he's never challenged me. He only bullies people he can dominate."

Kurimoto kept a steely gaze on him. "May I ask where you were this weekend?"

"I met with the board in Tokyo on Friday. My wife came up on the Shinkansen and we spent a long weekend in Hakone."

Hasegawa was about to take over when Kurimoto said, "You mentioned that a violent crime in this—well, it's little more than a hamlet, really—would be hard to believe. If someone at the university—"

"If you're thinking of murder for a promotion, that would be far-fetched, even at a big, vibrant school. At JGU, it would be like elbowing one's way to a window seat on the Hindenburg—as it was burning."

Hasegawa asked, "The situation is bleak?"

"In the post-bubble years, the university's financial health slipped from fair to dire. When our founder passed, it became grave."

"University politics are tense?"

"You have a gift for understatement. We're almost sunk, and President Satō is bailing with a teacup."

"Did Ikenami-*san* have trouble with the president?"

"Not at all. I, on the other hand, have nothing but. Anyway, unfortunately for all, I suspect the end is in sight."

"What will happen?"

"JGU will close. Faculty will find jobs elsewhere, as will the lucky ones among the staff, the non-faculty employees."

Hasegawa frowned.

"It's more than sad. It's deplorable," said Yoshida. "The president has a responsibility to these people. It's probably too late, but I'm ready to tell the board of trustees that one of us has to go, either the president or me."

"Could someone have guessed this was coming?"

"I have told no one, but some might surmise."

"If they dismissed the president, would they call on you to step in?"

"That would be up to the board."

"If you became president, who would be dean?"

Yoshida smiled and shook his head. "No one internal. None of the Japanese faculty, including Ikenami, has the personality or gravitas to walk into corporate boardrooms and sell our programs. None of the foreign faculty speak Japanese well enough. Most likely, I'd fill both rolls."

Hasegawa asked, "What if the board backs Satō?"

"And I leave? Tribal warfare. The board will choose a new dean, probably from the existing faculty. The resulting politicking and alienation will rip the place apart."

"Who would the board choose?"

"As the most senior Japanese on the faculty, probably Ikenami."

"What if he were unavailable?"

Yoshida reviewed the senior faculty for the detective. All had some potential except for Malik, the senior IT professor. Yoshida said he was simply stupid. Hasegawa asked about Will, but Yoshida replied he was too new.

Hasegawa made more notes. "Thank you for the frank assessment. How about a student? It's said Ikenami-*san* was disdainful of foreigners and that the students," he read from his notes in English, "hated his ultra-nationalist bullshit."

Yoshida winced. "Likely not an uncommon sentiment."

"Any student who had especially potent feelings?"

"There was an Indian student a few years ago, a terrible scene right in the classroom. We would have fired anyone but Ikenami."

"He is special?" asked Hasegawa.

"He's the only remaining faculty from JGU's opening. The founder was fond of him. He's also well known in academic accounting in Japan."

"We understand he wanted to get rid of a young professor, Cook-*san*."

"By engineering a negative recommendation on Cook's contract renewal? No, Cook's the best young professor we've ever had. Unless Ikenami unearthed some dark secret, which for Cook—have you met him?"

Hasegawa nodded.

"Then you know that's ludicrous. It's more likely Ikenami was carried off by *Toire-no-Hanako.*"

Kurimoto chuckled at Ikenami falling victim to a restroom ghost, but Hasegawa rubbed his forehead as he looked through his notes. "Ikenami-*san* wanted to join the IT committee?"

"I doubt someone did him in over a committee assignment, but that was odd. He suspected university resources were being misdirected."

"Embezzlement? Theft?"

"He said 'IT resources'—but was not specific in his email."

"I see," said Hasegawa, but his attention was on what sounded like a heated conversation outside Yoshida's office.

There was a sudden knock, and Chieko burst in. "Come quick, please! Stop them!"

40

After a short quiz, Will's Japanese professor started on the day's topic, honorific verbs, but the class lacked its regular enthusiasm, so she paired them up to practice. Each pair contrived conversations doused with honorifics, except for Will and the Scottish student. Will struggled to keep his mind on task, but his partner was worthless, tongue-tied at every turn. To Will's relief, they soon changed partners, and he got one of the exchange students, who carried her side admirably. Even Will warmed to it.

The tension returned, however, as soon as class ended. Will had never seen the room empty so fast. Something was clearly happening, but there was nothing to do but return to his office and wait.

As he entered the stairwell to head to the second floor, Trinh was waiting for him. "What's going on?" whispered Will.

"There is rumor you killed Ikenami-*sensei.*"

As Will started up the stairs, he kept his voice low. "Probably from the fighting rumor you told me yesterday."

"No," whispered Trinh, "different people say it, that you killed him and throwed his body in the river, but you mistaked and dropped his phone."

"What are they saying about why I killed him?"

"No one says. Just, you killed him and about the river."

Will took a few steps in silence before he said, "Don't worry."

She grabbed Will's arm. "But *Sensei,* what if someone else saw?"

Will stopped and turned to her. "Someone *else* saw *what*?"

There was terror in Trinh's eyes as she looked up and down the stairs, but he could hear Laurie's voice just above them. He took a step up, freeing his arm, and whispered, "Conference Center. Ten minutes."

Will trotted up the stairs and found Laurie and her professor, but the professor dropped the conversation as Will emerged from the stairwell.

Will greeted them with a smile and bowed. "*Ohayō gozaimasu.*"

The professor replied in kind, then excused himself.

Laurie whispered, "Everyone was looking at me strangely this morning, and now that. What's going on?"

"There's a rumor I killed Ikenami and dumped him in the river."

"What?"

"They found his phone there Monday. I suspect it's that fact mixed with yesterday's rumor that we had a knock-down, drag-out fight in his office."

"Did you?"

"No, you know better than that."

"Well, I'm sorry, but you've been acting so weird the last two days."

Will walked on in silence.

"Does the fight rumor come from the argument you had with him, or is someone trying to make your life difficult?"

"I would have said Ikenami, but . . ."

They were both quiet as they approached Chieko's open door. As they passed, she called out, "Grames-*sensei*."

Will said, "*Ohayō.*"

Chieko smiled. "*Ohayō gozaimasu.* Can you do native English check of email to all students, staff, and faculty?"

Will quickly worked through it, then turned the paper toward Chieko. "Well done. Only a few minor changes." He read it aloud:

> In view of the many reports circulating on campus, we approach the entire university community with information and a request. We are sorry to inform you that Prof. Kiyoshi Ikenami is missing. The police are investigating. We urge anyone with information about Professor Ikenami's disappearance to come forward. You may contact a member of the administration or the police.

Will read the contact information and continued with the text:

> We also caution in this time of uncertainty and worry against trusting or repeating rumors. Hurtful rumors have been circulating. Such baseless talk not only damages innocent reputations, it interferes with the all-important police investigation. The Dean's Office will inform everyone of any news without delay. In the meantime, let us turn our

thoughts to Professor Ikenami and his family as we await his safe return.

Will said, "Good announcement."

Chieko looked at Will and Laurie with a sympathetic smile.

Will asked, "You heard the rumor?"

She nodded. "In Japan we say, '*Ikken kage ni hoyureba, hyakken koe ni hoyu:* When one dog barks, all dogs bark.'"

Laurie asked, "Any idea where the rumor came from?"

"No, it is ridiculous. I can't believe students spread it. Worse thing is I heard it from staff. Another sad thing: Mrs. Ikenami entered hospital last night, sick with worry he killed himself."

"This whole thing is awful," said Laurie. "It's torturing his poor family. What we're wading through's nothing like them, but these rumors—"

Chieko was looking at the doorway behind Laurie, her eyes wide in surprise. Will and Laurie turned to see Watanabe.

Through clenched teeth, he growled at Will, "Why?"

❧

Yoshida was first to the door, followed by Hasegawa and Kurimoto. The argument was in the hallway, and it surprised Hasegawa when Yoshida simply stopped and listened. Kurimoto translated in a whisper.

Will asked, "You saw me do it?" Watanabe was silent, but Will went on, a storm gathering in his voice. "Of course not. You'd have stopped me, at least called the police. If you didn't see, how do you know?"

"Everyone knows!" shouted Watanabe.

"How, Jirō? How if no one saw? And who told you? Who told you a lie like that? How'd he say he knew? Why did I do it? What possible reason could I have to kill Ikenami?"

Laurie gently tugged on Will's arm. "Will, let's just—"

"No! I want to know who told him. Who was it, Jirō? A student? Staff? Faculty? Who?"

"Yes, Professor Watanabe, we all want to know who," came Dean Yoshida's voice as he stepped into the hallway. Hasegawa was a step behind, followed by Kurimoto.

Watanabe's mouth flapped, making incoherent near-speech as he looked from face to face. Then he gathered himself, pointed his finger at Will, and shouted in Japanese, "Here's your murderer!"

Watanabe dropped his hand when Yoshida stepped close. As Yoshida glared down at him, Watanabe shriveled. Yoshida said in Japanese, "Murder is a serious allegation that could bring disciplinary action." Watanabe seemed to take heart. Yoshida added, "Against whoever makes such an incendiary accusation—unless he can prove it." He looked at Will.

"I assure you it's a lie," said Will in Japanese.

"Perhaps Professor Watanabe should discuss the basis of his accusation with Detective Hasegawa."

Hasegawa nodded.

"I'll show you to the chairman's office. It's just up the hall."

Yoshida strode down the hall, followed by Watanabe and the police. Will and Laurie looked at Chieko, who made an "Ooh" expression and motioned for them to come back into the office.

Once inside, Laurie asked Will, "You okay?"

He didn't look at her. "Yeah."

"You don't look okay. You look angry."

"Yeah? Now why is that?"

Laurie flinched.

"Sorry." Will rubbed his forehead. "There's no reason to snap at you." He turned to Chieko. "I'm sorry you had to see that."

She smiled. "I can understand if it upset you. I think you were very . . . you did not show all your anger."

"Restrained," said Laurie, and Chieko smiled and nodded.

"This is bad. Someone's making me out to be a killer."

Laurie frowned. "Later today they'll be talking about someone else."

"I think it was a heart attack," said Chieko.

Will looked at the ceiling and shook his hands to relax them.

Laurie tugged on his sleeve again. "Let's go."

"Where?"

"I think your office is far enough."

In the office, Laurie took Will's hand. "This place is getting . . . interesting. Can I hang out here more?" Will tried to smile. "You really okay?"

"Worried. And as far as you hanging out, I'd love that, but for the next few minutes, can you hang here alone?"

"How come?"

"Because Trinh knows something, and I have to find out—"

"Oh," said Laurie, as she dropped his hand and looked away.

"Let me finish. With Watanabe's accusation, I expect the police will come knocking any minute, and I don't want it to look like I'm hiding. So you'll wait here, smile when they arrive, and stall them. Please."

Laurie nodded but was not smiling as she shooed Will out of the room.

Trinh was looking out the enormous windows on the second floor of the Conference Center. As Will approached she had her brow creased. "I worry too much, maybe, but new rumor scares me."

"You were saying someone saw something?"

"Yes."

"Can you tell me what you heard and who told you?"

After a few seconds, Trinh took a step toward the windows. Almost whispering, she said, "No one told me. I saw."

Will moved closer. "Tell me."

Trinh hesitated, rubbing her arms through her coat. "I saw Ikenami-*sensei* fall in the stairway."

Will waited.

"I was coming down the stairs, and he said something, but I could not understand. You stepped in front of him, and you said he cannot decide about Anson's contract. He pushed you. You were ready to hit him, and he stepped back and fell."

"I wouldn't have struck him."

Trinh's voice was emotional. "But he fell."

"Yes. Then he got up and climbed right back up the stairs."

"He was angry."

"That was it. You saw the whole thing."

Trinh was quiet.

"Was anyone with you?"

Trinh shook her head. "No."

"Did anyone else see or hear it?"

She shook her head again.

Will looked out at the snow.

Trinh took a small step closer. "I didn't tell, but now rumor is you fighted."

"We didn't fight. He pushed me. That was all. I never touched him. You saw it all. He was okay."

"What will you do?" asked Trinh.

"When I talked to the police yesterday, I didn't tell them about him falling down the stairs."

"I will not tell. I promise."

"Maybe I should. If someone else saw it and tells them, they'll think I was hiding something."

Trinh turned to Will and whispered, "Please do not tell police."

"But—"

She reached out and took his hand.

"Trinh, it's safest to tell them."

Trinh looked panicked. "If you tell now, they will believe the rumor."

Will pulled her close and patted her on the back, and Trinh buried her face in his chest. "Hush. It'll be all right," he said.

"Please don't tell."

Will dropped his head back and sighed, but Trinh didn't pull away, so he let her go. He looked back and forth between Trinh and the snow. He checked his watch. "Okay, I won't tell. Stop worrying, okay? Tell no one except the police that you saw Ikenami. That way no rumor's coming from you. If the police talk to you, tell them Ikenami and I argued, he pushed me, and I looked angry; everything except him falling."

"Yes."

Will looked at his watch again. "I need to get back to the office. We'll swim today, like normal, just like any other day."

She nodded.

"We need to know where this rumor came from. Can you trace it back?"

"Yes, I will find out."

"Thank you. Someone knows something—or is making things up—and we've got to know who."

～

HASEGAWA TOOK HIS TIME. HE LOOKED OVER THE LARGE office, leafed through a book, poked at the keyboard of the unplugged PC, and adjusted the radiator. He sat and flipped through his notes, seemingly ignoring Watanabe. In fact, Watanabe had his full attention from even before they stepped into the room. It was more than noticing that the man hadn't washed his hair in days, wore shoes in desperate need of new soles and a shine, and had probably never worn a coordinated outfit since his mother last dressed him. It would have been impossible not to notice such a blinking, jerking ball of raw nerves. Hasegawa waited to see what Watanabe would do. Perhaps this was not the height of agitation, but something closer to a steady state. Hasegawa suppressed a shiver.

At length, Watanabe blurted out, "I just repeated what everyone's saying."

Hasegawa showed no reaction.

Watanabe, clearly expecting a question, glanced back and forth at Hasegawa and Kurimoto, but she mimicked Hasegawa's stone face.

Watanabe couldn't sit still. "Grames killed him and threw his body in the river, but he dropped his phone. That's how you know."

Hasegawa pushed his jaw forward. "Mmm."

Blink. "What?"

Hasegawa tilted his head, just a few degrees.

"What?"

Hasegawa meted out his words. "Killed him . . . threw him in the river . . ." He was silent for a few seconds. "That Grames is one cold-blooded fellow."

Watanabe nodded enthusiastically.

"What other cold-blooded things has he done?"

Watanabe blinked again, knitted his brow, and looked away.

Hasegawa waited a long while before he asked, "It's a sudden cold-bloodedness?"

"So he's not always like that. It was probably a psychotic break."

"What's that?"

Watanabe looked askance at him. "Somebody abruptly goes berserk."

Hasegawa stared at him again. At length, Hasegawa said, "To be more precise, it is an episode of acute psychosis in someone who has been asymptomatic, either completely or for a significant period. Its most common triggers are: psychoactive drugs, such as LSD or PCP; opioid withdrawal; or a shattering emotional loss, such as the death of a loved one."

Blink, blink.

"Which is it? Is he a drug user or did somebody die?"

Watanabe's voice was softer. "I don't know him that well."

"You knew him at," Hasegawa checked his notes, "the University of Illinois. Was he cold-blooded then?"

"I didn't know him well there either."

Hasegawa nodded and made meaningless scribbles, then sat and stared at the page. Without looking up, he tapped his pen on the paper. "He dumped the body. I get it. After killing him."

"Yes."

Hasegawa raised his eyes to Watanabe's and held them. "He killed him because . . . ?"

"They were fighting."

"About . . . ?"

"I don't know! But you can feel his disrespect. It's subtle, but it's there. When he speaks of senior faculty, like the dean, he calls him 'Yoshida-sensei.' But he says, 'Professor Ikenami,' refusing to call him '*sensei.*'"

"Isn't 'professor' the more respectful title?"

"In Japanese, yes, but he never calls him 'professor' in Japanese."

"What does he call him?"

"'Professor' in English."

"Ah." Hasegawa rubbed his chin. "They fought a lot?"

Watanabe was quiet for a few seconds. "Not so often."

"What did they fight about?"

"I don't know."

"Did you ever see them fighting or arguing?"

"Yes."

"Where was this?"

"In faculty meeting."

"Fighting?"

"Arguing."

"Yelling?"

"No."

"Threatening each other?"

"No."

"Then what?"

"Grames disagreed with Ikenami-*sensei*."

"Called him an idiot, that sort of thing?"

"No, just said he was wrong."

"I see. But he killed him."

Watanabe looked at his lap, where he was tearing the tips off the fingernails on his left hand.

"Where were you Sunday afternoon and evening?"

Watanabe looked up. "I went shopping on Sunday. In Nagano."

"What time did you get back into town?"

"I don't know, maybe four or five."

"Did you come to the university?"

Blink. Blink. "Yes."

"When?"

Watanabe dropped his eyes and hunched over. "Maybe . . . four or five."

Hasegawa could see Watanabe curling up inside himself. His voice was so soft that Hasegawa could hardly hear him. There was only one thing left to learn for now, though, and Watanabe had that much play left in him. Hasegawa leaned forward. "You were here at the right time. Did you witness a fight?"

"No."

"An argument?"

"No."

"You heard this from someone?"

"Yes."

As if she was wired in, Kurimoto leaned forward, too, as Hasegawa asked, "From whom?"

Watanabe looked away, but Hasegawa kept his eyes on Watanabe's. He saw him look down, watched the tension build until, barely audible, Watanabe whispered, "Just . . . everyone knows."

Hasegawa scowled at him impatiently.

Watanabe sat, eyes closed, for a long time before he shrugged and whispered, "I don't remember."

41

YOU UNDERSTOOD WHAT HE WAS SAYING?" ASKED DAVID. Will nodded. "He told the police I'm the murderer." Laurie was hugging him from behind.

David nodded at Will in admiration.

"You've got to learn the language sometime," said Will.

David grinned. "Got a teacher, but I don't do my homework."

"Oh yeah, who's that?"

There was a soft knock on the door. David opened it. Anson peered in and whispered, "What's up?"

Will pointed to a folding chair in the corner. Anson opened it and took a seat. "I heard the blowup but figured I should wait awhile before poking my nose in."

Will frowned. "These rumors are getting ugly."

Anson looked worried. "It's like someone's got it in for you. For me too. The police told me yesterday that Ikenami's going to torpedo my contract renewal."

"They heard that from me," said Will. "Ikenami told me Sunday, but don't worry, Yoshida decides that. You'll come through unscathed."

David asked, "Why does Ikenami want Anson gone?" He looked at Anson, who frowned.

Laurie sat up. "Okay, I'll tell it. You know Anson first came to Japan as a missionary?"

"I knew you're Mormon, or what is it? Something 'saints'?"

"He volunteered to go convert some new saints, they sent him to Japan, and one of his towns was Nagano."

"Ah, coming to JGU was like coming home. I get it."

"No, there's way more. I guess the missionaries can't date. Still, there was a very special, very saintly saint in Nagano and Anson fell madly in love—with Miho." Laurie grinned as Anson's face glowed red.

"Your wife, Miho?" asked David.

"Exactly! Anyway, he was a missionary, so he stayed mum."

"I couldn't tell Miho, not then," said Anson.

Laurie chuckled. "I heard after you left Nagano, you wrote her a letter!"

David was smiling. "The two of you got together?"

"No, while he was a missionary, they only wrote letters—"

Anson added, "A month before I went home, I sat next to her at a church conference. It was the most amazing feeling!"

"His two years were up, he went home—and the first thing he did was call her on the phone and propose."

"I didn't want her to get away."

David shook his head as he grinned. "You proposed without ever going on a date or anything?"

"I realize how wacko it sounds, but I was old enough to know I loved her. Anyway, she talked to her parents—"

"And they refused," interrupted Laurie.

"They were trying to protect her. I was barely twenty-one, and she was only a few months older. I hadn't even graduated from college."

Laurie said, "They kept sending letters—never meeting—as Anson hurried through the rest of his undergrad."

"And got into the PhD program at the University of Chicago," added Will.

"Her parents still refused to let them get married," said Laurie.

"We hoped they might relent if I was in a PhD program, but their minds were set. She visited Chicago one week each year, and I spent a week each year in Japan—"

"He worked like a maniac," said Will.

"Still took me four years."

"At that point, you were how old?"

"Twenty-seven."

"You'd been waiting for her since . . . ?"

"I met her the week before my twentieth birthday."

David shook his head again.

Laurie grinned. "It's great, isn't it? The day after he defended his dissertation, he flew to Japan with proof that he'd finished his PhD."

"I already had the job lined up here at JGU."

"He arrives in Nagano, stops only long enough to clean up and put on a brand new suit, goes to her house, diamond ring in his pocket, and asks Miho's father for her hand."

"Her parents relented?"

Anson nodded. "I didn't have a clue then that JGU's financial state would deteriorate like this."

They all laughed.

David looked perplexed. "I remember when word got out here of your wedding, people wanted to plan a welcome party or reception. Ikenami announced that, as the senior professor in Anson's area, it was his place to arrange it, but nothing happened."

"Well, we got married in April, and I didn't move here until August."

David shook his head. "That's not the reason there was no party. He's been treating you like something stuck to his shoe ever since you arrived."

"It makes me uncomfortable, talking about him that way," said Anson.

"This is what I don't get," said Laurie. "Why was he so upset?"

Will sat forward. "Are you kidding? Anson had the temerity to violate the purity of a Japanese woman—"

"No, I didn't. We were married before we—"

"No, not *that.*" They chuckled at Anson.

Will frowned. "Imagine what Ikenami thought when your baby was born."

"But Japan is a great country and the people—"

David waved his hand. "We all feel that way, Anson. If we didn't love Japan, we wouldn't be here. But there's a difference between being patriotic and being Ikenami."

"Anyway, his feelings toward my family are his," said Anson. "I still worry something's happened to him. I doubt I'm a suspect—I have an alibi—but the police sure spent a long time with me yesterday."

"Oh, no worries," said Will grimly. "Haven't you heard the rumor?"

"What?" asked Anson.

"It was me. I murdered him and dumped his body in the river."

ANSON'S ROMANCE WAS AN ENTERTAINING DIVERSION, BUT soon the office was empty, and Will was pacing. He assumed after Watanabe's accusation he'd be next on the detective's list, so except for his talk with Trinh, he'd stayed put. Had they simply dismissed Watanabe's ravings? Surely, they could see he was unhinged. Still, Will waited.

He'd wrung the muscles in his arm into knots.

I should have closed his eyes.

He sat in front of his computer and opened his lecture: "What is marketing?" He tried to run through it in his head, but the sun was so bright, and marketing wasn't about disposing of bodies or spending your life in prison—or torturing a widow so she ends up hospitalized.

I wish the police would come and ask. Ikenami's dead. He's in the field behind the Conference Center. It's all my fault.

He looked out the window, tears filling his eyes.

If the police find me crying, it really will be over.

Will looked up at the sky. There were clouds, not enough, but some. Glancing at the parking lot, he saw the police driving away.

42

OGAWA ASKED THE DOG HANDLER, "HOW DOES THIS work?"

Suzu's handler looked up from putting on his snowshoes. "She's an avalanche rescue dog. She's used to finding things, people, under the snow. When I take her off the leash, I'll let her roam through a grid."

Hasegawa nodded, and the handler, a wiry little man who looked like he could walk on the snow without snowshoes, set Suzu to searching the empty lot next to Ikenami's car.

"What happens if she finds something?" called Hasegawa.

"She digs," the handler called back.

Hasegawa looked at Kurimoto. "I could work with a dog."

"You realize that's mildly insulting?"

He shrugged. "Until you can find bodies in the snow . . ."

It took a long time for Suzu and her handler to work over the lot, and Hasegawa wished he had a cup of hot coffee.

Suzu's handler brought her back. "There's no one in this lot."

"All right, Kurimoto will go with you and Suzu. Check the neighborhood, any pile of snow big enough for a body. Work your way to the bridge and around both ends. Ogawa and I will wait for the tracker team."

A few minutes later, Hasegawa pulled his sleeve back to see his watch again: 1:07 p.m. "Why can't they have dogs that do tracking *and* avalanche rescue?"

Ogawa pointed. "Here comes the other team."

The tracking dog's handler was twice the size of the other handler, but he jumped around with the dog like a child. "You ready to find somebody, Nana?" He petted her. "You ready, girl? Yeah, good girl."

Ogawa explained the situation to Nana's handler and asked, "What do you need?"

"Something to give her the scent, and then a place to track from."

"We have two coats and some shoes, and she'll start from the car."

The handler gave Nana the scent, then opened the door to Ikenami's car to let her pick up the trail. Nana sniffed around in the car, then jumped out and sniffed the road, back and forth. The handler worked his way around the car, giving Nana ample time with each step.

Back at the car door, Nana's handler looked at Hasegawa, who made a circular motion with his hand, and the process started over. After Nana's second circle, they enlarged the search area.

Nana's handler came back after a few minutes and bowed. "She's finding no trail."

"Could the scent have washed away in all the snow? It's been two and a half days."

"The fresher the trail, the better, but there's *nothing*."

"You're saying Ikenami wasn't here?"

"I can't say so unequivocally, but yes."

"All right, we go to the bridge."

It only took a few minutes to walk to the bridge, where Nana sniffed up and down both sides without indicating a thing. They set her to checking the area around each end, which Suzu was already working over.

The two teams finished at about the same time, and everyone gathered at the end of the bridge. Hasegawa watched as the dogs wagged their tails and jumped on each other. "They're friends?"

"They are now," said Nana's handler.

Hasegawa watched the river flowing by, cold and fast. "Avalanche dog has nothing and tracking dog has nothing."

Nana's handler said, "Again, with the delay in starting the search and all the precipitation, I can't say definitively."

Suzu's handler said, "I can tell you he's not buried anywhere between here and the car, absolutely."

"So he's not here *now*." Hasegawa looked at Suzu's handler, then at Nana's handler again. "And as far as passing through, if you had to guess . . . ?"

The big man bent down and petted his effervescent partner, then looked back at Hasegawa. "I'd say your man was never here."

43

WATANABE UNDERSTOOD THE POLICE WERE RIGHT ABOUT the rumors. From their questions, he worried he might be a suspect.

I must be more cautious.

How many times had he promised himself he'd be more careful and then done the same careless, stupid things? He'd faced no dire consequences yet at JGU, but he would if he didn't get control of himself. He'd had to confess he was here Sunday evening. Someone might have seen him. He could not afford to be caught in a lie.

Now he needed something distracting, calming, if only for a little while.

He locked his office door. Back at his PC, he clicked through the hierarchy of folders until he got to his special one. He typed the password.

Which one . . . ?

One of the new ones from Saturday; the closeup in the sunlight, her hair sleek and smooth as an inky waterfall; the last one before she zipped up her coat.

44

WILL AND TRINH WERE STRETCHING IN ADJACENT LANES in the pool. Will rubbed his sore right arm.

"Are you okay to swim?" whispered Trinh.

"It's this or endlessly worry in my office."

"I will get information soon."

"Thank you." Their eyes met. "Really, thank you. You're—"

Trinh turned and was waving at someone. Will looked over to see Laurie emerging from the women's shower room.

45

CHIEKO WAS UNSURE WHAT TO DO WITH A PHONE CALL from Ikenami's research partner in Nagoya, so Yoshida took it. Given what the detective had told him about a likely suicide, it surprised Yoshida to learn that Ikenami's latest research paper was close to final acceptance at a premier academic journal. Yoshida confirmed, "A conditional acceptance? Was he having trouble making the changes the reviewers requested?"

"Not at all. We already exchanged draft revisions. He merely wanted to polish a few things. That's why I can't understand the delay."

Yoshida paused. "I'm afraid I have bad news. Ikenami-*sensei* has been missing since Sunday. The police suspect suicide."

"That's awful. Suicide . . . I can't believe it."

"We all feel the same way."

"No, I mean, I can't believe he'd do that. We just got the reviews back last week. We talked on Saturday, and he was still ecstatic."

"Oh?"

"Believe me, this paper is the greatest achievement of his career. Suicide is out of the question."

46

WILL AND LAURIE HAD LUNCH IN THE CAFÉ AFTER SWIMming. As they ate, Will stared out the window, his reticence bordering on creepy. Laurie tried to pry him open, but Will dismissed every question. She assumed he was still on edge from his run in with Watanabe. She talked about the girls, Will's class, even Trinh, keeping their conversation as far as possible from Ikenami.

They were almost back at Will's office when they ran into Chieko in the hallway. "We have special faculty meeting today at six p.m."

"What about?" asked Will.

"Ikenami-*sensei*."

There was no escaping him. As long as they were acknowledging the elephant in the hallway, Laurie had a question. "Any news?"

"Oh yes! My friend told me police search with dogs in town today."

Laurie asked, "Did they find anything?"

"No, or everyone would know by now." Will sounded dejected.

Chieko nodded. "Yes, I think I agree."

"Any new rumors?" asked Laurie.

"Not yet, but there will be. Always there are new rumors." As Chieko looked down the hall, Laurie saw her eyes narrow.

Watanabe. He was hovering at the stairwell, doing a nervous dance. Laurie regarded him with disgust. "What does he want?"

"Wants to talk to someone, looks like." Will spoke as if the breath was being squeezed out of him.

Laurie turned to Will. "You okay?"

Will's eyes flashed. "How many times are you going to ask that?"

She stopped herself from snapping back. Something was *very* wrong. She needed to get him alone, now. "Let's go to your office."

Will glanced at Watanabe, still dancing. "No, just go home."

The anger that had flared in his eyes a mere moment before was gone, and it made the hair on the back of her neck stand up. As his anger switched off, it took everything else with it. His eyes looked dead.

Will disappeared into his office without another word. Laurie was blinking hard, so Chieko led her into her office, sat her down, and got her tissues.

Laurie dabbed at her eyes. "It's that freak, Watanabe. Will's been different ever since this morning."

"Watanabe upsets us, both of us."

"How dare he accuse Will? I'll show him a murderer!"

"No, no, Watanabe is our only accounting faculty left." Laurie was still near tears, but Chieko added, "You wait. After we hire new accounting professor, then it is okay."

"He accused Will right in front of the detective!"

"Police will not believe Watanabe."

Laurie sat back and looked at the ceiling. She had squeezed the tissues into a tiny lump, so Chieko got her more. "Everything will be okay."

Laurie pressed the tissues to her nose as she stood. "Thank you. I should go home."

"You can stay here."

"No, it'll just keep hurting if I stay." Laurie's lip was quivering.

"I will watch for you. I mean, watch out for him . . . but for you." Chieko looked at Laurie in frustration. "You understand?"

Laurie nodded and squeezed Chieko's hand as she turned to leave.

BACK IN HIS OFFICE, WILL SLUMPED IN HIS CHAIR. LAURIE HAD said they'd use dogs. As long as it was in town, they wouldn't find anything.

Which meant they would realize Ikenami never made it into town? He should have realized that before he moved the body!

The plan had been to move Ikenami into town Monday night. They would have found him by now. His family would be planning a funeral. It should never have involved the police.

I should've left Ikenami where I found him.

I should've called an ambulance.

For all his understanding of his blunders and idiocy this week, he had precious little insight into what to do now, for the snow stood well below three feet deep, and the police were pulling into the parking lot.

47

WILL FOLLOWED KURIMOTO INTO THE CHAIRMAN'S LARGE, rarely used office. Yoshida was talking to Hasegawa. It was in Japanese, but Will could follow. "He said Ikenami was excited, giddy even. It's a major accomplishment. I'm going to the hospital now to assure Yōko he did not commit suicide."

After Yoshida left, Hasegawa motioned to one of the large, soft chairs. Kurimoto said, "Thank you for talking with us again, Professor Grames."

"Of course." Will sat up straight and looked at Hasegawa, who merely looked back. Will knew he was being studied, so he looked at Kurimoto, who regarded him with no expression at all. His arm hurt, but he left his hands in his lap, forcing them to look relaxed.

At length, Hasegawa said, through Kurimoto, "Rumors, so ugly."

"Especially when they're about you."

"About the detective?" asked Kurimoto.

"No, sorry. I should have said, 'Especially when they're about oneself.'"

Hasegawa's eyes were fixed on Will. "We often hear rumors in investigations." Hasegawa asked Kurimoto in English, "How often we are hearing rumor is completely false?"

"Completely false?" Kurimoto considered it. "I have almost never heard of such a thing. They always seem to have some bit of truth."

Hasegawa gazed at Will again and looked almost like he might smile. He spoke through Kurimoto. "Why do you suppose there is a rumor you killed Ikenami-*san*? What is the bit of truth in this?"

"I think this is a tiny community craving news and full of active imaginations. The rumor could stem from the fact I was on campus Sunday. Or someone may have seen me talk to Professor Ikenami." They'll never believe this. I wouldn't if I were in their place.

"You talked to him."

"I did." What more can I say? The more I try, the guiltier I'll look. Just be cool.

Hasegawa flipped back in his notes. He paused and looked up. "You were angry."

"Professor Ikenami was being spiteful."

"Spiteful?" asked Kurimoto.

"He was being mean."

"You argued."

"I told him he could not decide on Professor Cook's contract renewal by himself." No motive. No matter how interested, they'll find no motive.

"You fought."

"No, he was angry and left."

"You watched him walk away."

"That's right."

Hasegawa sat back, looked at Kurimoto, and threw up his hands.

Kurimoto asked, "If you didn't fight, where did the rumor come from?"

"I don't know," said Will. His right shoulder was uncomfortable, and he had an almost uncontrollable urge to flex it.

"We were thinking Ikenami-*san* might have killed himself, but Yoshida-*san* says he was delighted regarding a study about to be published."

"That would be exciting."

"If he did not kill himself, where do you think he is?"

"I have no idea." Will involuntarily drew his shoulder up toward his head in a circular motion.

Hasegawa cocked his head to the side.

Will felt the urge to flex his shoulder again like pressure building in a steam pipe. He willed it to be still, but the shoulder moved anyway.

"Your neck hurts?"

"Sorry, it's a nervous thing I often get at the start of a term."

Will tried to get a look at his watch as Hasegawa made a note, but he must have seen it, because he asked, "You're in a hurry?"

Will glanced at his watch. "Class starts in fifteen minutes."

Hasegawa nodded and went back to writing.

"I'm sorry I couldn't be more help." Will's shoulder flexed again.

Hasegawa nodded to Kurimoto, and she said, "We will talk again."

"All right. I'm not sure what more I can tell you." Shoulder flex. "I'll be happy to do whatever I can."

Kurimoto spoke for Hasegawa. "Thank you."

Will stood and exchanged bows with them, then let himself out and closed the door behind himself. As he turned toward his office, he caught a whisper behind him. "Will."

David was beckoning him, so Will slipped into David's office.

"How'd it go?"

"Fine," replied Will, as his shoulder spasmed again.

David looked serious. "Were you doing that in there?"

"Toward the end."

"What were they asking you about?"

"That rumor about me killing Ikenami."

"That's what I was afraid of."

"They said rumors have some kernel of truth, so where'd the rumor come from, and did Ikenami really just walk away after we argued."

David frowned.

"You think I'm in trouble?"

"Sorry, but you look like you're coming unglued."

"I told you it's a beginning-of-the-term thing."

"I've seen you before terms, Will, but never like this."

Will leaned back against the wall. "They want to talk again. They only let me go because I had class."

"Will, what's going on?"

Will's shoulder flexed again as tears welled up in his eyes.

David pressed his palms to his forehead. "Oh no."

48

WILL HURRIED TO HIS OFFICE, GRABBED HIS COMPUTER and handouts, and headed for the classroom. He had one minute.

It was still sunny.

Whatever. David had told him to forget about moving the body.

Now Will had to face the first section's seventy-three students. Each knew some story of how he had killed Ikenami.

Will strode into the classroom. "Good afternoon." He flicked the switches to lower the screen and turn on the projector, then connected the video cable to his laptop and opened the lecture file. Without looking up, he said in a loud, clear voice, "There is a rumor I killed Professor Ikenami and dumped his body in the river." Will put the slides into presentation mode and stood tall. "Who has heard that rumor?"

A few students looked at him. There were no hands.

"Okay, who has *not* heard that rumor?"

Again, no hands.

"One thing about this class you must learn now: when I ask a question, I expect an answer. This is a yes–no question. You have either heard the rumor or you have not. You *must* raise your hand. Again, who has heard I killed Professor Ikenami?"

A few hands went up, then more, until almost everyone's hand was raised.

"That's more like it!" said Will. "Do I have the rumor right?"

Brian called out from the back, "You dropped his phone."

"Mighty clumsy of me."

Someone said, "You have his body hidden in your house."

"Brilliant of me, don't you think?"

Some students laughed.

"You buried him in a watermelon field," said another.

"Fertilizer?" asked Will, to more laughter.

Will put his hands up to silence the class. "Why did I kill him?"

No one raised a hand.

Will stopped smiling and looked over the class with his jaw set until every eye was on him. "For the record: I did not kill Professor Ikenami.

When I saw him here on Sunday, I did not hit him, I did not touch him, I did not raise my voice to him. I do not know where the rumor's from." Will paused, and his voice was deeper as he went on. "But I think it's reprehensible."

Will turned and wrote "Reprehensible" on the chalkboard.

"English vocabulary word for the day. Look it up. Then when someone tells you Professor Grames is angry, you can explain why."

The room was silent as Will gave the handouts to the students in front to pass back. Trinh was beaming at him from the side of the classroom.

"This is the syllabus. Read it. You will regret it if you do not. Now moving on to our topic for today," he clicked his presentation mouse to move on from the title slide, "what is marketing?"

Will waited, but no hands rose.

"Again, when I ask a question, I expect an answer." He called on a young woman in the back and asked again, "What is marketing?"

"Marketing is the selling part of business."

"That's part of it." He called on one of his classmates from Japanese language class.

Her jaw dropped in surprise, and she looked at the woman next to her for help before she said, "Also advertising and products and things."

"Again, part of it. Brian, does Canada's population of a dozen or so know what marketing is?"

A few laughs.

"Yes, Professor, we've all learned to read, unlike most Americans." More laughter. "We can see from the syllabus that marketing is creating value for customers."

The laughter rose.

Will advanced to the next slide. "Marketing is all about giving people real value: a better product, better service, better price, better user experience—a better *something* that gives them a reason to spend their limited time and money on your offering. Know your customers' wants and needs and offer them better value than the competition. Do that, and chances are you'll make a profit."

49

IT NORMALLY TOOK WILL AT LEAST HALF AN HOUR TO decompress after class, but looking out his window at the snow—now only two and a half feet deep—in the fading daylight, class disappeared in an instant.

At least it's cloudy.

There was a gentle knock on the door, and Trinh slipped into the room.

Will asked, "How was class?"

"I learned very much."

"Did I look like a killer?"

She laughed. "No, you were great."

"Did you find out anything about the rumor?"

"People all say they heard from other students. I trace it back three times, three levels. It is the same six students, but they are second-years I don't know."

"Can you talk to them? I mean, can you get them to open up to you?"

"No problem." Trinh was smiling. "They are all guys."

WILL HAD FOLLOWED DAVID'S INSTRUCTIONS, LEAVING HIS office lights on and his door unlocked so the police would not assume he fled home. He entered David's office without knocking, and David killed the lights and locked the door. They spoke in whispers.

David shook his head. "Amazing. I can't believe you could lift him."

"You don't want to know the details."

"Or the exact location."

"David, what trouble am I getting you into by telling you this?"

"Ah, yes." David retrieved a piece of paper and a pen from his desk.

"What's this?" asked Will.

"Standard agreement for legal representation. I am your attorney."

"I'll have to trust you, since I can't read it in the dark." Will signed it and handed it back.

"Your wallet, too, please."

Will laughed.

"No, I mean it. Give me your wallet."

Will took it out and handed it to David, who extracted a thousand-yen bill. "This will suffice for the foreseeable future."

"Attorney-client privilege works if we're in Japan? I mean, you're licensed in the US somewhere. Are we on thin ice?"

"Ooh, nice wintertime idiom. My obligation to you remains, irrespective of legal jurisdiction or the silliness of your phrasing. But your worry: can they compel me to reveal anything you tell me? No, they cannot. They would respect our attorney-client privilege, as we would theirs in America. That is, of course, for anything you divulge concerning crimes you have committed. Crimes you may plan to commit are a different story, which is part of why you will not move the corpse. Is there any physical evidence to tie you to him?"

"His keys are in my desk. I was going to put them back in his pocket after I moved him so it would look less suspicious."

"They must not be in your desk."

"Understood. Then, bottom line, how much trouble am I in?"

"Hiding a body is surely a felony. A foreigner would go to trial, be convicted, likely have his sentence suspended, and be deported."

"How much trouble would the Japanese conviction be in America?"

"It wouldn't count as a felony conviction in America. Your academic career is another story. Some universities might overlook it, but not good ones, at least not for a great while. Failing to disclose it when asked a relevant question would amount to lying on your employment application, which would be just cause for termination when they found out. And they would find out. You've said it yourself: academia is a small community."

Will hung his head.

"But . . ."

"What?" asked Will.

"That's if you come forward. If you continue the deception and are caught, we could be talking prison time."

"How long?"

"Months, maybe more. I'd have to look into it."

"Then I should come forward now and hope for leniency?"

"That brings up a big 'if.' *If* they believe you, yeah, confessing might be best. But if they decide you killed him, you go away forever. You wouldn't get the death penalty, because they can't prove premeditation; you had nothing to gain. So perhaps not life, but you won't go back to America until you're an old man."

"Will they think I killed him?"

"Is there any possibility someone saw you move the body?"

"Anyone who did would've said something by now."

"What about the argument and him falling?"

"One person saw, a first-year from Vietnam, Trinh Nguyen."

"Is she talking? The rumors are coming from somewhere."

"She's in my Japanese class, and we've gotten to be friends. Just today, she told me she saw but has told no one. She won't either. I'm sure. In fact, I asked her to track down the source of the rumors."

"You trust her that much?"

"Yes."

"Back to whether the police will think you killed him. With an autopsy, what will the cause of death be?"

"I guess a cerebral hemorrhage or something like that, from the fall."

David tapped his fingers on the arm of his chair.

"What?" asked Will.

"It's too . . ."

Will waited.

"You remember the fall pretty well?"

"I've replayed it a hundred times these last four days."

"Watch it again. As he fell, did he hit his head?"

Will closed his eyes. He watched Ikenami pull away in alarm, as if Will was an animal about to attack. With sickening anticipation, Ikenami teetered, then fell. "He hit on his left shoulder, really hard. He rolled and hit on his right hip, bounced off the wall and down two steps on his butt. Then he rolled and landed flat on his back on the landing—his head up. It didn't hit the landing." Will opened his eyes. "It looked like he wrenched his neck trying to keep his head from hitting the floor, in fact."

"His head never hit hard on a wall or step?"

"No. I'm almost positive."

David frowned at him in the meager light that shone through his window from the parking lot.

"What?"

"Will, I don't think you need to feel so guilty."

"Why?"

"I think someone murdered him."

50

ALL THE FACULTY HAD GATHERED IN THE ADMINISTRATION building's first-floor conference room. Dean Yoshida, occupying the lone chair at the head of the table, called the meeting to order. He was irked this meeting was necessary at all. Someone had to take over Ikenami's Managerial Accounting course. It was required for all first-years. The faculty members were all on contract, and their teaching loads for the year had been set last spring. Yoshida wanted Watanabe, the only other accounting professor, to take on the extra work, but contractually, Yoshida could not force Watanabe to do it. After this morning's row, Watanabe would surely refuse. So Yoshida called a faculty meeting, hoping Watanabe would cave to peer pressure.

There sat Watanabe, close by, where Yoshida couldn't miss him, reading a book.

The passive-aggressive little toad.

Yoshida told everyone, "After Professor Ikenami arrived on campus Sunday, it's unclear what happened. Rumors are circulating, including a particularly vicious one. Please don't spread them. You are authority figures. If students hear you say something, they assume it's true."

Malik, IT professor and associate dean, had presumptuously taken Ikenami's usual chair to the dean's right. "I've heard, you know, sort of . . . scary things. But there could be some truth in the rumors, maybe. I think we should listen to some—"

"You think too much," said Yoshida with derision. He went on, "Other things you might want to know: Professor Ikenami's wife Yōko was admitted to the hospital last night. The strain on her has been heavy. I visited her today, and she thinks they may release her tomorrow. She told me Professor Cook's wife, Miho, has been taking meals for the children. She appreciates that greatly. Let me say, pulling together is what I hope a trial like this will bring out, not rumors and backbiting." He looked at Watanabe, who made a great show of turning the page in his book.

"If anyone else can help, I suggest you call Miho-*san*. She knows the family's needs now better than anyone. Matsuyama-*san* will also stay in touch with her. You can contact the dean's office with questions."

The door opened, and President Satō entered. He paused as he stared at the table's head, where all the nearby chairs were taken. No one stood for him, so he walked the length of the table, took a chair from the row along the wall, placed it at the far end of the table, alone, and sat.

David spoke up. "What will we do with Ikenami's first-year course?"

Watanabe shot him a searing look. "You expect Ikenami-*sensei* to be gone for the whole term?"

"Not at all. We should simply be prepared for that contingency."

Yoshida tapped on the table. "Yes. It's late to find an adjunct, so I was wondering whether Professor Watanabe could step up and help in this crisis."

Watanabe looked at the dean in shock, but Yoshida was sure he was feigning it. He must have expected this.

Before Watanabe could speak, Malik leaned far forward. "This is two sections. He already has a full load, and there's no time to prepare. I think that is sort of asking kind of a lot, don't you think?" He looked down the table for support.

Anson said, "It's certainly Professor Watanabe's decision, and it's a heavy load, but we could reduce his spring term load. Also, I could front-load my first-year finance course, double up on sessions for a few weeks, to give him time to prepare. Then his course could be backloaded."

"Thank you, Anson." Yoshida looked at Watanabe.

Malik leaned forward again. "Maybe you should, you know, give him some time to think about it a little."

Yoshida stared at Watanabe. The pressure was palpable and other faculty were shifting in their chairs. Watanabe was reputed to be a powder keg. He almost got fired for throwing a printer through his office window—which was closed at the time—before final exams last spring.

Finally, Anson said, "If it's too much of a burden, I could take the course. There isn't much to it. It's only basic managerial accounting."

Yoshida wanted to laugh out loud. Anson, for all his innocence, could be shrewd, needling Watanabe's pride.

It worked. "Someone who knows what he's talking about should teach it." Watanabe was almost shouting. "It *should* be an adjunct, but I'll do it. I don't need 'time to prepare.' I know the material."

Yoshida jumped on it. "Wonderful. Thank you."

Syed Baig, the junior IT professor, raised his hand. "Students are worrying and the whole campus is upset. A vigil could bring everyone together. If anyone knows anything, a vigil could inspire them to come forward."

Malik said, "If Professor Watanabe needs a little more time to decide, we can, you know, make some time for him, I think."

Yoshida scowled at Malik. "That's settled. Try to keep up, will you?"

"What we need is better security, so nobody else gets murdered," said King with a smirk.

Satō jumped up and pointed at King. "No one said Ikenami-*san* is murdered. No one said! I talk to police, first one to talk to police, and they do not say that. You should not say the thing like that. You stop that!"

Everyone looked at him in shock.

He sat. "It is not the proper thing to say."

Yoshida smiled at Satō. "Did you have anything more from the police? You must be in close contact with them."

Satō gazed out the window as if he hadn't heard.

Yoshida raised his voice. "President Satō!"

His head barely moving, Satō turned his eyes to the dean. Yoshida had no doubt Satō was ready to explode, so he said loudly and slowly, "Perhaps you could report on the investigation. What have the police told you?"

"I should not comment on police matter."

"You have met with them today?"

Yoshida would have waited for Satō's response, but Malik said, "We should all probably cooperate with the police. But I think maybe the police should concentrate on students. There are so many students and so few of us. You know, someone *has* to have seen *something*, I think, but you know, they can be sort of shy. Maybe President Satō," and Malik looked down the table and spoke louder, "can send out an email to everyone and sort of encourage them, you know?"

There was no immediate response. Soon, someone else said, "JGU Ski Day is on Saturday. Is it appropriate during this tragedy?"

David was leaning back. "I was not aware that this is yet a tragedy."

Malik jumped in. "Yes, we should, maybe, sort of consider the mood of the campus and not do something so . . . you know."

Danny Charles said, "It might be best to let the students go. I'm getting the feeling the present mood on campus is not so positive."

Yoshida tapped on the table again. "I must agree. The students need this."

"No, it is too . . . frivorisness," said Satō, to exasperated sighs.

"Do you mean 'frivolous'?" asked David.

Satō glared at David before he turned his scowl back on Yoshida.

Soon, everyone's attention was on the dean.

"We can raise this with student leaders. If no one has anything else—"

Satō jabbed the table with his finger. "I already answer Ski Day!"

"If there's nothing else about Professor Ikenami, we will conclude."

Everyone looked relieved—except Satō, who was trying to burn holes in the dean with his eyes. Yoshida gazed back at him, and without the slightest sign that he recognized the president's rage, he stood and left the room.

51

STEVE KING'S WIFE, RUMI, WENT OVER THE ACCOUNTS again.

Everything added up. They should've had barely enough to get through the next month, and they did. She had withdrawn the rest, fifty thousand yen at a time, over the last six months, draining their savings into a thin box she hid in the bedroom. The bulk of their money, their combined life savings, was still in the joint investment account. It would come last, a single transfer to clean out the account on her way out the door.

Like most Japanese wives, Rumi controlled the finances, and like most Japanese husbands, Steve got a cash allowance. She gave him enough for gasoline, lunches, and drinks, but not the other things she knew he craved. She checked his wallet, watching the yen dwindle until he was spending like a miser the last week of the month. He never had money left. The man couldn't sock away a hundred-yen coin if he won the lottery.

Rumi breathed out slowly.

So why was there a copy of *The Shining* in the bookcase, pages hollowed out, filled with ten-thousand-yen bills, 196 of them? Why was there a copy of *The Shining* at all? Her husband couldn't stand Stephen King.

52

IT WAS SNOWING HEAVILY AGAIN WHEN WILL CALLED HOME. He steeled himself for an icy response as Sarah called Laurie to the phone.

"You ready to come home?" asked Laurie.

"Can I apologize first?"

"No need."

Ouch. "I was a jerk this afternoon. I'm sorry."

"Yes, you were, but no need to apologize. I'll be there in a few minutes."

Laurie was no warmer when she arrived. When Will hugged her, she hugged him back, but stepped away. "Can we talk?"

"Sure. What about?"

Laurie sat. So did Will.

"This Ikenami thing. You're all jammed up, like you did something."

"We had that argument."

"Yeah, but what I'm getting is different. It's like," she faced him in her chair, "I know you can't be involved, but it feels like you are."

Will looked at her. He looked at the window.

"I'll ask you straight out so you can tell me no. Are you involved somehow? Is there something you're not telling me?"

Will sat back and looked at her again. He tried to stop it, but his shoulder flexed.

"Tell me, Will."

"I'm afraid to. You've seen me screw up a million times before." He glanced at the window again and got up to close the blinds.

Laurie waited.

Will sat. "But in all the time we've been together, I've never given you cause to be ashamed of me."

"What did you do?"

"I panicked." His shoulder flexed again.

"What do you mean?"

"The argument, I stepped in front of Ikenami as I was making my point, and he pushed me. I got angry and made a fist—for the briefest moment. I wouldn't have hit him. But he stepped back . . . and fell down the stairs."

"Was he hurt?"

"I walked off, but I looked back from down the hall, and he yelled that I'd be sorry—from the top of the stairs—so I assumed he was all right."

"You didn't push him?"

"Didn't touch him or threaten him, but he took that step back, afraid I might."

"And fell."

"I knocked on his door in the evening to apologize."

Laurie waited a long while this time, before she asked, "And . . . ?"

"He didn't answer, so I opened the door. He was dead on the floor."

"Oh, Will."

"I assumed the fall must have killed him. I imagined the police wanting someone to blame and putting me away forever. It scared me to death."

"What did you do?"

"I moved the body."

Laurie sat still.

"I decided to move it into town the next night, so no one would know where or when he actually died. In the meantime, I hid it in the *susuki* behind the Conference Center."

"Ikenami's in the field?"

Will nodded.

Laurie stood, so Will did too.

"I'm sorry, Laurie. I—"

Laurie slapped Will so hard that he fell against the bookshelves. She picked up the phone.

"Who are you calling?" Will was holding his cheek.

"Who you should've called the second you found him!"

Will hurriedly pushed the phone's cradle down. "Can I tell you something before you send me to prison for the rest of my life?"

"What?" Laurie hissed.

"I talked to David about it today after the police questioned me again. I asked him whether I should just confess, and he asked whether Ikenami hit his head as he fell. Laurie, I remember every detail. He did not hit his head."

"That makes it okay?" She was holding back tears.

"It means the fall didn't kill him."

"What did?"

"David thinks, and I'm beginning to agree, someone murdered him."

"Murder? That's ridiculous. What for?"

"That's the big question. Until we have an answer, the police won't look any further than me."

Laurie put the phone down and covered her face with her hands.

Will was about to pull her close, but someone knocked. Laurie turned toward the window. Will opened the door. It was David.

He came in and said, "I saw you pull up, and I wanted to see whether—"

Laurie broke into tears.

Will and David stood silently. At length, David indicated one of the chairs. "Sit. Let me tell you what I think we need to do." David got Laurie into one chair, and he took the other. Will perched on the edge of his desk. David lowered his voice. "I think someone murdered Ikenami. I think they're using his fall, blaming Will, to get away with it."

"Why?" asked Laurie, still crying.

"I don't know, but we need to focus on people he fought with recently. I'd bet one of those fights was a lot bigger than anybody realized."

"Who?" asked Will.

David pursed his lips briefly. "You said Watanabe's been a basket case. I'm not aware of any fight between him and Ikenami, but the way he's acting, it could be him."

"Okay, although he's always like that, and he worshipped Ikenami."

"How about the IT committee thing?"

Will knitted his brow. "The IT faculty? With Watanabe, we're up to four. Who else?"

"Anyone else in IT. It might be what the committee oversees."

"Like what?" asked Laurie.

"That must be a pretty big budget. IT is connected to everything in the university," said Will.

Laurie wiped her eyes. "What about plain old university politics?"

David gave her a smile. "A long shot, but we won't rule it out."

"Who would that add?" asked Will.

"Satō, I guess," said David.

"What about Yoshida?"

David sat back. "Beyond hard to believe, but I'll put him on the list."

"Is that all?" asked Laurie.

"For now," answered David. "I suppose it could be a student, but there's no one to focus on at this point." He asked Laurie, "Can you hold on until we have someone to point the police to?"

She looked at Will a long time before she stood and held her arms out. David smiled, but even as they hugged, Will knew she was boiling with anger hotter and deeper than she'd ever felt toward him before.

David stood. "You two go. The police car's still outside and I don't want that detective getting ahold of Will again today."

Laurie nodded.

"And no more tears. Sorry, but Will's acting weird enough. If you act odd, too, the police will know for sure he's involved."

"Okay, but what about Ikenami's family?"

She sounded like she might cry again, so Will took her hand and said, "It's not open-ended. We have a few days, that's it. Then . . ."

"The police get an anonymous tip," said David. "They dig the remains out, do an autopsy, and find out someone murdered him. They don't know about the fall—no one will tell them—so they don't tie the bruises to Will like he was afraid they would."

Laurie still looked worried. "You said someone's trying to use the fall to frame Will. The murderer must know about it."

"If he was going to come forward, he would've by now. My guess is the killer can't tell them without putting himself here and wiping out his alibi. With the autopsy showing murder, Ikenami's argument with Will is moot. With no motive to kill Ikenami, there's no cause to focus on Will."

"Then why not tell them now?" asked Laurie.

"Because if the autopsy doesn't show murder, you'll never see Will again. He was here, he's admitted arguing, and he was the last to see Ikenami alive. He's their prime suspect."

Laurie wiped her eyes again. "Okay."

"See you tomorrow," said David.

"Smiling and happy," said Will, as his shoulder flexed yet again.

53

I t was late and Ogawa looked put out that he'd had to wait at the station for Kurimoto and Hasegawa, merely to show them Ikenami's broken watch. Ogawa took it from the evidence bag with care and laid it on the table.

"How do you suppose he broke it?" asked Hasegawa.

Kurimoto could see that Ogawa recognized it as a test. "It's a sapphire crystal. Those don't break easily. You can crack one with a hard knock—shatter it, even—but it generally stays intact. Making one disintegrate like this takes a lot more force. Someone purposely broke it."

"Why would someone break a nice watch like this?"

"It has a date display, and it broke the same day of the month that the victim disappeared. That's no coincidence. I think this was a crime of passion. The watch represented the victim. By breaking the watch, he was symbolically breaking the victim, or his relationship with him."

"You sound like a profiler."

"Only trying to be helpful, sir."

"What brand is it?"

"Seiko."

Hasegawa frowned, so Ogawa looked again. "Grand Seiko."

"A lot of Seiko watches use battery-driven quartz movements, but this is a Spring Drive Chronograph. Any significance there?"

"More expensive. Even more likely to symbolize a relationship."

Hasegawa was still frowning. Kurimoto, standing behind the detective, caught Ogawa's attention. She looked at Hasegawa's wrist and back at Ogawa. He looked quizzically at her.

"Tell him," said Hasegawa.

"You might ask the detective to show you his wristwatch."

"It's a Grand Seiko? Or . . . may I see your wristwatch?"

Hasegawa removed his Spring Drive Chronograph and placed it next to the other one. "This watch is much more expensive than an average Seiko. There are plenty of watches that cost many times more, Swiss mostly, but you won't find a higher quality timepiece than this anywhere."

Ogawa said, "People are saying Ikenami is unusually nationalistic. Breaking his fine Japanese watch fits perfectly."

"Before you take your profile any further, let's concentrate on the evidence. Is there anything unique about this watch?"

"Grand Seiko?"

Hasegawa shook his head disgustedly. "The Spring Drive."

Ogawa looked puzzled, so Hasegawa explained, "While this watch has a quartz component, it's a mechanical movement. The whole thing runs off the energy in the spring. No battery. I'm guessing the killer thought hitting a battery-operated quartz watch hard enough to crack the crystal wouldn't necessarily stop it. You might have to hit it *much* harder, shattering the crystal. He didn't have to do that to this one, because it's mechanical, with tiny gears, and is much easier to break—but he didn't know that." Hasegawa looked around. "Give me a magnifying glass."

Ogawa handed him one, and the detective examined the watch on the table. He asked for gloves, picked up the watch, and checked it more closely. Finally, he put it down and handed the magnifying glass to Kurimoto. "This was no crime of passion, and I don't think the watch represents anything, except that Ikenami is dead. There's a tiny shard of crystal lodged under the minute hand, deflecting it. It was reset after being shattered. Someone was trying to give us a false time of death."

Kurimoto gave the magnifying glass to Ogawa. He talked as he looked. "There were crystal shards on the office floor."

"Suggesting that someone murdered him in his office." Hasegawa put his hands on the table and leaned forward, his eyes on the two watches lying side by side. "The killer wants it to look like he died in some way that could have shattered his watch—a fall or a fight—but he doesn't want us to know when it happened. He has an alibi for the time on the watch. Yet he drives the victim's car into town—carefully, too, never touching the steering wheel, preserving the victim's fingerprints—and plants the victim's phone on the bridge, pointing to suicide."

Kurimoto creased her brow. "Sounds like a colossal incongruity."

Hasegawa added, "And for a university type, none too smart."

∾

Kurimoto followed Hasegawa out. "We made a little headway today."

Hasegawa regarded her, then nodded. "Emphasis on 'little.' Anyway, I want to see the IT committee people again. Something's going on there. Oh, and Grames, definitely Grames."

Hasegawa was at his car before he remembered his gloves. As he reentered the station, the desk officer signaled he had a call.

"*Moshi-moshi.* This is Hasegawa."

"Detective, I am so glad I am not calling too late."

"I was just leaving. Who might this be?"

"Oh, I am sorry. This is Shinichi Satō, president of Japan Graduate University of International Studies. Please let me say how grateful . . ." Hasegawa looked for his gloves, unsure when Satō would get around to saying anything. At length, he heard, "I would have brought this up earlier, but it only hit me this evening."

"What's that?"

"I have been concerned for some time that the dean, Yoshida, is . . . how should I say this . . . ?"

"Directly is simple."

"Yes, yes, I suppose so. Please excuse my indiscretion in saying this, but Yoshida . . . seems to live significantly beyond his means."

"He may have some inherited money or large savings. He worked overseas for many years, didn't he?"

"As an academic. I assure you, it is not a profession that makes one wealthy. The point is, Yoshida may be involved in something illegal."

"Do you have any evidence?"

"No, but I fear he may be embezzling university funds."

"That's a serious charge."

"I do not make it lightly. My biggest fear, and the reason I called you, is I don't know whether he has done it alone. There's no telling how deep it goes. I am not sure we can do an internal investigation."

There are my gloves! "You realize the seriousness of this accusation?"

"I do. I hesitated to call you. But as you can well imagine, the implications for what may have happened to Professor Ikenami are horrifying."

54

Huong lay on Trinh's bed looking at the snow falling thick outside the window. "I heard you're asking everyone about who's telling rumors about your professor. Better be careful or people will talk."

Trinh focused on her computer. "I want to know where it's coming from. The rumors hurt everybody. What if the police focus on *Sensei* instead of what really happened?"

"You so sure he didn't—"

Trinh turned and glared at her friend.

"I can't believe this! He's married—with kids!"

"He's nice. I'm trying to help."

"You just like his butt."

Trinh laughed. "Who doesn't?"

"For an old guy butt, it is cute."

"He's not so old. You should see him in his swimsuit."

"You know all I brought is a bikini. I can't wear that to the pool."

"Buy a lap suit." Trinh gave her a grin. "It's worth it!"

"You and your married boyfriend! Don't you feel any shame?"

"For what? It's not like we're having an affair. Besides, you know I don't want to get involved with anyone. *Sensei* is safe. Nothing can happen."

"You see him watching you, and you grin wickedly as he sweats, relishing the longing in his eyes as he wishes he could act on his lurid desires, as he reckons the price: the end of his marriage."

"Ew! You should write trashy romance novels. I'm not ruining his marriage. I haven't touched him."

"Never?"

"His arm or something."

"Something?"

"His hand."

"In the pool?"

"No."

Huong laughed.

Trinh looked at her reprovingly, "You shouldn't be talking. How many guys have you slept with since we got here?"

"How many guys or how many times?"

"See what I mean?"

"It's not that many."

"You were drunk every time."

"So what?"

"So if he isn't right enough to sleep with sober, he can't be very right."

"Felt pretty right."

"Every time you wake up in a guy's room, you beg me never to let you do it again."

"Not *every* time."

"Oh?"

"All right, every time *so far.*"

Trinh sighed.

Huong shrugged. "I don't care. Forget your professor crush. Give me a man I can touch."

Trinh gave a coy smile and turned back to her computer.

Huong sat up. "You're going to do something with him!"

"No."

"Yes, you are!"

"Nothing bad, anyway."

Huong clapped as she laughed. "All right, I'll buy a lap suit tomorrow. I want to see the rest of Professor Irresistible!"

55

Usage of the Webmaster's first website was still way up. He wasn't sure why. Nothing on the website had changed since before usage rose in December. He thought the spike could have been rooted in loneliness with the New Year holiday approaching, but it was halfway through January now and things were still hopping.

It could be a winter thing.

He checked the statistics for the previous two Januarys. Usage was up every year. What was it about January that made men more interested in chatting with women as they stripped their clothes off?

Whatever the reason, more usage meant a higher probability of finding men who met his target profile. That was the entire purpose of his first site: to find users for his real business. The first site was simple. He bought interactive sex cam streams wholesale and resold them, with his servers as proxy. The site used a regular dot-com IP address, registered with the official Domain Naming System, on the Surface Web, the small part of the World Wide Web that the public knows and uses. It was not a problem that his profit margin on that site was almost nonexistent; that profit wasn't the point. He wanted to sift through the users for those addictive types who watched hours at a time every day. He was marketing to that thin slice who might pay dearly for a much more illicit treat. Those who bit on his invitation were given a special username and password. Then they were instructed to download the Tor web browser and access a site on the Dark Web, websites with no DNS registration and accessible only through an encrypted, untraceable network.

The Webmaster opened his second site to see whether viewing was still on the rise now that the students were back. He was especially interested in the middle of the day. It had always been a slow time, but two exchange students from Hong Kong had taken up volleyball in the afternoons. It had left them hot and sweaty every day this week. He clicked on the raw file that captured the stream from one's camera, advanced it to 3:02 p.m.—and smiled.

You could set a clock to this girl's showers.

Soon she was down to her underwear and disappearing into the bathroom, so he closed the file and went back to his usage statistics. Afternoon viewing would never match evening, but it was up. At this rate, requests for access would rise. He had to keep it capped, of course; if word got out, it would finish him. To join, an applicant had to respond to a cryptic but irresistibly intriguing invitation or be recommended by an existing subscriber—and reveal his true identity. While users knew him only as the "Webmaster" and each other only by screen names, he had the real-life details of each of his 307 special customers. Club secrecy was paramount, so each outgoing feed was watermarked, visually and digitally, for that specific user. If any videos showed up on other sites, he could destroy the subscriber who leaked it. That was mere window dressing, though. What truly kept the users in line was the fear of losing access.

He checked the exchange rate, pulled up his calculator and . . . almost thirty-three thousand dollars—every month! And he was at only three-quarters of his safe capacity. He pumped his fist in the air and grinned before checking the balance of his account in Zurich, which was mostly invested in the American stock market. He was a genius!

All that money coming in and no variable cost. That was the beauty of it. Modified wireless access points (he had the APs custom made overseas) and massive hard disk capacity were his primary costs, and they were fixed and sunk. The Webmaster used the university's bandwidth, which was wide enough to handle his outgoing streams without ever approaching its limit. There were no manufacturing or marketing expenses, salaries, taxes, nothing. Forty-four tiny lenses hidden inside forty-four wireless network APs in forty-four dormitory rooms. How lucky that the buildings' reinforced concrete construction limited the signal range and required so many APs. He simply had to get the sexiest girls into the rooms with cameras—and as a member of the Student Life Committee, he had a say in the assignments.

Of course, part of it was luck. Although it was easy to pick second-year girls, the Webmaster had to choose first-years based on admission application photos. They separated the obvious winners and losers, but they were hardly reliable. And there was no way to predict a girl's proclivity to spend her private time undressed. This fall, though, camisoles were all the rage and of his forty-four girls, half preferred lounging and studying in something skimpy. They were wearing more now that it was winter, but as the school year progressed, sexual activity picked up. Ten had boyfriends, so even if they used the boyfriends' rooms sometimes, he still had live sex streaming three to four nights a week at predictable times. Another eight were sexually active, although only two with any regularity. The most frequent show was an unremarkable looking and poorly performing Taiwanese girl. (She had inspired a hilarious ongoing discussion thread on why, after so much practice, she was getting no better.) Most of the other girls did something rousing now and again. All of them stripped down to nothing, the majority every day.

In the quest to create more value, over the winter break he augmented the top twenty rooms with infrared cameras. Users were jubilant. Still, the real key to success was the new girls. With girls like this every year, he could make millions.

He checked room rankings. All but one of the top ten girls had sex occasionally, although the volleyball girls were rising fast and might break into the top ten. Each subscriber had his favorites, of course, and the Webmaster helped them keep track of their girls. Each girl had a full archive, and he sent out discreet alerts to users' mobile phones when there was especially wanton activity. A drop in any subscriber's viewing brought emails with still pictures or short videos, lest interest wane. Those bits of personalized service were enough. Exclusive, secret access to real girls—beautiful girls who had no idea they were being watched—was too alluring. He had the perfect product, one that stoked all the endorphins the customer could muster, but was never quite real enough to sate his desire.

Looking at the numbers, the Webmaster wondered how much difference it made not to have held anyone back this year. Each of the first two years, he chose one girl as his own and kept her camera private. He had agonized over whether to do the same with Trinh. In fact, he had been trying to get closer to her ever since she arrived. She was outwardly warm, yet aloof to anyone but students. Still, he could take his time in her first year, become a friend, and still have a full year after that for more. Relationships with students were forbidden, but they could be discreet. The chance of a relationship with Trinh was worth the risk.

Although the Webmaster hoped to make Trinh his own, in the meantime, he had faced the reality of what a body like hers would do for the website. It was an incomparable marketing opportunity. Besides, she'd never know. Still, he would, and he feared the jealousy would gnaw at him. It took him two weeks to decide, but finally, sorrowfully, he switched her camera over for his subscribers and featured her in emails for the next month. As he expected, usage skyrocketed, easing the sting. More effective salve came with perfect customer retention after he raised prices by twenty percent. He might be able to push them up even more. Her curves were gold—creamy smooth, brown gold—and they might still be his.

V

Constrained Optimization
制約付き最適化

Thursday, 14 January 2010

56

YOU AWAKE?" ASKED WILL.

"Yes."

"You okay?"

Laurie didn't answer.

"I freaked. I thought of never seeing you again, not seeing the girls grow up. I was stupid, and I went to pieces."

"You can't get away with it, you know. They'll find him. What will that do to the girls? How could you be so selfish? It was evil, Will."

"I'm sorry. I just . . . fell apart."

"Being phobic of the Japanese police is no excuse."

Will watched his breath fog, rise, and disappear.

There were feet heading down the stairs.

"Sarah?" asked Will.

"Becka. Sarah went down before you woke up."

"How long have you been awake?"

Laurie turned away and pulled the covers higher.

Will lay quietly. There was surely something he should say.

Soft footsteps came trotting up the hall, Rachel's. She fumbled with the door for a second, then it slid open. She kicked off her slippers, scurried into the *tatami*-floored room, and jumped on Will. He hugged her before she burrowed between them into the *futon*.

"Are you still sleeping?" she asked Laurie.

Laurie gave her a kiss. "Yes, it's winter."

"But you're not bears. Bears hidernate all winter."

"Hibernate."

"Yeah, that. I saw it on television. They get fat, and then they go to sleep, and in the spring, they wake up all skinny."

Laurie's eyes were half-closed."That's right."

"Do they wet the bed all winter? Becka said they do."

"They don't have beds, but I imagine they're pretty stinky by spring. Are you ready for breakfast?"

Rachel nodded.

"Okay, you go down and I'll be right behind you."

Rachel padded off down the hall, and Will got up to look out the window. "Fog. If it's sunny—the snow must be over four feet now—it might not be trouble today, but it will be tomorrow. I should check the weather." When he turned to look at Laurie, she was already gone.

57

I GOT A PHONE CALL LAST NIGHT," SAID HASEGAWA AS THEY left the station.

Kurimoto glanced at him hopefully. "A break in the case?"

"Yoshida, the embezzler, killed Ikenami, the whistleblower."

Kurimoto looked at him. "Once again?"

"Satō, JGU president who can't remember where he put his teeth, is accusing Dean Yoshida, Italian brands and Hakone getaways, of embezzlement. He's afraid Yoshida has co-conspirators, so he wants us to investigate rather than doing it in-house."

"Isn't that what an auditor is for? Don't they have one?"

Hasegawa shrugged. "I've seen stranger things."

58

Z06 (HE'D CHOSEN HIS CAR AS HIS SCREEN NAME: FAIR-ladyZ2006) had windows open for both girls' livestreams, so he saw VietKitten leave her room and arrive fifteen seconds later in Viet-Goddess's. He wished they weren't such good friends. It was nice to watch them laugh when they were together, but they spoke Vietnamese and he couldn't understand them. Besides, together, they were never in their underwear.

Before long, VietKitten was heading out her friend's door. He maximized her window to fill the screen and waited with anticipation for her to enter her room. VietGoddess was higher ranked and unquestionably the better looking of the two, but he preferred VietKitten. She would have been in the top ten last year, and with VietKitten there was more to watch. VietGoddess only changed her clothes. She did it often, looking herself over in the long mirror on the bathroom door. She even admired herself in her underwear sometimes, but never naked, like VietKitten. The Webmaster had named her well. The best show from VietGoddess was watching her get her pajamas on—which was great—but nothing ever happened after that. VietKitten slept in next to nothing, and there was often a show at bedtime. It was better when she first arrived: the shows were on top of the bedcovers. These days, it was too cold for that. Still, the noises she made were fantastic.

VietKitten's door opened. She walked in and sat on the bed.

Come on, it's shower time.

She got up and sat at the desk. She was opening her laptop?

Don't toy with me. I have to leave soon.

She stood again.

Oh, she's the one. What I wouldn't give for a chance at that.

He leaned back. It was an interesting idea.

It wouldn't hurt to ask. The worst the Webmaster can say is no.

His breath came faster as her clothes came off.

He snickered as she stopped in front of the mirror. She might have been more enamored than he was.

I bet she works it all day long, loving every look she gets.
Yeah . . . it's worth asking.
How much to offer . . . ?

59

Laurie found Will after Japanese class at the edge of a group of students. As she walked up, a student was asking, "What happens at a vigil?"

Brian said, "Could be a brief speech, but mostly people stand around silently. Sometimes they hold candles."

"It's a time to think about the person in trouble or pray."

"Eight tonight?"

People nodded.

"Are you supposed to pray for someone who kills himself?"

Laurie took Will's hand and gave it a gentle tug. Will merely squeezed in reply, so she put her arm around him from behind, laid her forehead on his back, and closed her eyes. At least Will was only listening.

"He didn't kill himself."

"Yes, police looked for his body with dogs yesterday."

"I didn't see dogs."

"Not at here, in the town."

"What for? Dogs will not find him in the river."

"I heard his wife had a nervous breakdown from guilt over killing him."

"Why?"

"Why what? I would have killed him if I were his wife."

"Who would marry him in the first place?"

"Someone who knows all about the local *yakuza* said it was them."

"What is *yakuza*?"

"Japanese mafia, organized crime."

"They are tattoos—have, I mean."

"He had tattoos?"

"Ikenami-*sensei* was a *yakuza*?"

"No, he owed them money; gambling on horse racing or something."

"They beat you up for that. If they kill you, they never get their money."

"I hear they cut off your finger."

"No, their own fingers, the little finger, one knuckle."

"For initiation."

"For screwing up a job."

"He hides until finger heals or has shame of no finger anymore?"

"Forget the *yakuza*."

"He is drinking too much and fall down in the dark and freeze and die. That's what I think. Why no one else is saying that?"

"He probably died of a heart attack."

"And fell in the river."

"Give up on the river, okay? Someone killed and buried him. I'm sure."

Laurie pulled harder on Will's arm, and they peeled away from the group. Laurie whispered, "You're sure someone murdered him?"

"I don't remember his head hitting. Plus, the rumors. How does a rumor start that I killed him, yet no one's gone to the police? It's the killer."

"Watanabe?"

"He's weird enough. Maybe he got angrier than any of us has seen him? But I doubt it."

"Then who?"

"I don't know, but the rumors could be the key. If David's right that someone wanted to use the fall to mask the murder, the murderer must have seen it happen. He's using rumors to focus the police on me."

"Last night you said Trinh saw, that she was on the stairs."

"Trinh swore she hadn't told anyone. It could have been someone below us or above her, someone I never saw, like I never saw Trinh."

"I can't believe she told anyone. Not the way she looks at you."

"You said it was just a crush. Anyway, she's trying to trace back the rumors. If we can find the source, I think we'll get the killer."

"Then what?"

They rounded the corner into the administration building, and Laurie saw Trinh walking up the darkened hall ahead of them.

Laurie stopped. "You have someone waiting."

Will whispered. "There's no need to go. She'll talk with you too."

"I hope she can help. Bye."

Will said, "Bye," as Laurie hurried away. She wondered which would be worse, someone thinking she was fleeing because she went too fast, or someone catching her crying because she wasn't fast enough.

WILL TURNED TO TRINH AND SAW HER WALKING TOWARD HIM, so he motioned to her to follow and set off for the Conference Center. He walked over to a clutch of large chairs with thick high arms, all black leather, and chose one facing away from the windows. He had no desire to see that field. Besides, he needed to be aware if anyone else happened by. It took Trinh a couple of seconds to see him in the unlit room. Then she hurried over and sat in the next chair. "Should I not come to your office?"

"I think the police will talk to me again. I don't want to take a chance on them knocking on my door and finding you there."

"Ah, okay," she said, and then smiled. "I have news."

"New rumors?"

"No, last night I talked to guys I told you about yesterday. They all heard the rumor from same guy, second-year Japanese student."

"It's coming from a student?"

"Wait, listen. Last night I found him and said hi."

"That's all it took?"

"Sometimes guy is so simple. He talked, and I laughed, and soon he was open. I was sure if I wait, Ikenami talk will come. He said he heard you killed him, and I asked who told him. He did not want to say, but I used this face," she showed Will a soulful pout, "and I say, 'Please tell me.'"

"Did he?"

She nodded.

"You didn't have to do anything besides talk, did you?"

Trinh lit up as she shook her head. Will wasn't sure whether it was in pride or a reaction to his jealousy. He put his arm on the side of the chair and leaned toward her. "Who?"

Trinh leaned in, too, her arm tight against Will's. "Watanabe-*sensei*."

WILL HAD ONE MORE PIECE OF INFORMATION TO COLLECT, SO as he passed Chieko's door, he smiled and said, "Good morning."

"*Ohayō gozaimasu.*"

Will stepped around to the side of her desk, leaned over, and whispered, "Professor Ikenami wanted to be on the IT committee."

She nodded.

"Why?"

She got a serious look and whispered, "Why do you ask?"

"Because someone is making up rumors about me. Something's going on, it involves Ikenami, and that's the only odd thing—recently."

She rested her chin on her palm and rolled her pencil in her fingers. Turning to her PC, she brought up her email program and typed the dean's name and password. She scrolled through the messages, clicked one, and looked up at Will. "I get coffee. Would you like a cup?"

WILL KNOCKED ON DAVID'S DOOR, HEARD HIM CALL, "COME!" and stepped into the office with a smile.

David raised his eyebrows. "You swallow a canary?"

"We finally know why Ikenami wanted to join the IT committee. I saw his email to the dean."

"This?" asked David, holding a piece of paper.

"How'd you do that? And how'd you read it? It's in Japanese."

David just smiled.

"Unfortunately," Will said, "it's awfully vague."

"Allegations of IT resources being misdirected. What resources? By whom? For what purpose? He doesn't say."

Will frowned. "Yeah." Then he smiled again. "I have something else. Trinh found the source of the rumors."

"That was quick."

"She's good. She wrapped these guys around her finger. The last one didn't want to tell her, but she gave him a pout and he broke."

"Who are we up against?"

"She traced it back to a single source who heard it from Watanabe."

"I told you! That's why he was so eager to put the police onto you."

"Yeah, it fits, but why would he kill Ikenami? It took Watanabe two years to find a job. He worshipped Ikenami for hiring him."

"That was my second year here. It thrilled Ikenami to get someone Japanese."

"I don't think Watanabe did it. He's volatile enough to fly into a rage and bash Ikenami's head in, but not stable enough to keep his wits afterward."

"You're far more stable, and you couldn't hold it together just hiding the body."

Will looked down, stung.

"Sorry. But hey, that's a good thing. You want to do that and *not* come unglued? Anyway, if it's not him, why the rumors?"

"Trinh said she traced it to Watanabe, not that he created it."

"You think someone told him?" David looked unconvinced.

"Someone he trusts. But it's not like I can go ask him who."

"Neither can I," said David. "Ikenami warned him away from me at the start. I'm not sure Watanabe has ever spoken a word to me."

Will rubbed his sore shoulder.

"How about Trinh? She's got the skills; you said so yourself."

"What if Watanabe's the killer? I can't put her in danger."

David gave him a serious look. "Will, we have to know—now."

Will set his jaw and looked away, out the window, toward the snow.

David gave him a minute. "Bring up the idea. See what she thinks. I doubt it's so dangerous."

60

Hasegawa and Kurimoto re-interviewed Satō first. As they began, what Kurimoto saw most clearly was Satō slipping into senility. He told them things he had on Tuesday as if for the first time. When Hasegawa mentioned Satō's call last night, it took three tries before Satō realized what he was talking about.

"You've seen how Yoshida dresses. And he's never here during term breaks. Never. He's off to one place or another."

To Kurimoto's surprise, Hasegawa glanced at her and nodded almost imperceptibly. She shifted forward. "Maybe he likes to travel."

"Who has so much money?"

Kurimoto smiled. "Could you tell us where he's gone recently?"

Satō looked at her. "I believe he may have . . . visited companies."

"Oh? Why is that?"

Satō was suddenly animated. "That's the problem! He visits under the guise of recruiting students, but he's selling training programs."

"The university funds the trips, but he sells private training services?"

"Perhaps private. Yes, yes, it must be!"

"He does the training by himself?"

"Well, no, he uses other faculty."

"The companies pay the university?"

"He must skim money off the top. Or it could be kickbacks, too."

"Your accountants track the funds? These records are audited?"

"Audited?"

"An outside accountant checks the accuracy of records and—"

Satō flashed anger. "I know what auditing is. Of course, we're audited."

Hasegawa was about to speak, but he stopped. He looked at Kurimoto again.

He had told her just this morning, "You're a police officer. You don't have to defer to people in authority if you sense deception."

Kurimoto leaned forward again. "If they're audited, why the call last night?"

"I'm afraid my memory isn't what it used to be. You're young, so you wouldn't understand."

"I would," said Hasegawa with derision.

That took Satō off guard. "I . . . perhaps so." Satō glanced at the door.

Kurimoto asked, "What is your specific accusation?"

"I accused no one."

"What was your call last night?"

Satō looked at Hasegawa, who sat stone-faced. Satō told Kurimoto, "I was merely saying he lives beyond his means and it seems suspicious."

"Now you accuse Dean Yoshida of skimming money from training programs or receiving kickbacks?"

After an uncomfortably long pause, Satō said to Hasegawa, "I was mentioning possibilities, not making specific accusations."

Hasegawa said, "This is a serious investigation into a man's disappearance—"

"I know—"

"You are using it for your own petty agenda."

Satō sat up straight, head high. "That is enough from you, young man."

"Yes, indeed," said Hasegawa gruffly as he stood.

Kurimoto stood and waited. Satō rose as if it hurt.

Hasegawa glanced at Kurimoto, and she realized that as he had scolded Satō, she had retreated. Now she cast off that submissive posture. "If you have anything substantive to report, we welcome your input."

Satō ignored her and stared at Hasegawa. The detective headed for the door. Kurimoto followed, and they bowed. Satō turned his back on them without acknowledgement.

In the hallway, Kurimoto asked, "What do we do?"

Hasegawa took a deep breath and let it out slowly as he stared at the ceiling. Finally, he looked up the hall toward the dean's office. "Ask Yoshida whether he's an embezzler."

Kurimoto's mouth fell open. "We do?"

"We follow every lead, no matter how demented the source—briefly."

"How briefly?"

"Oh, a question or two should suffice."

As they sat with Yoshida in his office, Hasegawa did not give her a "go ahead" look, so Kurimoto was quiet. Hasegawa said, "There has been a report—vague, but we must follow up."

Yoshida's hands were behind his head, fingers interlocked. "Please, ask. I'm at your disposal."

"We appreciate that. Let me be direct. There has been a suggestion you live beyond your means as a dean and professor."

Yoshida lowered his hands and rested them on the arms of his chair. He frowned at Hasegawa. "Let me guess: the president has intimated, however indirectly, that I should be a suspect in Ikenami-*san*'s disappearance."

Kurimoto sensed no apprehension, no deception, only . . . disappointment? She looked at Hasegawa but couldn't read him. He sat there, impassive, watching Yoshida.

Hasegawa's stare unnerved so many, but Yoshida seemed unaffected. "Did he mention travel? My assistant has detailed itineraries for my trips, even personal. I often visit companies hoping they'll send a student or buy a customized executive education program from JGU. Did he harp on those? You are welcome to comb through my records, and I am sure our accounting staff and auditors will cooperate fully."

"Your financial dealings have been perfectly legitimate?"

Yoshida looked entirely calm. "Yes. I'm sure you have procedures, but I wish you'd focus elsewhere. There may be an actual crime here. It would be a shame to get sidetracked by an old man's delusions."

THE OFFICERS MOVED ON FROM YOSHIDA TO THE CHAIRMAN'S office, where they had a full day of interviews planned. Hasegawa knew Yoshida's answers did not satisfy Kurimoto, but for now, her training would have to wait while she concentrated on translation.

Malik strode into the chairman's office with a broad smile, dressed all in black, with loose-fitting trousers, a silk shirt buttoned only halfway up, and a leather jacket. Hasegawa watched as Malik settled in, making minor adjustments until his clothes draped nicely. He set his elbows on the high arms of the chair, letting his hands dangle off the ends. It was an exact replay of his entrance yesterday. Finally, he slid his left arm forward just enough to push from his sleeve the biggest Rolex watch Hasegawa had ever seen. It even outshone the diamond glinting on his little finger.

Hasegawa, through Kurimoto, said, "Ikenami-*san* has been missing for four days now. Where do you think he is?"

"I don't have any idea, really. I've heard, you know, rumors, that's all."

Hasegawa looked at him.

"I've heard it was suicide. I've heard it was murder."

"We think it was not suicide."

Malik sat quietly, his face still fixed in a near smile.

"Why would someone murder Ikenami-*san*?"

"I don't know. He was well liked, kind of popular, I think." Hasegawa gave him a skeptical look, and Malik said, "Or kind of, you know, well respected, very well, maybe."

"Who could want him dead?"

"I think I really don't know maybe why he's missing."

Hasegawa cocked his head to the side and waited for Malik to answer the actual question. When Malik simply sat there, Hasegawa was irked. "I'll ask again: who could want him dead?"

"Dead? You really think he's . . . oh, no one, I think."

Hasegawa stared at Malik for a few seconds, but Malik showed no reaction. "Yet rumors say someone murdered him. Why would there be such rumors if no one wanted him dead?"

"Someone could have lost his temper. I heard it was Grames."

Hasegawa nodded. "In our experience, such a violent explosion of temper is rare. In every case, there was some hidden problem before the violence. Who could have had such a problem with Ikenami-*san*?"

"Oh, I don't know. I don't know about problems between faculty."

"You think it was someone on the faculty?"

"Oh, no, I don't know. There are students, you know, but a faculty member could be, sort of . . . that's just, you know, what I hear, but a student could be, you know . . ."

Kurimoto looked like she was having a terrible time translating. Hasegawa stared at him, trying to decide whether he was being purposefully obtuse, or his mental processes truly were that muddled. Hasegawa checked his watch: 9:14 a.m. "Tell me again about the IT committee."

"Like I told you yesterday, it doesn't do much. It hardly ever meets. The IT Services staff handle everything."

"You chair this committee?"

"It's just a sort of formal title, you know, not a special responsibility."

"Why would Ikenami-*san* want to be on that committee?"

"I told you before, I don't know. Maybe he was sort of worried, you know, about IT here, I guess. I mean, why else? Or maybe not worried. Maybe just sort of interested, you know. I don't know. I don't really . . . so I can't, maybe, you know, help so much."

Hasegawa waited for more before he said, "So maybe yes, maybe no."

"Yes. I mean, that's right, maybe."

THE NEXT INTERVIEW WAS THEIR FIRST WITH DANNY, THE new English professor from Australia. He was good looking. He was also young enough that Hasegawa wondered how he had gotten onto a university faculty. Kurimoto was struggling with his accent, but it was clear within the first few minutes of her translation that Danny was too recently arrived to know anything. Kurimoto pressed him to share what rumors he had heard, but Danny refused, saying, "To give you names to go with the rumors would be irresponsible of me. I know nothing. I hear things from people who know nothing, and so I won't share them."

When they asked him about his assignment on the IT committee, Danny wasn't even aware of it. He speculated that he was supposed to help with English checking of the website, etc. Regarding Malik, he was slightly more forthcoming. "He came by my office on Monday and introduced himself. I had lunch with him on Tuesday. He talked about Professor Ikenami. He said the faculty is split. Some support the president and whatever direction he wants to go, and others the dean, who I suppose wants to do something different. Professor Malik said he was afraid Ikenami was joining the president's side. He said Ikenami wanted the president's help to force out faculty Ikenami did not like."

"Force out who?"

"Whom."

"Excuse me?"

"The correct response is, 'Force out whom?'"

Kurimoto nodded, embarrassed.

Danny smiled. "This rumor has a proper source, so I'll report what he told me: Ikenami wants to get rid of Peregrine, Grames, King, and Cook. I assume you've heard that, because you asked about most of them."

"Why did he want them gone?"

Danny shook his head. "I wasn't interested enough to ask."

TODAY, KING HAD PULLED HIS MOSTLY GRAY HAIR, WHICH hung loose the day before, into a short ponytail, revealing a small gold earring in his left ear. The same heavy gold chain as yesterday showed from the undone collar of his shirt. He'd rolled his sleeves up one turn, enough to show the edges of a complex tattoo. He entered the chairman's office with a put-upon air. "This is a waste of time. Nothing's changed since yesterday."

Kurimoto's smile seemed to mellow him, though, and before long he was reciting a litany of rumors he had encountered in the last day. At length, he smirked and said, "I don't know anyone who'd want to kill him, but people who hated him . . . it'd be easier to list his friends."

"Please do."

King laughed. "Can't think of a one."

"This is not a joking matter."

"Hey, just because I'm laughing doesn't mean I'm joking around. I can't think of a single friend the guy had."

"You say 'had' as if he is dead."

"Isn't he? You disappear for this long, you're either dead drunk, you met the lay of your life, or you're facedown under a quick foot of dirt. Since I've never seen him drink much and not even a working girl would give him the time of day, I figure that means dead."

Kurimoto didn't look as if she'd understood everything King said, but Hasegawa trusted she was giving him the gist.

"We heard he was interested in removing some faculty members."

"All foreigners, all *gaijin*, right? And I'm on the list? I married a Japanese woman. Ikenami hated that. But the son of a bitch wasn't worth hanging for. That's how you execute people here, right?"

"If he wanted to force you out . . . ?"

"The place is going broke. We're *all* gonna be out. Besides, he didn't have the power. If you ask me, Ikenami should have paid more attention to his own problems and left everybody else's alone."

"His own problems?"

"He must have had at least one great big life-or-death one, right? I mean, how else did he end up dead?"

~

Hasegawa shivered outside, smoking the last of this morning's allotment of cigarettes and watching the snow sparkle in the sunshine. 10:58 a.m. He had one minute—and a headache. Yesterday was better. Ikenami's broken watch was a real clue, and the dogs were so excited, friendly, even cute—and simple. No need to talk. What he wouldn't do to work with dogs all day.

Next was Will. The guy seemed a regular sort. His wife seemed nice, too. A guy generally can't be too bad if his wife is nice. Yesterday, Wednesday, when he had a class to teach, he wore cotton slacks and a button-down oxford shirt and tie, regular department-store stuff. Tuesday was jeans and a shirt from Uniqlo, no pretense. He knew Japan too. In fact, besides Anson, of the foreign faculty they'd interviewed, Will was the only one who fit here.

Still, Hasegawa sensed deceit. There was guilt—in Will's eyes, how he sat, his face as he spoke. Hasegawa could see it pressing on him, squeezing; he could almost smell it on his breath. Weird as it was, it wasn't enough guilt for an otherwise good person who murdered in a sudden rage, and there wasn't enough guile for someone who murdered with premeditation. He'd done something, but what?

~

Will's seat in the chairman's office felt more comfortable than it had yesterday. Maybe it was from his intervening talks with David.

Hasegawa said, "Thank you for talking with us again."

"I'm not sure how I can help, but I'll do my best. I still don't know where the rumors are coming from."

"Yes, that is a puzzle."

Will waited as Hasegawa looked at his notes.

"You said Ikenami-*san* would not renew Cook-*san*'s contract."

"He didn't want to, but it wasn't up to him."

"And no new contract for you?"

"Me? I'm not up for renewal."

"Ikenami-*san* wanted you gone too."

"I hadn't heard that. It could be true, but I never heard anything."

Hasegawa looked at him.

"I'm the senior-most marketing professor. There are no problems with my teaching evaluations, and I'm doing solid research. I don't think the dean wants me gone."

Hasegawa kept staring at him, so Will leaned back. "You look as if you have a question."

"The rumor. It is strange, isn't it?"

Will smiled. "Rumors are strange. I heard this morning that the *yakuza* killed him. Then I heard he was a member of the *yakuza*."

Hasegawa smiled. "What time did you see him at the stairs?"

"Just before four. Three fifty? Fifty-five?"

"Do you know we found a wristwatch in his office?"

"A watch?" Will tried to control his shoulder as he remembered he still hadn't tossed the shoes from that night. At least Ikenami's keys were now in the river.

Hasegawa stared, so Will asked, "It's significant?"

"It's broken."

Will waited.

"It stopped at four oh nine."

"You think it broke on Sunday? Right after I saw him?"

"It has Sunday's date."

"I remember it was before four, because I called my wife a few minutes later and it was exactly four. Here, let me check." Will pulled his phone from his pocket and brought up the call log. "Here. Four o'clock."

Hasegawa leaned forward, and Will held out the phone to show him. Hasegawa suddenly took the phone and started scrolling up and down. "All your calls are to your home or your wife."

Will smiled as his shoulder flexed.

Hasegawa clicked the phone a few times and started scrolling again. "Incoming calls too." He looked at Will. "You must be a good husband."

61

DAVID ASKED WILL, "HOW'D IT GO?"

"Pretty well. Not much nervous, unhinged twitching. They didn't ask many questions. They went to the rumor again, so I told them the *yakuza* rumors. That got a smile. They asked about his wristwatch. It was broken, stopped at four oh nine, so I took it off and put it in his desk drawer."

"Why?"

"Because I didn't want them to find him in town with a shattered wristwatch and no shards of the shattered crystal nearby."

"How about fingerprints?"

"Gloves. Anyway, I saw him before four, so it couldn't have broken in the fall. I figured it broke when he collapsed."

"My guess is whoever killed him broke it and set that time to strengthen his alibi. Who was around on Sunday?"

Will closed his eyes and looked at the courtyard side of the building in his memory. "Third floor: Watanabe." He did the same thing for the side facing the parking lot and listed three more faculty.

"Not Malik or King?"

"Nope. That's just whose lights were on, and that was hours after . . ."

David waited a few seconds before he nodded.

Will looked outside.

David asked, "The sun?"

Will nodded.

"How many sunny days can it take?"

"One's no problem. Two could be. I doubt it would last through three."

"We better get moving. We need an IT person. Anyone you trust?" asked David.

"No. No one I have a bad feeling about, either."

"Okay, I'll find someone. Have you talked to Trinh yet?"

"She's in class, but . . . I'll work on it."

David showed a stern face. "I don't like it either, but we need to know."

"What if I'm wrong? What if Watanabe's the guy?"

"I agree he might be dangerous, but he'd have to get worked up to act. Frustration, rage, and he snaps."

Will said, "Consider what Trinh will have to do. She can't just knock on his door and ask him. His defenses have to come down. She'll have to warm up to him, get him interested, as she did that student. So Watanabe's all excited, and she leaves? Or worse yet, he's worked up and then realizes she's playing him? If he could kill Ikenami, he could kill her."

"Will, the woman's beyond gorgeous, right? She frustrates every guy she sees. She's been dealing with it since she hit her teens. He'll talk."

"What if he's the source?"

"He won't clam up, because that won't score points with Trinh, and he'll be dying for points. If he's the source, a lie is his only option. So we follow it up. If it doesn't pan out, we know Watanabe's lying, and he's the source."

"I wish there was something faster and a hell of a lot surer."

"Lawyers deal with this all the time. Working within the law takes time, and you rarely get all you want, but it's what you've got."

"Modeling too. Constrained optimization. Maximize or—"

"You're such an academic," interrupted David with a smile.

62

T HE HARDEST PART OF ARRANGING TRINH'S HELP, OTHER than the sickening feeling of using her, was getting the chance to ask. The more people saw them together, the harder for her to investigate the rumors. He didn't have her phone number—which he was glad of when Hasegawa checked his phone—and he didn't want to chance creating a digital trail with an email. The pool was closed today, so class was the one place he knew she'd be. The problem was making contact without others noticing.

Malik's first-year MBA/MPA Management Information Systems course let out at noon, so the students would head to the cafeteria, café, and dorms. The snow forced everyone into two enclosed pathways. One led to the gym, pool, café and the east dorm, the other to the cafeteria and the west dorm. Will didn't know which dorm Trinh was in, or whether she would prefer the café or the cafeteria today. He dithered for a minute, trying to come up with some reason to choose one or the other, before he gave up and headed to the cafeteria. He dallied at the tiny convenience store next to the cafeteria until the first students emerged from the walkway, and he waded into the stream. He kept a lookout for Trinh as they flowed past, but he made it to the classroom building without seeing her. He looked through the glass doors into the classroom building. There she was, in the atrium, her back to him, talking with Professor Malik.

Malik threw his head back and laughed. For all his fuzzy speaking and his inability to keep up in faculty meetings, Malik was open and approachable with students. Will had heard he was a dynamic teacher. It was as if there were two of him, and every interaction with the vacuous one left Will feeling as if Malik wore his dunce cap on purpose.

Malik was laughing again. Will couldn't stand and wait. Trinh tilted her head, her luxuriant hair hanging long and smooth as she listened to whatever story Malik was telling.

Will frowned and headed for his office.

63

PRESIDENT SATŌ WAS TO CALL THE CHAIRMAN'S ASSISTANT with any news, but this was something the chairman needed to hear firsthand. That meant leaving a message and waiting, and Satō preferred to wait in his room in the Conference Center, where there were no ears.

The phone rang. "*Moshi-moshi.* This is Satō."

The chairman was gruff. "I only have a minute."

"Yes, yes. In faculty meeting yesterday, someone proposed a vigil for tonight. It has gotten traction. I don't think there's any way to stop it."

"What's the problem?"

"I thought it best to keep everything as quiet as possible."

"Is anyone unaware of his disappearance?" asked the chairman.

"I meant I'm trying to keep talk and speculation minimized."

"How's that working out?"

"I think it's helping," said Satō.

The chairman snorted softly. "Yes, I'm sure you do."

Satō pinched the bridge of his nose as he pressed his lips tight together.

"If that is all—"

Satō interrupted and said, "No, there's another matter. Yoshida wants to go ahead with Ski Day on Saturday, despite strenuous objections that it is inappropriate. I told everyone I was canceling it, but Yoshida is ignoring—"

"You want me to arbitrate your disagreement over a skiing activity?"

Satō was quiet.

"Then I'll decide. You know Yoshida is the only person keeping JGU afloat. If he feels a lack of support . . ."

Satō waited a few seconds. "So that means . . . ?"

The chairman snapped, "Yoshida's right, as usual. Anything else?"

Satō held the phone in a death grip. "No, that was all. Thank—" Satō clenched his teeth as he heard the click.

64

How long before the next one?" asked Hasegawa.

"Five minutes," answered Kurimoto. She'd seen the tension building and knew he was ready to snap. "But they're students. They can wait."

Hasegawa nodded and headed out the door.

Nicotine addiction: even without the cancers, why would anyone do that to himself?

She stretched and walked to the window to bask in the sunlight, taking in the courtyard below. It wasn't quite half-past three o'clock, but it had been a grueling afternoon. They had asked for students who were on campus on Sunday, and Chieko had delivered. They had been going since noon, twenty-one so far. Not even one remembered seeing Ikenami.

The JGU faculty was an odd bunch, though not much odder than her own college professors. But the students were fascinating. So far, they'd talked to ones from twelve different countries. None would be here much longer; not after the scandal that would bubble up from Ikenami's murder as if from a cesspool. And it was murder. She hadn't been a cop for long and was no detective, but she could sense the darkness in this place.

Hasegawa came back looking more like himself, and Kurimoto greeted the next student. Kurimoto invited her to sit, introduced herself and Hasegawa, and said, "Maybe you could start by telling us your name."

"Huong Nguyen. I'm from Vietnam, and I'm a first-year student."

"Do you know Professor Ikenami?"

"Who he is, yes, but I do not know him much."

"You were here on campus Sunday?" asked Kurimoto.

"Yes, mostly in my room in the dormitory."

"Did you see Professor Ikenami?"

"No."

"Did you see any faculty?"

"I saw Grames-*sensei* on Sunday night," said Huong.

"What time?"

"About ten thirty. He was going home. We said hi, and he talked to us. He is very friendly."

"We?"

"Me and my friend Trinh."

Kurimoto noticed a change in Hasegawa the moment the second Nguyen woman walked into the room. If they had not spent the last three days doing interviews together, she might not have sensed it, but she caught Hasegawa sitting up straighter. He had been keen as a cat on the prowl in his interviews with the faculty, but disinterested in the students, checking his watch every few minutes. With this one, he forgot about the time. He did the questioning, too (through Kurimoto), rather than letting her handle it on her own. In fact, he looked at Kurimoto expectantly as she translated the woman's first answer. "My name is Trinh Nguyen. Same family name as Huong, you just talked to, but we are not related. It is common in Vietnam."

"Do you know Professor Ikenami?"

"Yes, he always says hello in the hall, and he talked to me once in the cafeteria."

"Is it common for faculty to talk to students there?"

Trinh smiled genially. "Most professors are friendly. Second-year students told me Ikenami-*sensei* is not so much, and they teased me after he sat by me."

"Did he bother you?"

"No, he was nice. Everyone is nice here."

"He never tried to get . . . more friendly?"

Trinh smiled. "No, he was a gentleman."

Kurimoto had to fight not to laugh—an entire line of questioning driven by jealousy over a young woman Hasegawa had known for two minutes. And his eyes! How many times had he refocused on her face?

"Did you see him on Sunday?"

"Yes."

As taken as Hasegawa had seemed with Trinh, suddenly Kurimoto saw the cat again. "What time?"

"Four or a little before."

"Where was this?"

"He was climbing the stairs in this building, at the other end of the hall," and she pointed. "He was coming up while I was going down."

"Did you speak to him?"

"No, he did not see me. Grames-*sensei* was waiting to go down the stairs. Ikenami-*sensei* was looking at him. I was above, so I don't think they saw me. They said something to each other. I could not hear Ikenami-*sensei* so much, but he sounded serious. That was when I looked down and saw them. Grames-*sensei* looked upset."

"Angry?"

"Maybe not angry. Maybe . . ." Trinh looked down and said to herself, "Oh, that new word I learned today, what was it . . . ?" She looked up with a smile. "Annoyed. He looked annoyed. He said something in a serious voice too. It was about Cook-*sensei*. I think Ikenami-*sensei* was angry, and so Grames-*sensei* walked away."

"Grames-*san* walked away."

"Yes."

"Ikenami-*san* watched him go."

"Yes."

Hasegawa showed no reaction Trinh would notice, but Kurimoto saw his eyes flash and, as if she could see inside his face, the smile he concealed.

～

HASEGAWA HAD ONE SUSPECT, SO AT 4:17 P.M. HE HAD ANOTHER run at the lawyer.

"We have new information that makes suicide much less likely."

David nodded.

"Do you have any ideas about Ikenami-*san* disappearing, any reasons?"

"I hear rumors of murder, but I can't guess any motive. If there is one, I would guess someone killed him. In the meantime, I'd guess he died."

"A death implies a corpse."

David nodded.

"We haven't found one."

No reaction.

"Where would it be?"

"I heard his car was in town."

"We searched with dogs and could not find a body."

David gave a lazy shrug. "I would believe a heart attack before murder. He was only in his fifties, but he was overweight, diabetic—on insulin, I believe—so a heart attack seems the likely scenario."

Hasegawa's face showed nothing as he stared at David, but inside he was castigating himself. A rookie could have seen it! The wife told them Tuesday morning that he was on insulin. With the unknowns of travel, a diabetic on insulin would carry extra vials and syringes. So why, when Ikenami arrived back in town on schedule, had Hasegawa seen no unused insulin or syringes on the list of evidence from his car and office?

As soon as they finished with David, Hasegawa got Ogawa on the phone. "You're sure you didn't miss it? You looked everywhere?"

Ogawa was adamant. "Through every drawer, on every shelf, under, over, behind, everywhere. There was no insulin and only one syringe."

"Could he have had them on his person?"

"Maybe, but the logical places to keep it are his desk, his bag, and his suitcase. I found a kit in the desk, complete except for insulin and syringes. There was another kit in his bag, no insulin, one syringe. I'm sorry I didn't recognize its significance earlier, sir. It was a terrible miss."

"We all missed it. Anyway, follow up with the wife. Was he regular with testing his blood and giving himself injections? How much did he use? How much did he keep on hand? Who made the purchases? And tell her to have the pharmacy fax us his prescription records."

65

WILL WAS MEETING DAVID SOON. HE HAD TO TALK TO Trinh before that. It was a small campus and Will found her on the third floor of the library, although she wasn't alone. He needed to get her attention furtively, so he walked past the study tables toward the periodicals section. As she looked up, he glanced at the hallway, and she rewarded him with the subtlest of nods.

Two minutes later, Trinh stepped into the hall. Will was at the stairway, and once they made eye contact, he headed up to the library's rarely used fourth floor.

Will waited for Trinh to reach the top of the stairs. "Thanks for coming."

"Did something happen?"

"It's Watanabe and the rumor. Trinh, I trust your source. I can believe Watanabe told the students. But it's possible he was just passing it on."

Trinh nodded.

"The problem . . ." As Will paused, he looked at Trinh, her face turned up to him in devoted expectation. He looked out the window at the sunny courtyard and its melting snow, now only three feet deep.

Trinh asked, "What can I do?"

Will kept his gaze out the windows. "You're too involved already."

"Please. I want to help." She stepped closer and tugged on his arm. "*Sensei*, tell me."

Will looked down at her again. "You got the students to talk."

She nodded again.

"Can you do the same with Watanabe?"

66

T HE WEBMASTER ONCE AGAIN HAD HIS HEADPHONES ON when he heard a knock on Will's office door.

"Sorry I'm late." It was David.

"No problem," said Will. "Everything okay?"

"The detective had another talk with me. I can tell you on the way."

"I'm set. Let's go."

Will was confiding in a friend. The Webmaster should have planted a microphone in David's office and the chairman's last night when he did Will's. He would rectify that tonight. He wasn't sure how he could listen to the extra feeds. Maybe he'd pay less attention to this one. It hadn't yielded much.

He stopped himself as he realized he was being negative. He prided himself on being *maemuki*, optimistic. While he had gleaned no significant revelations from the bug, he had learned from his talk with the police that they did not seem to be focusing on him. In fact, the rumors seemed to be working. The detective had interviewed Will three days in a row. Still, it disturbed him they were taking so much interest in the IT committee.

He checked his PC and saw Trinh in Huong's room. She had her coat on, and Huong was getting hers. They must be going out.

He made his way to the main entrance, where the university bus would pull up in two minutes. Trinh and Huong were in line.

Maybe it was time to watch them directly. Besides, he could use some groceries. He returned to the office, grabbed his coat, then waited for the bus to leave. He could pass it in his car.

67

As they took the stairs to the basement of the library building, Will asked, "You're sure we can trust him? I thought the IT staff were suspects."

"We have to trust someone, and my person says he's the guy."

"Who is your person, anyway? And how did you get a person?" asked Will, but David stepped out of the elevator without answering.

Will followed David into the IT Services office. A young woman, the only one there, stood and stepped up to the counter. David said, "Professor Grames and I have been looking at the university website and have some questions. We'd like to talk with Itō-*san.*"

"Yes, Manager Itō does all JGU website, but not here now."

"I see. Will he be back today?"

"He left a few minutes. He is back, I think, in one hour."

68

The university bus kept a regular schedule, shuttling students into town to the bank, grocery store, hospital, and train station. At five p.m. Tuesdays and Thursdays and twice on Saturdays and Sundays, it headed for a larger town thirty minutes away. It only made one stop there, at a shopping center where the students could splurge at Aeon, a large discount retailer and grocer; Daisō, a hundred-yen shop; Hard-Off/Book-Off, a used hardware and bookstore; and Xebio Sports.

Huong planned to get a swimsuit, then groceries, but Trinh was checking her watch.

"Don't be impatient," said Huong. "I just want to see them all."

Trinh pointed at the meager selection. "It's January. This is it."

"They don't have any two-pieces like yours."

"There's probably a store with a better selection, but we'll have to get a ride from someone."

"Why doesn't JICA let us get cars?"

Trinh gave her an "I don't know" look. "They're a government agency that helps developing countries. What do they know about what students need? I guess they want us spending all the scholarship money on school. But swimsuits, remember? We're spending your scholarship money on a swimsuit."

Huong chose four. She asked a salesclerk about fitting rooms, but he didn't understand, so Trinh asked and he smiled and showed them the way.

"I said the same thing you did," said Huong, peeved.

"You did. I don't know why he didn't understand."

"I do. He wasn't listening. He was staring at you."

"You want him to stare at you? Step out here in that little yellow one."

THE WEBMASTER TRIED TO MOVE NATURALLY FROM COVER TO cover as he scouted for the girls in Xebio. They were not in the skiing section like he expected, so he started a long, nonchalant walk around the store and spied them looking at swimsuits. Happening by when they were shopping for something that personal would make them uncomfortable, so he stayed as far away as possible while keeping them in sight.

He knew Trinh swam but had never ventured into the pool to see her. As he thought about it now, he realized it could be the perfect place to pique her interest. Although he had never done it as a sport, he was a decent swimmer as a teenager, and his upper body wasn't in terrible shape. While he was not as young as the students, he was sure he could impress her. The girls in the entertainment district always commented on his physique. He had a low cut swim brief he got for a vacation to Phuket a few years ago, just the thing to get a girl's attention. He only needed a swim cap and goggles.

69

YES, MANAGER ITŌ IS HERE NOW." THE WOMAN LOOKED back, caught Itō's eye, and bowed her head.

As Itō approached, David stepped back into the hallway. Itō looked perplexed but followed him. "May I help you?"

David's voice was quiet. "We had some questions about the university network and website. Can we talk someplace?"

"It must be private?" asked Itō.

"I would prefer that."

Now Itō looked even more perplexed, but after hesitating, he showed David and Will to the server room, where they took seats at one end of a large table.

Itō looked at them expectantly, and David spoke. "You might have heard that Professor Ikenami wanted to join the IT committee."

Itō sat still, emotionless, for a few seconds and nodded.

"He told Dean Yoshida that computing resources were being misused."

Itō's face tightened. Will said, "Professor Ikenami was not accusing you. As far as we know, he never mentioned your name."

David nodded.

Will went on. "Now Professor Ikenami is missing, and the only unusual thing we have found is his interest in the IT committee."

"Why do you search for Ikenami-*sensei*? You are not police."

"No," said David, "but the police have been asking us a lot of questions and we're getting uncomfortable. We do not want to be suspects, so we're looking into it ourselves."

Itō looked at the two, then at the table, for a long time. "I have heard rumors . . ."

Will sat back. "About me?"

Itō's mouth was tight as he nodded.

"I seem to have become a suspect. I have to find out what's going on before it's too late. We," Will pointed back and forth between himself and David, "think Professor Ikenami disappearing has something to do with the IT committee. To find out, we need help."

Itō sat back and looked at the professors; one, then the other. He closed his eyes for a moment before he leaned forward. "Police also ask me about IT committee." He sighed aloud. "I think I am uncomfortable too."

70

AS THEY WALKED FROM THE CAFETERIA BACK TO THE FARther of the two dorms after dinner, Trinh asked Huong, "What do you know about Watanabe-*sensei*?"

"I know he gives me the shivers."

Trinh laughed.

"A second-year who had his class last term said he was all right, that he gets less freakish after the first few weeks."

"Does he spend much time with students?" asked Trinh.

"I don't know. Why the sudden interest?"

Trinh shrugged, but as they walked on, she said, "You know I was trying to find out where the rumors about *Sensei* were coming from."

Huong stopped and grabbed Trinh's arm. "Not Watanabe!"

"Hush, quiet."

Huong whispered, "Why would he make up rumors?"

"I don't think he made them up. I think he heard it from someone."

"Another student?"

"I don't know. The only way is to ask him."

"You can't ask him that!"

"Not yet, but he's taking over Ikenami-*sensei*'s course and we have that special makeup class tomorrow. I was thinking I'd sit in front."

Huong looked up at her friend. "I'll sit next to you like always."

"Yes, please. We'll sit in the second row. It'll look strange if I'm alone. Being so close, I'm sure he'll look at me, maybe a lot. When he does, please don't look over at me."

"Why not?"

"It'll only draw everyone's attention. No matter how much he's looking at me, keep your eyes on the screen."

71

KING STEPPED INTO MALIK'S OFFICE AND CLOSED THE door. King asked, "You talked to the cops this morning?"

"Yeah."

"They think somebody killed him."

"Maybe. I don't know. It sort of sounds that way, but they didn't say."

"What about them asking about the IT committee? That was weird."

"What did they ask you?" asked Malik.

"Probably the same things they asked you."

"Oh, yeah, maybe so."

King stood, waiting, but Malik said nothing more. King tried again. "Why do you think they were asking?"

"Oh, I don't know. I don't think the IT committee has anything to do with him disappearing."

"Why do you think he wanted to be on the committee? It must've been important."

"You think so? I don't know."

King knew pressing any harder would accomplish nothing. Malik was doing his stupid imitation. After four years of working together, King knew this was Malik's first line of defense. Malik would follow stupid with lies, then if someone pressed, escalating protests that the person was harassing, persecuting, and finally, physically intimidating him. Malik's reticence was evidence enough that he knew something.

72

WILL WAS WAITING FOR LAURIE WHEN SHE PULLED INTO the parking lot. He got into the van and she drove out of the university without a word.

"Laurie, if we don't give the police a killer, they'll take me."

"I know."

"We made progress today. I found out Watanabe's spreading the rumors."

"You think he's the killer?" She sounded odd, not disinterested, but flat.

"I doubt it, and I doubt he's making them up. He's getting them from somebody else, I think. I asked Trinh to see whether she can find out who."

Laurie didn't respond. Where silence had been a comfort yesterday, today Will couldn't take it. "We talked to Itō in IT Services. He agreed to help us figure out why Ikenami was interested in the IT committee."

Again, no response.

"We're making progress. We really are."

"When will you have actual evidence, something you can take to the police, not mere rumors and guesses?"

"Soon, I think."

"Weeks, Will. It'll take you weeks." There were tears in her eyes.

Will said nothing. The weight that had been too much for him to bear was mangling Laurie, too. The flatness wasn't just in her voice. She was being crushed. It was *his* burden. She was never supposed to have known.

73

A T EIGHT THAT EVENING, THERE WERE OVER THREE HUN-dred people in the JGU courtyard. The occasionally full pool's large island and the bridge from the administration building side had been cleared of snow late in the day. It was snowing again, but only a dusting. University staff were handing out candles and matches. Will and Laurie stood with David, Anson, and Danny.

President Satō, Dean Yoshida, and a few other university officials, along with Ikenami's wife and two teenage children, were standing on the cleared bridge, next to the pool of snow. At 8:05 p.m., Satō took a microphone to address the crowd. After an initial screech of feedback, they reduced the volume—enough that people had to strain to hear.

Although Satō had worked on his speech for much of the day, and got a native speaker to check it, his pronunciation and the low volume made him almost incomprehensible.

Still, somehow, Will caught it all. "Thank you, students, faculty, and staff, for coming together this evening. As you all know, our dear friend, colleague, and teacher, Prof. Kiyoshi Ikenami, is missing. We are a small community here. We are close, with bonds that are strong and lasting. His disappearance has shocked and saddened me deeply, as I am sure it has you. I have heard expressions of worry and grief from many students. They ask me, 'What could have happened? Where could our dear friend and teacher be?' Sadly, we must wait. As we wait, let us keep Professor Ikenami in our thoughts and in our hearts."

David whispered to Will, "Everyone who feels Ikenami was a dear friend, please raise your hand."

Will closed his eyes.

The president went on, "Let me introduce Professor Ikenami's wife, Yōko," and he handed her the microphone. One of the Japanese faculty stepped forward with another microphone to translate. No one could hear her tiny voice at first, so they boosted the volume. Laurie hugged Will's arm tight as she talked. "Thank you for coming out on this snowy night. I love the snow. In the small town in Niigata prefecture I am from, we had meters of snow every winter. I grew up loving it." Her voice cracked. "Now I feel it crushing me."

Laurie buried her face in Will's shoulder.

"Sunday night, I expected my husband to come home. I got snow instead. Each day, I wait—"

As she stopped, Laurie cried harder. Will turned and held her.

"I wait for him, but all I see from my window is the snow. Please, if anyone knows where he might be . . ." Her voice trailed away, and she stood there crying as everyone looked on. Finally, Yoshida stepped forward, took the microphone from her, and shepherded her back to her children.

Satō held out his hand for the microphone, but Yoshida ignored him, stepped forward again, and said, "Please now light your candles and observe a minute of silence."

They had positioned staff to turn off the hallway and library lights, and soon the courtyard was lit by the soft golden glow of hundreds of candles. People bowed their heads. Will assumed most were praying, but he had little doubt he was the only one praying for forgiveness.

Laurie clung to him and cried.

～

AFTER A FEW MINUTES, PEOPLE DRIFTED AWAY, LEAVING THEIR lit candles in the large pile of snow that surrounded the pool's island. David did the same with his. Will and Laurie had been in no shape to light their candles, so David took them, lit them, and placed them in the snow. He gave Will's shoulder a tug. Will moved with him, and Laurie followed along, glued to Will's arm. At the bridge, David gave Will a gentle push toward the administration building and the parking lot beyond. "Go home."

He watched the two of them walk off before he surveyed the scene in the courtyard. The president was gone. Ikenami's family had made their way inside with the dean. Kurimoto was taking in each face in the dissembling crowd. But Hasegawa was staring steadfastly at him.

VI

Restructuring
リストラ

A Brief Return to Last Sunday, 10 January 2010

74

IT WAS MURDER, PER SE, BUT THE WEBMASTER PREFERRED TO see Ikenami's death as restructuring the JGU faculty, a slight downsizing.

Still, murder is troublesome business. Airtight alibis are a myth. If the police suspect murder and you have a motive, even a secret one, they'll ferret you out in the end. Even an accident can look suspicious.

But the Webmaster had needed Ikenami quiet. That hadn't necessarily meant dead, but dead would do. Ikenami happened by at the wrong moment, that was all. He saw the Webmaster's secret rack of servers. It wouldn't have been much of a leap for him to guess what the Webmaster was doing. He obviously hadn't suspected how blatantly illegal it was. Otherwise, he would have gone straight to the university president, if not the police. That the whole thing had not come crashing down on the Webmaster's head simply meant Ikenami had kept quiet up to that point. It wouldn't last.

As the days passed after final exams ended, the Webmaster had hated how the fat man weighed on his mind. The holidays should have afforded days of total debauchery. Instead, he agonized over whether to do away with Ikenami, and if not, how to keep him quiet. He had doubted money would outweigh Ikenami's glee at humiliating him. Even if money were enough, paying Ikenami was unthinkable.

After all, money is winning, and winning is all that matters.

The Webmaster much preferred killing him.

If only he hadn't started his holiday maintenance and upgrade work early, his server closet would never have been open at that time of evening. Perhaps that was what bothered him most: this was all his own fault. If he'd stuck with his normal precautions, it would never have occurred. The Webmaster lived by a few general rules, though, and one was: Never pay for your own mistake when someone else could pay instead. He didn't know how much Ikenami had seen, but the man would pay dearly for his curiosity.

The Webmaster puzzled for days about how to make it appear like some natural cause. He considered stuffing a rag down Ikenami's throat, choking him to death, and replacing the rag with a piece of food, but Ikenami was a big man and he'd have to fight to subdue him. An air bubble in the bloodstream can kill, but he would have to get it into a vein. He checked the internet anyway and was disappointed to learn they're rarely fatal. As he investigated other ideas, he'd grown increasingly frustrated. Nothing was foolproof, and he could not bungle this. Winter term was nearing, so he had no choice but to try. He finally settled on the simplest, least detectable method, for which Ikenami himself would supply the weapon: an insulin overdose and fatal hypoglycemic shock. Given Ikenami's diabetes, the medical examiner would assume a heart attack and forego an autopsy. There would be a funeral, a cremation, and what was left of the man, always so puffed up, would fit into an urn. Problem solved.

Or almost. Did Ikenami carry enough insulin with him to do the job? The Webmaster had stolen a master key shortly after he started working at JGU. That made searching Ikenami's desk simple, and he was rewarded with a full vial. That would do it. Whatever Ikenami was carrying would be insurance. He knew Ikenami might not expire immediately, but it didn't matter how long he was comatose before he died, only that he couldn't talk.

The sole remaining problem was incapacitating Ikenami long enough to inject him. It did not have go into a vein, but needles leave marks, so it would have to be where Ikenami injected himself or someplace the medical examiner wouldn't see. That meant a struggle, but it couldn't be helped. He would just have to make it quick.

Ikenami was returning on Sunday. (As associate dean, Ikenami had to leave his schedule with Chieko, the dean's assistant.) It was perfect. Sunday was the quietest day of the week. And Ikenami would surely come to work. He never missed a day. He couldn't help himself.

As Sunday approached, the Webmaster's anxiety grew, but there was excitement in the fear. That afternoon, he started a program on his home PC that would browse a long list of websites. Then he headed to the university on foot, entered from the deserted western side, and waited.

He passed the time watching videos, but he had not thought to use the bathroom at home. Ikenami arrived so late that the Webmaster had to sneak into the women's restroom on the third floor of the administration building. With only one woman on the faculty, he was unlikely to be seen.

As he looked out the window after thoroughly washing his hands, Ikenami's car pulled in. Ikenami got out. The Webmaster's heart beat faster. He had done nothing this reckless for far too long. As he listened at the restroom door before leaving, he heard soft footsteps, but they passed and entered the stairwell. He opened the door, hands sweating, peeked out, heard Ikenami puffing up the steps, and went to look.

The footsteps were Trinh's. He watched her silently descend toward the landing between the third and second floors. Then she stopped. He strained to listen. Ikenami was talking to . . . Will. Trinh kept out of sight, and he almost laughed. He hadn't realized he and Trinh were so alike. And then a most wonderful surprise: Trinh drew back in shock as Ikenami fell!

He waited, watching, listening. Ikenami climbed back up the stairs and screamed at Will. The incident over, Trinh leaned out farther and took a long look before heading down.

The Webmaster reviewed his plan. It was perfect! With the fall—which the police would find out from Will himself, the prig, or if he kept quiet, from Trinh—no one would question a blow to Ikenami's head.

On his way to see Ikenami, he used the master key for one last stop: the new English professor's office, where he had seen a cricket bat while perusing the young man's things a few nights before. (He often looked through offices in the evenings. You can learn such interesting and useful things.)

He approached Ikenami's office warily, listening for any activity. He knocked softly on Will's door first. No answer. He tried it. Unlocked. Will wouldn't hear, but he might return soon. The Webmaster needed to get this finished.

He double-checked the insulin vial and syringe in his pocket, then took a deep breath, fairly bouncing in anticipation. He knocked. It surprised Ikenami to see him, of course. He looked oddly at the cricket bat as he spewed a few vile words. Then the Webmaster distracted the fool with nothing more than wide eyes and a finger pointed at the window. Up came the cricket bat, and he swung hard. One blow was sufficient.

He locked the door and quickly prepared the syringe. He undid the man's pants, pulled them down, and although it made his skin crawl, pulled open his rectum, shoved in the needle, and pushed the plunger. The irony was almost poetic. He reloaded and injected until he had drained the full vial of insulin. He found the kit in Ikenami's briefcase and pumped in its nearly full vial, just to be safe. With the insulin kit stowed, minus the used vial, he got Ikenami's pants back up, put his coat on him, and arranged him face up on the floor. The bruise from the blow to his head would be against the floor, as if from a fall. Then he sat by the door and waited for Ikenami to stop breathing. It took less than half an hour. He felt like screaming with joy, but pumping both fists into the air had to suffice—that, and opening Ikenami's eyes and spitting in them.

As he turned off the heater, it occurred to him to break Ikenami's watch and reset it to the time of the fall. Around 4:10 p.m. would be close enough. But then, with a smile, he set it back one more minute to 4:09. A vaguely gruesome number in Japanese, it would be his own private subscript. He even left the door ajar so they would discover the body sooner.

Sneaking back home under cover of darkness, he was all atingle. Ikenami was dead, and without a single witness! He was brilliant. He had to admit the fall was luck, but the plan and its execution were altogether, absolutely, undeniably brilliant.

There are superior humans, a natural ruling class, and for us, there are no rules.

So how was it the corpse up and walked away?

Song One: Greeting
一曲目：挨拶

Heart briefly syncopates, then halts its beating.
Naught to hold his soul in, life so fleeting.
All known as real melts into luminous haze,
And then it dawns:
He's mutely witnessing his end of days.

On a close-cropped lawn he stands alone.
So where's the escort who will shout him home?
If not acclaim, at least a Guardian meeting.
He taps his foot,
Impatiently expecting Heaven's greeting.

Who waits to honor him?
Who will genuflect to him?
Will they bestow laurels,
Or is his crown more glorious?

A distant hilltop with a shining tree,
Splendor inspiring curiosity.
Perhaps they're waiting there with choirs to sing
His praise, then all
With welcoming chorus, him to heaven bring.

(But) There's nothing there except the gleaming leaves
Blindingly shimmering in an unfelt breeze.
Restively he chafes at vain delay.
And frets
To which imperious god a prayer to pay.

They shall not ignore him.
Glory lies in store for him,
Shouts of approbation,
Deserved exaltation.

Hosts have minded all his unvoiced cries.
(But) They ever watched in life and long surmised
He worked for nothing, save his own short name.
Who here could care
In makeshift time, he'd garnered meager fame?

And so the wait for one to volunteer,
A friend from life who felt his heart sincere,
Just one who knew a kinship born of love,
Who now could
Reach out and lift him from a place above.

Is it any wonder   *[Nobody came]*
Hope is blown asunder?   *[Only himself to blame]*
To all disdain he meted,   *[Eyes devoid of charity]*
By karma now he's greeted.   *[Still not cast, pleading, heavenly]*

VII

Cognitive Dissonance
認知的不協和

Friday, 15 January 2010

75

THE WEBMASTER'S ALARM RANG AT 6:40 A.M., BECAUSE Trinh set hers at 6:50 on weekdays—even Fridays, when she didn't have Japanese class. He rubbed his eyes, rolled out of bed, and opened the blinds to what would have been a sunrise but for the mountains in the way. He checked the exchange rate and prices on the stock exchanges, then logged onto his website and clicked on Trinh's video stream. As she slept, he sat and drank her in.

Surely he would have heard something if she had come forward with what she saw on the stairs. He could not understand why she hadn't. She was supremely confident, smart, active, popular—an upstanding girl everywhere but his imagination—so why stay silent? He thought the rumor of Will and Ikenami fighting would nudge her to tell, but even with people saying Will killed him, she was quiet. Why protect him?

Unless she was using it! The Webmaster should have thought of that sooner! He, of all people, should have recognized her smile and easy laugh as finely crafted artifice. Had she made demands, or was she waiting, letting Will twist in the wind? He grinned at the thought. What would make her turn him in? If she was shrewd, she'd trade this secret only for something truly valuable.

It was 6:49, so he muted his PC. He hated Trinh's alarm, like a blast from an air-raid siren. It worked, though, and he always smiled at her slapping the clock as she sat up in shock. This morning, she stayed sitting, gazing at her pillow. At length, she stood, stepped over to her dresser, and pulled out fresh underwear. He watched with disappointment as she disappeared into the bathroom. In the fall, she walked out naked, drying her hair with a towel, and dressed in the room. When it got colder, she took clothes in with her.

He headed to the kitchen for breakfast, his mood buoyant. Any blackmail would likely happen in Will's office, so with the bug he planted two nights ago, he would hear. If not, at least today he had a worthy challenge: finding what would make Trinh talk, a lure that promised her more reward than pulling Will's strings. Or if not a carrot, perhaps a stick. There must be something she would protect, a dream too dear to abandon, a beloved treasure—or, if he was lucky, her own secret.

76

WITH THE NIGHT'S ACCUMULATION, THE SNOW WAS WELL over three feet deep again, and it was still flurrying, so snowpack was not an immediate problem. On Fridays, Will left Laurie in bed and got everyone off to school. Laurie generally thanked him in the shower. Today, Will knew she was not just sleeping in.

Should he say something? He decided to simply dress and leave.

Soon, he was ready to go, but as he looked at her curled up in the *futon,* Will knelt next to her. "Hey."

She didn't respond, but she was awake.

"I'm going to go."

He waited.

"I can't lose you, Laurie."

I'm so on the brink of losing everything else. I can't lose my family too.

ON HIS WAY OUT, WILL NOTICED A NEIGHBOR BURNING TRASH in a barrel near the street. He watched the unattended fire for a full minute before he grabbed the plastic bag that held his shoes from

Sunday night. He walked over, tossed the evidence into the fire, and walked back to his van.

77

As Kurimoto took the turns into the mountains, the elevation rising, the snow quickly deepened. Hasegawa's eyes were closed, but Kurimoto knew he was awake. So it was no surprise when he blurted out, "Four oh nine. Is that supposed to be a joke?"

"If it's not a coincidence, it's kind of sick, death and pain in the same number."

Hasegawa opened his eyes. "What time did Grames say he saw him?"

"A little before four o'clock."

"Grames fights with Ikenami, kills him, puts his watch in the desk so we'll know what time it happened, and admits he was not only at the university, but argued with Ikenami minutes before. It's ridiculous."

"We're sure either Grames or the Vietnamese woman, Trinh Nguyen, was lying. Grames said Ikenami walked away. She said Grames did. It's small, but it must mean something."

"Or else the two fabricated the argument." He was quiet for a few seconds. "Never mind. Too stupid."

Kurimoto looked over at him. "The victim could've caught them in an affair. She's got to be tempting."

"Why make up an argument? Why create a reason to suspect him?"

"What if it wasn't an argument, but a fight? It gets out of hand, Ikenami dies, and the lovers make up this story to cover it."

"But why this story? It makes more sense to alibi each other."

They were silent as Kurimoto drove on.

Hasegawa looked out the side window. "Or is someone else using the fight to cover a murder?"

"According to Grames, it wasn't much of an argument."

"But we already know he's lying."

"What's the point of disposing of the body if the killer already has Grames framed for the murder?"

"Why the lie?" asked Hasegawa, mostly to himself.

Kurimoto added, "How weird are all the rumors about Grames? I mean, why him, when only Trinh has offered the flimsiest 'I saw' or 'I heard' and zero physical evidence? Someone knows Grames is the killer and is creating rumors rather than coming forward? Or the killer knows whatever Grames is hiding and is using rumors to frame him?"

"Liars so far: Grames, or the woman, but I'm guessing Grames; the lawyer; that IT professor, Malik; and the other one, King. Also, Watanabe; maybe the IT Services manager, Itō; maybe the dean."

"You're passing on the wife?"

Hasegawa looked out the side window. "After last night . . . yeah."

"The students felt credible, all but Trinh. But I haven't felt good about a single professor. It's enough to make me believe they all killed him."

Hasegawa chuckled. "Caesar?"

Kurimoto smiled. "Perhaps not daggers in faculty meeting, but it fits as well as any other theory."

"What about Ikenami having no insulin even though he'd been traveling?"

"I followed up with Ogawa," said Kurimoto. "He called the wife last night. She told him she was the one who picked up all the prescriptions. She had the pharmacy fax his records, and I looked them over this morning. Regular insulin purchases, and all fast-acting ten-milliliter vials, none of the once-a-day kind, and then an extra vial before his trip. I estimated a range of usage rates from the purchases, and even at the high end, he should have had at least half a vial left, if he used the extra one at all."

"There was nothing in the kit in the desk or the one in his bag."

"Get this: Ogawa also asked whether Ikenami kept a reserve. She said she took it as her responsibility to make sure he did—always. One full vial at home, one in his office."

Hasegawa sighed.

"He almost never used the reserves. In fact, she had to rotate in fresh ones so they wouldn't expire. If he did tap into one, she always replaced it the next day. He could've taken the office vial on the trip, but with the extra she picked up, there was no need."

Hasegawa looked like a bloodhound on a scent. "There's a reserve vial at home?"

"She said so. We can check when we see her today."

Hasegawa took out his notebook. "At last, another real step forward."

"You think so?"

"I'm sure. We know the murder weapon."

78

STEVE KING GLANCED AT THE BOOKCASE AS HE PULLED HIS pants on—and stopped with them still around his knees. Where were his books? Where was *the* book? He had nearly two million yen in there! That was over twenty-one thousand dollars!

He yanked his pants up and bounded to the dining room. "Rumi, where's my books?"

She looked up from the newspaper with surprise. "What books?"

"The ones I had in the little bookcase in the bedroom!"

"Why you are so bother? They were all old. You never read again. We needed a space, so I tied them up and put them with trash."

"Here?"

"No, outside, in trash holder."

"You *what*? Wait, when's trash day?"

"Yesterday."

"*Gone?* You brainless—You—How dare you throw out my books?"

Rumi's eyes flashed. She picked up her fork and threw it at him.

With that, their screaming started in earnest.

79

WATANABE'S HEAD WAS POUNDING. WHAT A WEEK. HE'D had less than two days to prepare for the first lecture of a course he'd never taught. He should've let Anson take it. It would've served the sycophant right.

If Watanabe was going to teach it, he wanted to start as soon as possible. If he waited, class would have to meet three times a week.

The students would have enough trouble handling the material with the regular schedule. To compress it would only make things worse.

Watanabe looked down from his third-floor window at the students streaming into the classroom across the courtyard. The first time teaching anything was rough, but this was a required course in the two biggest programs, more students than he'd faced in his life.

I know the material. Like Anson said, it's just basic managerial accounting.

As he headed to the classroom, he rehearsed his opening lines.

He'd be fine. He could do this.

Turning the corner into the classroom building, seeing the dozens of students milling outside the room, he slowed, stopped—and ducked into the restroom.

He closed his eyes and tried to regulate his breathing.

You have to do this. You *can* do this.

I can?

Yes. Of course!

He would take command, intimidate them. If he got too nervous, he'd do what his mother had told him: imagine them as toddlers.

As much as he'd tried to prepare for it, however, as he entered the classroom, he stopped again, staggered by the sea of faces staring at him. Except for the first two rows, students packed the classroom's eight tiers. He looked at those hundreds of eyes. A sense of hunger pervaded, not for knowledge, but for the glee of watching him crumble.

He looked back at the door.

You have no choice.

He focused on the table in the front of the room. He set down his laptop and attached the video cable, then lowered the screen and started the projector.

After one final deep breath, he steeled himself and looked up—and there, directly in front of him, smiled the young woman who had been his most cherished dream from the first day he saw her.

Watanabe lectured mostly to the walls, like he always did. He concentrated on them harder this morning. He glanced at a face now and again—he had to; they expected it. But every time, he had to force himself not to look at Trinh. He was twenty minutes into his lecture before she caught his eye. It was nothing odd, a mere smile at something he said, but sitting right in front of him, it was impossible to miss.

Then he slipped. It was only a moment, an impulse unchecked as he tried to get the right words out, his brain disconnected from the muscles of his eyes as his gaze moved from her eyes . . . to her mouth . . . to her breasts. She was wearing a blouse buttoned only to the fullest point, and there was—

He looked down at his laptop as he realized he'd stopped talking. As he looked away, he could see it, as if the image was seared into his consciousness. There was so much skin; smooth, soft, so perfectly—

Deep breath. Deeper. Look at the slide. Say something about it.

Watanabe had to read the entire slide before he remembered what to say. He looked at the back wall and started speaking again. He talked to the clock. It had a face. It wanted to learn managerial accounting, didn't it? What clock wouldn't?

Ten minutes passed before he glanced at the back row. Time and again, he fought the urge to stare at Trinh, but over the next half hour, he worked his way down until he was looking at the top five rows. With fifteen minutes left, he ventured forward to one more line of faces.

He made it through a pair of eyes on each side of the room. Next would come the center section. She was there, down one more row. He couldn't help himself. Who could? He looked—

Oh yes!

But oh no no no.

She was smiling at him, looking directly into his eyes and smiling *at him*! It was pure ecstasy! How was he supposed to teach now?

He was still looking at her! She was still smiling!

The slide, look at it.

He started talking again, but with only half a brain. The other half was buried in Trinh's eyes and lips and blouse, and it took his eyes with it. He tore them away, but soon they strayed back, waiting to meet hers.

She did it again! Her impossibly big brown eyes were looking into his! She wasn't just smiling; she was smiling shyly, as if she liked not only the lecture, *but him*!

Trinh's friend, sitting next to her, was looking at him too.

They're all looking at me.

A young woman in the back raised her hand.

Trinh turned her head to look toward the back as the question started, and he watched as she turned her shoulder, as the blouse pulled tight—

He strained to hear the question.

He asked the woman to repeat it.

An answer. He was supposed to answer. He knew the answer! He told the clock all about it.

He looked down, where Trinh's warm eyes were staring at the screen.

Look into my eyes again. One more time!

His eyes dropped lower, to her blouse.

He glanced at the clock again. Five more minutes.

He forced his eyes to the screen, then to his laptop. Three more slides. He had timed the lecture well.

Don't look. Don't look. Don't look.

Ooh yes.

No! Focus on the screen!

He read the content off the screen without thinking about the words. He did the same with the last two slides.

Finished.

Trinh was reaching down to get her bag. He let himself just stare. Suddenly looking up—sensing his gaze?—her eyes claimed his. Oh no! He'd had no harassment complaints at JGU, but what if she told someone he was looking down her blouse?

This can't happen again!

80

WILL AND DAVID SAT IN THE CONFERENCE CENTER AND looked outside at the sun glistening off the crystalline whiteness as they talked in hushed voices. David worried about it melting—it was back below four feet—but he didn't bring it up. Will looked weaker today, deforming almost before his eyes, despite the progress they were making. He couldn't go more than a couple of minutes without his shoulder spasming.

"Trinh will work on Watanabe today?"

"I expect so. He's got Ikenami's class for the first time. I'll see her in the pool later. She'll give me some indication."

"Trinh in a swimming pool. If you can resist, you're a better man than I."

"Not better, only married."

David chuckled, then looked out the window for a second. "How's Laurie today?"

"I left her in bed."

"I'm worried about her, Will. And you. I empathize, but this doesn't look good. You've got to pull her out of it."

"The only thing that gets me over here is fear of what the police will think if I don't show up. I remember about his wife and . . ."

David gazed out while Will pulled himself together, his shoulder twitching again and again.

"David, I want to lie under the eaves and let the snow thunder down off the roof and bury me."

"You've got to ignore it, Will. *He's* the one who pushed *you,* as I recall. A fist clenched in a moment of anger is a far cry from one raised, which is a world away from throwing a punch. He provoked an argument, began a physical altercation, and stepped off into space. Not your fault. And the result? Bruises. That's all. Somebody else killed him—murdered him, Will. He's dead regardless of whether he falls down the stairs first, regardless of whether he happens across you on Sunday at all."

"I understand what you're saying. I have to end the cognitive dissonance. Marketing's half psychology. But I know—in my core—hiding his corpse was repugnant." Will paused to compose himself. "You saw his wife last night. Keeping quiet is depraved. This anxiety's *not* going away."

"Sorry, but either the anxiety goes away, or you do. You want to stay with your girls? Stop dwelling on his family and cultivate contempt for whoever killed him. Because *you* didn't." David softened his voice. "Once it's solved, grief at his death will swallow up their pain."

Will was blinking hard.

"Guilt won't bring him back. You're already doing all you can. The genuine tragedy would be if Laurie and the girls lost you."

Neither spoke for a minute before David sat up. "We should get back."

They stood and started walking.

"Why don't you take her to a movie?"

"Closest theater's an hour's drive away."

"If it gets the two of you out of town, all the better."

Will nodded. "We don't need a babysitter. Sarah's old enough to watch the little ones. Still, she'll want Trinh to come over. Sarah idolizes her."

"Not a bad thing, Trinh as a role model. She handles herself with as much grace as I've ever seen. As a dad, you might not want to hear this, but Sarah's likely to be every bit as stunning in a few more years."

"If that's supposed to displace my anxiety . . ."

"Hey, anything to distract you."

81

T RINH KNOCKED SOFTLY ON WATANABE'S DOOR. THERE WAS no answer, so she knocked louder. She was about to leave when she heard, "Come in."

When she opened the door, Watanabe popped up from his chair like he'd sat on a live wire. She kept her eyes turned down as she entered. Her steps were short, her feet turned inward. She'd seen Japanese high school girls. She knew how to do it.

"*Sensei,* I was wondering . . . I know you are busy, but . . ." She looked up. "May I ask a question?" She looked at her shoes.

"Oh yes! Of course! That's what I'm here for, anytime!"

Trinh's father taught her to fish in the Mekong River with a length of bamboo, some line, and a hook. She had a talent for casting, for feeling the first timid nibbles, but even more, for setting the hook. She watched this one struggle for another moment. Could he get any redder? She bit her lip and looked around his office, then back at him. "I enjoyed class."

"I'm glad. Thank you."

She took a tentative-looking step toward the chairs in front of his desk. "You had to prepare so suddenly, but still it was so good, so easy to understand." She caught his eyes and held them. "You impressed me."

He lit up. "I admit, the last two nights were late, but it's simple material, easy to teach."

She looked down again. "Maybe for you."

He smiled and pointed to the chair. "Would you like to sit?"

Hook set.

"Thank you." She sat and leaned forward to put her bag on the floor.

"Are you interested in accounting?"

"Yes, but I'm interested in everything. I have not chosen a concentration yet. I am thinking finance, accounting, maybe marketing."

Watanabe smiled. "I vote for accounting."

Trinh laughed even as a shiver ran up her back.

Those eyes!

Although she wanted desperately to glance away, she kept her eyes on his. "Yes, you should vote like that."

He laughed.

She bent down again and fished a notebook and pen out of her bag. As she sat up and prepared to write, she gave him ample time to look away, but still caught him staring when she raised her eyes.

Trinh asked him about accounting courses. It was easy to get him talking about something he knew. She did her best to gaze into his eyes, but never lasted more than a few seconds. He was pleased by her interest, and each time she wrote something, it was like she was petting a puppy.

At last, it was time to land him. "Who will teach accounting courses if Ikenami-*sensei* does not come back? Do you have to teach them all?"

"We'll have to hire someone. In the meantime, we'll find adjuncts."

"Will he come back?" Trinh had no trouble looking worried as she lowered her voice. "I hear terrible things. Most students say he is dead. Some say someone murdered him, even another professor."

"I heard that too."

"Can you believe it? All the students say Grames-*sensei*. I know him from Japanese class, and his family too."

Watanabe spoke with confidence. "I heard all the same things."

"It is only students' rumor. Students don't know."

"Other people say it too."

"Not students?"

When Watanabe nodded, Trinh's shock was genuine.

"Who? Do they know?" she asked.

"It could be true. Grames argued with Ikenami-*sensei* on Sunday."

"Someone saw?" She leaned forward—one more tug as she readied the net. "That is terrible! Who saw? Who said?"

He opened his mouth, but then his eyes lost their wide, nervous look, and after staring at her blouse once more, they flicked away. Trinh waited, but even as she kept her gaze fixed on him, she felt the hook pull free.

82

Hasegawa and Kurimoto spent two hours with Ikenami's wife. She reviewed his insulin usage in detail, showed them the home supplies, and agreed there was no reason for his office not to be stocked.

Back at JGU, they re-interviewed the IT committee yet again, but it was all shrugs and shaking heads and memory lapses. They'd lined others up for the afternoon, along with a few students and the last couple of faculty. Still, Hasegawa was on edge. They were just covering the bases, asking the same questions, not chasing some new clue or hunch. They were losing the scent, despite the university being thick with it. There was a corpse somewhere, people knew it, but no one was talking. It was as if there was some grand conspiracy, but of people with no apparent reason to protect each other. It was maddening. Staring out at the snow sparkling brilliantly in the sunshine, Hasegawa couldn't help thinking it was mocking him, as all he could do was grope about in the dark.

83

Zo6 watched VietKitten check her new swimsuit in the mirror. She poked, lifted, turned around, and looked over her shoulder at her back. She rummaged in her purse. Soon she was standing up straight, her phone held out to the side, taking a picture of her back in the mirror! Oh, VietKitten was a fun one!

She pulled and tugged and took another photo, which must have satisfied her, because she tossed her phone on the bed. As she faced the mirror again, she ran her hands up and down the smooth fabric, a bright yellow with blue accents that made her appear curvier than she was. She grabbed her jeans and pulled them on. She was wearing her swimsuit under her clothes?

He opened another browser window and called up the JGU website. The Webmaster wanted to keep secret what university it was, but did he think the subscribers were idiots? It had taken Zo6 all of half an hour of keyword searches to figure it out. Some girls' pictures were on the university website! Looking there now . . . JGU had a pool, although according to the website, it didn't open for half an hour.

He leaned back and watched her slip her shoes on.

Have a pleasant swim, lover.

After she left, he was restless. He thought about what it would be like to have his hands on that swimsuit, his hands inside of it. He could if the Webmaster agreed. Even if the Webmaster refused, he could simply drive there.

To find her alone, though, would be impossible. The only way would be to buy access to her from the Webmaster. He had seen hundreds of molestation and rape videos, even briefly groped a girl on a crowded train and then quickly fled, but had gone no further. It would be an amazing experience. He clicked on VietKitten's archive and opened a video of her undressing. She'd be ten times better if he tied her up.

It would be a hundred times easier if he had a key to her room. Did the Webmaster have that kind of access? He clicked on the contact button and a message screen popped up. How much to offer . . . ?

He watched the video for another minute.

He had the money. What else was he going to do with it?

After he typed his message, he read it. He scrolled over the "Send" button. He stopped and read it again. It was a shocking amount of money. So what? The Webmaster wouldn't agree, anyway. The cursor hovered.

Click.

Five minutes later, he was surprised to get an answer. He paused the video he was watching and opened it.

The reply to his generous offer was a single word, "No."

At least the guy was prompt.

84

HUONG DIPPED HER TOES IN AND JUMPED BACK. "IT'S COLD!" "Not once you swim," chided Trinh.

"You mean it's always this cold?"

"Once you get moving, it feels good."

Huong sat, put her legs in up to her calves, and held herself as if she was shivering.

"You're such a baby."

Huong kicked her legs and pouted. "Fine, if I freeze, he better be cute."

Trinh laughed. "Do a lap. I want to watch."

"Why?"

"To help. Go."

Huong jumped in, dunked herself, and pushed off the wall. Trinh walked along the side, watching Huong's stroke. It was fundamentally correct but showed a beginner's inefficiency.

Trinh was in the water when Huong finished her lap.

She stood, panting. "That's hard. How many laps do you do?"

"Thirty, usually more."

"Will I look like you if I do that many?"

"Of course. By the way, you have a nice stroke."

"I do?" Huong smiled broadly.

"You need to practice. You'll get a lot faster as you do."

"So thirty laps for you aren't like thirty for me."

Trinh ducked under the lane divider.

"We don't use the same lane?" asked Huong.

"You're too slow," said Trinh, and with a deep breath, she was gone.

THERE WAS ONE STUDENT HEADING THROUGH THE POOL DOOR from the showers. His suit surprised the Webmaster. While skintight, it covered his thighs. No matter, his own suit would make him even more desirable by comparison.

The Webmaster stepped into the shower to wash. It was a long process every morning and evening, but the girls might already be inside, so he rushed. He washed his hair, then scrubbed his skin. He caught himself taking too long and moved to another spot. Time and again, he hurried himself. He still felt vaguely dirty when he turned off the water, but he had to get in there.

Once he had his swimsuit and cap on, he did a few quick pushups. He looked for a mirror but couldn't find one.

Each pool lane had a sign: Fast, Medium, Slow, Walking. It looked like Trinh was gliding along in the fast lane, Huong was next to her in medium, and the guy was in slow, although he was almost as fast as Trinh. He had hoped not to share a lane with either of the girls. For a relationship, the girl must trust you, and that takes time. He had learned long ago not to come on too strong or be too open. To stay out of their lanes meant either using the slow lane, hardly a good first impression, or swimming in the walking lane as if he couldn't read. Then it occurred to him that the second-year student watching Trinh swim was a lifeguard. The Webmaster approached him with a question.

"Can I swim in the walking lane?"

"Sure, as long as no one's walking."

"Thank you."

"Anytime, *Sensei.*"

85

W**HAT'S A VLAN?" ASKED DAVID.**
Itō answered, "Virtual local area network. Think of network two ways. One way is hardware: server computers and client computers and cables and wireless transceivers. Another way is software. Inside one hardware network can be many software networks."

"Software networks are virtual."

"Yes. We have so many VLAN for administration offices, faculty, IT Services, Computer Center, library, and six around campus for students."

"There's no extra VLAN? One that shouldn't be there?"

"No. No extra LAN equipment, either. We would see it."

"Yet with high traffic . . ." David folded his arms. "A little or a lot?"

"Two times what it should be. Not so high now. It is high at night."

"So Ikenami was right about IT resources being misused."

"Yes, I think so."

David leaned on the wall as he looked through the long line of windows into the brightly lit server room.

"We should tell police?" asked Itō.

David considered it. "Do we have any idea what that extra traffic is?"

"No."

"If the police look, can the person hide it so they can't find it?"

Itō nodded. "I think so."

"Then it's best to work quietly until we know more."

"Should we tell Satō-*sensei*?" Itō looked apprehensive.

David gave him an odd look.

"Yes. Not him. Yoshida-*sensei*?"

"We don't know who the extra traffic might be linked to?"

Itō shook his head.

"The fewer people who know, the less likely the culprit is to hide." Itō didn't understand, so David rephrased. "Our search is secret. If more people know, maybe we cannot keep the secret."

"Ah, yes."

"Can you find the source of the traffic?"

Itō considered it. "If the traffic stay high, yes. All we need is they does not be scared and stop."

"What's next?"

"Tell everyone about the audit in a meeting."

"That should light a fire under the culprit." Again, Itō didn't understand. "Whoever it is will get scared and come here secretly, right? I mean, this is where all the internet traffic is controlled."

"Yes! So now we send email."

"To whom?"

"IT committee."

"Who's that?"

"IT professors: Malik, King, and Baig; new English professor: Daniel Charles; and some staffs. You help me with the English, please."

86

TRINH WAS GLAD TO SEE WILL'S FAMILIAR SHAPE AT THE end of her lane. She stopped at the wall, stood, and lifted her goggles. "Hi, *Sensei.*"

"Hi. You beat me here today."

"I brought Huong to try swimming. She bought a new swimsuit."

Will smiled. "I saw. I mean, not that it's new, but I noticed—I better shut up. If I say anything to her about the suit, they'll fire me."

"You can say!"

He laughed. "No way. It's a nice suit, though."

"Just nice?"

Will blushed. "Are you free tonight? I want to get Laurie out of town, away from all the rumors and accusations, to a movie."

Trinh bounced up and down and clapped. "Babysitting? Yay!"

"Thanks. The kids adore you."

Trinh grinned.

Will lowered his voice. "Do you know anything more?"

"A little." She looked at Huong, only a stroke away, and back at Will. "We talk later?"

"Conference Center. No afternoon class, right?"

Trinh nodded. As Huong reached the wall, Will showed Trinh three fingers, and she nodded again.

Trinh expected Huong to pop up out of the water. When there was no splash, she leaned around Will to see whether Huong was all right. She was emerging—with a big smile.

Will turned to her. "Hi, Huong. How do you like it?"

"Like it?"

"Swimming."

"Oh, I like it." Huong looked at Trinh. "I like it *a lot!*"

Trinh told her in Vietnamese, "Don't you embarrass me!" and Huong grinned all the wider.

Will smiled with her. "I'm glad. Trinh comes all the time, but there's rarely over five or six of us. Today must be newbie day."

Huong looked lost. "What is 'newbie'?"

"Someone new, like you and the guy in the far lane. I've never seen him here either. In fact, I believe it's Professor Malik."

～

Huong finished before Trinh, so she sat with her feet in the water and watched the others. She had not paid much attention to the student in the next lane. He was an excellent swimmer, though. His body was lean and strong, and he swam lap after lap, never stopping. In fact, she wished he would.

Even as good as he looked, he did not swim like Trinh. Huong was sure no matter how much she practiced, she never would either.

Then there was Will. Huong had always thought he was good looking—and she liked his warm, if unexciting, personality—but now she understood why Trinh was so over the moon for him. As cute as he was in jeans or facing the class in slacks and a necktie, he was meant to be in water. He moved through it with such ease. A few strokes and he was at the far end of the pool, where he would disappear with a small splash just before the wall. A couple of seconds later, he would reappear a quarter of the way back—all effortless.

What would Danny Charles look like in the pool? There was a potent daydream!

Huong noticed the person in the walking lane on the far side of the pool had stopped swimming. As he stood, she saw it was indeed Malik-*sensei,* and she looked away, not wanting to see him undressed. She wasn't sure what the difference was. Will wasn't that much better looking. Malik had a handsome enough face, and he might have been taller than Will, but he had the middle-aged, marshmallowy body of someone who got little exercise. Undressed, he could not have strayed onto a less advantageous stage. On one side of Huong was a young swimmer who was surprisingly pleasant to gaze at, and on the other, a god and goddess risen from the sea.

Now Malik was lifting his goggles and looking right at her, smiling!

Huong hopped back into the pool. As she fumbled with her goggles, it looked like Malik might get out. She got the rubber strap around her head. Yes, he was getting out. His swimsuit was tiny and disgusting—and he was still watching her!

Huong pushed off and swam hard until she reached the wall at the other end. As she stood there, panting, making a show of adjusting her goggles, Malik sat on the pool deck to stretch. She wanted to get back underwater.

Better yet, give me gills.

It was another five minutes before Trinh coasted to the far wall and stopped. Huong swam back to her. As Huong stood, Trinh stopped rubbing her eyes and asked in Vietnamese, "How was the swim?"

"Fine. So are the guys, except," whispered Huong, and with her body shielding her hand from Malik's view, she pointed at him.

Trinh peeked over Huong's shoulder. "What's he doing?"

"Stretching."

Trinh shivered.

"At least he's sitting down," added Huong.

"Why?"

"His suit. It's like something he bought in a sex shop."

Malik was facing away, so Trinh stood, looked, and dropped back into the water. "It's an old-style lap suit, but even for that, it's small. He sits there like he's on display."

"Can *Sensei* tell him to get a different suit?"

"He'll probably never come again. Almost everyone stops within a week or two."

"Why can't he stop and go away *now*?"

Huong saw Trinh glance down. "He's looking at us?"

"No, worse."

"Hi, Trinh. Hi, Huong," came Malik's voice from above her.

Trinh kept her body in the water, but looked up and greeted him. "Hello, *Sensei*."

Huong looked up for an instant. "Hello."

"Do you swim a lot?"

Trinh shrugged and her voice was soft. "Sometimes."

Huong kept her eyes on Trinh. "Not so much."

"Anyway, I wanted to say hello."

Trinh gave him a weak smile, which Huong echoed. She suppressed a sigh of relief as he headed for the showers. Trinh's face went involuntarily sour. When Huong's did, too, Trinh put her hand over her mouth to cover a laugh. Huong looked over her shoulder at Malik strutting away, and she got the giggles, too. She gave an exaggerated shiver, but as she did, Trinh suddenly looked down. Huong froze. She shivered for real, and glancing behind her, she saw Malik turn back toward the shower room door.

Malik slammed the door of the shower stall and glared at the wall. He had saved Huong from being raped by Zo6 and this was how she repaid him? Shivering as if a mouse had run across her bed? And Trinh laughing!

His whole body was tense. They would regret this. He had more power than they could imagine!

He turned on the shower, stripped off his suit, and washed.

Women longed for him. He made them pant and shake and scream. What did these two understand about love from a man with his skills? They thought joy came from guys like those two mere boys swimming along next to them? They would compare him with them? In the social clubs of Nagano, every girl's face lit up when he walked through the door. They fought for his companionship. When he had to leave, they pouted as they asked when he would return, genuine sadness in their eyes. They worshipped him. There, where he had no reason to hide that he was clever, he cast off the cloak of dull-wittedness that made him blend into the background. It had served him since boarding school, stopped his classmates from expecting normal emotional responses or making armchair diagnoses of sociopathy. He'd done fine in his studies, where it counted. And now he did fine with women, where it counted. But laughter? From a student? From a *girl*?

No! Girls are for sex. Period.

He was scrubbing harder now.

He should've told Zo6 he could have Huong anytime. The price was ten percent of the site's monthly revenue.

I could sell live video access to the others!

He'd never done a pay-per-view event.

I could give him her room key!

The male student who had preceded him into the pool walked into the shower room. Malik stopped scrubbing, put his hands on the wall, and leaned into the hot water.

What if a subscriber thought it was too much and notified the police? It was too risky. Everyone knew they staged even the most realistic-looking rape videos. Viewers suspended disbelief and fantasized, that was all. Those who take comfort in the underlying innocence of it might not appreciate the real thing.

In the end, subscribers' qualms were irrelevant. The police might investigate the rape.

Only if she reported it, though. Lots of girls don't. Even if she wanted to, going to the police in a foreign country might be too intimidating.

But if she did . . . he'd have to pull the camera from her room as a precaution, upsetting her fans. And if the police caught the guy, it would blast Malik's life to hell. The revenue stream was too important. It would be stupid to jeopardize it merely to humiliate her. He could do that in class.

Malik turned off the water, but as he opened the stall door, he realized he had left his towel on a shelf by the pool. He slipped his suit back on, but paused before stepping out. It was important to appear as if nothing had happened. He would smile and be pleasant.

He opened the door. The girls were still in the pool, both facing away from him, talking to—

That wasn't a student in the lane with Trinh; it was Will!

At the shelves, Malik pretended to search for his goggles.

The girls laughed. Will spoke, and soon they were tittering again. White-bread Will. Saltine-cracker Will. The man was *tōfu*! And they were babies who'd never tasted meat.

They were getting ready to climb out of the pool. Will was first. He sprang from the pool and stood, all in one long, smooth motion. As Will stepped away, Trinh's eyes never left him. No wonder she hadn't come forward.

87

Rumi King boarded the Shinkansen for Tokyo and collapsed into her seat. She felt the box cutter in her pocket, fished it out, and dropped it into her bag. Her plan had been to leave in the spring, but after this morning's ugliness, today was as good a day as any.

Steve had a class in the afternoon, so he would likely be at JGU all day. After that, anger over the fight would keep him away until well after midnight. Then he'd stumble through the door reeking of beer, or some cheap tramp's perfume, or both. But any chance he might discover her before she escaped had stoked Rumi's morning with adrenaline. She had done it all. When he got home, he would not find a single possession of hers. She had been sending what she could, one box at a time, to her sister to store for her in a self-storage trunk room. She had already boxed much of the rest, so she only had to pack eighteen boxes today, plus all their luggage. The delivery service arrived to pick them all up in plenty of time for her to leave the professor with a parting gift.

Rumi began her last trip out the door by shredding Steve's clothes: what he had in the closet, the drawers, those stored in boxes; every shirt, tie, hat, and sock. Next came his books, slicing the pages out of every volume with her box cutter, then the furniture and bed, lest he have a place to sit or sleep. She gathered all his photos, negatives, diplomas, and other treasures, along with his passport and every document that could have been any use to him. (She'd already pulled and packed the PC's hard drive.) With it all gathered into the kitchen, she set a wire-mesh wastebasket on the cooktop, turned the exhaust hood on strong, and burned the lot.

Once their dishes and glassware lay in shards throughout the apartment, Rumi smashed the kitchen appliances with a hammer. Then she wrecked his beloved television, DVD player, and the fiber-optic modem and wireless hub that connected Steve to his favorite porn sites. She destroyed the air-conditioning/heating units high on the living room and bedroom walls. Let the man freeze to death. The food was especially fun. She poured it all into a pile on the living room floor, dry items on the bottom, wet on top, and doused it with their entire stock of wine, the bottles then broken on the floor. She even took a hammer to the toilet. Finally, as she made her way to the door, she shattered the lightbulbs one by one.

It was with deep satisfaction that Rumi locked that loathsome apartment for the last time. After she pulled the key from the lock, she turned, looked into the sun in the western sky, and threw the key as far as she could.

Rumi clutched her bag to her chest now and waited for the chime signaling that the train's doors were closing. With that, she would be safe at last. He would never find her. She had sixty-six million yen, over seven hundred thousand dollars. It was mostly cleared out from their joint investment account into a temporary account she would empty and close tomorrow. That much money would provide all the anonymity she would ever need. The ten percent of it Rumi carried in cash could take her to the ends of the earth.

88

TRINH WAS WAITING AS WILL ENTERED THE CONFERENCE Center. He took a seat in the next chair. "Thanks for coming. Did you talk to Watanabe?" His shoulder, aching, spasmed again.

She looked at Will with concern. "Yes."

"It went all right? You're okay? Was he scary or threatening?"

Trinh smiled. "It was not easy, but he is not dangerous. *Sensei,* he knows something. He said someone saw you and Ikenami-*sensei* on Sunday."

"Who?"

"He did not tell me."

"Who told him?"

"I asked, but he just said it was not a student."

Will sat back and stared out across the room.

"I think he will tell me. I can talk to him again. He will tell."

Will looked at her. "Do you think he saw?"

"No."

"Could he be lying? He could have started the rumor."

"No, *Sensei,* I can tell when a man is lying. Someone told him, and he will tell me who."

89

Malik looked out Watanabe's office window at the snow. "I'm so worried about Ikenami-*sensei.*"

Watanabe gave him a somber nod.

"Have you heard anything?" asked Malik.

Watanabe leaned his head on his hand. "No, it's all rumors."

Malik had not heard such a reserved response from Watanabe all week. If he was losing interest, it could be problematic. No one else on the faculty was so open to suggestion, and like Yoshida said, rumors from a professor carried the ring of truth. It might still work. He had seen the way Watanabe watched her in the cafeteria.

"Rumors . . . mostly, I guess, sure, but still scary. You know, there has to be some truth there. Like Grames fighting with him on Sunday."

Watanabe looked unconvinced. "Yeah, Grames admitted it, but before that, how would we have known whether it was true? We don't know who saw it."

"I just sort of believed it when I heard it, I guess. It sounded true, like the kind of thing Grames would do, you know."

"Who told you?"

Watanabe had never asked anything like that. "Oh, it was . . . some-times it's best to . . . I don't want to, you know, say and cause trouble or something for the person."

"Yeah, that was my response exactly."

Malik probed apprehensively. "Your response?"

"What I would have said. If someone asked."

"Ah." This was getting dicey. If Watanabe wasn't up for his daily dose of scandal, it might be better to wait. Should he try getting a drink into Watanabe before telling him?

No, it was Friday night and there were promises to keep to his girls in Nagano. It was time the police forgot about IT and arrested Grames.

Malik looked back out the window. "I still think it was Peregrine or Grames, or maybe both together. You know, Grames is like a trained dog. He'll do whatever Peregrine says."

Watanabe shrugged.

Malik hesitated. "You know, I've been sort of hearing things about them for a while. I thought they must be made-up stories, you know. But I saw something today that was sort of, I don't know, disturbing, I think."

Watanabe looked up at him.

"I've been hearing things, rumors, you know, that they were having affairs and things with students. I didn't tell anyone, you know. But today I saw Grames with a girl in the pool, and they were, like, sort of giving each other, you know, little hidden touches they thought no one could see."

"Grames and who?" asked Watanabe.

"It surprised me so much too. But now I think the rumors must be true. And it's so wrong, because the girl is really nice, you know, sort of innocent. He's taking advantage of her."

"Who?"

Malik played it coy. "You might, you know, get a bad opinion of her or something. And it might not be what it looks like, you know, not be an affair, and she might not be pregnant, so I can't say."

"Pregnant?"

That may have been too much. I better back off. "That's what I heard, but I don't believe it."

"Who?"

"I shouldn't say. I think it's been going on for a while too."

Watanabe leaned forward. "I could check into it."

"It might be best if someone did. If Grames is, you know, whatever he's doing with her, someone should stop him. We can't afford to have a predator in the faculty."

Watanabe spoke almost to himself. "On top of Ikenami-*sensei* disappearing, a sex scandal could sink the school."

Malik felt a chill run up his back. If Watanabe started thinking of the good of the school, he might clam up.

But he was so close. "It might, but I think maybe other people saw, maybe word is already out. I just keep worrying about Trinh and—"

"Who?"

Malik widened his eyes. "No one. I didn't say anything."

"You said, 'Trinh.'"

"Oh no, I think you heard it wrong."

Watanabe was sinking into his chair, deflating as if someone had stuck a pin in a balloon.

"Like I said, she's a nice girl. And Grames, he makes me so—"

"I don't care. I have a lecture to prep." Watanabe turned abruptly to his PC.

90

IT committee members:

There will be a special meeting of the IT committee tomorrow (Saturday) at 8:00 a.m. I'm sorry to take your time on a weekend, but it is an urgent matter, and everyone's attendance is required. I expect the meeting to conclude in time to participate in JGU Ski Day.

Best regards,

Itō, Manager, IT Services

Malik spun in his chair. The IT committee met perhaps twice a year; there was no such thing as an "urgent matter." Besides, Itō's English wasn't this good.

∼

WITH WHAT THE POLICE SAID ABOUT IKENAMI WANTING TO JOIN the IT committee, King wondered whether the police would be at the meeting. They might have found Malik's porn site on the JGU servers.

King's heart was racing, so he leaned back and closed his eyes.

He wasn't absolutely sure it was porn Malik was streaming, let alone whether he was using the university servers. It would be stupid for Malik to take a chance like that.

He's none too bright, though, and he's such a greedy son of a bitch.

Still, hosting the site using JGU's network would be idiotic. It must be hosted elsewhere. And Malik having paid him to design a streaming portal didn't necessarily mean porn.

With Malik's tastes, what else would it be? Why use the Tor network instead of standard encryption? He had to be serving not just porn, but something illegal if he was that intent on hiding the files.

It could be child porn. Malik was twisted enough.

So what? It's only my problem if they can tie it to me.

They would never find King's name in any of the code he'd written. He had not used his usual formatting, so it wouldn't resemble his work. There was also no email traffic. Malik made every request in person, and every time King transferred a file, he used Malik's USB drive.

He was safe.

Unless Malik murdered Ikenami.

Who would kill someone over a porn site? Even if he was hosting it on JGU's machines—even if Ikenami, who understood nothing about IT, had stumbled onto it—all Malik needed to do was scrub it off the machines and say Ikenami was persecuting him. He'd seen Malik use that ploy. To kill for a porn site would be nothing short of psychotic— and King knew psychotic. He went to high school with it. Half his friends were psychotic, and the other half ended up in prison.

He'd keep quiet. There was nothing to gain by coming forward, and nothing about which to feel guilty. *He* had done nothing wrong—except taking payment in cash to keep it tax free, but everybody did that.

He would keep away from Malik, to be safe.

And forget helping Malik with TrueCrypt, the steganography software?

No, he could still help. King smiled. Malik was such an idiot. He set up the hidden volume on the disk and couldn't enter the right password to access it again. It was good Malik hadn't lost all his data, or he wouldn't be willing to pay such a hefty price for help hiding the rest.

With my idiot wife having thrown out my cash stash, I need the money.

If he had trusted Malik in the first place, he would have hidden the money in his office, not where his wife could toss it out with the trash.

Still, he had to get free from Malik before things got any riskier. Which left just enough time for one last payment.

91

Hasegawa saw Kurimoto looking at him. He was the brilliant detective who kept the other detectives on their toes and the rookies quaking, and he had no idea what to do next. He was tired, had a headache for the second day in a row, and wanted a drink. It was necessary for him to say something, though. "Is that everyone on our list for today?"

"Yes."

He checked his watch: 5:33 p.m. He walked over to the window and looked down at the snow shining in the courtyard lights. Someone had a motive for murder, but how to float it to the surface?

"Sir, if I may . . ."

"What is it?"

"Someone murdered Ikenami. I'm not sure why I'm so willing to say he didn't collapse and get buried in the snow. It just feels more like murder."

Hasegawa nodded.

"And it was premeditated. I think you agree."

He nodded again. He might as well let her run with this.

"Someone has a motive, but I don't think more interviews will help. No one's talking, and we have no leverage."

She was right about that. "What do you suggest?"

"It's in the IT, something worth murder. I can't explain why I'm so sure of that. Perhaps it's that everyone says Ikenami wanting to be on that committee was weird and all the IT people acting like they're hiding something. It's . . . a feeling I guess—"

"That doesn't make it wrong."

"If I'm right, then our only chance to catch them is if whatever is hiding in the IT stays there."

Interesting.

Hasegawa nodded again.

"If I may suggest, let's come in *big*, like a SWAT team, only with IT people. Let's walk in, no warning, take over, and pick it apart until we find the clue we need."

"It will take a day or two to set up."

"Yes, sir, I was about to suggest we go back to Nagano; leave them alone for the weekend. That way, the killer is complacent, and when we swoop in at dawn on Monday, the evidence is still here."

It was a good idea.

Hasegawa stepped over to the cabinet that held their coats and put his on, then held hers out to her. He'd never done that for her. She looked embarrassed but appreciative.

As they passed the president's office, Hasegawa stepped in and pointed to the president's room. The assistant nodded, so Hasegawa spoke to the president from the doorway. "We're going now, I'm sorry to say."

Satō looked up, startled. "Excuse me?" His eyes looked unnaturally large through his reading glasses.

"I'm afraid the case has gone cold. It's looking like natural causes. We'll continue searching, but I have little hope we'll find Ikenami-*san* alive."

Satō kept staring at him. "I see."

He looked like he might say something more, so Hasegawa said, "We'll inform you of any developments. In the meantime, farewell."

"Goodbye," said the president, looking bewildered.

They repeated the conversation with the dean, then headed for the car.

Kurimoto drove again. As she was pulling out, Hasegawa spoke softly. "A weekend off."

"If you think that's all right."

"Oh, definitely. It's just . . . I haven't had a weekend off in six weeks."

"Yes, sir, I was aware of that."

Hasegawa studied her. "Would you mind telling me your name?"

He was afraid she might blush, and she did. "It's Yoshie."

"Mine's Yūji, not that it matters."

She showed a self-conscious smile, so he turned and stared outside as he thought about all the partners he'd been through. It was six years since the last one who was any good. Even that one wasn't as bright as Yoshie. He'd never had a woman partner. But they could never promote Yoshie out of step with her entering class.

That doesn't mean I can't take her along wherever I go. I could also tell her to lose the uniform and wear a suit.

At least he could try.

92

DAVID COULD SEE THAT THE ENGLISH HAD ITŌ STUCK, SO he said, "It's okay, I think I understand."

"Sorry, I forget electronic dictionary when I came to server room."

"No problem. You'll do an audit of all the traffic on the main line that connects the university to the internet. We find out what kind of packets, where they're coming from, where they're going, everything."

Itō nodded.

"When will you do it?"

"I set up a program to audit if traffic goes over one hundred fifty percent of normal daytime load."

"What if that catches nothing strange?" asked David.

"It audits every time. Audit over and over. We will find it."

"When can you do it?"

Itō smiled. "I start already."

~

MALIK LISTENED TO THEIR CONVERSATION, BEMUSED BY David and Itō trying to ferret out the truth. From what he knew, Itō could barely find his way around the JGU network. Moreover, Malik had hidden things masterfully. He had three data flows. The first was the video from the forty-four dorm rooms he had outfitted with cameras. It was huge, but the university, at his urging, had installed a network that could handle video. Of course, everyone else imagined incoming streams, such as video lectures, but it could also be used for Malik's outgoing ones. The feeds from the cameras, encrypted and disguised as DNS traffic to get past any filters, piggybacked on the dorm VLANs. He'd written a special routine that stripped his traffic off and routed it to his system. He'd reconfigured the line carrying it to look like any ordinary equipment uplink.

The second data flow was tiny, the incoming requests from subscribers to Malik's streaming service. Malik depended on the main router to send those packets to his system.

The third flow was the biggest. Malik had to serve all his subscribers at once. He had King design the portal to handle 500 streams, but he set the cap at 401. He had three-fourths that many now. Of course, one blabbing subscriber could bring the entire business tumbling down. More subscribers meant more risk, but Malik felt 401 was safe enough. (Truth be told, he had always thought prime numbers were lucky, and 401 felt good.) He couldn't get that much data through JGU's firewall, so he put in a bypass. It connected to a media converter tying the university's system into the phone company's fiber-optic line, linking his goldmine to the world. A new wire entering the existing switch box might be noticed, so Malik installed a second, secret switch box in the fiber-optic line. He hid it in the mass of cables under the server room floor.

The server setup was Malik's crowning achievement. The dormcam website ran on a rack of hardware hidden in a closet in the next room. These days, the library used the room to store old furniture, and the lone key to its closet—Malik had changed the lock—never left Malik's pocket. The closet and server room shared a wall, so Malik put in special venting that drew cool air from under the server room's raised floor and vented it back into the space above the server room's drop-ceiling. He also backed the closet door with sound-absorbing foam. Even from centimeters away, the hum of the fans was almost inaudible.

Regardless of all his stealth, the audit would be troublesome. The only way not to trip the audit routine would be to throttle his servers' bandwidth. He could default to low-resolution, but his users would not be pleased. At least the audit was only on the main line to the internet service provider. He could still capture and store the full-definition camera streams, and users could enjoy them later.

Fortuitously, when King programmed the streaming site, he'd set it up to change the video resolution with the flick of a software switch. Today, Malik's main job was to prepare an email to the subscribers about a "problem with the ISP." He made it long and abstruse. The less they understood, the less they expected. He left out any estimate of how long it would last. That way, if it took more than a day or two, he would only have to grant credits to those who complained.

93

HASEGAWA SAT ON HIS SOFA WITH HIS SCOTCH BOTTLE ON the table before him and a glass of ice in his hand—merely sat, watching the ice melt, never pouring a drink. His wife, who was off visiting their daughter in Morioka, did not approve of him drinking, so he didn't. She didn't approve of him smoking either, but that was harder to stop. Still, he was trying his best. Refusing to toss the scotch bottle was his minor rebellion.

He had not taken the cap off the bottle for six years. There was no point. His wife had poured out the scotch and replaced it with a mixture of apple juice and oolong tea. That was her minor rebellion. He laughed hard the night he discovered it—she made a valiant effort to get the color right, but he could tell—and he had pretended ignorance ever since. When it got cloudy, she changed it, the color slightly different each time. Games, the silly things people do for little or no reason.

They do evil, too, and they have reasons for that.

He picked up the tumbler, the glass cool on his fingers. He tipped it one way and another, watching the ice slide around in circles.

In a circle as small as JGU, so isolated, so confined, a puddle teeming with that many lies, someone's guilty, and someone knows.

Ice . . . He swirled it around . . . Slippery stuff when you warm it.

Who to light a fire under . . . ?

He pressed the glass to his forehead. It might be time to arrest the lot.

94

THEY WERE ON THEIR WAY BACK FROM THE MOVIE, DRIVING silently through intermittent snow showers, when Laurie said, "Will . . ."

"Mm-hmm?"

Laurie didn't respond right away. When she did, her voice was quiet. "Why doesn't guilt ever go away?"

"You mean for a monumental screwup?"

"I mean for taking a piece of gum from the K-mart when I was eight."

Will drove on in silence.

"I could list a thousand things I still feel guilty for. And while I watched a movie with my husband, Ikenami's widow waited for hers."

Will was silent for another minute. "It might not disappear, but it'll fade."

"No, I think it's something we're meant to bear, like an enormous basket of rocks we have to carry, or like pins stuck into us." It was a minute before she continued, voice thick with emotion, "I love you, the bright, confident, innocent you I married. It breaks my heart to think of you spending the rest of your life with this pain."

"I won't. It'll get better."

Laurie was quiet.

After another minute, Will said, "David quoted a Buddhist monk the other day."

"He has a friend who's a monk? How does he meet these people?"

"No, one from centuries ago. Anyway, the quote was something like, 'If righteous people can get to heaven, how much more so the wicked ones.'"

"Sounds backward."

Will gave her a wan smile. "Yeah, I thought so too."

"If it's true, our chances of making it went way up this week."

"David keeps telling me I'm not the one who killed him. Whoever murdered him planned it. I was in the wrong place at the wrong time."

"Maybe so."

It took Will awhile to respond. "No, we both know I'm not innocent. We'll solve it and go on. My big rock will flake away. Just . . ."

"What?"

"Give me your rock, 'kay? I can carry this, but the idea of you—"

"Hush."

95

THERE WAS NO SOUND BUT THE SOFT RUMBLE OF THE TIRES on the road. The car was warm, so Trinh unzipped her coat.

Or perhaps it wasn't the car.

Trinh couldn't think of anything worth saying, so she watched the snow stream past. She had been alone with Will before, but the white outside seemed to set the minivan apart, like a cozy bubble, and she had the vague feeling that words might pop it. She sank back further into her seat as she watched Will's hands, strong but relaxed, on the steering wheel.

Her father told her one day when they were fishing, "Comfortable silence is one sign two people are truly close." Comfortable as she was with Will, this was not at all like being with her father.

Before reaching JGU's entrance drives, Will asked, "Which dorm are you in?"

"East, but *Sensei,* maybe you should drop me off at the main entrance, not the dorm. Everyone in the lounge stares when cars pull up."

"Trinh, you can call me *sensei* at school, but when it's only us, how about just Will?"

"Okay." Her voice was softer now.

Will pulled into a parking space by the administration building but left the van running. He let go of the steering wheel and turned to her. "Thanks for watching the kids tonight. The rumors have been hard on Laurie."

"Did it help to go out of this town?"

Will flexed his shoulder. "I don't know. I hope so."

"I hope so too. I enjoy to babysit. We have each other's phone number and email address now, so please call me to do this anytime. When I am with your family, I am not homesick anymore."

"We could share them."

"Your family?" Trinh put her head back and laughed. "Sarah taught me a new word tonight."

Will smiled at her.

"'Skyrofoam.' We went outside and snow was falling so tiny round shapes and she said it is like Styrofoam pellets, balls, but from the sky."

Will laughed and turned off the headlights. "There's actually a word for that kind of snow that hardly anyone uses, graupel."

She returned Will's smile.

"Before you go . . ." He paused. "The rumors and Watanabe and this whole mess . . . you don't have to do this. If things get too out of hand, you'll tell me, you'll stop, right?"

"I think maybe it is already out of hand. Or worse than out of hand."

Will looked down.

"No, *Sen*—no, Will, not the thing about you. Just everyone here wants to talk about wild stories all the time. It makes me want to scream."

"I'm glad I miss most of them. Even so, I feel . . . stretched, like suddenly nothing in my life fits."

"You will feel right when I get a secret from him."

"I still don't feel good asking you to do it."

"I want to know too."

Will sat still for a long time, and when he spoke, he stopped himself.

"What? Please say."

He patted his fingers on the bottom of the steering wheel. "I'm scared, I guess. Scared for you too. I'm pushing you to the edge of something. I wish I understood what."

"Don't worry. It will be okay in the end."

He smiled, but it looked more like resignation, so Trinh reached over and squeezed his arm.

Will put his hand on hers while he stared out the window. Finally, he looked back at her. "I better get home."

She nodded.

Then he leaned toward her, arms outstretched.

Perhaps they were at an edge, one they could lean over together, and look.

～

WATANABE WAS STEPPING OUT OF THE ADMINISTRATION building when Will's vehicle pulled up, so he ducked back inside. Will's office was at the other end of the building, so Will would use the other door. A few seconds of waiting and Watanabe wouldn't have to acknowledge him. Standing in the shadows of the cold, dark hallway, Watanabe watched his breath. He knew how foolish he was being, but Will soon extinguished his headlights, so Watanabe waited.

There was no Will going in the other door.

Watanabe looked out. Steam was still blowing from the tailpipe . . . and it looked like there was someone—

Watanabe turned away and shut his eyes tight. He leaned his head back against the wall. He wanted to bang it, hard. It was better to know, though, better not to be so ridiculously naive, so hopeful, and so stupid.

He peeked again. They were sitting, talking. Maybe they were friends.

Friends who go on drives together at this time of night?

The van was in front of a conference room window, so Watanabe backtracked up the stairs, traversed the second floor at a full run, bounded back down to the first floor, and slipped into the conference room. The blinds were down but not closed, so he was sure they could not see him as he approached the window.

Whatever they were talking about, it brought no smile to either of their faces. They weren't arguing. It was just something serious. They looked . . . worried? His thoughts raced with all the things that could worry a couple in a warm van on a frigid Friday night.

He looked at them, so relaxed together, at Trinh, her enormous eyes, her full lips. She licked them—only for a moment—but he'd heard it's a sign a woman wants to be kissed.

No, not Trinh. Anyone but Trinh.

He picked up a chair and slammed it into the floor. He did it again, then again, time after time, until the legs broke off. As they leaned close to hug, Watanabe brought his fists to his eyes and cried.

96

Trinh and Huong paid no mind to the snow cascading past the window. They were curled up on opposite ends of Huong's bed in their pajamas.

"*Sensei* said he liked your swimsuit."

"No, he didn't."

"He said he couldn't tell you or they'd fire him."

Huong laughed. "You tell him he's welcome to flirt with me anytime. But that Malik gives me the creeps."

"What did he think he was doing?"

"People say he's so nice, he cares so much about students, blah, blah, blah. I guess he's a good enough teacher, but there's something off about him."

Trinh lay on her back. "The good teaching evaluations—he gives everybody an A. People who have him as a thesis advisor say he's terrible. I heard he only had two students last year, and both asked to switch."

"Did they let them?"

"One, but I guess if he has none, he doesn't meet his teaching require-ment, so they made the other stay with him."

Huong looked sympathetic. "Poor thing."

"She complained to the dean, and he basically became her advisor, even though Malik's name was on the thesis."

"He won't be my advisor. After seeing his bony frog-butt strutting around in that . . . *thing* today. It turns my stomach just remembering it."

Trinh, overcome with sympathetic shivers, rubbed her arms.

Huong rolled onto her stomach. "How'd it go with Professor Blinky?"

"I didn't get it out of him. I was close, though."

"Still can't believe what you did."

"I just smiled at him."

"You made eyes at him. That's a lot more than a smile."

Trinh put her arm over her eyes. "Please don't tell anyone, ever. I'm disgusted enough already. If anyone else finds out, I'll die."

"Making him think he was getting someone's heart . . . no more morality talks from you, big sister."

"It's not like he had his hands on me, but . . ."

Huong said quietly, "You feel like he did."

"Kind of. Like he touched me and I let him. But what he's doing, spreading those rumors, is worse. I'll work him tomorrow too. I don't know how else to open him up fast, and I need to know where he's getting this stuff. But pretending I'm interested . . ."

"For discombobulating a guy, sister, you've got the tools. Use them quick and get it done. Tomorrow's only one more day."

They were quiet for a minute.

"Does *Sensei* realize what you did?" asked Huong.

"That I led Watanabe on, but no details."

"He's okay with it?"

"Not so much. He was worried. It was cute."

"He's jealous."

Trinh smiled up at the ceiling. "Maybe a little."

Huong sighed. "I wish I had a guy who was jealous."

Both were quiet again.

Trinh looked over at the desk. "Can I have a *mikan*?"

Huong got up, tossed one to Trinh, and took one herself. "You know if you can't peel it in one piece, it means you're a monkey."

Trinh laughed as she sat up. "I could never do it with an orange, but I can with these."

Neither spoke as they tried to peel like humans.

Huong finished first. "He really said he liked my suit?"

Trinh smiled and nodded. "Mm-hmm."

97

STEVE KING HAD TROUBLE WITH HIS KEY. WITH AS MUCH AS he had drunk, he had trouble even seeing the lock. After a few tries, he got it in and opened the door. As he stepped into the *genkan,* he tripped. The *genkan* was full of shoes? What was she doing, dumping them all out? Why didn't she leave the light on for him? Vindictive witch.

He found the hall light switch, but it didn't work, so he put down his bag, kicked off his shoes, and started down the dark hall toward the living room. Three steps in, he screamed in pain.

There was broken glass on the floor.

"Damn it, Rumi! What'd you do? You bitch!" he screamed.

Silence.

He made his way back to the *genkan* on his hands and knees, clearing glass out of his path as he went.

I'll kill her. When I catch her, I'll wring her scrawny neck.

He had a small flashlight in his bag, and standing at the edge of the *genkan,* he used it to inspect his foot. There was no glass in the cut, but it was deep and bleeding profusely.

He shined the light at the *genkan* floor. There lay the shoes he'd shed a minute ago, and underneath them was every other shoe he owned— sans toes. He panted with rage. "I'll slice *you* up!" he screamed as he hurled a mutilated shoe down the hall.

He needed a bandage—a towel, a sock, *anything*—to wrap his bleeding foot. He put his one good right shoe on his one good foot and hopped down the hallway. The flashlight beam sparkled back, broken glass everywhere—and the lightbulb was shattered in the socket. The living room light switch didn't work either. He figured none would.

As he shined his flashlight into the room, it sank in that his wife was gone for good. Yet the totality of the destruction which lay before him was too much to fathom. There were pages of books strewn everywhere, stuffing sticking out from the sofa and chairs, a disgusting puddle of food in the middle of the room, and a lifetime's mementos smashed into so many pieces on the floor. A tornado would have left more intact.

He stood there, staring, unable to think, until he felt blood dripping from his throbbing foot. He still needed something to stanch the flow, so he hopped back up the hall to the bedroom.

Shining the flashlight around the room, looking for anything intact, he was unable to process what he was seeing. Each circle of light was like a photograph: shots of a disaster's aftermath, possessions shattered, torn, strewn everywhere, like shots from some horrific newspaper story, but everything was his. On the wall, in lipstick, he found her farewell. "BTW, never told you Stephen King is my favorite author. Go party with that!"

He scanned the room once more. At least he had bandages galore. Every piece of clothing in the apartment was now a rag.

VIII

Hazard Models
ハザード・モデル

Saturday, 16 January 2010

98

LYING IN BED, WAITING FOR THE ALARM, KURIMOTO COULD not get the Nguyen woman, Trinh, out of her head. The answer to Ikenami's fate was somewhere in the JGU network—she was sure—but Trinh was tangled up in it, too. She had a hunch it was something Trinh would never tell Hasegawa, but would he let her approach Trinh alone?

She checked the clock: 6:58 a.m. She switched off the imminent alarm. Hasegawa had said he wanted her to talk, that she should not wait for him to ask.

But waking him up on a Saturday morning?

7:02.

He didn't specifically forbid it.

You must take chances, her father had told her, and with chances come mistakes. Just make sure they don't make enemies, and as a cop, make sure they don't get you killed.

Hasegawa wouldn't kill her.

He answered sleepily, "*Moshi-moshi.* Hasegawa."

"Sorry to wake you, sir."

"Kurimoto? Don't I have the weekend off?"

"Yes, sir." She paused. "You just don't get to sleep."

"You'll pay for this."

"There's no need to state the obvious, sir."

"Why are you calling?" Was that a smile in his voice?

"I'd like to visit JGU and talk to Trinh Nguyen."

"You can't wait till Monday or ask over the phone?"

"I think she's . . . not hiding something, but there may be things she'd only share with . . ."

"You want to have some girl talk."

"You're so understanding, sir. Thank you."

"I didn't say I approved." He paused. "You're grinning, aren't you?"

"I'm afraid so, sir."

"Go."

"Thank you."

"Just . . . if it's girl talk, better leave the uniform at home."

"How unconventional of you, sir."

"I've created a monster."

99

THE SNOW THAT STOPPED IN THE NIGHT STARTED AGAIN before dawn, so Will was shoveling when the pocket of his jeans buzzed. He got his glove off and fished his phone out. "*Moshi-moshi.*"

"Will?" came Trinh's voice. She was crying.

"What's wrong?"

"There is a new rumor."

"What is it?"

"Oh, Will." She cried loud and hard.

"Trinh?"

No words.

"Go to the entrance to the university. Now. Throw on your coat and boots and go. Walk out toward the road. I'll pick you up."

Will took only enough time to tell Laurie where he was going before he left. As he turned into JGU, he saw Trinh walking up the road. He stopped the minivan, and she opened the door and looked at him, eyes red.

"Hop in. We'll take a drive," said Will.

He didn't know where to take her, so he started down the road to town as Trinh cried softly.

"Can you tell me?"

He realized he should have thought of a handkerchief before anything else. He pulled his out of his jeans pocket.

"Sorry, guy handkerchief," he said, as he handed it to her.

She wiped her eyes and held it to her face. "I was waiting for the library to open to study before skiing."

"JGU Ski Day?"

"Yes, but now I will not go."

"What happened?"

"My friend came, but she looked strange at me, so I asked what is wrong." He waited as Trinh cried harder. "She heard . . ."

"What?"

"We are lovers."

"You and I?"

Trinh nodded into the handkerchief.

He drove on, unsure what to say, as Trinh sobbed.

The parking lot at the train station looked like a suitable spot to stop and talk. Will parked away from the other cars and switched off the wipers. He left the engine running. "Was it Watanabe again?"

"I don't know. I didn't ask anyone," she said.

"You shouldn't. You can't trace this one back. Why this? Trying again to destroy my reputation and get the police interested in me? Or were you getting too close to something?"

Trinh shrugged and covered her eyes with the handkerchief.

"It's going to be okay."

"Everyone will hear. Everyone will think I am . . ."

Will sat awkwardly for the next couple of minutes. "I feel honored, actually."

She tried to smile.

They sat without speaking as Trinh got control of herself. After a few minutes, she spoke. "Before babysitting, Watanabe-*sensei* never came to his office, so I did not find out who told him some rumors."

"After this, it's too dangerous. Let's give up on it."

"No."

"But—"

"No, Will. He cannot hurt people so much and not pay for it. He will tell me. Then he will tell police. He will tell *everyone*."

~

WILL SAT IN THE LIVING ROOM NEXT TO BECKA AND RACHEL, who were watching *SpongeBob SquarePants* in English on satellite television. Laurie was sitting on the floor, trying to finish the Christmas jigsaw puzzle. With a flourish, she put in a piece and exclaimed triumphantly, "I got one!"

"Congratulations."

"That's enough for now. Come help me in the kitchen."

Will followed, and as soon as he closed the door, Laurie asked, "What did she tell you? I know it's bad, Will. It's all over your face."

"A new rumor. People are saying we're having an affair."

"Will!"

"It's not true!"

"I didn't think it was. But this is awful!"

"She was crying and . . ."

Laurie stepped closer and put her hands on his chest. He drew her in tight and held her.

Suddenly, she pulled away. "You need to go."

"Where?"

"Back to school. Get Trinh and bring her here. She loves the girls. They'll perk her right up. Then we're going skiing."

"Laurie, a day skiing with people who will all have heard the rumor will hardly make her feel better."

"I don't know. Going to that movie helped me a little. Besides, we're going to show up with her at the university café as a happy family for a late breakfast. Then Trinh and I will sit next to each other on the Ski Day bus. Someone's trying to use Trinh to crucify you, Will. I'm not letting that happen to either of you."

Will called Trinh, who had not quite made it back to her room, and told her he was coming to bring her home with him.

"No, please."

"Trinh, don't be embarrassed. Laurie knows the rumor is a lie."

"But—"

"You can come home with me or with Laurie. You know once she decides something, that's it."

Trinh was quiet.

"I'm leaving now to come get you. Same place."

"Okay."

~

Laurie was waiting when Will got back with Trinh. Trinh gave her a sheepish look, slipped off her boots, and stepped up into the house, whereupon Laurie hugged her and whispered, "I'm so sorry, Trinh."

"No, I am sorry."

"We will fight them, okay?"

Trinh nodded, tears in her eyes.

"Dry your eyes. The girls don't know you're here. They'll be so excited."

Trinh smiled and wiped her eyes with Will's handkerchief.

Laurie stepped into the hallway and called out, "Hey, girls! There's someone here to see you!"

The living room *shōji* slid open, Becka and Rachel saw Trinh, and they ran to hug her. Sarah appeared on the steps and grinned. Rachel held her arms up and bounced, so Trinh picked her up and they all headed into the living room.

"Are Mommy and Daddy going to another movie?" asked Rachel.

"I don't think so," said Trinh.

Laurie said, "In a little while, we're going to the café, and then we're all going skiing."

"Trinh too?"

"Trinh too."

The girls cheered in perfect unison.

100

WATANABE ROLLED OVER AND COVERED HIS HEAD WITH his pillow, but light ignored didn't cease to exist. Neither was there any way to peel visions of Trinh and Will out of his mind like the wrapper off a candy bar.

He sat up, screamed, and threw his pillow against the wall.

He checked his refrigerator: cheesecake from the day before yesterday and curry from a week ago. The freezer had ice cream . . . and ice.

He got a spoon and carried the ice cream and cheesecake back to bed.

A few spoonfuls in, he decided he needed something to stare at.

He opened his laptop. There was always email.

His favorite news sites might have something.

He considered throwing the laptop against the wall, too.

Eventually, he'd listened to the siren singing long enough that he gave up and opened Trinh's picture file. He clicked on the first one and stared. She was in the library by the third-floor windows, studying. They worked together so often in fall term. She would study while he read the latest academic papers, worked on research, or prepared his lectures. He drew strength from having her there, close enough to see out his office window, so disciplined, so devoted to him. It was his most productive term ever.

Someone who had done so much for him, seen him through grueling days, stood by him and believed in him, beat back his self-doubt when it rose all-consuming—he owed her respect, even after last night's betrayal. For every immoral act, though, someone must pay, as he had paid. As a boy and even a teenager, he had taken his whippings. He had made humiliating apologies as a college student. He had followed the protective order taken out against him. He had learned from it, and no one had ever gone to the police again.

Now the prices were his to decide.

He started on the cheesecake.

Who—obvious—but how much, when . . . ? He had more to consider than desserts to cover it. No matter; 7-Eleven was only a five-minute drive.

101

DAVID WAS IN EARLY FOR A SATURDAY. HE WANTED TO hear about the bandwidth audit before Itō's IT committee meeting. The two of them talked in hushed voices in the café.

Ito spoke soberly. "I thought maybe this will happen. Audit of ISP main line shows no high traffic."

"Ikenami was wrong about there being an IT problem?"

"No, maybe he is right."

David was puzzled. "How can the audit not show anything?"

"Traffic was not high, but do not say, 'not show anything.'"

"Why?"

"Because bandwidth was so low," said Itō.

"Someone manipulated the audit?"

Itō opened his electronic dictionary and looked up "manipulated." His eyes lit up. "Yes! Someone shuts down a thing or uses less bandwidth."

"There can't be many people capable of that, right?"

With a self-satisfied smile, Itō held his hand up to David, fingers spread. "I can count on one hand."

"Wait, how would anyone know about it?"

"We talked."

David was taken aback. "I sure as hell didn't tell anyone."

"I also tell no one."

"Then how—" David's eyes widened.

"Now you see why we talk in café, not in server room."

"Then the next step is . . . ?"

"Eight o'clock," said Itō.

"Everything's ready?"

Itō nodded as he smiled confidently.

102

KING OPENED HIS EYES, LOOKED WHERE HIS ALARM CLOCK once sat, and remembered that it was in several spots now. He checked his watch, thankfully still intact. It looked like he was not going to the IT committee meeting that started two minutes ago. In fact, his wife had filled his waking thoughts with a single overwhelming question: how to be asleep again as soon as possible, or put another way, how long until the next pain pill?

Actually, he had a second question: how to kill the bitch?

First came sleep. He pulled another pill out of his pocket and swallowed it. As he lay there waiting for it to work, he thought again of the money in the book, the money he should've hidden someplace she couldn't have grabbed it and run—

He sat up with a start, rushed to open his bag, and pulled out his laptop. As it blinked to life, he cursed it, then remembered his internet connection depended on two small boxes that were no longer rectangular.

King pulled on his pants, slipped on his shoe and coat, slung his bag over his shoulder, and hopped up the hall to the door. His foot ached like it had been severed and sewn back on. It took five minutes to get to his car through the snow on the crutches they gave him at the hospital last night. He started the car, then opened his laptop and waited for—

No unprotected networks.

He cruised the neighborhood, searching . . . and found nothing.

As he drove down the main road to another group of buildings, he searched again . . . hoping . . . yes! At the webpage for his brokerage account, he waited. He entered the password and held his breath as the account summary loaded, waiting for the number, large, reassuring, denominated in trustworthy US dollars . . .

Load, damn it. Six digits before the decimal point. Six big, beautiful . . .

He stared at the screen, unable to breathe.

She took it, every penny.

He slowly closed his laptop.

Pain pills don't fix everything. Some things need whiskey—which, unfortunately for King, took money, and he had precious little left.

103

RATHER THAN HEARING, "WHAT'S GOING ON?" FROM EACH person as they showed up, Itō planned to enter the server room after everyone was there. When King did not arrive, he waited, but at 8:06 a.m. he walked into the room and started the meeting. "Thank you everyone for coming today. I also asked IT staffs to be here. I wanted to—"

"You know, you do not chair this committee," said Malik, after he had made a show of checking his watch when Itō entered. Now he glanced around the table, as if eliciting support. "You should not call meetings, you don't run them, and you don't invite staff."

The junior IT professor, Syed Baig, looked impatient. "Everyone's here. Let's get started."

Itō began again. "I wanted to—"

Malik popped up from his chair. "I said you are not the chair of this meeting!"

Itō paused, nodded, and took a seat.

Malik finally had the floor. "Now, why are we here?"

Danny laughed, and Malik scowled at him.

"May I begin?" asked Itō.

Malik stood tall. "Yes." With that, he sat.

"In December, Ikenami-*sensei* asked questions about IT resources."

Danny narrowed his eyes. "Asked whom?"

"Asked me. Also, IT staffs."

Malik was leaning his chest on the edge of the table, resting his chin on his hands. "You know, I don't think a few questions, and so long ago, way back in December, that's not, you know, really a good reason for a special meeting." He looked around the table again. "Everyone is busy. And you know, the police are sort of investigating and asking questions and everything already, so maybe we should not, you know, get involved for now."

Itō said, "Ikenami-*sensei* thought someone is misusing IT resources."

Malik raised his head and was about to speak, but Danny spoke first. "He wanted to redeploy them, use them in another way?"

"No, he thinks someone uses IT maybe for illegal thing."

The two office managers and the IT staff looked at Itō in shock.

Baig glanced from face to face. "Oh, I think the police should hear this, not the IT committee."

Malik leaned forward. "You know, that's what I was kind of saying. We should let them handle this, not get in their way."

Danny was having none of it. "No one's said anything about getting in the way. Perhaps we can help."

"I think now we know, you know, what Itō-*san* had to say, so we are done for now." Malik straightened up. "So I adjourn the meeting."

Danny laughed. "No, you don't."

"I chair the committee and I say this meeting is over. You can go." Malik waved his hand as if shooing everyone from the room.

Danny perused the faces around the table. "I would appreciate it if everyone stayed a little longer to discuss this."

People looked at each other. No one stood.

"What illegal activity?" asked one of the IT staff.

"He did not say."

"What *did* he say?" asked Malik.

Before Itō answered, people started talking on top of one another in Japanese.

"It was something illegal on the network?"

"Inside JGU or outside?"

"It might be a cheating scandal."

"Someone hacking email accounts."

"No, it has to be something much worse, something worth killing for."

Malik stood, leaned over the table, and yelled, "I asked a question."

"Yes, you did," said Danny.

"I know I did! You don't tell me that!"

Danny smiled and shook his head.

"So, what is your answer?"

"What did you ask?" asked Itō.

Malik was turning red. "What did he say?"

"Who?"

Danny laughed.

"You know—He—You stop laughing!"

It took five minutes for things to calm down enough that Itō could offer any coherent answers. By that point, Baig had excused himself and escaped, and Malik had ordered Danny to get out. Danny didn't move. Malik repeated, ad nauseam, that it was a matter for the police, not the IT committee. Eventually, Danny asked what Itō planned to do, and he responded, "We will start a full audit tomorrow morning of all packet traffic in and out of JGU."

Malik's eyes shot to Itō. "*All* the traffic?"

Danny got everyone's attention. "Will that be disruptive? I mean, will we still be able to access the network and the internet?"

Itō said, "Can still access after a short time when we shut down all traffic."

Danny nodded. "Once things are back up, will the audit slow things down?"

"You will not know it is happening," said Itō.

Malik appeared flummoxed. "How long will this last?"

Itō was about to say, "Only a day or two," when Danny asked Malik, "If it's not disruptive, what difference does it make?"

Malik spent most of the walk from the meeting to the café thinking of Danny cut into pieces and tossed in the river. He was about to open the café door when he saw Trinh sitting with Will's family, beaming, his daughter in her lap. If this was how they countered the affair rumor, it was brilliant. He might have enjoyed how they were turning this into a chess match if he had time. But every day that passed without Will arrested was another day his business was in danger.

And tomorrow, Itō would start his bandwidth audit. Thinking it best to wait and see what happened in this morning's meeting, he had left the website throttled down. Itō auditing all the traffic, regardless of whether volume reached the trigger level, had shocked him so badly he was afraid his surprise had shown. He was still safe for today. He had encrypted the outgoing streams and disguised them as DNS traffic, like the internal camera feeds. Itō might wonder why DNS traffic was so high, but he would have no answer, and no way ever to get one without dismantling the network. Still, it would be far safer to shut down the site during the audit.

Only a few subscribers had complained so far, but messages would pour in if this continued. He would rather the police were doing it; a single long shutdown, and then he'd be up and streaming with no worries. Itō had total access to the JGU system any hour of the day or night. If the IT committee backed Itō, he could stretch his audit out interminably, obliterating Malik's subscriber base.

Malik abandoned the café and plodded back to his office. They should have arrested Will by now! The setup had been perfect, except for the corpse disappearing—and not knowing Trinh and Will were friends. She was still the only witness—

Malik stopped dead in the darkened hallway. He should have realized it before. It was so obvious: Will moved the body! It was fantastic! Once the police got ahold of him, he'd crack, and that would seal his fate. Only a murderer would move a body!

Trinh was the key. If she described the fall, they'd take Will away, he'd confess which canyon he'd dumped the body in, and that would be that!

If Trinh talked.

To increase the pressure on her . . . shake her up somehow . . .

As he started walking again, he thought of Trinh in her room, undressing for him Tuesday night; sitting to his right, halfway back, in his Thursday lecture; lying on the bed with Huong last night, eating a *mikan.*

Huong, the bitch, she'll pay for—

They were best friends! If something happened to Huong, the police might talk to Trinh for hours. Eventually, exhausted, she would let it slip that Ikenami fell. How could she not?

104

*G*OMEN KUDASAI!*" CALLED DAVID AS HE SLID OPEN WILL'S front door.

Laurie opened the *shōji* to the *genkan* and smiled. "Nice Japanese. Someone's been studying."

"Merely listening to what people yell when they open my door."

"I'm getting the girls ready for skiing. If we're early enough, we can ride on a student bus."

Laurie showed David into the kitchen, where Will was washing dishes. He looked up and smiled. "How's it going?"

David took a seat. "Can't complain." He looked at Rachel, who had a Japanese children's book out on the table. "Hiya, Rachel."

Rachel didn't look up as she answered, "Hi."

"Hey, what are you doing? You're not old enough to read."

"Sure I am. I'm four. That's old enough."

"Do the other kids at kindergarten read?"

"What's kidner-garden?"

Laurie said, "That's German for 'yochien.'"

"It's *yōchien,* Mommy, *yo-u.*" She looked at David. "Are you German?"

"I don't think so."

"Then how come you—"

Laurie picked her up. "Why don't you check and see whether Sarah's ready to go?"

"Okay." She scampered out the door.

Laurie poured juice as Will wiped his hands. "I'm staying away from the office today."

"That may not be necessary. There's no police car. The snow stopped. It's back to four feet, so no big worries about melting."

Laurie looked surprised. "The police are taking the day off?"

David raised his eyebrows. "We can hope. Anyway, I got news from Itō about the IT meeting this morning. Oh, and Itō suspects someone's bugged the IT Services office and server room."

"You've got to be kidding," said Laurie.

"Nope. Don't let it surprise you. If it is an IT-type doing this, bugging offices would be child's play."

Laurie whispered, "You think . . . ?" as she pointed at the ceiling.

David shook his head. "No, but think what you've said in your office this week."

Laurie looked at Will in alarm. "We talked about it. I mean, you told me right in your office. All three of us sat there and—"

Will had reached out and taken her hand. "No, the murderer would've tipped off the police by now."

"It's possible you got bugged since," said David. "Anyway, the IT meeting. Everyone was there except King."

"You think that means anything?" asked Will.

David posed a hypothetical. "If you're the killer, would you miss a meeting where they might discuss the reason for the murder? If anything, King looks more innocent. Anyway, Itō opened by saying that Ikenami thought there was a misappropriation of IT resources for something illegal."

Laurie's eyes opened wide. "Wow."

David nodded. "Yeah, all hell broke loose. Malik kept insisting Itō should talk to the police, not the committee."

Will frowned. "Doesn't that clear Malik? Why would a murderer insist Itō work with the police?"

Laurie asked, "The IT committee scares him more?"

David sat back. "He *wants* the police involved if he's framing Will. He thinks Will's cornered. The cops take him, problem solved. Anyway, yesterday Itō set up a tiny camera outside the server room. He's caught no activity that's worthwhile yet. The only people to venture down the hall were IT staff, and Itō checked on them. Nothing suspicious."

"Did anything helpful happen this morning?" asked Laurie.

David leaned forward. "Itō got things calmed down and told them he'll do a bandwidth audit."

Will asked what that was, and David explained it.

Laurie looked puzzled. "If the murderer's there, why warn him?"

David spoke with authority. "Because of that camera in the hallway."

She gave him a puzzled look.

"Smoke." David sat back again. "Now we wait for him to come out for air—which, for him, is the server room."

105

VIETKITTEN WAS ADMIRING HERSELF IN THE MIRROR IN HER ski coat and pants when VietGoddess came bursting in. Zo6 couldn't understand them, but VietGoddess was wearing ski pants too. The tight waist came up so high it acted almost like a corset . . .

Zo6 was losing himself in the fantasy when a guy stepped through VietKitten's open door and said in Japanese, "Wow, you two look . . . great! Now if you can ski a little . . ."

VietKitten answered in Japanese, "I heard skiing is not so hard."

"You'll get the hang of it, but you'll end up on your face a few times. On your butt even more. Still, you'll love it. Even falling down you'll look . . . let's just hope you don't melt the snow."

VietGoddess made a mortar and pestle motion with her hands. "Grinding sesame."

"What's that?" asked VietKitten.

"Means he's trying to flatter us."

VietKitten laughed. "What's wrong with that?"

Zo6 loved it when they spoke Japanese, and he smiled as everyone laughed. He looked again at the message the Webmaster sent an hour ago:

> As to yesterday's request, I changed my mind. VietKitten is yours at price you offered. Saturday night only! Reply if still interested. I will send instruction.

Tonight.

He needed to answer soon.

It would only be a four- or five-hour drive, perhaps less.

Why bother, though? He'd never actually do it. It was ridiculous.

He maximized VietKitten's window, so it filled the whole screen. She was laughing again.

106

A T LEAST I'VE STILL GOT A CAR, THOUGHT KING. HIS FOOT didn't ache as much as it had this morning. Now he needed something to wear besides the clothes he had been in since yesterday. He couldn't even wash them: his wife had smashed the controls of the washing machine and slashed the hoses.

King had never bought clothing locally. Now he opted for the best value he could think of, Uniqlo. There was a McDonald's next door. After this much pain, he deserved a little comfort food, so he stopped there first.

After a Value Meal, King was ready to face the prospect of a few weeks in ugly clothes. He needed shirts, slacks, underwear, and socks.

The clerk took things to the register as King chose them. It was a great help, since he was still on crutches. He hated them. They rubbed under his arms, and he was already sore.

I could use some rags for padding.

The clerk scanned the tags and told him the total: a little over thirty thousand yen. King handed over his credit card.

"In how many installments would you like to be billed?"

"One."

"Yes, sir."

King's foot was hurting again.

I should have thought to bring the pain pills.

"I'm sorry, sir, but they refused the credit card."

The thieving bitch canceled the Japanese card?

King opened his wallet and took out his American Express card.

"I'm afraid we don't take that."

He put it away and pulled out his US credit card.

Soon she said, "I'm sorry, but they also refused this card."

She canceled all the cards?

"Fine, sorry." He pivoted to go, banging one of his crutches into a display table.

"Or we take cash."

King freed his crutch and hobbled toward the door. "So did she."

~

"What happened to your foot? That looks bad." Malik was seemingly amused at King's pain.

King had his foot propped up on his desk. "I cut it. Needed a few stitches. No big deal."

Malik smiled. "Anyway, you figured out the TrueCrypt configuration?"

"Yup. Even spy agencies can't crack this. You can do all the setup remotely. I've got instructions all written so you can create the hidden disk volume. Even if someone hacks your disk or forces you to give them your password, they only get to the innocuous files in the outer volume. You encrypt the whole disk, so there's no way to tell the hidden volume is there. Looks like empty space would on a normal encrypted disk."

"So how do I get in?"

"When you go to mount the disk, you type the password for the hidden volume. It doesn't match the one for the outer volume, so the software searches the hidden volume header, if there is one. If it matches that password, up come your files."

Malik knitted his brow. "I tried it like that before."

"Well, you must have done something wrong. Make sure the hidden volume's password is nothing like the outer volume's. No 'icecream1' and 'icecream2' right? You don't want them cracking both. In the instructions, I've suggested passwords that are easy to remember. You can't mess it up with what I've prepared."

Malik didn't smile, but King saw his eyes brighten. Malik reached into his pocket, pulled out a USB drive, and held it out, but not far enough that King could reach it with his foot up on the desk.

King sat impassively, so Malik stood and leaned over the desk with it. "I guess you don't move so good with your foot." When King still didn't take it, Malik looked wary. "What's the problem?"

The problem? I've been wearing the same stinking underwear for two days, I spent too much of the little cash I had on a soggy hamburger, and my car's almost out of gas. "Payment up front this time, that's all. That and the price has gone up."

Malik was silent for a few seconds. His voice was cold and dead when he continued. "We agreed on a price."

"And we'll agree on a new one, no problem."

Again, Malik stayed quiet. King was, too, so Malik asked, "Why?"

King folded his hands on his stomach. "Because I want more money. Because what I've got for you is worth it. Because with all the questions people are asking about IT, I shouldn't be giving it to you at all."

Malik's jaw tightened.

"Mostly, because you need it."

Malik's eyes narrowed. He waited. When King didn't speak, he asked, "How much?"

"Double."

"No way."

King smiled. "Fine, try to get TrueCrypt working on your own again. Lose the rest of your files."

"I can do it. I was only paying to make the setup go quicker."

King shrugged. "Maybe. With the cops circling like sharks, you don't have a whole lot of time, do you?"

"It's got nothing to do with the police. It's sensitive files is all."

"Whatever. I don't care. But if you keep on making like it's nothing, I'll charge you triple. Double's the special sale price, good for sixty seconds."

Malik glared at him but didn't move, so King sat, silent. After half a minute, King looked down at his watch and back at Malik.

Malik pulled out his wallet. "I only have enough for the original price."

"Go to an ATM."

"I don't have time today."

"It's Saturday. When you make up an excuse, give it a shred of truth."

Malik had been tense, but now King saw him shift his weight forward onto the balls of his feet. Hidden by his left sleeve, King slipped the fingers of his right hand into his shirt until he felt the knife's handle.

Go ahead, lunge for me. Try to take me out like you likely did Ike-nami. Find out how it feels to suck your last breaths through a hole in your neck.

Across the desk, Malik hovered, so King prodded. "Four, three, two," he looked Malik in the eyes, "last chance . . ."

Malik turned toward the door. "I'll be back in an hour."

107

WHEN TRINH TOLD HER THAT MORNING WHAT LAURIE was doing, Huong had clapped and laughed out loud. There wasn't room for Will and his family on the bus, so they gave Trinh a ride to the ski resort. They offered her a ride back to campus, too. Trinh refused for long enough that Laurie gave in. Still, Huong smiled as she watched Laurie make sure they were in plain view of the students at the bus before she gave Trinh a long hug. Hugs followed from each of the girls—Rachel's after Trinh lifted her up and pressed their foreheads together, to the crowd's collective, "Aw."

Huong saw Trinh wince as she took her seat on the bus. "Are you okay?"

"No, I'm sore."

"I didn't see you take any nasty falls."

"Then you weren't watching. I'm more tired than sore. I can't remember the last time I was this wrung out."

Huong wasn't listening. Professor Danny the Surfer was walking up the aisle. Huong let a student pass, then stepped far enough into Danny's way that he would have to say something.

He approached her with a smile—then looked at Trinh, "May I?"

Trinh gave a little bow and scooted over for him.

She has a professor already; it's my turn!

"How was it?" asked Danny.

Trinh winced. "It hurts. I think I was on my back more than my feet."

"Some nasty spills?"

"Not so bad, but I have to get up so many times. It hurts now, all over."

Huong said, "You were better than you are saying."

"Not as good as you."

"Maybe." Huong shrugged. She told Danny, "If I was better, this is the first time for anything."

"She can't be better at everything." He laughed as he turned to Trinh.

Brian, Huong's "had been more than a friend" from Canada, was coming up the aisle. "Was it as much fun as you thought it would be?" he asked with a big smile.

Huong glanced back down at Danny for a moment. "No." She looked at Brian again. "Or maybe, I guess, yeah."

Brian put his hand on her waist as if to get by, but prodded her up the aisle. "What did you like best?"

She scowled at him.

He gave her another nudge.

She looked away.

He pressed again, more gently.

At last, she smiled.

～

ON THE DRIVE BACK TO JGU, DANNY TURNED OUT TO BE QUITE an entertaining fellow. He wasn't the man Will was, of course, but he made for a fun bus ride. In fact, Trinh paid no attention to Huong in the back of the bus with Brian, or to the 2006 Nissan Fairlady Z that drove past as they arrived at the university.

108

Z06 STOPPED HIS CAR AND WATCHED THE FIRST STUDENTS get off the bus. He felt his pulse quicken at the sight of a girl he knew. Soon came two more. They were only twenty meters away, near enough to see them smiling—in real life, the actual girls, with no lens distortion!

He wanted some excuse to go into the university, but it was too risky. He couldn't afford to have anyone remember a stranger on campus today.

Would anyone remember, though? Who noticed him—ever?

Keeping an eye out for VietKitten, he pulled in and parked. He was getting out of the car before he realized he had thought of no excuse.

He might not need one. In a place like this, there wasn't likely to be much security.

He pulled his collar up high and turned to face the bus. The girls were closer now. They were standing by the bus, talking and laughing. They were so much prettier in real life! As he walked, he fought to keep a leisurely but self-assured pace. Starstruck at girls he had been watching for months, he wanted to go slower, just gape—and faster, too, for his legs to catch up with his racing heart. He tried not to focus on anyone for too long as he made his way past the crowd. There were four girls he recognized. He stopped at the campus map on the wall of the building and looked back again. Yes, this was worth *any* amount of money.

Still, he needed to get out of sight. Perhaps there was someplace he could watch undisturbed. Students were heading to covered walkways on either side of the parking lot. They probably wouldn't notice him if he simply got back in his car.

As he looked at the bus again, he noticed a black-and-white Toyota topped with a rack of red lights on the other side.

I should go.

He saw another girl emerging, talking to someone behind her. As she stepped from the bus, she looked forward, her long, rich black hair shining in the sun; and forgetting all the people, all the eyes, even the police car, Zo6 stood and stared.

VietKitten was the last off the bus. She was talking with some foreign guy. Zo6 hadn't seen him in her room, but he never saw guys there. They looked like they were close, though. VietGoddess soon joined them. It was wonderful to see VietKitten smiling; she was so cute. Still, his eyes kept going to VietGoddess. He wanted to ask her a question, to listen to her voice as those enormous eyes focused on him.

Soon, the students were gone. The final straggler was a girl he often watched last year. He had gone to bed with her more times than he could count.

The email from the Webmaster had said to go to the Conference Center, so he walked back to the middle of the classroom building, where it was visible. He would have to take the skyway; the path was under a meter of snow.

Once there, he found himself in a large room with floor-to-ceiling windows facing out on a huge open field. It relieved him to find it deserted, and he hurried over to the chairs. He counted five from the east end, then slipped his hand between the bottom cushion and the arm. He felt up one side, across the back, and down the other side before he discovered a manila envelope folded lengthwise. It was fatter than he expected, with something soft inside. He tore it open.

A piece of paper, a key, cotton gloves, a condom, and a nylon stocking. He slipped the key into his pocket. The paper was a campus map with "E610" noted on the east dormitory building and a note in poorly written Japanese: "Let's not leave any evidence behind. Wear stocking over head as a mask or not, your choice. By the way, it will be Pay-Per-View, so give a good show."

Underneath, the ass had drawn a smiley face.

109

Kurimoto's visit was official police business, so she drove a police car to JGU. When she arrived, she was disappointed to find it all but deserted for Ski Day. She did not know whether Trinh had gone but took a pass through campus hoping to bump into her: the more casual, the better. With a steady stream of interviews, JGU had seemed, if not bustling, at least active. Walking through the halls late Saturday morning, she realized what a tiny, quiet place it was.

Kurimoto asked someone what time the skiers would return. Then she drove into town for lunch. On her return, she curled up in a comfortable chair in the library to read a Hideo Yokoyama crime novel.

Sunset was approaching, overcast, the entire world slipping into the gray of the sky, before Kurimoto spotted a bus disgorging skiers in the parking lot in front of the administration building. She saw Trinh and hurried out to catch her. Trinh did not seem to recognize her at first, then worry flickered across her face before she showed the officer a pleasant smile and bowed.

Kurimoto used a friendly manner. "You need not bow so low."

"Always be polite to police."

"No, I'm not the police today. See? No uniform."

Trinh looked surprised. "No interviews today?"

"I just wanted to look around. I'm considering graduate school."

Trinh smiled. "You should come here."

"I was thinking it's almost dinnertime. Have you eaten?"

Trinh retreated a half step. "Not yet, but I have to study."

Kurimoto realized her hope of getting Trinh away from campus for a leisurely meal might be unrealistic. "I don't have much time either, but I would love to hear more about JGU. I'm buying. Would you like to grab something quick?"

Trinh glanced at the students disappearing down the walkway and seemed to weigh her prior conviction. Then Trinh's eyes moved to the administration building and Kurimoto saw . . . revulsion? "Okay. I should not study hungry, maybe."

Kurimoto laughed and bounced on her toes. It was affectation, but she needed to shed as much as possible of Trinh's memory of yesterday's uniformed interview. "I can wait while you change."

"Okay, but if you want to know JGU, you must come to the dorm."

Kurimoto hung around in the hallway, talking to a young woman from Nepal and another from Thailand until Trinh was ready to go. She emerged wearing form-fitting jeans and a hooded sweatshirt, her coat in her arm and a backpack slung over her shoulder. Despite Trinh's obvious intention to study, Kurimoto gave a longer meal one more try. "I guess we can eat here on campus, but you must be awfully tired of the food here. Is it any good?"

"Not very."

"I have a car," said Kurimoto. "We could go someplace close."

"I don't know anyplace."

"Ooh, I tried a good little restaurant, Italian. It's five minutes away."

Trinh seemed about to say no, but relented with a smile. "I love Italian."

Kurimoto gauged Trinh's reaction as they pulled up in front of Trattoria Napoli but saw only excitement at visiting a new restaurant. As they got out of the car, Kurimoto got no sense that the spot where they found Ikenami's car held any meaning.

Kurimoto let the conversation wander from the weather to life in Japan, Trinh's plans after graduation, and JGU. They were eating before Kurimoto put on a discouraged face. "This whole Ikenami thing is turning into . . . oh, but you don't want to talk about that."

"I can."

Kurimoto sighed. "It's so hard. No one knows anything. Or . . . it's more that someone knows but isn't saying."

"Yes, I think so too."

"You can tell?"

Trinh nodded, "I hear things."

"Those are just rumors."

"Maybe."

Kurimoto lowered her voice. "You think they're more than rumors?"

Trinh was quiet, the end of her fork cupped in her spoon as she twirled a bite of spaghetti on it. Kurimoto waited, as Detective Hasegawa would. After a minute, Trinh spoke. "I think you heard rumors that Grames-*sensei* killed him. I did not believe it, so I asked who said it. I tracked a story backward, and it comes from one person."

"Who?"

"Watanabe-*sensei*."

"He knows something? Or hates Grames-*sensei*? Why is he doing it?"

"I don't think he makes up the stories. I think he hears from someone."

"Do you know who?"

"Not yet. I think I will know soon."

"How?" As Trinh glanced at her, Kurimoto saw anxiety in her eyes. "What are you going to do?"

Trinh said, "I already tried once. He almost told me."

"Watanabe . . . I don't know how you feel around him, but he makes me want to run away—and I have training in fighting! I feel sorry for him, but he still leaves me . . . I guess 'uneasy' is a nice way to say it. Did you talk to him?"

Trinh nodded.

Kurimoto affected a shiver. "How could you stand it?"

Trinh gave a little shrug and looked down.

Kurimoto waited.

"I know if I distract him, he might talk without thinking so much."

"Let his guard down. How did you—" The image of Trinh distracting Watanabe burst upon Kurimoto, and she blanched, eyes wide, duplicity fled, as she shivered for real.

"I let him be thinking I was interested."

"I don't think I could do it. His eyes!"

Trinh made an uncomfortable face. "I wore a shirt that guys always stare at, and he let his guards down."

"He didn't tell you?"

Trinh shook her head.

Kurimoto said, "You know, we can talk to him again, Detective Hasegawa and I. This is not your job."

"The rumors are about Grames-*sensei* . . . someone wants to blame him, and he did nothing."

"You're doing this for him?"

Trinh stared at her plate.

Kurimoto lowered her voice. "I liked a teacher once, too, an instructor at the police academy, but I never talked to him." She paused, judging how far to take it, and decided to push. "As much as Watanabe scares me, I worry about you and Grames-*sensei*. He is married. We met his wife. You will get hurt."

"No, it is okay. We are friends."

"You feel more."

Trinh gave a laugh as she shrugged. "A little more maybe. It is okay. It is not affair."

Kurimoto let her concern show.

"Do not worry about him. He is the sweetest man you can know, so gentle. I know his whole family. I babysit his girls. They are so cute!" Trinh grinned. Then she looked at Kurimoto, altogether serious, and said in a hushed voice, "I want to know who is making up rumors. I think someone murdered Ikenami-*sensei*, and that person starts rumors."

"You think Watanabe will tell you? He might be the murderer!"

Trinh nodded. "I take a chance."

"When?"

"Tonight, if he comes to campus."

"What makes you so sure he'll tell?"

Trinh looked at Kurimoto for a long moment before she sat up straight and tall. "Because men who live in fantasy world imagine so much."

"I have never been . . . pretty like you. What is it like to have someone be in a dream over you?"

Trinh frowned. "Most of the time it is not nice at all."

"Maybe not. You think his fantasy will make him talk?"

"If he wants something so badly, he hopes for more now and for a next time. It is awful, but I know his dreams."

"Ew."

"If I smile and pretend, he cannot say no."

It was lightly snowing again when Kurimoto accompanied Trinh to the third floor of the library. She sat in another comfortable chair and tried to read, but her mind was on Trinh, who kept looking at the administration building. After twenty minutes, Kurimoto walked over to Trinh's table and sat next to her. "He's here, isn't he?"

"That is his office." Trinh nodded to a nearby office with lights on.

"You don't have to do this—or I can go with you."

"He would never say with you there."

"Then I'll wait outside."

Trinh smiled. "You have a gun?"

Kurimoto said earnestly, "I could kill him with my hands."

Trinh covered her mouth as she laughed. She whispered, "You don't need to kill him. I will be all right."

"I would like to stay."

"No, really. Go."

"You will call me after?"

Trinh nodded.

"You still have my number?"

Trinh took out her phone, found Kurimoto's number, and showed her.

Kurimoto nodded and reluctantly stood. In an almost scolding whisper, she said, "No matter what happens, you call me tonight!"

Trinh nodded again. "I will."

110

TRINH'S EYES WERE DRAWN YET AGAIN TO WATANABE'S office window. She checked her watch: 8:04 p.m. Kurimoto was long gone, and Watanabe might leave any minute. She remembered his eyes and squirmed in her chair.

She couldn't just keep waiting. Will needed this.

Trinh stood, and determination took over. At the top of the administration building stairwell, she stopped and peeled off her sweatshirt, but hesitated. She closed her eyes in the dark hallway and thought of Will. As she opened them again, playing through the upcoming scene, she paused. Imagining Watanabe's eyes, she took a step back—and ran to the restroom at the far end of the hall.

Pacing, she tried to focus on accounting questions. She could ask something from the textbook, but it was a flimsy excuse. As distracted as he was yesterday, though, she could say almost anything. She checked herself in the mirror. It was a different look from her last visit, a tight, cherry-blossom-pink sweater that was so fuzzy soft it begged to be touched. Was she going too far? It wasn't low cut. Still, she would have been more at ease with Officer Kurimoto waiting outside.

Trinh faced the restroom door, steeled herself, and stepped back into the hallway. She strode up the hall, calmed herself again as she stood at Watanabe's door, and knocked.

"Come in."

She opened the door, keeping her eyes down in a shy facade. "Excuse me, *Sensei*," she said before she looked up—and froze. Watanabe showed none of the embarrassment he did yesterday. In fact, he looked . . . angry. "I'm sorry. You are busy. It can wait until next week."

Watanabe stared—normal for him—but today his eyes were narrow. She waited, hoping he would say something, before she lowered her eyes again, said in Japanese, "I was rude to intrude when you are busy. I am sorry," and stepped out.

"Did you have a question?" asked Watanabe in English.

"I'm sorry. Yes, I did."

"You're here now. Ask."

She bowed, stepped back in, let the door close, and bowed again before she sat in a chair. Setting her bag on the floor, she pulled out the textbook and put it in her lap. Scared as she was, she still remembered to be careful with her posture—spine straight and shoulders back—as she flipped through the pages. She looked up at him. "*Sensei*, are you all right?"

He looked away. After a few seconds, he stood, turned his back to her, and stared out the window.

"*Sensei*, is something wrong?"

He was quiet for a long time before he spoke. "I saw you."

She waited.

"Friday night, I was there. I saw."

"Last night? Did I do something?"

"With him," said Watanabe.

"I don't understand."

"I saw you with Grames—in that van of his."

She drew back in the chair, eyes wide, and looked at him staring out the window. She waited for more, but he stood there, arms crossed. The one hand she could see was closed in a fist.

Her voice came, quavering and soft. "I was babysitting for Grames-*sensei* take his wife to a movie. His girls are very nice and asked me to come."

He said something in a voice so small she couldn't hear.

Her manner was timid. "Excuse me?"

He whirled around and glared at her. "And the hug?"

Trinh's mouth opened in shock. "Hug? He is my friend. His children hug me too. Laurie, Mrs. Grames, hugs me every time I see her." Faced with his psychotic eyes, tears came easily. "I did not do wrong thing!"

She saw him soften, so she moaned and turned on the faucets. "I did no bad thing. Never!"

He took a step toward her. "No. I meant . . . I was just . . ." He leaned over the desk and whispered, "I'm sorry. Please don't cry. It's just . . . I heard a rumor."

"What rumor?"

He stood straight and looked away again.

Still crying, she kept her gaze on him. "Tell me. If you can be so cruel already, you can say rumor too."

He started to shrug but immediately lowered his eyes.

"Tell me."

Without looking up, he quietly said, "I heard . . . well, that you and Professor Grames . . . someone said . . ."

"What?" She was more strident as she cried. "What did someone say?"

Watanabe's voice was so soft she could barely hear. "You are lovers and . . ."

"And *what*?"

"You're pregnant," whispered Watanabe.

It was exactly the provocation she needed. Trinh jumped up so suddenly that the chair fell over backward behind her. "What? Who tells such a lie? Who said that?"

Watanabe looked at her in dismay. "It was only a rumor. Please forget it."

"Tell me!"

"I shouldn't—"

There was no acting anymore as she pointed her finger at him and growled, "You tell me *now*! Who told you this lie?"

Watanabe, easily twice her size, cowered before her.

"*Who?*" she shrieked.

"Malik. It was Malik!"

111

AS HUONG DRIED OFF AFTER HER SHOWER, SHE LOOKED AT herself in the steamy mirror. She would meet the right guy. That was fate, right? Someday.

How many men does one woman get? Soon enough, one would take her body with only a shrug. She let it happen, every time, from the boy in his school uniform when she was seventeen to Brian in his ski coat an hour ago. Then there was the right one, the one she let her father refuse . . .

Beer would numb it. The campus store was only three minutes away.

She held herself and looked at the bed. Sleep would numb it better. Except she wasn't sleepy.

She faced the mirror again. To turn the lights out with beer . . . a lot of calories. She was fat enough already. She didn't see it yet in the looks she got from guys, but she would. It was only a matter of time until she looked like her sister, mother, grandmother . . .

An evening with Trinh would be free: calorie-wise, cash-wise, and Trinh wouldn't think she was having a breakdown when the tears came.

Huong pulled on sweatpants and a T-shirt. Three doors up the hall, she knocked.

She tried the doorknob.

Back in her room, Huong slipped her shoes on and grabbed her wallet and coat. The campus store had whiskey too. Faster than beer, and less fattening.

112

LAURIE WAS SITTING AT THE KITCHEN TABLE WITH A SMALL mirror, doing her makeup. The door rattled as it slid open. It was Sarah. "Better be careful driving tonight. It's snowing again."

Laurie smiled at her, then returned her concentration to the mirror as she put the finishing touches on her eyes.

"Is Trinh coming over again?" Sarah asked.

"No, sweetie, she was here this morning. That's twice this week."

"I know, but tomorrow's Sunday, so all the times will be *last* week and she won't have been over *this* week at all."

Laurie laughed. "She's got classes to study for, including your dad's. Speaking of which, coming over now kinda makes her look like the teacher's pet."

"But every family needs a pet, right? She's way more fun than a hamster or something."

Laurie laughed. "I'll tell her you said that."

"You'll ask her to come over next week?"

Laurie closed her mascara. "If I see her, I'll ask whether she has time."

"She's gonna be there?"

"Not at the restaurant, but we might see her. Anyway, if so, I'll ask."

113

DAVID WAS SUPPOSED TO BE LEAVING FOR THE RESTAU-rant to meet Will and Laurie, but Itō got priority, so he was back in the café instead. He was concerned that Itō's spirits weren't as high as this morning.

Itō said, "There was no one on a video last night, and no one comes in today. Someone should come in to work on a system, but nothing."

"Whoever it was already turned things off before last night, right? That's why the audit showed no high traffic."

Itō looked troubled. "Yes, but still, I thought someone would come."

"What do we do now?"

"I found one strange thing in nighttime audit. DNS traffic is high."

"What's that?" asked David.

"In internet, each thing, each website, is on a domain. Each domain has a number. When you go to the site, your query goes to Domain Name System to get the number, like a phone book. Some kind of traffic a filter can stop, but DNS traffic always goes. If I am sending secret data, I maybe change it to look like DNS traffic."

"Can you trace that back to its origin within JGU?"

"Everything on a surface looks fine," said Itō.

"You can dig deeper?"

"Yes . . ."

"But . . . ?" asked David.

"It takes time."

114

WATANABE SAT AT A STUDY CARREL ON THE THIRD FLOOR of the library and looked outside at the air thick with snow. It could have been New Year's confetti if it had come just over two weeks earlier—and if there was anything to celebrate.

He had meant to go home when he left his office an hour ago, but ended up wandering around campus. After skulking about the library and peering through the windows at the students in the café and the cafeteria, he bought a candy bar at the campus store. He had no notion what he would do if he found Trinh. He couldn't talk to her; not yet, anyway. But he would make it up to her. Perhaps it was guilt, perhaps passion, but if it took the rest of his life, he would undo the shame he'd caused her today.

From this window on the north side of the library, he had a clear, if oblique, view of the side of Trinh's dorm that faced the gym. Trinh's sixth-floor room's light was on. If not for the snow, he might have caught a glimpse of her. With his binoculars, he might have been able to sneak a glance at the window and make out her face again. As it was, all he saw was light diffused through the snowflakes, and once, a flicker, someone moving.

Home would be the rational place to go—where he could sit by himself, watching television, eating whatever stale food he found in his kitchen.

A restaurant would provide a better meal, although he'd still be alone.

No, he could stay at least until her light went out—or they closed the library. Hopefully, in that time, there would be another flicker.

115

H UONG WAS CRYING. "WHAT IF HE BLABS?"
Trinh held her friend. "Hush. He won't."

"Yes, he will. Guys talk. Their dirty little mouths are connected to their dirty little penises."

"Mm-hmm, I know." Trinh rocked Huong gently.

"I need another drink."

"No, you don't."

Huong pulled away and looked at the glasses and the half-empty bottle on Trinh's desk.

Trinh frowned. "Whiskey won't fix it."

Huong leaned over and picked up her glass. "Won't make it any worse." She took a mouthful and swallowed hard, then handed Trinh's glass to her. "Don't make me drink alone. Only drunks get drunk alone."

Trinh swished the pale brown liquid around in the glass. At least Huong seemed to be stopping crying. She was watching, so Trinh took a sip.

Huong moved farther back on Trinh's bed and leaned on the wall. "You can cry too."

"What for?"

"Being in love with a married man."

"I am not."

Huong took a sip and rested her head on the wall. "Yeah, you are."

Trinh looked at her glass. "He has a wife, and he loves her. His kids too. It's enough if Will is happy."

"Ooh, he's 'Will' now? What happened?"

"Just . . . trying to find out who's spreading these awful rumors, we've had to meet and talk. We're a little closer, that's all."

"Did you get your pervert to talk, or did he just look down your shirt again?" Huong's words were slurring.

Trinh leaned back against the wall. "He talked."

"What did he say?"

"That he'd heard the new rumor, and worse . . . plus, who told him."

"Worse than the affair rumor? Who?"

Trinh lifted the glass and downed it all in two swallows.

Huong blinked in surprise, then laughed as Trinh opened her eyes wide and gasped. Huong put down her glass and flopped over on the bed.

The whiskey brought tears to Trinh's eyes, and it took her a minute to see straight. She wiped her eyes with one hand as she stroked her friend's hair with the other. At length, she sighed. "I can't do anything—*that* kind of anything—with Will. I'd never be able to live with myself."

Huong moved up on the bed, laid her head on Trinh's pillow, and closed her eyes. "It might surprise you what you can live with. Besides, there's no shame if his wife never finds out."

"You could stand the idea of sleeping with a married man?"

Huong was still.

Trinh's voice was quiet. "Who was he?"

"My boss. First job out of college."

Trinh looked at her in shock, but Huong didn't see. "Didn't you feel guilty?"

"I don't know, maybe. You're the first one I've ever told. Like I said, if no one knows, where's the shame?"

"Even so, you must feel . . . I don't know."

Huong rolled onto her back. "You try to forget what your mom drilled into you all the time you were growing up. Still, it's hard to ignore the voice in your head that nags at you that you're no better than the bar girls. You're not a sex worker unless you take money for it, right? But you're right: it still hurts. So after some months, you go to bed with someone else, and for a short little while, everything feels wonderful. Then, whether it's hurt about that or loneliness you'll never find someone, you climb into another guy's bed, and another." She put her arm over her eyes. "It works, sort of. It stops hurting very much. Maybe each guilt wipes away the one before. Eventually, though, people do know. I can tell you, whatever guilt I felt pales next to the shame."

Trinh took her hand. "You don't have to do it with anyone else this time. You can stop, and when we leave, no one back home will know."

"Yeah, I know." Huong paused to compose herself, but it didn't help. "I'll promise myself not to do it again. And I won't, for a while. But sooner or later . . ." She smiled even as she cried again. "Besides, that new surfer professor, I bet he could wipe away a *lot* of old pain."

Trinh kissed her on the forehead. "Let's stick with whiskey for now, little sister." Standing up to pour them each another, Trinh could feel the whiskey. She made this round smaller. Then she sat next to her friend and pressed a glass against her hand. Huong took it, eyes still closed.

116

MALIK RAN TO THE LIBRARY BUILDING. HE'D SUSPECTED ItŌ might start the bandwidth audit tonight instead of tomorrow morning. When the JGU website went down, he realized it was under-way. At least he'd had the hours he needed in the afternoon to finish setting up the TrueCrypt steganography software, so all the files were encrypted and couldn't be hacked. Now he just needed to shut down the server without being seen. Otherwise, the ISP's data flows and the audit's data flows would not match. Then it would only be a matter of time before they discovered the extra switch Malik had hidden under the floor.

How to get to his server? The library basement would be too risky now. Itō was surely in the server room. Malik could try crawling up the hallway, but if spotted, he might as well phone the police and turn himself in. He cursed himself for not installing a remote power switch.

He stopped at the entrance to the library and thought about the lay-out. There was no way in without being noticed, and it was impossible to cut the power to his server without—

Malik smiled as he turned and hurried around the outside of the library.

117

Z06 PULLED INTO THE PARKING LOT OF THE RESTAURANT and turned off the car. He got his laptop from the back seat and powered it up, hoping for an unprotected Wi-Fi connection, then plugged in his wireless modem.

Waiting . . .

He opened the website and logged in.

VietKitten's camera . . . no one there.

VietGoddess's? There they were. Drinking? Whiskey? He laughed.

He would have liked a little himself, or better yet, a bottle of liquor with a *mamushi* pickled in it. Did the snake's potency really make a man more virile? There would be no better time to try it—except that he had to drive. He'd heard it was expensive, too. He might find *mamushi* extract in a drugstore, or *suppon* extract—although he'd never understood how soft-shell turtle could be as effective as a venomous snake.

First, dinner!

He was about to close his laptop when the site went dead.

Maintenance? He must have missed the notice. The Webmaster always underestimated how long things like this took. It might be down for hours—or all night. Fate? Or at least luck. Perhaps he would have a use for the twine and box cutter he brought with him after all.

118

Laurie, Will, and David were just taking their seats at a restaurant in town when David asked, "I was pulling up at that new Italian restaurant, and who do you suppose was coming out?"

Laurie was surprised. "Wait, you already had dinner?"

"I . . . yeah, a little. Anyway, who?"

Laurie knitted her brow. "That's what I want to know. Who was this earlier dinner with?"

"Fine, I'll tell you," said David. "The young female officer who does the translating."

"You were having dinner with her?"

"No, she was leaving the restaurant when I pulled up."

"Who was in the car with—"

David interrupted. "Let me finish. The female officer—and Trinh."

Will's eyes opened wide in surprise.

Laurie looked at Will. "You think that's a problem?"

Will sat back "It's okay. It might even be a good thing. If they were talking about the case, Trinh would just complain that they've falsely accused me."

"They looked happy enough as they were leaving, anyway," said David.

After the server took their orders, David leaned forward and whispered, "Has Trinh gotten anything more out of Watanabe?"

Will shook his head. "Not yet. Or at least, she hasn't told me. She's supposed to get ahold of me as soon as she knows anything. What about Itō?"

David sighed. "He's sure something weird is up with the university's bandwidth. He's still looking, and he's confident he can solve it, but it'll take time."

Laurie sighed. "I've had enough waiting."

"Hey, don't you do waiting-time models or something?" David asked.

Will nodded. "Mm-hmm. Hazard modeling, survivor analysis. In marketing it can be used for purchase timing."

"Does Itō have any idea what's going on?" asked Laurie.

David said, "I don't understand all that stuff, but the traffic has settled down. Itō still thinks whoever it is must know what Itō's up to. Anyway, there's too much of some kind of outgoing traffic."

Laurie creased her brow. "Where's it coming from?"

"That's what he's working on. He said the sophistication has him thinking it's not his staff, so he's got two of them helping."

"What do you think it is?"

Will mused, "If it's outgoing traffic, someone's probably serving an internet business using the university network."

Laurie picked up the moist towel next to her chopsticks and wiped her hands. "That sounds like staff. They can program well enough, know the network, and have administrator access."

David rested his chin on his hand and looked out the window. "A business to kill for . . ."

"Doesn't make much sense, does it?" asked Will.

David didn't seem to hear, but then he made an "Ooh" face and turned to Will. "Ikenami finds out one of the computing staff is running a dot-com from the JGU network. What does he do?"

"I don't know. Tells Itō, I suppose," said Will. "Or if he doesn't trust Itō, then Itō's boss or the dean or the president. You think it's someone on the staff and Ikenami suspected Itō was in on it?"

"Possible, but you're right for any staff: Ikenami takes it to some manager, and right away. So why would Ikenami wait?" David raised an eyebrow.

Laurie smiled at him. "Tell us. You're obviously dying to."

David grinned. "Faculty. If it was someone he detested, he'd wait, gather evidence, and accuse the person with no warning in front of everyone. This is Ikenami we're talking about. It's all about public humiliation."

Will sat back in wonder. "A faculty meeting bombshell."

"IT faculty?" asked Laurie.

David nodded. "Probably. I'd say either King or Malik, not the junior guy."

Laurie looked at David. "You're sure it's not the IT guy?"

"He's been vouched for. He's also been an enormous help so far."

Laurie turned to Will. "Who?"

Will sat back and nodded. Finally, he said softly, "Malik."

THEY WERE EATING WHEN WILL GOT A MESSAGE ON HIS PHONE.

"What is it?" asked Laurie.

He read it, then handed it to David.

"I'm your wife," said Laurie. "I'm supposed to get it before him."

"Once again, the plot thickens!" David passed it to her.

> He talked! Also, power is out here. So strange.
>
> Trinh

Laurie handed Will his phone, and he sent a reply:

> Great! Talk tonight? What time?

Will set the phone on silent, put it on the table between himself and Laurie, and everyone watched it as they ate. It buzzed with a message after a few minutes. Laurie grabbed it and read it aloud:

> Yes, tonight. Huong is blue. Might take long time. I message when she feels better. Oh! Power back on.

"Sounds like there's time for dessert!" said David.

Laurie typed a reply:

> BTW, Sarah wants you over again. She doesn't care whether
> you seem like the teacher's pet. She says we need one and
> you're it.

Trinh's message came back a minute later:

> HAHA! Tell her she must feed me and give me box to
> sleep in!

~

LAURIE WAS QUIET AS WILL PULLED OUT OF THE RESTAURANT parking lot an hour later and started the cautious drive home. The air was thick with snow. As they crossed the bridge, she asked, "Will, is there something wrong?"

He glanced at her. "Yeah. I'm sorry. It's all horribly—"

"Not Ikenami. I mean . . . it's all vague, but I have an awful feeling."

Will frowned. "I've had a bad feeling all week. At least it'll be over soon."

"No, that's not it. It's something else, something new."

"Like what?"

"I don't know." She was quiet for a few seconds before she crossed her arms tight in front of her. "Will, drive faster."

He looked over at her.

"Please. I'm scared, and I want to get home."

119

MALIK KNEW IT WOULD BE ONLY MINUTES BEFORE THE facilities staff got to the main electrical power board in the university's physical plant behind the library and turned the power back on. A momentary outage was all he needed: once his server rack went down, it took an actual click of the power button to restart.

Now, with JGU's electricity restored, Malik stood by his office window and drummed his fingers on the wall as he listened to the microphone he'd hidden in the server room. Someone, probably Itō, was typing. As long as Itō was at the university, Malik couldn't restart the server. Even after Itō left, it might not be safe, but if the JGU website was up, he'd risk it. He didn't know what time Zo6 would summon the courage to start, but he doubted the man would go through with it. He was a thirty-six-year-old construction inspector for the city of Yokohama, still living with his parents. (Malik researched him more before he set this up.) Except for New Year's Eve, he hadn't missed a night of streaming in three months. He was hardly the type to explore new horizons.

Malik looked at his car disappearing under the loathsome snow: freezing-cold bird dung by the tonne. But ready access to Japanese girls meant working in Japan, and this job came with four months of white.

The typing stopped. A door closed. Malik let himself into the chairman's office across the hall with its perfect view of the courtyard. Itō appeared, wearing coat and boots, heading toward the classroom building. Malik wondered why he didn't just walk through the administration building's hallway. There was no reason to get out into the awful snow. Malik waited for a minute, then headed for the Conference Center. From a window there, he watched Itō clear off his car. He waited until Itō pulled out before he headed back to his office and checked the JGU website. It was up.

He hurried to the basement of the library and opened his closet. It only took a few minutes to get the server restarted and everything working smoothly. He could stream within JGU with no audit problem. If he streamed out of the university, though, it would cause data flows not to match in the audit. So he restricted access to himself and started only two live streams. He connected the stream from Huong's camera first. She was curled up under a blanket, with no sign of Zo6. Then Malik brought up Trinh's stream. It was too much a part of his daily life to go without, at least not willingly. It was comforting to see her asleep under a blanket too.

Malik needed an alibi for the time of Huong's rape, so as soon as he got home, he set about creating proof he was there. The woman who lived in the next apartment had complained when he vacuumed last month, saying it woke her up. Tonight, he did it with vigor, banging the vacuum into the wall to make sure she was awake. He didn't stop until the doorbell rang. That would be the pizza he ordered before he left the university. Heard and now seen, Malik relaxed and grabbed a beer from the refrigerator.

It wouldn't hurt to have one more bit of evidence. He picked up the apartment's landline phone and dialed a local number.

Voice mail.

Another number got him voice mail again.

Who could he call at this hour?

He frowned. He had not talked to her in a month.

120

I HAVEN'T SEARCHED PHYSICAL CONNECTIONS.

Itō had been home for all of thirty minutes. He was filling the bathtub and still hadn't had dinner. Did he really need to go back?

The snow's so thick tonight.

But whoever it is might think the audit's done and start again.

In the morning, I can see whether traffic spiked tonight.

I ought to go in and check, though.

121

THERE WAS A LARGE ROOM ON THE GROUND FLOOR OF THE east dormitory. Zo6 had peeked in earlier and seen sofas, chairs, and a big television. It had huge windows, but slats protected them from the crush of snow that piled against them where it fell from the roof. Now Zo6 heard loud laughter as he approached from the parking lot. No one had paid him any mind as he walked around the university's central buildings in the late afternoon, but this was a much more private space. It was only 11:32 p.m. Maybe he should wait.

He looked up at the snow pouring out of the sky in utter silence, like soft white coins from a secret jackpot. The whiskey had warmed him enough that he had not bothered to zip his coat. If he closed it and pulled his hat low, they might not even notice him. The later it got, the greater the chance that someone seeing a stranger might question him. Fortunately, he had checked the website, and it was still offline, meaning no one would see—unless it came back online in the middle.

He approached the building warily and looked through the door. The big room was to the left through a glass door. The elevator was straight ahead. All he had to do was walk through the small lobby, press the button, and go.

He stood, trembling, and wiped the sweat from his forehead. What slim chance was there that he could reach VietKitten's room without being seen, enter without waking her, and subdue her before she brought her neighbors running?

Even if she screamed at the first sight of him, he could still touch her. He thought of VietKitten answering his knock in her pajamas, only one button done, like she wore them when she was alone.

He tingled with adrenaline as he realized he really would do this, and before the feeling could fade, he opened the door, strode across the small lobby, and pushed the elevator button. It opened immediately, and he hurried in and pressed the button for her floor.

Two. He put a glove on as the car rose.

Three. He slipped on the other glove.

Four. He felt for the key in his pocket.

Five. A deep breath, then another.

Six. The doors opened, and he listened. He stepped halfway out of the elevator. All clear. He moved into the small vestibule—and let the elevator doors close off all that his life had been before.

There was a small commons room across the vestibule, but the lights were out. To the left was a door to the north wing, and to his right, one to the south. Numbers and arrows on the wall confirmed VietKitten's room was south, as on the campus map. He checked the north anyway, looking through a little window in the door. Two girls were talking far down the darkened hallway. VietKitten's hallway was dark, too, not a soul in sight. He eased the door open and stole down the hall. The numbers were rising by twos. That would make the fifth door . . . E610, as he'd thought. There was a nameplate: Huong Nguyen.

VietKitten had a name! He wanted to shout it.

His hand was shaking as he got ready to knock. One more deep breath. The tingling was back. He rapped softly on the door and listened. He felt in his pocket for the key. Slowly, silently, he slipped it into the lock in the center of the doorknob. He turned the key, and the knob turned with it . . . with no click. She hadn't locked it. He cracked the door, listening again. Zo6 checked the hallway once more, then stepped into the room and locked the door behind himself.

He stood, heart racing. His eyes were already adjusted to the hallway's darkness, so he could see clearly. To the left was the closet, to the right, the bathroom door he knew so well, and beyond that, her bed. The foot of the bed was visible. He could see her toes, which was odd: VietKitten always slept under the covers.

He took the stocking from his pocket and pulled it over his head. As he crept into the room, again he felt like shouting. He was in Viet-Kitten's room—no, Huong's! How many times had he imagined this?

And this is it!

He trembled in anticipation, especially his hands, as he neared the bed. There she was, facing the wall, under a throw blanket, thick black ponytail hanging off—

He froze and stared down at her, the stocking over his head the only thing that kept his mouth from gaping open. It was VietGoddess!

~

TRINH AWOKE TO HER PHONE RINGING AND ROLLED OVER. With all Huong's tears, she'd forgotten to call Will. She opened her eyes—

The hand was on her mouth before she could make a sound. She threw a punch, but it was a glancing blow, and before she could swing again, his fist flew down and her stomach exploded in pain. She curled up and gasped for breath—and bit his hand. He yanked it away as a fist hit her mouth, hard.

He grasped her tight again. She tasted blood. His? Her own? Through tears, she looked up at the dark form above her and struggled for air.

One scream, one breath!

He hit her hard in the eye and points of light sparkled in front of her like snowflakes while the room slowly turned. Surfacing from the vision, she felt her mouth break free, but before she could scream, he stuffed something into it.

He sat straddling her, and she kicked—hard.

His fist again.

Blackness.

～

MALIK BANGED ON HIS KEYBOARD AND TWO LARGE COMPUTER monitors bathed his room in a soft blue light. Talking to his wife in London always put him in a foul mood.

He pulled from his wallet the tattered sheet of paper that held the usernames and passwords which allowed him to remotely access the PC in his office. From there, he could access Huong's feed and pipe it to himself, disguised as DNS traffic, through the regular JGU network. It took a couple of minutes to make all the connections.

Damn it! I missed the beginning!

Despite the regular outgoing feeds being down, all the raw camera streams were being saved on hard disk. He could catch it later. Zo6's size surprised him. The man was enormous. Or perhaps it was just his coat. Why was he leaving it on? Malik couldn't see her. He saw her arms bent over the head of the bed. Zo6 must have tied her hands to the bed frame. He had her legs tied down, too, although it didn't appear to be rope. For all his anticipation, the man had not bothered to learn anything about the art of binding a woman?

Malik focused on what he could see of Huong: naked legs, young and smooth. It roused the echo of the first girl . . . How many since then had offered themselves to him gladly, even humbly, asking to be bound? He thought of the last one, a professional in every respect, including her level of service. How many years since he had been forced to settle for an amateur? He'd certainly left the last pro smiling. But that was his gift, to leave women feeling their womanhood all the stronger. They loved him for it.

Still, Malik could understand the attraction of force. To overpower a woman, to push harder than her body could resist, would be a heady feeling. It wouldn't be like overcoming her self-control, though. Having a woman bend to your pleasure, to your whim, was far more intoxicating than taking her against her will.

But Huong, she needed to be humbled, to realize she was not the sort of woman who could laugh at men with impunity, particularly a man like Malik. He smiled. It was nice to know she would carry this lesson with her for the rest of her life. So would Zo6.

How many women had Zo6 done this to? It was entirely possible this was his first. For all Malik knew, this could be his first, period.

As Malik leaned back and watched, he felt a twinge of envy. The first is such a uniquely exciting experience. But even Huong couldn't match his own.

Zo6 was shuddering.

That was quick. Rookie.

Malik had been waiting to see Huong's face, but the idiot had worn his coat the entire time. In fact, she seemed unconscious almost until the end. The torn panties hanging from one knee and shreds of pajamas around her ankles punctuated the scene nicely, but overall, it was not the show Malik had hoped for. With such a poor performance, it was good he had not tried to sell it on pay-per-view. He laughed as he imagined Zo6's reaction when the man read Malik's note.

Through the microphone in Huong's room, Malik heard loud voices in the hallway. Zo6 must have, too, because he raised his head in alarm. Huong was writhing, trying to scream. Zo6 sat up and grabbed her pillow.

Yes, muffle her. Put the pillow over—

Malik lurched to the edge of his chair and gaped at the screen.

Trinh?

Trinh!

The stupid—he raped the wrong girl!

Trinh's mine!

~

AT LENGTH, VietGoddess stopped struggling, but Zo6 held the pillow to her face as the steps continued up the hall. The sound of keys. Doors opened. Good nights. Doors closed. Zo6 breathed again.

He whispered in Japanese—he'd heard VietGoddess speak it enough to know she'd understand—"I'll take the pillow off. Try to scream and I'll beat your face in."

He raised it a little. She was quiet, so he lifted it the rest of the way off. Was she pretending to be unconscious again? He held the pillow at the ready as he gave her cheek a soft slap.

No reaction.

He stood and poked her hard in the ribs.

His throat began to tighten in panic.

He pressed his hand to her throat and felt for a pulse.

He grabbed her wrist, then released it and put his ear to her chest. She wasn't breathing.

He couldn't hear her heart!

He recoiled, falling to the floor, and scurried away until his back banged into the desk.

She was dead? He'd *killed* her?

He stood, yanked the stocking off his head, and desperately did up his pants.

~

MALIK watched with increasing horror. When Zo6 stood, Malik waited.

Move . . . Trinh, move! Breathe!

No!

No, no, no!

Damn it! He killed her!

Malik jumped up. He had to go!

Taking a step toward the door, he fell, his pants around his ankles. He hastily pulled them up and grabbed his coat.

He was at his front door before he remembered he needed to cut the video. Back at his PC, he pulled up the control page and killed the outgoing feed from Huong's camera.

When he got downstairs, he hurried to his car. He stopped as he grasped the door handle. People knew his car.

He turned around, looked back to the car, then toward the university. He glared up into the sky at all the despicable flakes pouring peacefully down. And he ran.

122

Laurie woke as Will slipped into the *futon*. She checked the alarm clock. "It's late."

"I waited, but she never called. I sent a message and even tried calling, but no answer."

"Whatever she was going to tell you can wait until morning."

"Yeah."

"You going to be able to sleep?"

"I don't know."

"C'mere. Let me hold you."

123

So what if it's late? Trinh said she'd call, thought Kurimoto as she listened to the phone ring.

Asleep. I knew I should have called earlier.

Asleep is what I ought to be.

She climbed back into bed and closed her eyes—for two minutes.

Maybe there's something on television.

124

Malik lived close enough that it took only fifteen minutes to run to campus. He went straight to his server closet in the library's basement, where he grabbed a little bag of tools and one of the original wireless APs he had switched out. Then he rushed to the dormitory. It looked like there were still people in the first-floor lounge, and there were lights shining from windows scattered throughout the building. At least on the sixth floor, they were almost all out—on this side of the building, anyway.

He entered cautiously and was about to call the elevator when he stopped short. The stairs were safer.

He had to stop three times to catch his breath, but he finally reached Huong's floor. There was no sound from the hallway, so he opened the fire door and peeked in.

Still, dark, deserted.

Malik took the master key from his pocket and slipped silently down the hall. Huong's door was wide open. The imbecile! Malik locked the door behind himself.

He went to the bed. It was indeed Trinh. He felt her neck for a pulse, then listened for a heartbeat.

He leaned against the wall and stared at her body, silhouetted in the darkness. The police would find it all. He would replace Huong's AP tonight, but when could he replace Trinh's? Once they found her, they would seal both rooms and that would be the end.

Unless there was no body.

She would be easy enough to lift and carry, but then what? Take her in the elevator? Carry her down the stairs? Ludicrous.

He sighed and turned slowly around.

The window!

She deserved better—alive—but dead, what difference did it make? He removed the screen, slid it open, and looked down. There was nothing but white below him. Under the window, a meter from the building, was a huge, dense berm of snow that had fallen from the eaves. From this height, her corpse would slam into it like a rock and probably penetrate half a meter. Even if it didn't, more would slide off the roof before dawn. No one would find her until spring. They would do an autopsy and find she'd been raped—perhaps. By spring, that evidence might be gone. Anyway, the rapist would be long dead; Malik would see to that.

He looked back at Trinh, lying still, eyes closed, in the faint light from the window. Even in death, she was one of the most beautiful women he had ever seen. He stepped back to the bed and used his pocketknife to carefully cut the twine that bound her hands and feet. She'd bloodied it; she had struggled so hard. He sat next to her, took the cloth from her mouth, delicately cleaned her bruised eyes, and wiped the traces of blood from her nose and lips. He caressed her still-warm face and stroked her long ponytail, sighing deeply. How he wished he could have done this in life. He squeezed her breasts softly. She would have moaned. She would have loved him. And he would have made her happy.

Malik kissed her.

Trinh's pajamas and panties were so badly torn that there was no point in trying to redress her, so he cut them off. He used them to clean the blood from between her legs. He wiped off her wrists and ankles.

Malik stood. He didn't want to do this. He cared for her as much as anyone he had ever known. But it was time to finish, so he crossed her arms over her chest and lifted her naked body from the bed.

She was surprisingly heavy.

He carried her over to the window, got her head and shoulders out, and set her back on the sill. With great effort, he got underneath her. With one hand on her lower back and the other on her buttocks, he bounced her gingerly as he counted: one . . . two . . . three!—and pushed as hard as he could, up and out. He got his head out in time to see her hit. It wasn't clear through the densely falling snow, but it looked like she had landed face up, arms and legs demurely folded. She was deep enough that no one would notice before tonight's snow buried her.

Malik shut the window, replaced the screen, and pulled the curtain closed. It only took a minute to replace the wireless AP. He grabbed Huong's towel from the bathroom and wiped off anything he or Zo6 might have touched. There was blood on the bedspread and pillowcase, so he gathered her pajamas, panties, and the lone stocking on the bed next to the lengths of twine and the gag. Then he balled it all up, throw blanket and pillow, too, in the bedspread and tucked the bundle under his arm. He would find a place to burn it all tonight.

After grabbing the wireless AP, her phone, and his tool bag, he took a last look around before he crept into the hall. He didn't bother to lock the door. There was nothing to see. And the more people who contaminated the scene, the better.

Song Two: Safe-Folded
二曲目：安らかに

Quiet, my wounded child,
Hush and be thankful.
Hear now the voices mild singing you home.
Safe-folded in light to rest, heart at peace, tranquil,
Let sorrow flee your breast.
Well you have come.

Why not your love invest?
Why let me suffer?
You, who could so have blessed, succored, and led?
Why was I left alone, frightened, to wander
Till, every mercy flown,
My blood was shed?

My part, to let you sail.
Your part, to venture.
Though, in part, all would fail, you must be free.
Joy you would choose, but know: pain was your treasure.
Now from your heart may flow
True charity.

If pain a treasure be,
How was I failing?
With vilest indecency I had to die?
See how I tremble still, soul on fire, wailing.
Would not my cup have filled—
Brimmed—by and by?

There is no torment sore
I've not partaken.
I knew your pain and more. I suffered all.
Your life, the merest sting, o'er now—awaken!
Peace to you I can bring
If you but call.

(Then) Whisper again to me.
Lead me to meekness.
Your voice, all quietly, pierces my soul.
Bind you my wounded mind, shore up my weakness,
Own now my pain, and find
If I can be whole.

Already owned, my child,
Merely release it.
(Though) By it you feel defiled, you hold it fast.
Loosen your grasp and see: it falls to pieces.
Now from your burden free,
At rest, at last.

I would partake your grace.
Let it spill o'er me,
Faltering, still with place for hate and strife.
All those I wounded deep, heal them before me.
Thus, I'll cast off the sleep
That clouded my life.

IX

Real Options
リアル・オプション

Sunday, 17 January 2010

125

HUONG LIFTED THE PILLOW OFF HER HEAD. THIS WASN'T her room. Seeing the bottle of whiskey on the desk, she remembered.

Where was Trinh? She checked the time on her phone: 7:50 a.m.

Monday.

Most likely.

Trinh must have left for Japanese class. Huong pressed the speed dial and closed her eyes. It didn't hurt as much that way. She listened to the phone ring . . . and ring and ring. That was odd. Trinh always answered.

She was probably talking to Will.

Eyes still closed, she dropped the phone on the bed and thought of him in the pool . . . Trinh's Will . . . so cute . . . She needed to get one of those . . . but later, when her eyes were open.

126

THE RINGING PHONE JARRED MALIK OUT OF SLEEP. THE ringtone was wrong.

It was Trinh's.

Malik sat up and found himself on his sofa, dressed. He looked at his watch. He'd wanted to pull the hard drives out of his server closet, but Itō would be in by now. It would be impossible to blithely walk out with three dozen hard disks. He should have done it last night. That was stupid. But tonight would work. Someone would miss Trinh by nightfall, but they wouldn't involve the police until tomorrow.

He picked up Trinh's phone and scrolled through the logs.

Will? Why would he call Trinh in the middle of the night? He smirked. Perhaps they really were having an affair.

Next was Kurimoto. The cop? The hair on his arms stood up.

He checked Trinh's email and messages. Nothing from the cop, but Trinh was going to meet Will. She never messaged him back, so they never met?

As if it made any difference.

He should have left Trinh's phone in the room! With the phone call and messages, the cops would have suspected Will.

He could still put the phone in Will's office.

Malik powered down the phone. Yes, this could still work out fine.

It wasn't until Malik was in the shower that he realized last night's full tragedy. He stood in a stupor, shampoo dripping off his head, as the road ahead narrowed and disappeared. The only witness, the only one who saw Ikenami tumble, the linchpin of everything Malik had been orchestrating, lay dead in the crush of snow from the dormitory roof. Most likely, she never told a soul what she saw.

127

WATANABE SAT AND STARED AT THE STEAM RISING FROM his two bowls: one held a pair of soft-boiled eggs, the other, rice. During the predawn hours, he'd formulated a plan, but in the morning light, his resolve was evaporating. Trinh would never agree to be alone with him for the few minutes it would take to confess his love. Knocking on her door would likely bring a harassment charge, not a sympathetic ear.

I need a real option.

He frowned. In his PhD program, he'd studied real options valuation, future choices becoming a series of probabilistic outcomes.

What future decisions do I get to make? What positive outcomes can I even hope for?

He slumped in his chair. White bowls, white food . . .

He picked up an egg.

A man with options? No, he was an egg: boiled, peeled, and then what? *Who remembers eating an egg?*

He held it in his hand.

What's a world with one less egg?

He gripped it tight and felt the heat, painful, on his palm. He squeezed, fighting back tears, watching as the tendons in his wrist tightened, until yolk and bits of white, still steaming, oozed between his fingers.

128

Z06 LAY CURLED UP IN HIS *FUTON*, HOLDING HIMSELF. *What kind of imbecile accidentally smothers someone to death?*

He didn't even know her real name.

He'd been excited—and so scared. He'd never been that scared in his life. It was glorious to feel powerful for once, to take what he wanted—but the tears, the agony on her face, the hate in her eyes . . . *What woman would ever look at him with any other emotion?*

I killed her. For a few moments of . . . what?

He hated it: having devolved into nothing more than the brief span that now defined his life; no love, no sympathy—nothing but an insatiable craving that no woman would ever willingly relieve.

He could confess to the police, accept the consequences—and hang.

Or I can lie here, remembering how soft she was, how warm.

129

KURIMOTO GRIPPED HER PHONE TIGHTLY AS SHE RAN. There was no music this morning, only her body nagging her to stop—and Watanabe's eyes, wide, unnerving, and possibly psychotic. She should never have let Trinh do it.

If she did, in fact, do it.

Trinh could have lost her nerve, so she never called, despite her promise.

That didn't explain why she still didn't answer.

130

HUONG SURFACED AGAIN. SHE NEEDED A TOILET. She sat up and rubbed her eyes. Was it time to go back to her room?

Where were her keys? Huong was sure she locked her room when she came here last night. She remembered them being on Trinh's desk by the whiskey bottle. Huong searched the room to no avail. Maybe Trinh took them to go sleep in Huong's bed. Still, Trinh would have returned them when she left for class.

Unless she was still asleep. Trinh never missed class—
It's Sunday.
Isn't it? Yesterday was skiing—and Brian. Yeah, it's Sunday.
I should be in bed.

Huong went to her room and found the door unlocked. Trinh wasn't on the bed. Huong's keys were on the desk. Trinh must have gone to study. It was weird of her not to lock the door.

Leaving the bathroom, she glanced in the mirror. She had looked worse, but sleep would help. She looked at her bed. Where was her bedding?

Huong checked the other room to see whether Trinh had left any-thing there, but she hadn't. Did she get sick in the night?

If Trinh had gotten sick, she would have put the soiled things in the wash before she left. Huong returned to her room, pulled on jeans and a sweatshirt, and headed to the laundry room. Her things weren't in any of the washers.

Whatever. She'd find them later. She wanted to lie down. She chose Trinh's room. Trinh had a blanket and a pillow.

131

MALIK PULLED OFF HIS TALL RUBBER BOOTS AND SLIPPED on his shoes. The snow was coming fast, dense, and wet, and he hated it. At least he was inside his office now. He turned on the radiator under his window and sat down to think. The problem of how to get Will arrested squeezed his brain like a vise. He had used those rumors masterfully—to no effect. Even though he had told the police Will should be a suspect, they had not interrogated him.

He had Trinh's phone, of course. It would be easy to plant. Then what? The affair rumor wouldn't spur them to search Will's office. And if Will found the phone, he'd just give it to the police, saying someone planted it. Since he surely had an alibi for last night, they would believe him.

I can call the police and tell them Grames has Trinh's phone.

What a stupid idea.

Whatever he came up with for Will, there were other pressing tasks. He had to destroy every bit of evidence about Trinh. He'd dismantle the whole server closet: pull the servers, the RAID enclosures, the rack, wiring, ventilation—everything. It would take a week's worth of nights. The drives were the most important.

If I get those out today, that will be enough.

He needed to erase any trace of the website from the Dark Web— although it would remain in users' histories.

I should inform the subscribers first.

That would mean restarting the website. And what about refunds? There were two weeks remaining in the month and someone might complain.

To whom?

The website would be gone. But an irate customer might try to track down the Webmaster. Refunds would be safer.

That also meant starting up the website. He could do it from the server closet this morning, a tiny stream of data too brief to track.

It would also be safer to destroy the disks, their encryption notwithstanding. Only if the files were gone would he be perfectly safe.

All those files gone.

All he had created, countless hours of girls who stripped naked for him at night and looked up at him from their seats as he taught the next day—all gone.

Or I could stash the disks somewhere until this blows over.

Trinh's camera was far more dangerous than any hard disk. But with any luck, he could swap out that wireless AP tonight. The police wouldn't search other rooms, so the rest could stay in place until summer.

But if the cameras are staying, why not the servers? Why lose that income?

None of the subscribers saw the murder, so no one was going to contact the police. Still, if anyone discovered his server closet and somehow tied it to him, the circumstantial evidence would bury him. He'd have no choice but to flee the country. If everything stayed hidden, though, with a few months' hiatus, it could begin again. A new incoming class in August would be a perfect start-up special. It was always fun to watch the new girls arrive in their rooms, look on as they unpacked, as they undressed.

He needed to send a message: hiatus, gala August restart campaign, even more girls, no refunds. Then he'd pull the disks and hide them somewhere no one could ever find them. And wait.

I need to wipe the server closet for fingerprints.

And get Grames arrested.

And kill that bastard Zo6.

132

Itō had scheduled a nine o'clock meeting with David in the Conference Center when they talked last night. David was early and waiting. At 8:52 a.m., Itō arrived. After the briefest of greetings, he told David, "Outgoing traffic is down suddenly, very much."

"Since when?"

"About midnight. It drops and stays down."

"So . . . ?"

Itō shook his head. "Without traffic, we cannot know who was using it."

"Can you search the physical connections or something?"

"Yes, but maybe the user disconnects."

David nodded. "He would have to disconnect in the server room, right?"

Itō thought. "Probably in server room. Possible outside, but *must* be in basement of library building."

"Can you keep people out of the basement?"

"My staff must work."

"Can you give people access *only* to the office?"

Itō thought again. "There is the fire door in the hall between office and server room. I can close it."

"Fire doors don't lock."

"Don't need lock. We still have—"

As Itō's eyes widened, David asked, "What?"

"When power cut last night, I forgot to restart software that records feed from the camera!"

"So whoever it is may have already accessed the server room?"

Itō covered his face with his hands.

133

David stared out the café window. "Can you believe this weather? Over five feet and no sign of letting up."

Will frowned. "No worries there, I guess."

David changed the subject. "What are you dressed up for?"

"Last week, Becka asked, 'If we're Christians, then why don't we go to church?' We start today." There were students at a nearby table, so Will lowered his voice. "I wasn't able to talk to Trinh last night, and I haven't been able to get through to her this morning."

"She likely slept in."

"It's nearly ten."

"That's not so late for Sunday."

"It is for her."

Will's worry had David concerned. "You want to go knock on her door?"

"With the rumors?"

As Huong opened the café door, a bell rang and the two employees shouted in welcome, "*Irasshaimase!*"

When Huong saw Will, she walked straight to his table and looked at one of the empty chairs as if asking permission to sit. Will nodded, and Huong asked, "Do you talk to Trinh this morning?" as she took a seat.

Will said, "No, I called, but she didn't answer."

Huong looked scared. "I cannot find her anywhere. I called her before eight. The phone rings, but now it says no service, call again later."

David said, "The library isn't open yet. She's probably hiding somewhere quiet, studying."

"Her bag, backpack, books, and notes are all in her room."

David leaned forward. "Perhaps she's with a guy friend?"

Huong cast big eyes at Will for a second. "No way!"

Will whispered, "She's been checking into rumors about—"

"Yes, she told me. She was trying to find out who starts it."

"Last night—"

"She talked to Watanabe-*sensei*."

Will said, "He told her who started the rumors."

"Yes—"

"She told you who?"

Huong shook her head. "She did not want to talk about it."

Will sat back and folded his arms.

Huong's voice was emotional. "Last night we were . . . I was . . . we talked, and we drank a little. Or more, maybe. I fell asleep on her bed. I think she sleeped in my room, and now my blankets and pillow are gone, my blankets and pillow and Trinh. She was in pajama, but no pajama in my room or her room. Where can she go in pajama all morning?"

David leaned forward. "She must be in the dorms. Can you talk to her friends? She's probably wrapped in your blanket, sitting on some bed, talking."

"Then why doesn't she answer phone?" asked Huong.

"I don't know. You know who her friends are?"

"Okay, yes, I will look now."

David was about to offer final words of encouragement, but Huong popped up with such determination that all he had time to say was, "Come to my office and tell me what you find out."

She looked back and nodded as she headed for the door.

Will gave David a sullen look.

"Go," said David. "Your family's waiting."

134

THE LIBRARY DID NOT OPEN UNTIL TEN A.M. ON SUNDAYS, so at five minutes after, Malik left his office and headed over. With his master key, he could have entered earlier, but if anyone saw him, it would have been hard to explain how he got in. Sunday mornings were the quietest time of the entire week. Anyone who saw him leaving with a box would pay no attention, let alone remember. Also, IT Services would be closed, Itō and his staff nowhere in sight.

Stepping out of the stairwell into the basement hallway, Malik was surprised to see the fire door closed. It stood just past the door to the IT Services office, and as Malik approached, he could see under the door that lights were on in the office. Itō was about, but was he in the office, or the server room, beyond the fire door?

In all Malik's years at JGU, he had never seen a fire door closed. He'd heard no alarms. There was no smell of smoke.

He stared at the door.

He started looking at the walls, up and down, and the ceiling, but he saw nothing. Malik had his hand on the fire door, ready to open it, before he realized the camera he had been looking for was more likely to be inside the door. It would catch him the moment he peeked. He needed to inspect the hallway without being seen.

The camera in his phone!

He opened the door enough to slip his phone in and snapped a photo. It took ten shots before he saw the tiny camera dangling from the ceiling.

Itō, Itō, Itō, you fool, trying to catch a master.

Still, the server closet was out of reach—for now.

MALIK WAS ALMOST BACK AT HIS OFFICE BEFORE HE REALIZED he had another problem. Until yesterday, King had always been not only circumspect in their programming transactions, but docile. Malik's generous payments had seen to that. With Trinh's disappearance, King's arrogance yesterday became more than an expensive annoyance. King knew Malik was streaming video. It would be a leap, but hardly impossible, for King to wonder whether the video was coming from the dorms.

King was the only person who knew, though. Malik was sure King had told no one of his programming work. King had joked once he'd have to kill him if Malik ever told King's wife, Rumi, about the money. It had been three years, and Malik still felt indignant at King's joking threat.

"King." It was Malik who had the blood of royalty.

Hobbled as King was now, killing him wouldn't be difficult. There was no reason it would have to look like natural causes, not with a life as sordid as King's. Malik could simply beat him till his head caved in.

135

WHATEVER NEFARIOUS THING MALIK WAS DOING, KING knew TrueCrypt would keep it hidden forever.

It's not my responsibility.

So what if he's streaming porn using the JGU servers? What difference does one more porn site make? To use JGU equipment might be technically illegal, but aside from the JGU administration, who would care? It's not as if porn has victims. If they get Malik, it'll probably be for tax evasion.

136

S IR, I'M SORRY TO BOTHER YOU AT HOME AGAIN," BEGAN Kurimoto.

"I'm not at home," said Hasegawa.

"Oh, I'm sorry. I can call back another—"

"It's fine. What did you need?"

"I was going to tell you . . ." She paused. "You're at the station, aren't you? You went in today!"

"That's what you called to tell me?"

"No, but if you'll be there a little longer, I'd rather come in and talk about this."

"THIS WAS SUPPOSED TO BE A DAY OFF," CHIDED KURIMOTO.

"Which shows from the way you're dressed," said Hasegawa.

He had never commented on her clothing before—but this was the first time he'd seen her in anything but her uniform. Were jeans and a turtleneck sweater inappropriate dress for the station? "I'm sorry. I suppose I should have changed before coming in."

"What for? You look . . . good."

She saw him glance again. What did that mean?

Hasegawa asked, "Did you get to talk to the Vietnamese woman yesterday?"

"Yes. That's what I wanted to talk about. She told me she's been tracking down the source of the rumors about Grames and Ikenami."

"Why?"

"She seems to have a schoolgirl crush," said Kurimoto.

"Isn't she old for that?"

"Think of it as a crush all grown up. She said she's traced the rumors back to Watanabe."

"The owl?"

Kurimoto covered her mouth as she laughed and gave him a quick nod.

Hasegawa shook his head. "How could anyone look so constantly startled? Anyway, what does he have against Grames?"

"She thinks he's parroting the rumors."

"The ultimate source is . . . ?"

"The murderer, she suspects," said Kurimoto.

"Who is . . . ?"

"She's cozying up to Watanabe to find out."

Hasegawa looked worried.

"That's my concern. She was going to do it last night—"

Hasegawa's eyes widened.

"Not *that.* She was just leading him on."

Hasegawa looked worried. "You think that's safe?"

"She isn't as guileless as you may think."

"I get the picture." Hasegawa took out his cigarettes, looked in the pack, shook it, and looked again.

Your last one of the morning. Don't use it yet, not on this. Hold on.

He put it back in his pocket, and Kurimoto sighed silently.

"Anyway, I had a friendly talk with her. I trust what she told me, and I think she's onto something. As we speculated before, Grames may be hiding something, but it's not murder."

"Okay, follow up with her. I want to know where this goes," said Hasegawa.

"That's the problem. She was supposed to call last night—I made her promise—and she never did."

"If she didn't talk to him, there'd be no reason to call."

"I've been calling her all morning and her phone is off," said Kurimoto.

"You never turn your phone off?"

Kurimoto looked down.

"You're worried."

She nodded.

"She's probably studying. We'll be back there tomorrow morning."

Kurimoto hesitated. "I'm sorry to have troubled you."

"It's no trouble. Instincts are important. Don't ignore them. Just trust that not every bad thing you imagine is real."

137

LAURIE WAS ALONE IN THE LIVING ROOM WORKING ON THE jigsaw puzzle again when Will came in. She sat up and stretched her back. "Thanks for going to church this morning. I think it's important for us to be united in that."

Will nodded. "I agree. Always have."

Laurie returned to the puzzle.

Will asked, "What did the girls think of it?"

"I think they've missed it. At least, there was no heel dragging when I told them we were going and no negative comments afterward. Although I'm sure they had more fun on Ski Day."

Will smiled. "We'll make Sunday-church-going Christians of them yet."

Laurie laughed. "We need to make Christians of *us.*"

Will frowned as he clicked through channels on the TV.

Laurie took his arm. "Hey."

"What?" answered Will without looking at her.

She got up, stepped to the sofa, and sat close to him. "You're being sensitive."

Will sighed. "I went to church and got all stoked up on guilt. I sat for that hour as if I was innocent, and I got to contemplate what an awful thing I did—am still doing—while his widow waited for the truth I could tell."

"You're trying to find the killer. If you tell one piece of the truth, more important parts will be lost forever. And nobody there was innocent. Who is? What would've been the point of church if we were?"

Will turned off the television. "Some people are innocent—completely. I think the girls still are, especially Rachel. I guess that's one thing I've always had trouble with."

"What?"

"Original sin. I mean, looking at our perfect baby girls, could you accept they were damned from the get-go?"

Laurie frowned. "I'm too busy thinking about all the bad things I've done. Original sin gets lost in the background."

Will sighed. "Ikenami puts it in the background for damn sure."

138

Ｉ
T WAS AFTERNOON BEFORE DAVID CALLED TO TELL WILL
that Huong still hadn't found Trinh. Will left for the university
immediately. He was heading for the Conference Center, his stomach
tied in a knot, when he ran into David in the hallway. They looked out
at the huge mound of snow in the courtyard, now over six feet deep,
and spoke in hushed voices.

"I shouldn't have asked her to talk to him," said Will.

"She wanted to," said David.

Will's shoulder twitched. "I shouldn't have let her."

"As if you could've stopped her? Besides, you got messages from her
after that. She likely just wants to be alone."

Will's voice was low. "I should talk to Watanabe."

"A cooler head might have a more productive talk with him."

"You're handling the IT end of things. The rumors are mine. You
said yourself, he hates you."

"He was accusing you of murder," said David.

Will frowned.

"Tell you what," proposed David, "we *janken* for it."

Will looked askance at him.

"Hey, it's the Japanese equivalent of a coin flip, isn't it?"

"You learn that from your teacher?"

"One of many things." David smiled.

"Fine. Winner talks to him."

They each held a hand out as they said in unison, "*Jan, ken, pon!*"

They both showed "paper."

"*Ai-ko desho!*" they said together.

David showed "scissors." Will showed "rock."

～

I
T TOOK WILL OVER AN HOUR TO CALM HIMSELF ENOUGH THAT
he thought he could confront Watanabe with the requisite self-
possession, but the sun approaching the western horizon lit a fire
under him. He settled himself again as he stood at Watanabe's door. He

would only have one chance, so he needed cool precision. Will thought of Trinh's smile, of Rachel's. He practiced smiling.

Will knocked.

Watanabe didn't respond, but his light was on, so Will knocked again.

Still no response.

Will hoped the door wasn't locked. He put on his most pleasant, unthreatening face—and quickly turned the doorknob and threw the door open. "Hi, Jirō." Will stepped into the office and closed the door behind himself before Watanabe could say anything.

Watanabe recovered from his surprise. "You can't come in without me asking!" He paused. "Or without you asking. Anyway, I'm busy, so—"

"Sorry to intrude, but there's something we need to talk about." Watanabe was about to protest again, so Will said, "Something urgent."

Watanabe frowned. "What?"

"You know there've been rumors I killed Professor Ikenami."

Watanabe glared at him.

Will continued, unflinching, "It's come to my attention that you are the one who's been spreading them."

Watanabe growled, "Get out."

"A student traced them back to you."

Watanabe leaned forward more menacingly. "I told you to get out."

"Trinh Nguyen. You admitted to her you told the rumors to students. In fact, the two of you talked about it yesterday evening."

Watanabe whispered vehemently, "She can't say I did anything," and the hair on the back of Will's neck stood up.

"No, and you did not make them up, but you were spreading them, including the latest one."

"What latest one?" asked Watanabe.

"That Trinh and I are lovers."

"No! Did she say I—? I wasn't harassing her. I never touched her. Never! That rumor—even when I thought it was true, I hardly—"

"Oh, so now you don't believe it?" asked Will.

"She told me what Malik said about her being pregnant was a lie, and I believed her."

Pregnant? I have to stay focused. "Malik."

"Yes. That's what she told you, right?"

"Was the source of all the rumors."

Watanabe looked perplexed. "Isn't that what she told you?"

"No, she didn't."

"What?"

Will waited.

Watanabe blinked at him before his eyes opened even wider. "She didn't say it came from me!"

Will responded flatly. "No, she said nothing. After she talked to you last night, sometime late, she disappeared."

"Trinh?"

Will nodded.

"Is she all right?"

"Dis-ap-peared."

"But . . . she must be . . ." Watanabe recoiled. "You don't think I—"

Will tilted his head to the side.

Watanabe stood. "I could never do anything to Trinh! Never! I—"

Will folded his arms.

Watanabe pointed his finger at Will. "You can't blame *anything* on me!"

"I can tell the detective what I've learned about you and Malik and the rumors. He'll be interested, don't you think?"

"This is nothing but revenge!" Watanabe jumped out from behind the desk and stepped toward the door.

Will backed up against it and put his hand out to stop him. "Whoa, whoa. Hold it."

Watanabe stopped beyond Will's reach, his eyes darting frantically as he bounced back and forth on his feet, as if he was waiting to run. "Get out of my way."

Will stared back, his whole body tense. He sensed something was coming—but Watanabe's lunge was too fast.

He grabbed Will's throat and choked him hard as he pulled him away from the door.

Still blocking the door, Will tore at Watanabe's hands. He had to free himself.

He struggled to breathe. Watanabe was cutting off his . . . weakening . . .

Self-defense class!

Will brought his hands together, fingers interlocked into a single fist. He jabbed straight up with all his remaining strength between Watanabe's arms.

That broke his grip.

Will brought his clenched hands down hard into Watanabe's nose.

Watanabe staggered back a step.

Will sprang forward and drove his knuckles full-strength into Watanabe's throat.

Watanabe crumpled into a heap on the floor. He crawled away behind his desk, gasping for breath.

"I'm calling the police," said Will.

"You can't accuse me! I didn't do anything!"

"That's for the cops to decide."

Watanabe stood.

Will braced for another attack.

Watanabe hovered behind the desk, tense, his eyes flicking between Will and the door. He suddenly turned, unlocked his window, and slid it open.

"Go ahead, call for help," said Will. "The more people we have up here, the better."

Watanabe looked out, then took hold of the window frame, put his foot on the sill, and lifted himself into the breach.

"You'll break your neck!" shouted Will, alarmed.

Watanabe crouched there, looking down.

"Get down. If you've done nothing wrong, the police are no threat."

Watanabe's weight shifted forward.

"Jirō, this is ridiculous! Get down!"

Watanabe coiled his legs, let go, and leapt.

Will ran to the window, looked down in fear—and saw a deep hole in the snow that filled the courtyard's pool. Watanabe had made it just past the pool wall. From the shape of the hole, which had collapsed in on him, Will guessed he landed almost flat on his stomach. Was he injured? Conscious? Even alive?

There was a stirring in the snow. Watanabe stood, covered in white. Will almost laughed with relief—until Watanabe started climbing out. There was no recourse but to watch as the snowman ran, limping, for the parking lot.

Will burst into David's office. "He jumped out the window!"

"What?"

"He tried to throttle me, but I hit him and he backed off. Then he opened the window and jumped."

"Did you call an ambulance?" asked David.

"He made it into the courtyard pool. The snow broke his fall. Then he ran to the parking lot."

David turned to look out the window, Will joined him, and they watched taillights, dim for their thick coat of snow, leave the lot.

"Damn," said David. "I should've thrown 'paper.'"

139

Malik decided the simplest place to beat King to death would be at King's apartment. He needed to get in a hard swing with a length of heavy pipe right at the start. That would keep King from getting off a scream that would bring the neighbors.

The bigger question was, when? If it was tonight, the police would be busy with King when Trinh's disappearance came to light. If the police discovered the servers and the website, they'd blame King. It might even look like the *yakuza* had been behind it all and had killed him. The police would eventually put the whole thing to rest.

It was unlikely they would find the servers, though, and mixing King into the mess could divert attention from Will. Would it be best to wait a few days before killing him?

But if the police already had Will in custody, King's death could make Will look innocent. Besides, once they discovered Trinh was gone, what if King put it together? He could easily have surmised Malik was up to something illegal. What if he threatened to go to the police with his suspicions? He might not stay quiet—not without an ever-increasing price.

Still, there's no need to be hasty. I can kill him just as dead tomorrow night.

He still had Zo6 to kill.

No, King came first.

Suddenly, the microphone in David's office came to life. Malik listened. Watanabe . . . out his window? And fled?

Oh, this was interesting indeed.

140

HASEGAWA'S ADVICE TO WAIT AND NOT WORRY LASTED for two hours before Kurimoto's instincts—which he also said were important—were screaming that she had to go. She did not bother to change clothes. She just bundled up, grabbed her keys, and headed for her car.

It was afternoon when she left, but a car sliding sideways in the icy slush triggered a head-on collision far ahead of her. That turned a fifty-minute drive into three hours. It was dusk when she arrived, and after trying Trinh's phone one more time, she entered the library. She searched it from bottom to top, asking students whether they had seen Trinh, but came up empty. She took a quick pass through the classroom building, cafeteria, gymnasium, café, and finally, to the east dorm, where Trinh's room was.

Kurimoto knocked on Trinh's door. No answer. She tried the knob. The room was unlocked, but dark. She stepped inside and turned on the light. Everything seemed in order. Her purse was on the desk. She checked it and found a wallet, but no phone.

She was about to check the bathroom when the other Nguyen woman, Huong, burst in and said something excitedly in Vietnamese—before she saw who it was and stopped dead. Kurimoto smiled. "Hello Nguyen-*san*. I was looking for your friend Trinh. Have you seen her today?"

Huong shook her head. "Did Peregrine-*sensei* or Grames-*sensei* call?"

"No. Why? Is something wrong?"

"I cannot find Trinh all day. She is gone this morning when I waked up."

"Gone?" asked Kurimoto.

"I sleeped on her bed last night. She sleeped in my room, I think, but this morning there is no Trinh, and my blanket and my pillow are gone."

"Show me, please."

Kurimoto followed Huong and looked over her room. It, too, looked perfectly in order except for the missing things from her bed. She was about to ask for more details when there was a commotion in the hall. Huong stepped out, followed by Kurimoto. Someone was saying breathlessly, ". . . stood on the sill and jumped!"

"Who?" asked a head poking out of a doorway.

"Watanabe-*sensei*! He jumped out his office window!"

"What floor is that?"

"Third floor! Can you believe it?"

"Did he break anything?"

"I don't think so. He jumped all the way into the courtyard pool. He was lucky it was full of snow. I was in the library and saw the whole thing."

"Why did he jump?"

"I don't know. Grames-*sensei* must have been in his office, because he looked out the window right after that."

"He's okay?"

"Watanabe? Yeah. He ran off."

"I'll be back," Kurimoto said, and she hurried to the elevator.

Kurimoto heard enough within her first five minutes in the courtyard that she called Hasegawa straightaway. The detective's response was short and direct. "Call the local police. Have them pick up Watanabe. Then find Grames and sit on him. I'm leaving now."

It took a few minutes, but once the local police understood the situation, they said they would go after Watanabe immediately and send an officer to the university. Next, Kurimoto headed to Watanabe's office. It did not surprise her to find people there looking out the window. She escorted them out one by one, asking each what had happened. None were eyewitnesses. She wrote down their names nevertheless.

With Watanabe's office closed and a sign on the door forbidding entry, she set out in search of Will. His office was unlocked, but he wasn't there, so she knocked on offices. She could see from the lights under the doors which were occupied. The third one she knocked on was David's.

"Come!" she heard him call out.

Kurimoto opened the door and found David and Will standing at the window. She flashed them her most disarming smile. "Hello, professors. I'm sorry to trouble you, but I heard something so shocking. Professor Watanabe jumped from his office window."

David motioned to the chairs. "Please, have a seat. You're in luck. Will was there and can tell you all about it."

It didn't take Kurimoto long to make thorough notes of what Will had to say. His assurance that Watanabe did not know Trinh was missing did nothing to assuage Kurimoto's dark sense of foreboding. She would have preferred to go in search of Watanabe, most likely the cause of whatever had happened to Trinh. But she had a responsibility to keep track of Will and David until Hasegawa arrived. So she dragged out her talk with them. Finally, after directing them to wait for Hasegawa, she sat in the chairman's office, facing David's, making sure they stayed put.

∼

Will told David, "I'm scared."

"We're just going to tell Hasegawa all the same things we told Kurimoto," said David.

"Not about talking to the detective. I'm scared for Trinh. This is . . ."

"Yeah, I know." David had a look of concern—for Will. He thought it might be best to distract him from his worry. "When you tell the story about Watanabe, Hasegawa's going to ask if you defenestrated him."

"What's that?"

"The act of throwing someone out a window."

"There's a special word for that?" asked Will.

"There is in English."

Will shook his head. "How do you know these things?"

"The law is a constant teacher, my friend."

WHEN HASEGAWA ARRIVED, IT SURPRISED KURIMOTO THAT he'd brought Ogawa from forensics. "Sir, we don't have a request yet to start an investigation into Trinh's disappearance."

"We have an open investigation here at JGU, don't we? While Ogawa was driving—badly; we're lucky to be alive—I called the dean's assistant to start a formal request. The university is the Nguyen woman's official sponsor, so they can act on this. Yoshida is off to an academic conference. She can't reach him until tomorrow, so we're left with Satō. Anyway, I want to hear what the Americans have to say."

Kurimoto gave a one-minute synopsis of her interview with them, then stepped across the hall and ushered Will and David into the chairman's office. It was the same discussion she had just finished, and Hasegawa's reactions paralleled her own. He was unconvinced that Will had acted purely in self-defense. Why were they carrying on their own private investigation without notifying the police? Lastly, it was deeply disturbing that Will occupied a central position in both the Ikenami and Nguyen cases. As a precaution, when the interview was complete, Hasegawa told the local officer to collect passports. He also had Ogawa call police headquarters in Nagano to get the Immigration Bureau to block Will, David, Watanabe, King, Malik, Itō, Satō, and Yoshida from leaving the country.

GIVEN WHAT WILL HAD SAID, MALIK WAS THE NEXT PERSON on Hasegawa's list.

Malik looked as if he was trying to look innocent. "I don't understand."

"Watanabe told Grames that you started the rumors," said Hasegawa, with Kurimoto translating.

Malik was leaning back, his hands relaxed on the arms of the chair. "What rumors?"

"Of Ikenami's death."

"But that's not a rumor, you know. He's dead, isn't he?"

Despite herself, Kurimoto let the edge of her anger show as she narrowed her eyes and set her jaw. She could feel Hasegawa's frustration, too, so she did not answer Malik.

Malik dropped his hands and shifted his weight. "Well, you know, we talked about things. Maybe something he heard from me, but I heard new things from him, too, you know. It was just talking, right? You know, no one knows what's happening and everybody's sort of wondering and talking and then you maybe hear things and, well, you know."

Kurimoto glanced at Hasegawa, but he kept his eyes glued to Malik. "You were trying to start a new rumor."

"Oh no. I just talked a little, and all so private-like, you know. And I was just sort of telling him what I heard."

The officers waited.

"What new rumor?" asked Malik.

"Grames is having an affair with a student."

"He is? So it's true? I heard that. I think it's awful. And I don't think it's the first one. Or maybe not, you know."

"The student is now missing."

"She left the university?" asked Malik.

"No, she has disappeared."

"Oh no, that's awful. She must have run away."

"Unlikely."

"You think he did something to her, like he did to Ikenami-*sensei*?"

Kurimoto sensed Hasegawa was ready to explode. Part of her wished he would. She waited. Hasegawa stood. "We will speak again tomorrow. In the meantime, you will surrender your passport to the local police."

"My passport?"

"Do you have trouble hearing? Yes, your passport!"

"Oh, well, okay, you know, if that's what you want."

"What I want," said Hasegawa in English, "is the truth."

～

HASEGAWA CHECKED HIS WATCH AS THEY MADE THEIR WAY TO the east dorm: 7:11 p.m. Kurimoto called ahead, so Huong was waiting. She reported she had kept her and Trinh's rooms closed and no one had been inside since Kurimoto left. Hasegawa set Ogawa to processing the two rooms while he and Kurimoto escorted Huong to the small lounge by the elevator. Word spread, and when they finished thirty minutes later, a gaggle of over two dozen students crowded outside the door.

Hasegawa had Kurimoto talk to them. "Thank you all for your concern. Ms. Trinh Nguyen may be missing. She was last seen last night at about eleven o'clock. Anyone up after that who saw or heard *anything,* no matter how unimportant, please wait here. Please do not talk to each other about it. We need your raw accounts. Others' stories might bias you."

Not a single person walked away.

Worry increased on Kurimoto's face. "Looks as if we need a list."

"Have Huong-*san* do it. Schedule them at five-minute intervals. I want to see anyone who knows anything *tonight.*"

141

LAURIE CALLED WILL AND TOLD HIM, "THE POLICE CAME TO the house and asked for your passport."

"Did it upset the girls?"

"I told them they're collecting faculty passports until they solve the case. Can you do anything more there? Should I come get you?"

"Yeah. David will stick around and keep an eye on our boy."

"You don't think it was Watanabe, even with him jumping?"

"Not after what he said."

"Who then?"

Will paused. "In the van."

142

WITH TRANSLATION, MANY OF HASEGAWA'S FIVE-MINUTE talks turned into ten. As the hours stretched on, it was harder to sit still. It frustrated him to the point of anger. The process was torturing Kurimoto, her anxiety was rubbing off on him, and there was so little information.

Ogawa was waiting for them when they finished at 0:08 a.m. "I processed both rooms. I've got fingerprints to check, but apart from that, I have only two things to report. First is the relative lack of prints in E610, Huong's room, where she thinks Trinh slept last night."

"Show me," said Hasegawa.

Ogawa walked them to Huong's room and let himself in. "She gave me the key." He handed it to Hasegawa. Students followed, so Hasegawa closed the door.

Ogawa gave them a tour of drawer handles, the desk, the window frame, and a dozen other places that should have had fingerprints. "There's nothing here, not even smudges. One of the Japanese students helped me interview the young woman about her cleaning habits. She said she's cleaned none of those spots since she got back after the New Year's break. Some she doesn't think she's ever cleaned."

"What's the other thing?"

Ogawa stepped over to the bed. "She told us her bedding was missing, so I processed everything here especially carefully. Look down here." He knelt by the foot of the bed and pointed to the floor below the corner of the bed frame. "See this? Looks like dust? I collected samples from below both corners at the foot of the bed, and below the center of the head of the bed."

They were all on their knees now. Hasegawa straightened up and rubbed his forehead.

"What?" asked Kurimoto.

Hasegawa didn't answer as he stood.

"What is it?" she asked Ogawa.

Ogawa hesitated, still kneeling, and looked up at the detective.

Kurimoto stood.

"Collect your things," Hasegawa told Ogawa. "Seal the other room. Have Huong-*san* get whatever she needs out of here. Then seal this one too. We'll be out presently."

Ogawa stood. "Yes, sir."

As the door closed, Hasegawa stepped closer to Kurimoto. He could see her consternation, but he had to tell her, so he kept it clinical. "The particles he found . . . it's what rubs off at the attachment points between metal and rope or twine made from natural fibers, particularly the rough, inexpensive—"

He stopped as she wheeled around, her hands covering her eyes.

Hasegawa suggested Kurimoto take a walk while he pushed the paperwork forward for a formal investigation. He started with the dean's assistant, but she still hadn't been able to reach Yoshida. He tried President Satō, who seemed to be waiting for the call. He gave Satō a brief explanation, during which Satō gave no signal he was listening or understanding. When Hasegawa finished, Satō remained silent.

"Excuse me, are you there?" asked the detective.

"Yes."

"Do you want to file a formal request for an investigation? I can have one faxed to you immediately."

"Such a hurry . . ."

"Certainly."

"As I was about to say, wouldn't a hurry warrant a call hours ago?"

"We moved as quickly as we could. We had to ascertain basic facts."

"I suspect you tried to contact Yoshida hours ago. Yet I am hearing from you for the first time now, in the middle of the night."

"He lives here. You live in Tokyo."

Satō was silent.

"I can fax you the form."

"I don't have a fax machine here."

"Your local police can deliver it to you."

"You needn't trouble them. I'll have fax access in the morning."

"We were hoping for your cooperation but will investigate regardless."

"Investigate? What about Yoshida's improprieties? You haven't even looked! Our accounting people told me. You want my cooperation? Why do you ignore me? Don't tell me you need my help and then—"

Hasegawa hung up on him and checked his watch: 0:39 a.m. He went to find Kurimoto.

Kurimoto was at the administration building's main entrance. She looked at Hasegawa expectantly. "You got the request?"

"Forget it. What do the local police know about Watanabe?"

"They're contacting his family and people who know him. They seem to be covering every avenue, but they had no progress to report. I told them to contact us if they need any support."

Hasegawa spoke with confidence. "They'll turn him up."

Kurimoto looked at him uncertainly. "Then we wait?"

"Until morning, yes."

"Where's Ogawa?"

"I told him to check whose passports they've collected and then go straight back to the station." Hasegawa took a step toward the parking lot and told Kurimoto, "We'll take your car."

She didn't move. "I feel we ought to be here."

Hasegawa glanced back at her before he said softly, "Yoshie . . ."

He rarely addressed her as "Kurimoto," let alone used her first name, so it was no surprise she hesitated. "Yes?"

"You want to beat down every door, squeeze people until they confess, *fix it.* I don't want to sour you on a police career, but that frustration, resign yourself to it—now. The worse the case, the more frustrating. From this moment on, this feeling will gnaw at you almost every day. You put up with it and keep going, because you never know when you'll break the case."

She blinked and looked away. "I understand."

He walked toward the lot, and she followed.

"Which car is yours?" asked Hasegawa.

"The white Honda Fit."

Kurimoto was pulling out when she said, "I get what you said about the feeling, but . . ."

"What?"

"I hate it!"

Hasegawa closed his eyes. "Good."

143

Z06 SAT IN HIS CAR, PARKED OUTSIDE HIS HOUSE, AND stared out the window.

Pay-per-view. How many saw? The site was down now, but that was probably because the murder had gone out live. Why else would it still be down?

Each livestream had a window where subscribers could chat about what they were watching. What were the comments last night? Derision as he fumbled trying to tie her up, laughter as he . . .

It would only take one phone call. These people weren't his friends. One with enough conscience to draw the line between rape and murder would end it all. One anonymous call.

Yet who'd alert the police to a crime he took part in by paying to watch?

Someone with a shred of decency. Someone who hadn't flushed what insignificant life he had down the toilet. Someone who had the sense to give a false name and address on his subscription application.

He caressed the steering wheel.

Someone with something to live for besides a car.

144

DAVID NEVER STAYED THIS LATE, SO MALIK ASSUMED HE was waiting for the police to leave. When they did and David stayed, Malik realized David, right next door, might be watching him. He could do nothing with an audience, so he left his office noisily, locked it with a great jangling of keys, and tromped into the stairwell. In the parking lot, he started his car and headed home.

Malik waited half an hour before going back to the university. As expected, David's light was out and his car was gone. Malik hurried to the library building. He carried a small flashlight, as well as a laser pointer to blind the camera in the basement hallway long enough to get past. It was risky, but after the detective's questions, he had to remove the hard disks. The only remaining evidence was that video. At least it was encrypted. Should he also swap out Trinh's wireless AP tonight? It might be safer to wait. Either way, he'd take one of the original non-camera APs from the closet, since he might not get back in for days or weeks.

The university buildings were closed and dark, so Malik made sure no one was watching before he entered the library. He headed for the stairs and trotted down to the landing between the ground floor and the basement. He turned on his flashlight and fished his master key out of his pocket again. Itō would lock the basement doors, after all.

Malik stopped before he reached the bottom of the stairs. He stared, dumbfounded, at the doors. There was a chain wrapped through the handles. It was padlocked.

X

Return on Investment
投資利益率

Monday, 18 January 2010

145

HIS WIFE WAS SNORING SOFTLY, SO HASEGAWA ROLLED HER gently onto her side. She got back to town while he was interviewing students at the university. He was glad. Better the occasional snoring than sleeping alone.

5:42 a.m. Better yet, actual sleep.

As he closed his eyes, he was staring at the bed in room E610. He saw the twine tied to the bed frame, to her ankles and wrists, as she lay there, dead. It was the only explanation. From what Kurimoto said on the drive back from JGU, Trinh was not the kind to succumb without a fight. The attacker either had a weapon—at her throat the moment she woke up, or she'd have screamed—or he beat her unconscious before tying her down. His escape: she was bound and gagged, unconscious, or dead. There was a minuscule chance he kidnapped—

Hasegawa fumbled for his phone as it buzzed and answered quietly, "*Moshi-moshi.*"

"Sorry to call you at home, sir, and so early—oh, sorry, this is Kurimoto." She'd obviously been crying.

"I know," he whispered. "What is it?"

"He threw her out the window, didn't he?"

Hasegawa was quiet for a few seconds. "Call Ogawa. He needs to head there now. Have him get the avalanche dog."

"Yes, sir."

"Then tell him to call the local station. I want four officers with shovels to meet us at the university, and we'll need some from Nagano to control the crime scene. How quickly can you be ready to go?"

"I'm ready now."

"I'm not. We leave the station at six thirty."

146

AS MALIK ATE BREAKFAST, HE SORTED HIS PRIORITIES FOR the day. Number one was getting the hard disks. Itō would lock the doors to the basement again tonight, so he would have to do it while the IT Services staff were there. They would attend to things elsewhere, but he had no way of knowing when. He'd still have to get past the camera Itō had rigged on the hallway ceiling. Early morning, when Itō was there alone, might be the best time, but it was already a quarter to seven. Malik ate faster.

After lunch, he needed to go grocery shopping. He was almost out of bread and eggs.

Maybe I can kill King in the afternoon.

No, evening would be better. He could scout it after the store.

He also needed an escape plan if things got out of control. But how without his UK passport? It had the entry stamp Japanese immigration would look for when he tried to leave the country.

The trickiest thing—even more important than the hard disks—was getting Will arrested. The rumors had put Will in the detective's sights, but Hasegawa had done nothing. Watanabe must be their prime suspect after disappearing like that. He needed something to force Hasegawa to act on Will.

And dish soap. He forgot last time. He grabbed a piece of paper. For the groceries, at least, he needed a list.

147

Aren't you going to work?" called Zo6's mother through the bedroom door.

"No."

She slid the door open. "Are you sick?"

"Yes."

"Then we should go to the doctor."

"If I need one, I'll go myself."

She knelt next to his *futon.* "Your office—did you call them?"

"No."

"You should do that. Let me get your phone for you."

"No."

"You need to—"

"It's none of your business! Get out!"

"Don't talk to me that way!"

He pulled the quilt over his head and lay there.

"Fine. If you want food later, come and say so."

148

Hasegawa thought it best to have Kurimoto drive, even as emotional as she was. It would occupy her for the hour it would take to get to JGU. Lest thoughts of Trinh still intrude, Hasegawa asked about their other cases. "How are the searches going for Ikenami and Watanabe?"

Kurimoto said, "In English, they'd say, 'Ikenami's gone cold.'"

Hasegawa frowned. "A little too apropos."

"I'm sorry, sir. I wasn't being flippant."

"We still have no clue where to search?"

"If he was murdered in his office, the killer concealed the body."

"We might never close this."

"Unless we get a confession," offered Kurimoto.

"Watanabe?"

"He must be guilty of *something,* no matter what Grames said last night."

"Where is the flying squirrel?" asked Hasegawa.

"Local police have staked out his home, and he's not with family."

"Still driving?"

"Possible," said Kurimoto. "We got his credit card and bank records in the night. He hasn't used his credit card or ATM card. If he's on the road, it's all cash. Or he might've paid cash for a rail ticket."

"He could be anywhere, if he had enough cash with him."

"Yes, sir, so I was thinking . . ."

"Go on."

"What if he had little cash? Where could he stay on the cheap?"

Hasegawa nodded. "You'd start with . . . ?"

"Local love hotels."

149

WATANABE ROCKED ON THE BED IN HOTEL AMORE AS HE tore at his fingernails. The police were certainly looking for him by now, and they surely suspected him of Ikenami's murder.

At least he didn't break his leg. His ankle was terribly swollen, enough that walking wouldn't be wise—

"Wise," he said aloud, pressing his palms to his eyes.

When was I ever?

What about Trinh? What if she was missing like Will said? Why would she run away? Was Malik right? Was she pregnant?

That would mean she'd lied when she said the rumor wasn't true.

Yet why else disappear? If Will did that to her, he'd pay with his life!

But then her baby would have no father. He couldn't do that to Trinh—

Unless . . . I became the baby's father . . .

Finally, a ray of hope.

First, change hotels—as far out of town as the gas in my tank will get me.

150

ALTHOUGH HE FELT UNHYGIENIC, MALIK SKIPPED HIS morning shave and shower and made it to the library at 7:32 a.m. The basement doors were unlocked. Malik cracked one open and peeked down the hall. The IT Services office door was closed. If Itō was in there and not the server room, Malik could walk right past and blind the camera with his laser pointer. Then he'd power down his system and pull the disks. He'd wipe everything for fingerprints and be out before Itō opened the office. But if Itō was in the server room, it would be impossible to get past him.

Malik crept to the fire door, slipped his hand in, and snapped a picture of the server room.

Itō.

151

AS DANNY LOCKED HIS CAR, DAVID WALKED BY AND ASKED, "You found one?"

"Yeah. It won't turn any heads, but the price was right."

At the administration building, David seemed about to say goodbye, so Danny said, "If you've got another minute . . ."

"Sure. What's up?"

"That's what I wanted to ask you."

David looked surprised. "What do you mean?"

"There's something funny going on."

"Funny?"

"Poor choice of words. Not funny at all. Something . . . not to be melodramatic, but it feels . . . vile."

David did not respond, but his smile was now gone.

Danny spoke soberly. "You know what it is. I haven't been here long, but I'm not blind. You and Will Grames are . . ."

David was looking past Danny. He turned and saw a line of four police cars coming up the entrance drive, red lights flashing. They quickly parked. As the police streamed out of the parking lot, Danny recognized Hasegawa and Kurimoto, and he counted ten others. "That's a lot of cops."

David said gravely, "Like you said, something's vile."

152

WILL HAD BEEN UP IN THE NIGHT, SO HE KNEW IT HAD snowed heavily. It was deeper despite significant compacting. Areas of snowpack undisturbed since the original *neyuki* were not much deeper than Will was tall, despite meters of snowfall.

As Will parked the minivan at the university, Laurie asked, "We don't get to see what's going on, do we?"

"David said it looked like they'd be digging. Best if I wasn't around."

"We go to Japanese class?"

Will nodded. "By the time we're out, Matsuyama-*san* will have found out what's going on. No one's as connected as she is."

LAURIE AND HER JAPANESE PROFESSOR TALKED FOR A FEW minutes, alone, before Will came into the room.

"No students in your class, either?" asked Laurie.

Will shook his head.

"I guess we go see."

The snow was too deep for many students to venture near where the police were digging into a high berm of snow next to the east dormitory. At least thirty, though, were leaning out of dormitory windows. Laurie and Will found David, Danny, and Anson on the second floor of the library. They were watching out a line of windows with two dozen others, all staff, since the library, while unlocked, was not actually open yet.

"Are they still digging?" whispered Will.

David nodded.

Laurie whispered back, "I see no—"

A shovelful of snow flew out of the hole.

"They had to dig that deep?"

David shrugged, his brow knit in worry.

Over the next fifteen minutes, as flurries started again, students began to ignore the library's posted hours and filter in. There were hushed conversations, but Laurie, Will, David, Danny, and Anson watched in silence.

The police officers around the hole motioned for the few students nearby to move back, then kept them going until they had them out of the space between the dorm and the gym. An officer approached with a German shepherd on a leash. The digging stopped and two officers emerged from the hole. A murmur rippled through the library as the dog's handler bent and took off the leash.

The dog put its nose to the snow, approached the hole, sniffed, and disappeared into it, but it scampered out a few seconds later. The police backed away as the dog moved along the great pile of snow that had fallen from the dormitory roof. After only a few yards, it started back. It moved back and forth, narrowing the search, then stopped a yard from the hole and dug into the snow. The handler approached and pulled the dog away. The two officers with shovels started digging.

From their vantage point in the library, the spot was behind the top of the berm, which soon obscured the hole. As the diggers slowly sank, the crowd in the library unconsciously inched toward the windows, many holding themselves as if standing on the edge of the hole. Laurie thought of how close Will and Trinh were. She knew if the diggers found what they were looking for, she'd have to hold it together for Will. He was in worse shape every day, his shoulder tic now totally out of control. She sidled closer to him, took his arm, and held tight. She looked over the faces of the students leaning out of dorm windows and saw Huong watching from a room on the third floor, directly over the hole.

Suddenly, the diggers emerged with their shovels.

The library was perfectly still.

Hasegawa jumped into the hole, bent over, and disappeared. Laurie waited, tears welling in her eyes, hoping for the detective to reappear and set the officers back to digging. But moments later, Huong's scream ripped through the frigid morning air, and Laurie wailed as Will collapsed in her arms.

153

THE PARKING LOT WAS SO FULL OF POLICE CARS BY THE time Malik returned to the university, he had to park by the Conference Center. He rushed to the main courtyard, but there was no one there, so he circled around and entered the library. There was a crowd by the windows on the north side, so he hurried upstairs before anyone saw him. The third floor wasn't empty, so he went on to the fourth. There were students watching from dorm windows, but he could not see what they were looking at. Then he saw snow being shoveled between the dorm and the gym.

It was only a moment that he watched, heart racing, before he did his best to walk nonchalantly to his office.

154

WILL STARED OUT THE WINDOW IN CHIEKO'S OFFICE, WET handkerchief in hand. Chieko and Laurie sat crying. David sat in a chair next to Chieko. He said to Will, "You're putting too much stock in what you heard seconds before the guy jumped out his office window. She talked to him and wound up murdered *that night.* Will, it's got to be Watanabe."

"You didn't see the look on his face. He had no idea Trinh was missing. He's not that good an actor. Malik's name came out only because he thought Trinh had already told me. It's Malik. I'd stake my life on it."

David frowned. "You may get that chance."

"How can this happen here?" asked Chieko as she sobbed.

David asked in a gentle voice, "When does the dean get back?"

"I called him right away. He leaves now and will be here after noon. But he already say to stop all business school classes. I called Yuriko and told her. Then President Satō announce all JGU classes are suspended."

Laurie asked, "What will happen?"

David rubbed his forehead. "The police intensify their dragnet for Watanabe. They interview Malik again. And us again. I expect the gloves are off. If they don't like someone's answers, that person's driven off to Nagano for interrogation."

Laurie looked anxiously at Will.

David kept his voice down. "Leaping from a third-story window trumps any duplicity by us. Anyway, if it's Watanabe, they'll find him. If it's Malik—"

"It is," said Will.

David went on. "Then we have to hope the police take him before they take us."

Laurie stood and joined Will. "How do we make that happen?"

Will rubbed her arms. "We pray he panics first. And we make it happen *today*."

155

Someone knocked on Malik's door. He debated whether to respond. Sooner or later, Will and David would go to one of their offices, and he wanted to listen. But if it was the police and he seemed to be hiding, it would draw suspicion away from Will. Will had to get arrested *now*.

Malik turned on the light, opened the door, and was surprised to see Danny.

"May I come in?"

Malik stared at him. "Yes, I guess so."

Danny didn't sit. He looked earnestly at Malik. "I believe there is something underhanded going on at JGU."

Malik's eyes narrowed. "Under who's hand?"

"Something bad."

"Oh yes, I think so. You're right. I'm worried, very worried."

"I believe it has something to do with you."

Malik opened his eyes wide. "You think I did something?"

"No. Sorry. I believe someone may be trying to blame you."

"Blame me? For what?"

"Ikenami and Trinh's murders."

Malik stood, his mouth gaping. "Trinh Nguyen, the first-year student?"

"How did you miss this? Someone attacked her, murdered her, and threw her out of the dormitory window."

"When?"

"The police found her body this morning."

"So you think someone's trying to blame me?"

"Peregrine and Grames. Possibly with help from Itō in IT Services. I suspect they're trying to get you arrested—soon, maybe today."

"Did you tell the police?"

"No."

"Why not? You should."

"No proof," said Danny. "I won't point the police at people on a hunch. For all I know, they're innocent and you're the guilty one. I hope the police put away whoever did this—forever. But faculty have no business arranging who gets taken, so I'm here fulfilling my moral obligation to warn you."

"I think you should, you know, talk to them, to the police, I mean."

Danny stood. "No. I warned you. My conscience is clear. If you're innocent, I wish you well today. If not, I hope you burn in hell."

"But . . ." The words died on his lips as Danny turned and walked out.

Malik stared at the door for a minute before he locked it and turned out the light. Back at his desk, he donned his headphones.

My surprised look was good. He believed it, stupid Australian. Probably descended from penal colony stock.

He switched between the various microphones.

How to get Grames arrested *today* . . . ?

156

S OMEONE WAS SERVING SOMETHING USING THE UNIVERSITY network, Itō was sure. They killed Ikenami for merely suspecting. Whatever it was, though, was gone now. Outbound traffic was down by eighty percent. Oddly, the ridiculously high internal DNS traffic remained. Where was it going?

Itō scanned the server room.

One of these machines . . . and one of these hundreds and hundreds of wires . . .

A physical search, unplugging wires one by one, shutting hardware down piece by piece, could take the whole day.

He sighed.

I better put on a sweater.

157

Your relationship with Watanabe-*san*, what is it?"

"Oh, we both work here, you know," answered Malik.

Hasegawa scowled, so Kurimoto did not bother to translate. Hasegawa leaned forward, and said through Kurimoto, "In case you are unaware, we found one of your students murdered this morning. One of the last people she talked to was Watanabe. Do you know what they talked about?"

"Why would I know? I wasn't there. I don't know anything—"

"They talked about you and the rumors you are spreading."

"I told you I only talk a little about what I hear, and only when other people sort of bring it up. I hardly talk to anyone. And Ikenami-*sensei* was maybe my best friend on the whole faculty. And I have no reason to—"

"Why were they talking about you? Why did Watanabe say he got all the rumors he spread from you?"

Malik stayed cool. "Oh no, I don't think he said that. That would not be true. You know, I heard most of these things first from him."

Hasegawa glared at him, and Malik glanced toward the door.

"Ikenami-*san* thought IT resources were being misused. He wanted to be on your IT committee. Saturday evening, Watanabe talked to Nguyen-*san* about you, and that night, someone murdered her."

"I thought you said the murder was last night."

"No."

"Then how did you find her body this morning?"

Hasegawa set his jaw. Kurimoto did not hide her contempt. "You cannot pretend you are not central to all this."

"Yes I can. I don't know why you talk to me. I couldn't hurt anyone. Trinh was an athletic girl. Do I look like I could murder her? Do I look that strong? I don't think so. And Professor Watanabe, you know, I don't know why he would blame me. I thought we were friends. But you know, there is so much discrimination here, so many people hate foreigners. But I thought, you know, maybe Watanabe was different."

Hasegawa told Kurimoto in Japanese, "Handcuff him. We'll interrogate him at headquarters."

Suddenly Malik sat forward. "How do you know what they said? Did Trinh tell you? Did Watanabe tell you? I bet it was Grames. Someone, Danny Charles, the new English teacher, he told me Grames and Peregrine and Itō are trying to frame me, make it look like I'm a murderer. Grames has always hated me. I don't know why. I never did anything to him. Maybe it's because I'm Malay. Grames is a racist and a liar if he told you. He lies to students about the university and President Satō, to his wife about affairs with students, to everyone. I really did hear he was sleeping with Trinh. I heard she was pregnant. Ikenami-*sensei* knew, I think, and that's why Grames killed him."

Hasegawa sat back. His face showed nothing, but Kurimoto could see a smile in his eyes. He waited a few seconds, staring at Malik. "Who told you Nguyen-*san* was pregnant?"

"Who? Oh, I don't know."

"Surely you remember hearing something so shocking."

Malik spoke slowly again. "Well, you know, like I said, hardly anyone talks to me. So what I hear is, you know, sort of hearing what other people say, you know, to each other. So I can't maybe remember who was talking. And I never told that."

"Our source says you told Watanabe that, and we heard it from no one else." Kurimoto leaned forward and added, "And believe me, professor, we've talked to so many people, we've heard *everything*."

"Maybe it's not true. I hoped so. That's one reason I never told anyone. And Trinh was a good student. I wouldn't spread a rumor that would sort of destroy her reputation, you know, especially if I don't know if it's true."

Hasegawa was quiet.

"You should talk to Grames. He was the last person to see Ikenami-*sensei* alive. And everyone was talking about his affair with Trinh. I don't know how you can say I'm a central person. He is much more central than me. I hardly have anything to do with anything. I'm hardly even, you know, in the circle. Even a big circle. And I don't think it's right to blame this on me because I'm a foreigner. And to accuse me just because Grames said something. I don't think that's fair. You can ask anyone what a liar he is. Maybe they won't know, but some will."

"Not fair," said Hasegawa with a slow nod.

"Not at all. But I'll cooperate with you. Like now. I am answering all your questions even though you are, you know, sort of being unfair to me. So talk to Grames. See what he says. See why he wants to blame it on me. I can wait. I'm not going anywhere. Just ask him some questions and try blaming him. But you shouldn't be so unfair, you know, to me, I think."

～

Hasegawa said through Kurimoto, "I'm sure it won't surprise you that Malik-*san* denies starting any rumors. He says what you told us about your conversation with Watanabe is a lie."

Will's demeanor was intense. "When you find Watanabe, he can answer that for you. I believe Malik murdered Professor Ikenami, used my argument with him for cover, and is using rumors to focus your investigation on me. The solution to this puzzle is in the university's IT and he does not want you to dig there. He's been doing his best to frame me, pulling Watanabe's strings."

"'Frame.' That's the same word he used about you. He also told us Trinh was pregnant, and that's why you murdered her." Kurimoto saw Will's hands tense. "He says Ikenami knew, so you murdered him."

"Trinh and I were friends. My daughters think of her as a big sister. I told you about the pregnancy rumor Malik tried to start through Watanabe, but Watanabe wasn't willing to spread it. For him to say that's why she was killed . . ." Kurimoto saw his jaw tighten. "He's still using rumors, even after she's dead. You'll do an autopsy, and you'll see she wasn't pregnant. You'll find Watanabe. He'll tell you."

Hasegawa was silent. Kurimoto looked at him, unsure whether to go on with questions of her own. Hasegawa was merely watching. As Will pulled out his handkerchief, Hasegawa pursed his lips and exhaled.

"Do you have any more questions?" asked Will.

Hasegawa was still watching him.

"Because if you don't, I'd like to sit with my wife and figure out how to tell our daughters Trinh is gone."

158

TWO HOURS LATER, WILL CLOSED DAVID'S OFFICE DOOR and asked, "Is it safe to talk here?"

"Hey, it's you and Itō he's worried about, not me."

"You remember how I told you there's nothing with the body that the police could tie to me?"

"Oh no," said David.

"No, it's not anything right there with the body. I've been looking all over for the gloves I wore the night I was digging."

"Did you ever take them off while you were out there?"

Will said, "Yes! Leather gloves and a hat, I was so hot. I have the hat, but . . ."

"If anyone finds them, can you say you lost them?"

"Yeah, but what was I doing there?"

"Acting like a moron," muttered David.

"Yeah, thanks. Thanks so much. What am I supposed to do when they melt out in the spring a few yards from the body? Your sarcasm's going to make this go away?"

"Calm down. Think! *If* they search the field—Wait, where in the field?"

"I was a third of the way into the parking lot from the Conference Center side. I walked straight out into the field, a straight line . . . maybe twelve meters, into the *susuki* where it was high and thick."

"A third of the way, then twelve meters? Are you sure? You couldn't find the body when you looked," chided David.

"I've thought about it a thousand times. I'm sure I'm remembering it correctly now. When I dug, I was a little too far west. I couldn't have missed by more than a meter, two at the most."

"I swear, Will, that field is the most idiotic move I can imagine."

Will asked, "You think I don't know? I don't need you telling me I screwed up. What I need is a way to get out of this mess!"

"Keep your voice down."

They looked at each other in tense silence.

David rubbed his face. "Okay . . . okay . . . body in the field . . ."

Will waited, and David looked at him.

"What?" asked Will.

"Okay, I told you before, it would be a bad idea to move the body."

"Yeah."

"As your lawyer, I cannot advise you to do anything illegal."

Will said, "But . . ."

"But if you *were* to move it, how could you be sure to find it this time?"

"Best thing: use a dog like the cops did. Second best, walk a grid over the area, punching a pole into the snow like an avalanche searcher, until I hit something."

MALIK LEANED BACK AND SHOOK HIS HEAD AS HE SMIRKED. Ikenami was on campus the whole time! What was Will thinking putting the body there? It was hardly hidden. If the police had ever brought the search dogs here, they would have found him. Was he planning to leave the body all winter and let it appear in the spring?

This idiocy was Malik's salvation. He could alert the police to the—

How could he explain knowing where it was?

He could make an anonymous call.

Stupid.

And when they found the body, then what? There was no guarantee they'd find Will's gloves.

ANSON LEANED ON THE HALLWAY WALL. WILL AND DAVID were his friends, two of the most decent people he knew at JGU. They couldn't—

Suddenly David's door opened, Will appeared—and stepped back in astonishment when he saw Anson.

Anson popped up off the wall and looked at Will.

Will glanced back into the office, looking worried. A second later, he stepped aside as David emerged.

"Hi Anson," said David. "I was going to the café to buy Will a cup of coffee. Why don't you join us?"

"I . . ." Anson was back on his heels. He looked at each of them, then toward his office. He answered timidly, "No thanks, I don't drink coffee."

"Oh, yeah. Cocoa, then." David locked his office door.

"I should get back to—"

"Nonsense." David extended his arm as he took a step and caught Anson at the waist. Anson stared, bewildered, at David as they veered down the hallway together. What he'd heard couldn't be true. He knew they were good men.

But if you *were* to move it, how could you be sure to find it this time?

Anson stopped. David and Will halted a step beyond, turned back, and looked at him as if to say, "What's wrong?" Under their critical gaze, Anson said, "David, Will, let me be honest with you. I overheard something just now. I was about to knock when I heard you tell Will to keep his voice down, and . . . well, I should've knocked, but I listened instead."

David folded his arms. His voice was quiet. "What did you hear?"

Anson glanced back and forth at them before he whispered, "Talk of moving a body."

Will looked at David. David kept his eyes on Anson. No one moved.

Finally, David spoke in a low, somber voice. "Anson, you've made some big decisions in your life. I daresay you've made them all correctly, so far." He paused and stepped closer. "You're about to make another. I'd rather you didn't do it in this hallway."

None of them had coats, so as Will and David slow walked Anson from the café back to the administration building, they held their drinks snugly—two medium coffees and a large hot cocoa—drawing warmth through the paper cups.

"Why didn't you call the police?" asked Anson.

"I panicked. If someone saw the argument, saw him fall, and told the police . . . I had visions of Japanese prison for the rest of my life."

"You didn't touch him?"

"No, but when I found him, I thought I'd caused it. He stepped back because, for that moment, my temper got the better of me."

Anson frowned. "Not to be judgmental, but I wish your compassion had gotten the better of you when you discovered him."

David took a sip of coffee. "We think Malik killed him. Murdered him. It's connected to IT here. He's doing something twisted. Itō is digging, trying to figure it out, and he's found serious irregularities, but so far, nothing conclusive."

"I guess what we're asking for—" began Will.

"Is for me to stay quiet," said Anson.

David nodded. "In a nutshell. Not for long. We'll solve it soon."

"Soon," repeated Anson. "You realize that means nothing."

"There's no schedule. It breaks when it breaks. But we're close, I'm sure."

Anson looked pained. "In the meantime, his family agonizes."

David was stern. "If we tell, the police take Will and Malik gets away with murder."

"Just what are you waiting for? What will suddenly change?" asked Anson.

"Itō says he's close, and whatever it is, it was worth killing for," said David.

Anson looked at Will. "This will not end well. Even if you prove someone murdered him, that it was Malik—even if you can tie him to Trinh's murder too—it's . . . bad. You reap what you sow, Will. I understand it sounds like a cliché," he looked Will in the eye, "but it's true. Bad does not beget good."

Will sighed, eyes down. He looked back at Anson. "Just so it doesn't beget unspeakable horror. Or, if I'm allowed to hope, let it beget the killer convicted without my role having to come out."

"Facilitated by my staying quiet," said Anson.

"That is all we ask," said David.

Anson looked at David. He looked at Will. At length, he spoke. "Sometimes you're sure what to do because it's obvious, such as calling the police when you find someone dead. Sometimes, although it's not obvious, you can feel what to do, such as guiding a friend through his legal morass after he moves the body instead of reporting it."

"Which one is this?" asked David.

"Neither." Anson took a long drink of cocoa and walked again.

David asked, "What are you going to do?"

Anson studied the snowy sidewalk for a few more steps, never looking up. "Pray until I get an answer."

159

Itō was radiating confidence. "The answer is in the odd DNS traffic. I'm sure."

It was 12:46 p.m., Hasegawa was tired, and the passion in the IT manager's voice made Hasegawa uncomfortable. The detective closed his eyes, his jaw set, and gave Itō some time to calm down.

As he waited, he could hear Kurimoto tapping her fingers on the arm of her chair. She was far too emotionally invested in the case, but he couldn't yank her back now. She would just have to deal with the pain and remember not to do it again. Some things are most effectively learned the hard way. Still, Hasegawa knew it was his fault. He should have given her a good verbal slap when he first saw it. His fault or not, it left him feeling a pressure he'd never experienced: needing to solve a case for the emotional well-being of another officer—and she wasn't even his partner.

"Fine." Hasegawa was gruff. "Let's assume you're right. How do we turn odd traffic into evidence with a name on it?"

"Find out where it's coming from and where it's going," said Itō.

"Sounds simple enough. Why haven't you done it?"

Itō's weariness showed. "Because the outgoing DNS traffic stopped the night Trinh was murdered. All we have left is the odd internal traffic, and I can't track it."

Kurimoto interjected, "It must be tagged with an IP address."

"That's the weird thing. It's not," said Itō.

She looked at him quizzically. "Then how can it be DNS traffic?"

"Now you see my frustration, and my conviction that this puzzle's the key."

Kurimoto said, "Someone's disguising network traffic as DNS packets to skirt filters."

Itō nodded. "Yes. But it's encrypted. Now the staff is physically disconnecting systems one by one to find the source. It seems to be coming from the dorms."

Kurimoto folded her arms. "That's a wireless LAN, right?"

"Yes. The traffic could come from anywhere," said Itō. "All someone needs is the network password. It could even be someone unconnected to JGU. With so many people privy to the password, there's little point in having one."

"The encrypted packets have to be routed somewhere, right?" asked Kurimoto.

Itō sat back and nodded.

Hasegawa saw the hunter in Kurimoto's eyes as she leaned forward. "Then it can't be someone from outside. The decryption key must reside on one of your routers."

160

W ILL SLIPPED INTO DAVID'S OFFICE.
"What's up?" asked David.

"A single glimmer of hope in an otherwise demoralizing day."

David waited.

"I found my gloves," said Will.

"That's more than a glimmer. Where were they?"

"The bottom drawer of my desk."

"You're hopeless. You realize that, right?" asked David.

"A minor celebration is in order. Buy me lunch."

"I bought you coffee."

Will said, "Okay, I buy you lunch."

~

MALIK TOOK OFF HIS HEADPHONES AND LISTENED TO THEIR footsteps disappear into the stairwell.

Gloves. Worn while digging, they had to have Will's DNA in them.

161

WHEN WILL AND DAVID ARRIVED AT THE CAFÉ, ANSON and Miho, sleeping baby strapped to her back, were finishing a late lunch. They had eaten in peace at the café for the first time since their baby was born. The pall of Trinh's murder kept away the normal crush of cooing students. As Miho headed for the door, Anson stepped over to Will and David's table and said, "Come by my office."

~

WILL KNOCKED ON ANSON'S DOOR THIRTY MINUTES LATER.

"Come in."

As David and Will stepped into the office, David asked, "What's up?"

Anson was dour. "My answer."

David raised an eyebrow. "I figured, 'pray till I get an answer,' was your way of saying we had the time we needed."

"No, sorry, I meant exactly what I said." Anson motioned to the chairs and David and Will sat.

"I will not turn you in—"

"Thank you," said Will. "We *will* find the killer."

Anson narrowed his eyes. "Fast, I hope."

Will smiled. "Count on it."

David said gravely, "I don't think that's what he means."

Anson leaned forward on the desk. "David, as a lawyer, you're in a unique position. You're obliged to stay quiet."

David waited.

"Correct me if I'm wrong, but if I stay silent, I become an accessory."

"After the fact."

Anson looked down. "If that comes to light, they can prosecute, convict, and fine or imprison—or more likely, deport me."

"In the very unlikely event that it comes to light, yes."

Anson sat back with a frown. "Understand, Miho isn't American like Laurie. If they deport me, it would be . . . well, the end of the world."

David asked, "How long are you giving us?"

"I still think you talking to the police would be the simplest, cleanest option. I'm sure my coming forward now isn't the right thing to do, but neither is waiting indefinitely—or very long. The police need information I have; I'm duty-bound to give it to them. Ikenami's widow is going through hell. That must end."

"When?" asked David.

Anson leaned forward. "I got the answer, 'a day.' It wasn't the answer I wanted, so I pushed for more time."

"And?"

"The answer remained 'a day.' That's for a 'smoking gun' kind of arrest."

David frowned. "When you say 'answer,' you mean what, like a voice?"

"Don't," said Will.

David looked at him. "You realize how important this is? This could—"

"David, if anyone knows . . ." Will looked past Anson, out the window. "I'd do anything to have that Sunday night back. I'm staring at the end of everything good in my life—and it's the most terrifying . . . It's as if I'm standing in front of a train, watching it barrel down the tracks at me, just standing there, unable to move."

David said, "I can only imagine, but—"

"You can't begin to imagine. We'd be asking Anson to join me on the tracks, David, to wait there, one step behind me. I can't ask that."

David sighed deeply and shook his head. "What happens after a day?"

Anson shook his head. "I wish I knew exactly. If the police find a smoking gun, so to speak, and it's all over, I can probably forget I ever heard anything."

"'A day,' what does that mean?" asked David.

Anson rubbed his forehead. "I'm not sure, but . . . twenty-four hours, more or less."

David frowned in frustrated resignation. "That'd be a day, more or less."

162

IT HAD TAKEN HOURS TO PROCESS THE CRIME SCENE AND send Trinh's corpse to the medical examiner. At 4:10 that afternoon, Hasegawa called to get an estimate of when an autopsy would be performed. The medical examiner answered, "Minimum, four days; maximum, a full week."

"Why so long?"

"She was frozen when she arrived. It's not like we can put a corpse in the microwave and hit 'defrost.'"

Hasegawa said, "No, I wouldn't expect—"

"We must keep her in a refrigerated environment, so the external tissue doesn't degrade before the internal organs thaw."

"Can you tell me anything now, given the condition of the body?"

The medical examiner was matter-of-fact. "He bound her. She was strong. She fought—hard. The abrasions are deep, and they suggest cord, such as packing twine, not rope."

"That fits with the crime scene. Can you guess as to cause of death?"

"I took a preliminary look and there appear to be petechial hemorrhages inside her lips and nostrils. I'll have to wait to examine her eyes. It's likely suffocation with something like a pillow, as I didn't see bruises that would suggest either ligature or manual strangulation. But this is premature. I can't even give you preliminary toxicology. Again, it will be days before I have anything definitive."

Hasegawa rubbed his forehead. "So whether she was pregnant . . . ?"

"We'll have an answer in . . . let's say five days."

"And DNA from the likely sexual assault?"

"Another two to four days after that."

Hasegawa was silent.

"I'm sorry, detective; we just have to wait. If you're wondering how to proceed in the meantime . . ."

"Yes?"

"My suggestion: gather your suspects in a cell and lock the door."

163

THAT EVENING, CHIEKO, STILL AT WORK, WAS SURPRISED TO get a call forwarded from the university's main phone number. It was from Trattoria Napoli.

"We have a student here, a young woman named Huong Nguyen."

"Is there some problem?"

"She's upset. We've tried to ask her what's wrong, but she doesn't understand. We hoped you could come."

"Yes. I'll come right away."

Chieko slipped on her boots, grabbed her coat and bag, and locked up the office. She was already on the stairs when she thought to tell Will she was leaving. She hurried back to his office and knocked. When he opened the door, she motioned for him to step out into the hall. She whispered, "The Italian restaurant called. Huong-*san* is there, and something upset her. Malik does nothing strange since we talked, but I cannot help watch anymore. I must go help Huong-*san*."

CHIEKO SPOTTED HUONG SITTING ALONE AT A TABLE LITtered with tissues. Chieko hurried over and sat next to her, but before Chieko could speak, Huong held out her phone.

Chieko took it. "What's wrong with—"

"Read it," said Huong, pointing frantically at the phone.

Chieko looked at the screen—and blanched.

> sorry I missed you saturday night. but i'll see you soon enough.

It was from Trinh.

∽

Kurimoto looked drawn after the wrenching morning and a day of translation and IT work with no break. At 7:07 p.m., Hasegawa suggested she call it a day, take the car, and return to JGU in the morning, but Kurimoto resisted. "Sir, I think I would be of most use with the IT staff."

Hasegawa gave her a dour look but relented. "I suppose having an officer monitoring their search—"

Hasegawa took the ringing phone from his pocket. After listening, he said, "We'll be right there," and hung up.

Frowning, he told Kurimoto, "Sorry, but I need you to translate."

"What is it?"

"Our murderer sent a message."

164

As Will sat down across from David's desk, the worry showed on David's face. "You look like you saw a ghost."

"I got a phone call," said Will.

"From?"

"No name, a woman, foreign accent, so I'm guessing a student. She said she saw what happened on the stairs and she's been feeling as if she ought to go to the police."

"Then why was she calling?" asked David.

"She wants to talk first, listen to my side, because she's afraid going to the police will ruin me, and she doesn't want to do that unjustly."

"Sounds positive."

Will shook his head. "Here's the weirdest part. She says she's in Nagano, that she was heading to police headquarters but had second thoughts. She wants me to come to Nagano and talk to her."

"Definitely weird."

"I don't see that I have any choice."

"It's snowing again. It'll be a long drive, and it's almost eight," said David.

"I don't know how long the talk will take, either. But it's not as if I have anything else going on." Will stood.

"You're going?"

"Have to. If a witness comes forward, everything falls apart. I've got an address in Nagano where she says she's waiting."

"Just . . ."

"What?" asked Will.

"Be careful, especially in what you say. This feels . . ."

"I know."

~

MALIK SAT WITH HIS FEET UP ON THE DESK, LEANING FAR back, grinning at the ceiling. The girl had performed flawlessly, and he would show his appreciation soon enough. The address she gave Will was a downtown office building. By the time he looked around, worried, looked some more, finally gave up, and drove home, Malik would be prepared. He would tell the police he caught Will digging and that Will ran when confronted. When the police dug deeper into the snow and found Ikenami and Will's gloves, they would arrest Will. He'd be helpless in the face of Malik's accusation, because he'd have no alibi. It was brilliant.

And no less brilliant was sending the text to Huong from Trinh's phone. The police would search for it and find it hidden in Will's desk. If only he could have seen Huong's face!

Malik listened as Will left. Seconds later, Will was jogging through the snow to his vehicle. Soon, taillights lit the parking lot red, and the minivan accelerated away, its headlights a great stream of white peering into the snowfall.

Malik slipped into light gray sweatpants and a windbreaker to blend in with the snow. On his way toward the Conference Center, he made the briefest of stops in Will's office, where he deposited Trinh's phone and retrieved the gloves Will wore while digging.

165

HASEGAWA SPENT MOST OF THE TIME AT TRATTORIA NAPoli waiting while Kurimoto and Chieko tried to calm Huong. His patience seemed to pay off. Huong had stopped crying. Now Chieko was asking whether there was a friend whose room she could share for the night. It surprised him when Danny entered the restaurant and strode over to their table.

"Officers, I wanted to talk to you."

The ladies looked up in surprise, but Hasegawa simply glanced around for another chair. As Danny sat, Hasegawa said nothing. He checked his watch: 8:24 p.m. He looked at Danny expectantly.

Danny looked earnest. "There is something quite wrong at JGU."

Hasegawa nodded.

"Lines are being drawn," said Danny.

"Lines?" asked Hasegawa in English.

"Peregrine and Grames on one side, Malik on the other."

Hasegawa waited, but Danny said nothing more. Through Kurimoto, Hasegawa asked, "Do you have information for us, or only suspicions?"

Danny sat back and frowned. "For now, suspicions. It will take some time to explain, but I believe you ought to hear them and how they lead back to the university—tonight."

166

Malik's plan was brilliant in its simplicity. Once he found Ikenami, he would plant the gloves close enough to the corpse that the police would find them when they retrieved the body, but far enough that Will could have lost them while unsuccessfully searching days ago. Then he would regale the police with the story of how he found Will digging in the field tonight, and how Will ran off.

Malik had bought a bamboo pole and a shovel today and secreted them outside the Conference Center. Now he took the pole and walked to the spot in the parking lot that Will had described, one-third of the way from the Conference Center. He put on snowshoes—the snow was far too deep to walk in—and headed due south into the field, measuring out four lengths of his three-meter-long pole.

Malik pushed the pole into the snow until it hit something solid. He moved the pole thirty centimeters and pushed it in again. Same depth. With that baseline, Malik spiraled his way out from that spot. He pushed the pole in again and again, always to within a few centimeters of where it had stopped before, as the spiral grew.

It was hard work pushing the pole through the compacted snow. The first meter out from the center took him twelve minutes, and the next, forty.

He was fifteen minutes into the third meter and losing hope when the pole came up thirty centimeters shallow. He moved it and pushed again. Shallow. He worked the pole around over the next few minutes. The shallow spot was about the size of a human torso.

Malik left the pole stuck in the snow and headed for the parking lot. He tried to run, but in the snowshoes, he ended up hopping. He amused even himself. Would the youngest of his lady friends giggle if he donned her bunny ears and hopped about on the snow for her? At the parking lot, he released the snowshoes and scampered to the Conference Center to retrieve his shovel. He peered up at the normally cursed snow. It was pelting him, thick, fast, and wet, and for once, he didn't care. Soon, snowshoes on again, he was ready to dig.

As difficult as the search had been, digging was far worse. Malik didn't last five minutes before he had to stop and rest. As he worked his way down, he had to throw the snow higher to get it clear of the hole. He had to rest after every three shovelfuls. He checked the time. Thirty minutes of digging so far and half a meter of the densest compacted snow to go. He decided to concentrate on one spot and try to get to whatever was underneath.

Ten minutes later, Malik pushed the shovel in and struck something hard. A troubling end to his hard work; it didn't feel like a body at all.

Oh! He's frozen!

Malik laughed out loud as he dug in little shovelfuls down the final twenty centimeters and found . . . a coat!

Malik jumped up and down with glee, dropped the shovel, and did a victory dance in the snow.

A coat!

He punched the side of the hole like a boxer working over a heavy bag.

I'm a genius. I'm a bona fide, unstoppable, world-conquering genius!

Malik realized he had to calm down and finish.

But he was a genius! He laughed again.

With the body found, Malik pondered where to place Will's gloves. Close enough and far enough at the same time . . .

Or Grames could lose the gloves tonight!

Why hadn't he thought of it before? Even simpler, it was all the more brilliant! Will didn't leave them when searching days ago, but tonight when Malik caught him digging and scared him away!

Malik dropped the gloves and stopped to consider whether to sprinkle snow on top, when suddenly, from above him on top of the snow, he heard, in thickly accented English, "You lose something?"

A chill ran from the backs of Malik's knees all the way up to his scalp.

It was Hasegawa.

167

THREE DARK FIGURES, SILHOUETTED AGAINST SNOW BATHED in red, looked out through the wall of glass on the Conference Center's second floor. There were lights flashing on so many police cars that the vast open field looked like hell itself, and the falling snow like blood floating down ever so slowly in great crimson drops. The three had watched the return on their investment since before the digging began, all in perfect silence. Their hate for the man the police were leading away was too visceral. There were no words that intense.

As a forensics team set up lights to start the work of uncovering Ikenami's remains, David took Will's shoulder in his hand and squeezed hard. Will, who had merely gone home for a few minutes, sure that Nagano was a ruse, blew his breath out slow and deep and studied the sky. Itō pressed his lips together, straight and tight, in what might have been satisfaction, but without the slightest hint of joy.

Suddenly, behind them, the door flew open with a bang. The three turned in unison to see Danny trotting toward them. He called out, "I stayed to help with Huong, and . . ." He stopped next to David and stared out at the scene below. "Sod it all, I missed it."

XI

Degrees of Freedom
自由度

168

H ASEGAWA LIT ANOTHER CIGARETTE, TOOK A DEEP BREATH, and blew a long stream of smoke toward Malik. After a few more leisurely puffs, he said, through Kurimoto, "I want to hear the story again."

"Story?"

Hasegawa smiled. "Yes. It is so imaginative. Please tell it again."

"What story?" asked Malik.

"About digging in the snow."

Malik leaned forward on the table. "It's like I told you. I sort of overheard Grames tell Peregrine he hid the body, you know, in the field. He told Peregrine right where it was. I thought someone needed to do something, so when they left, I went over, you know, hurrying over to the spot and started digging. I couldn't stand Professor Ikenami's widow worrying, so tragic. And the body was exactly where Grames said it would be."

"How clever of you."

"Not such a big thing, really. It was, you know, sort of my duty. Anyone would have done it, maybe, don't you think?"

"So thoughtless of Grames to speak in front of you."

"Well, you know, he's sort of . . . I didn't think it was, you know."

"You wouldn't say it was thoughtless of him?"

"Of him?" asked Malik. "Oh, well, you know he's kind of not so bright. I guess you can know that from what he did with the body. Pretty stupid, I think."

"What was the first thing that went through your head when you heard him say where it was?"

"The first thing?"

Smoke rose in a narrow stream from the tip of the cigarette as Hasegawa held it and, still smiling, stared at Malik.

"I didn't think about anything," said Malik.

"When you heard them talking about the body, what went through your mind?"

"About the body?"

Hasegawa scowled at him. "Yes, what was your first thought?"

"First . . . was . . . you know . . . I don't know."

Hasegawa narrowed his eyes.

"Or maybe I thought how terrible this is. Yes. And how I thought it was Grames all along. And I thought, oh, how tragic, that I was right."

"Never occurred to you, for example, to call the police?"

"Oh, you know, I have great respect for the police. Japan is so safe."

"You didn't call us."

"Oh, I guess . . . I couldn't believe what he was saying at first. So I thought . . . sort of, I should maybe investigate before I trouble the police. It was kind of hard to believe, don't you think?"

Hasegawa nodded. "Terribly hard to believe. You are so thoughtful not to trouble us."

"Oh, not so much. I try, that's all. We all have to be something."

"The gloves. Tell me about them again."

Malik gave him a look as if he didn't understand. "What gloves?"

"The ones in the snow."

"The gloves? I found them, that's all. I was digging. That's how I found them. I thought it was odd, sort of. But I didn't think about it so much."

"That's what you said."

"He . . . you know, I think he dropped them. He must have."

"That's why they were perfectly dry?" asked Hasegawa.

"Oh, I don't know. I think maybe they were sort of wet and snowy, you know, when I found—or not wet. They were snowy, I think. But you know things can be sort of dry in the snow. Snow isn't so wet, I think. You can shake it off or something. It's so cold, things stay sort of dry."

"You know what I think, Professor Malik?"

Malik smiled inquisitively.

"No, of course you don't." Hasegawa took a long drag on the cigarette, leaned on the table, and blew it hard into Malik's face again. He smiled at Malik's sour expression. "I think I am tired of listening to your lies."

~

Two hours later, Kurimoto was pouring a cup of coffee when Hasegawa approached. "Don't drink that."

"Sir?"

"It'll keep you awake."

Kurimoto said, "It'll be a long—"

"Not for you. Go home."

"I'd like to see this through, hear him confess."

Hasegawa lowered his voice. "You'd like to jump out of your chair and punch him in the face."

"Wouldn't everyone, sir?"

Hasegawa fought hard and suppressed his smile. "Yes, but I learned something about you earlier today."

She looked at him, baffled.

"You're an expert in Krav Maga."

"Yes . . ."

"You sent an academy martial arts instructor to the emergency room."

"Inadvertently, sir. I thought he would move in the other direction."

"So I don't want your career ended over human refuse like Malik."

"I have no intention of—"

"You don't, but that doesn't mean you won't," said Hasegawa.

"I can assure—"

"You're too involved." His voice was sharp as he brought it down even lower. "At least be honest with yourself about that."

She scowled, looking away.

"Listen, Malik's stupid act could last for days," said Hasegawa. "We can't both work him to the breaking point, so we'll tag team him. I'll take the rest of tonight with another interpreter. You interpret tomorrow when our normal shift takes over. That way, one of us is always here."

Still frowning, Kurimoto nodded understanding.

Hasegawa blurted out, "Why Krav Maga? Why not *karate*?"

She smiled as she poured out her coffee. "There was this American TV show named *Alias*. The heroine was awesome. I wanted to kick ass like her, so . . ."

It was 3:42 a.m. and Hasegawa was weary, so he chose a large pair of officers to do some screaming. He watched through the mirrored glass as Malik cowered before of them. How much longer would he last? He seemed distraught, but every time they posed him a question, he either told the ridiculous story or he talked and talked, saying nothing. It had flustered Kurimoto when she had been translating. It took her a few passes to realize it was not an issue of lacking English fluency; he really was talking gibberish. At first, Hasegawa had assumed Malik was simply an idiot. But the more he watched, the more he suspected the odd mannerisms—the imprecision, his inability to understand even simple questions, oblique statements that weren't actual answers, the appallingly poor memory—were all carefully crafted. So, too, surely, was the cringing.

An officer was throwing chairs. Nice touch.

Tears.

Were they persecuting him, as he said, violating his fundamental rights? Hasegawa wondered how common discrimination was. He hadn't seen it as far as he knew, but he had no experience outside of Nagano prefecture and this was his first murder involving a foreigner.

Oh, the officer flipped over the table!

MALIK LAID HIS ARMS ON THE NOW UPRIGHT TABLE, RESTED his head on them, and tried his best to concentrate on the silence. It was a welcome respite after the yelling. It was likely six a.m., but they had taken his Rolex, so there was no way to be sure. He couldn't tell by how tired he was, because they kept bringing him coffee. It helped too. He calmed himself with the warm steam rising out of the tall cup, pretending he was at Starbucks watching girls order their coffee, imagining what they'd look like naked. Each time he played his coffee game, he appeared to be more cooperative, and they eased up on him. They gave him the fourth cup a few minutes ago, and Malik desperately needed a restroom. When they brought the last cup, he'd asked them, but the officer didn't understand.

They would be back soon.

He sat up and took another sip.

If the police had shown up an hour later . . .

It was too risky to tell them about catching Will digging in the field and scaring him off. There was no telling how long they'd been watching.

So what were they doing now? He'd given them no facts to check.

They ought to slap handcuffs on Grames.

And they would if there were anyone left who had seen Ikenami fall. He would kill Zo6. All he needed was a free day to get to Tokyo and a hammer; just bash the bastard's skull in, laugh, and walk away.

Suddenly, the hair on Malik's neck stood up.

What if Zo6 is the reason I'm in custody? What if he talked?

The caffeine accentuated the sudden tremor in his hand, so he set the cup on the table with both hands. He closed his eyes and tried to focus. He crossed his legs.

Damn, I need a restroom.

169

HOBBLING FROM HIS CAR TO HIS OFFICE, KING OVERHEARD a clutch of students talking as they waited for the university bus.

"It was Malik-*sensei*?"

"They took him away last night. Didn't you see all the lights?"

"He killed Ikenami-*sensei*?"

"How did you miss this? They were out there digging for hours."

"In the field?"

"By the Conference Center."

"He really is dead?"

"You're hopeless."

King didn't slow his pace or show any interest, but he smiled as he headed for the elevator.

They caught the son of a bitch. It's about time.

King slumped into his office chair and perched his injured foot on his desk. He reviewed his work for Malik. Was there any evidence of his role in whatever scheme was so nefarious that Malik had murdered to hide it?

King woke his PC and started deleting the files he had created for Malik. King's name was nowhere to be found in any of them—he'd been careful of that—but now they needed to disappear. He opened his email, but his Malik correspondence was all JGU business.

If the police ask, I can say I did some work for Malik. If I don't deny it, they can't catch me in a lie.

He could deny he knew what it was for, though. There was no evidence he designed the site. If they tried to say he was Malik's partner, he'd challenge them to find a money trail. It was all cash, so there was no trace. King frowned. All but that last payment was gone for good.

170

AFTER EITHER WORKING ON OR OBSERVING MALIK ALL night long, Hasegawa turned the interrogation over to another detective and went home to rest. It was only nine in the morning when the telephone woke him from a sound sleep. He rolled over, picked up the phone, and mumbled, "*Moshi-moshi.*"

"This is Kurimoto. I'm sorry to bother you at home, sir, but something has come up here—"

"The suspect confessed?"

"No, sir. It's . . . I'm not sure what to say."

Hasegawa yawned. "I'll believe anything at this point."

"It seems he may be innocent."

Hasegawa rubbed his eyes. "Say again?"

"Innocent. It looks like he might be telling the truth."

"Impossible."

"One of the other faculty, a foreigner, came to the station this morning. We're hearing things that corroborate the suspect's story. He says someone moved the body."

171

DAVID RUSHED TO WILL'S OFFICE AT THE SIGHT OF THREE police cars, lights flashing, pulling into the parking lot. Not bothering to knock, he opened the door and found Will staring out the window.

"You have any idea what this is?" asked Will.

"Not a clue."

David joined Will at the window and watched as Hasegawa, Kurimoto, and four uniformed officers strode toward the building.

"Malik had an accomplice?" asked Will.

"Could be King's not innocent after all."

"He's not part of the murder. Can't be."

David shrugged. "Do we wait circumspectly here or go upstairs and watch them haul him away?"

"I don't suppose we know what else is going on. There aren't enough degrees of freedom in this—"

"Degrees of what?"

Will said, "Our minuscule information isn't enough to account for all the variables—"

Will and David turned toward the door in surprise as they heard footsteps approaching. There was a loud knock.

Will looked at David quizzically before he said, "*Dōzo, o-hairi-kudasai.*"

Two uniformed officers entered, followed by Hasegawa, who announced, through Kurimoto, "William Grames, you are under arrest for the murder of Kiyoshi Ikenami."

One officer approached Will, turned him around, and held him in place as the other officer cuffed Will's hands behind his back.

David stepped around the desk and told Hasegawa, "Hold on now. You caught Malik. He was out in the snow *with the body*! You can't believe Professor Grames is the murderer."

Hasegawa stood stoically.

"On what evidence? What could make you think Will is guilty?"

"A witness came forward this morning to confirm Malik-*san*'s story, another professor at your university, Cook-*san*. He says Grames-*san* put the body in the field, just as Malik-*san* says."

Hasegawa turned to go and David looked back in shock at Will. "Stay mum," he ordered quietly.

"Call Laurie," Will responded as they pushed him out the door, his shoulder spasming.

172

KING WAS IN THE MEN'S ROOM ON THE THE SECOND FLOOR of the administration building and saw the police walking to their cars in the parking lot, leading Will in handcuffs.

No way in hell. It was Malik, you morons!

What was he supposed to do, open the window and yell at them? Explain that he knew Malik was guilty because he wrote code for him?

No, far better Grames in handcuffs than me.

King frowned as the cars pulled out, lights still flashing.

He headed back to his office on his crutches.

There's no point in feeling guilty. I can't go to the police.

He let out a long sigh.

Okay, if they try him for murder, maybe I can do something. But until then . . .

173

WILL PROTESTED, "THE GLOVES, I'M TELLING YOU, THEY'RE not mine. A DNA test will prove they belong to Danny Charles. You know he didn't kill Ikenami because he was in Tokyo that day."

Hasegawa said, through Kurimoto, "DNA test takes many days. And I am not asking about the gloves."

"Don't you see? Malik was trying to frame me with the gloves because I talked about them. He planted bugs, microphones, in our offices. Knowing he was listening, I talked about the gloves, and he took the bait and tried to plant them where Ikenami's body was."

After listening to the translation, Hasegawa leaned forward. "It is the body I am interested in. How did he know where to find it?"

"You're assuming he did not put it there?"

"Why would he?"

"To hide it, obviously."

"Why, if he is framing you?"

Will sat back, jaw clenched.

Hasegawa leaned back. "To frame you using the fall on the stairs, as you claim, he wants us to find the body, to see the bruises. He wants someone to hear the argument and come to the police and tell. To hide the body makes no sense."

"But the gloves. Why did he have Danny's gloves with him where he was digging? That makes no sense either."

Hasegawa sat back and lit another cigarette.

"You are the last to see Ikenami-*san* alive." Hasegawa exhaled smoke. "You admit arguing with him. You never told it, but now you admit he fell on the stairs in your argument."

"What did the autopsy reveal? Did he die from the fall?" asked Will.

"You tell me."

"I don't know what killed him, but I'm sure it wasn't the fall."

Hasegawa nodded.

"But the gloves: you don't need to wait for a DNA test. Ask Danny. He'll tell you how we set up the whole ruse, and that the gloves you found are his. If Malik was planting gloves, it proves he's guilty!"

"It proves that Malik-*san* stole gloves. We can settle whose soon enough."

"Then let's settle it, and you'll know Malik is the killer!"

Hasegawa frowned as he shook his head. "Grames-*san,* you are smart. Tell me, use all your intelligence and explain so rationally: how did you know where the body was?"

"It's Malik that says that, and he's a liar—and a murderer!"

"Why does Cook-*san* also say you know the location? Is he a liar too?"

Will sat back again. Hasegawa had him cornered. Will glanced at the door, then back at Hasegawa, who was calmly drawing another breath through his cigarette as he stared at Will.

It was a lost cause—the hollow in Will's insides testified to it—but he sighed and affected his most sincere attitude. "I don't know what Anson heard. I don't know who he thought was talking. I have no idea."

174

DAVID STOOD, ARMS CROSSED IN IMPATIENCE, AS HE WATCHED Itō type at a computer in the server room. "How much longer?"

Itō didn't look up. "Not a long time."

"We don't have any time. We need conclusive evidence now."

"Con . . . ?"

"We need proof it's Malik," said David.

"And I need to search. There is no short time way. Let me work now."

David frowned, hands on hips. He was turning to go when he saw Itō pick up an electronic device shaped like a short wand. "What's that?"

"Toner."

"What does it do?"

Itō looked distracted. "We use it to trace wires."

"Will it take long?"

"It will take more time if we keep talking."

David shut up, and over the next five minutes, he watched the IT staff file into the server room.

"Is there a meeting?" asked David.

Itō said something in Japanese and the staff all started taking up sections of the raised floor. Underneath was a veritable spaghetti bowl of wires, hundreds upon hundreds, going all directions.

Itō turned to David. "We follow all above floor wires and compare them to server room schematic chart. All wires match schematic. Now we check to see if there are extra wires under a floor."

The staff gathered around Itō and he showed each of them a different sheet of the server room schematic drawings. One by one, they set off on their tasks. Finally, Itō asked David, "Would you like to follow the main line to the ISP?"

"Anything that helps us get this done."

Itō walked him over to a small electrical box. "This switch is interface that changes from our copper LAN cable to fiber-optic cable to ISP. You see two cables, just as it should be. Now we follow fiber-optic line."

"Using the toner?"

"No, that is only for copper cable. We follow with eyes and fingers."

David nodded and started tracing the fiber-optic line down to where it dipped under floor level. With some of the floor tiles out already, he could keep following the cable across three sections of the floor. "I need more floor removed," said David.

Itō hurried over and took out another section, then waited for David. After another couple of feet of tracing the cable, David frowned.

"Problem?" asked Itō.

David slipped his hand under a mass of cables. "The fiber-optic cable disappears under this bunch of stuff, but if I can get my hands underneath it a little . . . bit . . . farther—"

David looked up at Itō in surprise.

"What?" asked Itō.

"Is this cable supposed to attach to something?"

"Just attach to another cable."

David pulled gingerly on what he had found, and it moved. He slid it out from under the mass of cables. It looked exactly like the copper-to-fiber-optic switch they had been looking at two minutes ago, except that this one had three wires going into it instead of two. David looked at Itō again. "What's this?"

Itō knelt and examined the box before he glanced at David and smiled. "A back door."

175

I T WOULD BE IMPOSSIBLE FOR LAURIE TO GET TO NAGANO and back before the kindergarten bus dropped off Rachel. The question was whether to wait and then take Rachel with her to police headquarters, or to find someone to babysit and leave right away.

It would be better to have an adult there, even for Sarah and Becka, on a day this awful. That was especially true if the girls somehow found out about Will's arrest before Laurie could get back and explain the world was not ending. Laurie had used so few babysitters, though. Of course, Trinh came to mind first. At the next name, she pressed her hands to her temples and fought the rage that came with it.

Stop it. He only did what he thought was right. It was Will who hid the body.

Laurie took deep breaths. She could not cry. There was too much to do.

He can help with the trauma he's caused. He and Miho both. He can drive and translate for me with the police. She can stay with the girls.

Setting her jaw against her resentment, Laurie dialed Anson.

176

WHY IS THERE ANOTHER SWITCH?" ASKED DAVID.
Itō replied, "Someone wants to access ISP without go through JGU firewall. This is small switch but big thing to find."

"Now we use the toner thing?"

Itō pulled the toner wand from his pocket along with a tiny box. It had two wires protruding from it, each ending in an alligator clip. He pressed a button on the box and a green indicator light came on. "This switch you found has two fiber-optic cable. One goes to ISP, the other to JGU main switch. This third one is LAN cable, copper wire."

From another pocket, Itō retrieved a small knife. He gingerly cut through the outer sheath of the LAN cable and peeled it back to expose four pairs of thin twisted wires, each a different color. Even more carefully, he stripped just enough sheathing from each of the wires in the brown pair to attach an alligator clip. Then David learned why the device was called a "toner": it sounded a tone as Itō held the wand to the wire. Itō moved a couple of feet down the incomprehensible mess of cables under the floor and held the wand to individual cables until the toner sounded. By now the staff had all abandoned what they were doing, and everyone was watching Itō trace the cable. As he moved steadily across the room, staff removed sections of the floor. The process went on until they got to the wall on the far side of the room.

"What we're looking for isn't here?" asked David.

"In next room," said Itō with excitement.

Everyone hurriedly trooped out of the room and up the hallway. David asked, "What's that room used for?"

"It is a storage for library. Maybe I never go inside." Itō tried the door, but it was locked.

"Do you have a key?" asked David as Itō pulled his keys from his pocket. He tried one, and another, but neither worked. Itō glanced back at one of the staff, and the fellow took off at a full run.

"We have a key soon."

"What are we going to find?" asked David.

"Maybe computer or router, maybe more cable, like a chain."

"As long as we find the end today."

Itō looked pensive. "Yes, today, I think so."

"What's wrong?"

"Think what we will do when we find end of a cable."

"We'll see why Malik murdered Ikenami," said David.

"See how? Do not think we can open what we find and look inside."

"What do you mean?"

Itō stepped closer to David. "Someone was careful to be hiding everything and disguising network traffic. What we find will also be deep in security."

"Okay, but translate that into time for me. How long till we break through whatever security it has?"

"Do not say, 'how long.' Say, 'if.'"

David didn't try to hide his worry, but Itō offered no reassurance. Noise on the stairway called their attention down the hall. It was the IT staffer with a security guard close behind.

The guard had the key, and soon Itō was stepping through a room full of old furniture to a closet in the east wall. Itō looked back at the guard, and he inserted his master key, but the closet's lock wouldn't budge.

"He changed the lock?" asked David.

Itō frowned as he looked at the closet.

David was exercised. "Hey, we have to get into that closet—now! Get a fire axe or something. Break it down!"

As he said it, David saw Itō brighten.

"What?"

"It is closet," said Itō.

"Yeah. So?"

"Closet doors open out."

David looked at the doorframe and broke into a smile. The hinges were on the outside. They merely had to pull the pins.

177

*M*OSHI-*MOSHI*," SAID LAURIE.

"It's David. Hey, when can you leave for Nagano?"

"I just did. Anson picked me up five minutes ago."

"Well, come back to JGU and get me."

"Can't you follow?"

"Yeah, but believe me, you'll want to hear what we've found, and I can't drive and talk on the phone at the same time."

DAVID WAS WAITING AT THE UNIVERSITY ENTRANCE. HE GOT into the back seat of Anson's car, and before he closed the door, he blurted out, "Malik was piggybacking a web business on JGU's infrastructure."

Laurie asked, "How did you figure it out?"

"Itō did it. I tell you, he's good. It took so long because Malik wired his setup into the network with its own secret connection. They only started checking those connections today."

"What did they find?"

David talked excitedly. "There's a storage room in the library basement that backs onto the server room. Malik outfitted a closet there as his own little server space. He has racks of servers, routers, and I don't know how many terabytes of disk space. There are dozens of drives. It's impressive."

Anson asked, "What kind of business?"

David shook his head. "I don't know. Itō and his people are working on access, but everything's password protected. They tried getting into the files on the disks, too, but they're encrypted."

Laurie looked back at David. "How long is it going to take?"

"That's the bad news. Itō says it's unlikely they'll ever break it."

"The encryption's that good?"

David's voice sounded suddenly tired. "Remember, this isn't a team of security specialists, they're staff who set up passwords for new students."

"Can we get the police to help?" asked Laurie.

"You'd need the American NSA. Really, it may be impossible. Itō suspects there's more than encryption. The disks were mostly random noise, precisely what we'd see if Malik used steganography software to hide the files."

"Where does that leave us?" asked Anson. "Can we conclusively tie the setup to Malik?"

David nodded. "Itō was smart. As soon as he saw what was inside the closet, he told his people not to touch anything and they called the police. But I pushed him, told him Will's already in custody and we can't afford to wait. Itō had his people put on some of those white cotton gloves everyone in Japan seems to have and plug in a fresh keyboard so they could work on accessing the server. When that didn't work, they attached one of our PCs to the hard drive setup and found out they're encrypted. There's bound to be Malik's fingerprints—and no one else's—everywhere."

"But David, that won't help," said Laurie.

"I admit it's all circumstantial, but together with Ikenami suspecting someone was misusing IT resources, the pieces fit."

"That's not proving anything."

David said, "Hey, I'll take even implications at this point."

Laurie sniffed hard and looked out the window. David was quiet. After a minute, he reached forward and rubbed her shoulder reassuringly. "We'll get him out of this. I promise you. If he keeps quiet until we get a lawyer in there . . ."

Laurie opened her purse and retrieved a handkerchief. "Have you been able to find a lawyer for him?"

"An excellent criminal attorney from Tokyo. He can't get to Nagano until the morning, though. Will has to hold on for today."

Anson slowed as he caught up with a line of cars following a big rotary snowplow.

"Damn plows." Laurie glared out the window. "Is there any way to pass it?"

"If you want to end up crashed, yeah, we could try it," said Anson.

"Why can't anything just go right?" she asked as she teared up.

Anson parked the car while Laurie and David hurried into Nagano's police headquarters. When Anson got inside, he found them trying to talk to the officer at the front desk, but her English was not up to the task. Anson intervened in Japanese. "We are here to see William Grames. He is being held here. The woman is his wife, and the man is his lawyer."

"What is the name again?"

"William Grames." Anson spelled it for her.

"Please wait a moment."

As the officer made a phone call, David asked, "What did you tell her?"

"That Will's wife and his lawyer are here."

"Some lawyer," said David.

Laurie whispered, "I want to see him. I have to see him."

David put his hand on her shoulder. "He'll be okay. He needs to stay quiet for a few more hours." David looked at Laurie. "He will stay quiet, won't he?"

Laurie closed her eyes and shrugged. "He's been such a mess."

The officer hung up the phone and said in polite Japanese, "I'm sorry, but Grames-*san* is not allowed any visitors."

"It's his lawyer," said Anson.

The officer looked at David and asked Anson, "Does he have a license to practice law in Japan?"

Anson quietly asked David, who frowned and shook his head.

The officer needed no translation. She announced in English, "No visitor. I am sorry."

178

Y OU MOVED THE CORPSE FROM THE OFFICE TO THE FIELD," said Hasegawa.

Slumped in his chair, staring at the table, Will nodded as his shoulder twitched.

"Still, you insist you did not kill him."

Will was barely audible. "We had a brief argument, he apparently thought I might hit him, and he stepped back and fell down the stairs. I never touched him."

Kurimoto's voice was sharp. "Please speak up."

Will raised his voice a little. "He fell. I did not push him."

"When you found him unconscious, why didn't you call an ambulance?"

"He wasn't unconscious, he was dead. I checked."

"Are you a doctor? Can you be so sure someone is dead?"

"He still had his coat on," said Will. "It looked as if he stepped into his office and fell over dead, and the argument was four hours earlier. He wasn't lying there on his office floor unconscious with his eyes wide open for four hours. I listened for a heartbeat. I'm sure he was dead."

"Then why didn't you call the police?"

"I thought the fall killed him, that I'd be blamed, and I panicked."

"And hid his body in the field?" asked Hasegawa.

"I was going to move it into town the next night."

"It snowed, and you couldn't find it."

Will nodded.

Hasegawa had his arms folded on his chest. He sat silently for a minute, but Will never looked up.

"You knew Ikenami-*san* was diabetic?"

Will rubbed his face. "Most people knew that."

"You knew where he kept his insulin."

"No, I never saw him use it."

"You could guess," said Hasegawa.

"I don't know, maybe. Why?"

"Because you knew the fall did not kill him."

Will sighed. "Yes, I said that."

"So you killed him with his own insulin."

Will sat up. "What?"

"Do not act surprised. We suspected it early. The medical examiner will confirm it when the remains thaw and he can do an autopsy. He will tell us that Ikenami-*san* died of extreme insulin shock."

"I explained it to you. I didn't kill him. I just moved the body."

Hasegawa leaned forward. "Moved the car, moved the body, planted his phone on the bridge, exactly as one might expect a murderer to do."

"Malik killed him."

"Malik also killed the Nguyen woman?"

"I don't know, probably," said Will.

"Why? There were no rumors linking them, no rumors of an affair with him, no rumors she was pregnant with his baby. We found her phone in your office, not his office."

Will sat forward in the chair. "Malik made up those rumors. He obviously planted the phone. It's all coming from him!"

Hasegawa cocked his head to the side and stared at Will.

"I did a stupid, awful thing when I moved the body. I swear to you, I did not kill Professor Ikenami."

Hasegawa nodded. "We have talked enough about the first murder for now. Please explain now why you killed your lover, the Nguyen woman."

179

Although Laurie could do nothing to help Will, she wanted to stay at the police station. Anson suggested that with Will being held incommunicado, being home with the girls was best. Laurie knew he was right, so she made Anson try one more time, unsuccessfully, to get a message to Will before she gave up and took the long, silent drive home.

Laurie told the girls one at a time, doling out the story that each was old enough to grasp. Only three days after hearing of Trinh's murder, it was far too much for any of them. They all cried—Rachel mostly because she walked in on the tail end of Becka being told and saw Becka's tears. Laurie was a rock: no tears, no mistiness, only calm assurances that there was ample proof that Malik had murdered Professor Ikenami. She assured them the police would release Will as soon as they sifted through the evidence. She chose not to tell the girls that Will found Ikenami dead, panicked, and hid the body. They could learn about that idiocy later.

Now Laurie checked on the girls in their beds, first Sarah, then Becka, then little Rachel. All were asleep.

Asleep.

Dear God, please let Will just keep his mouth shut and sleep.

As Laurie entered her frigid bedroom, finally, the tears flowed.

180

DAVID HELD CHIEKO'S HAND AS THEY STROLLED ALONG the snow-packed sidewalk.

She looked up at him. "You did all you could."

David shook his head. "It wasn't enough."

"Your best is always enough."

"Will's in custody, his lawyer's not here yet, and we still don't know what Malik was doing."

"Do the police still keep Malik?"

David shrugged. "I hope so. His fingerprints must be all over his server setup. Itō says the cops worked on it into the evening before they sealed the storage room and left."

"There is nothing you could do there. You feel too much responsibility. You did not hide the body."

"We had it all worked out so perfectly."

"Such a clever scheme, and Malik fell into your trap, just as you thought," said Chieko.

"Damned Anson. Will would be free now except for him."

"Will would be free if he did not do such a bad thing. It is his fault. But yes, if Anson could be quiet, it is better."

David sighed. "It's like everything's black and white in his odd version of the world."

"He helped you at a police station."

"He did. He calmed Laurie down too."

"Does Itō-*san* still try to open Malik's files, or do police make him stop?" asked Chieko.

"Stopped, I assume, when they sealed up the storage room."

"We do not know why Malik killed Trinh?"

As David slipped his arm around Chieko's waist and pulled her close, he sighed in resignation. "Not a clue."

181

MALIK'S LAWYER GOT HIM OUT! IT WAS ALMOST MIRACUlous, except for the price, which was so high Malik wondered whether there was a bribe involved. Anyway, he'd been told not to leave the jurisdiction, and they assured the authorities that, without his British passport, he was not a flight risk.

Malik hadn't bothered to fold the few clothes he took; he'd just thrown them into the suitcase. The police had Will—finally—but there was no guarantee they'd settle on him as the killer. And if Zo6 talked . . .

The Shinkansen was nearly to Tokyo, but where to go from there? He'd looked into this, but the chances of pulling it off . . . ?

But I'm the genius, right?

182

KING SAT ON THE FLOOR AND STARED AT HIS WIFE'S BELligerence piled in the middle of the living room. As he sat, hating her, the image of Will in handcuffs haunted him.

The guy didn't do a thing. He's got a wife—a good one—and little kids.

Malik's the cancer. Killing that student. She didn't deserve to die like that.

King might be able to help prove it was Malik.

He pulled his injured foot as far into his lap as he could and checked the dressing. It would still be days before he could walk without crutches.

The bitch. I'll find her and . . .

Then what, really? Kill her like Malik killed Ikenami?

King frowned as he shut his eyes.

Sleep would be nice.

Malik deserved to hang. They'd need evidence, though.

King smiled wryly. He could channel his hate for his wife into sending Malik to prison. It would be a real joy to watch him squirm at a trial.

King frowned again.

As if that would do anything for me?

It wouldn't even help me sleep.

Damn the bitch.

183

FAIRLADYZ2006 WAITED ON THE TOKYO-BOUND PLATFORM. The Yokohama-bound side would have served as well, but the next train to Tokyo was an express. He shuffled his feet nervously. This was the last inbound express tonight. If he was going, a late train was best. He had caused enough trouble as it was, and this would leave them with plenty of time to get the trains back on schedule for the morning rush.

He heard the warning bells from the road crossing at the far end of the station. It was time.

There was a fence at the edge of the platform. He walked over to it and looked down at his car parked in the pay-by-hour lot shoehorned between the street and the station. She truly was a fair lady, with such graceful curves. He had never loved anything as much as her. Tears welled in his eyes. He shut them tight and shivered in the January darkness. As often as she had warmed his heart, tonight she wasn't enough.

He could see the gleam from the train's headlight. The station was on a curve, so he wouldn't be able to see the train itself until it was almost at the station.

He waited, watching the light grow brighter.

A recorded announcement told everyone to stand behind the yellow line on the platform as the express train passed.

There it was, moving fast.

He set a large manila envelope (wallet, keys, and a long yet too-brief note) on the platform.

There was a deafening blast from the train's horn as he climbed off the platform and took his place between the rails. Although his whole body was trembling, he stood facing the train to take it full on, with courage. He squinted, then opened his eyes wide with wonder at the tranquil fog of his last breath hanging luminous in the light that hurtled toward him: a brilliant, blinding whiteness, like one last dawn. It was the most blessed thing he had ever seen.

Song Three:
Blood on the Tracks Blues
三曲目：血濡れた線路のブルース

I was waiting, anguished, marking time, 'fore everybody knows.
I was waiting, crying, dreading when my momma even knows.
So I went down to the station, where that express train never slows.

Trembled frantic for a moment, when I saw that speeding light.
Felt to flee, a frantic moment, in that hurtling, screaming light.
Then it warmed like one last morning, slivered day before the night.

Left it all at that last station, where I spilt my blood like rain.
I kept nothing at that station, where my blood, it fell like rain.
Every bit of hope forgotten. How's each whit of shame remain?

Now what's it Heav'n's expecting? How's a shameful soul atone?
Even death has found me wanting, so how else can I atone?
Can't some kind soul quell this gleaming, give me night to hide, alone?

God, bless me with an evening, wicked brief, just like that dawn.
Tell me when will come the evening, heartbeat-short, like my last dawn?
As I wither in this shining, where's my blessed darkness gone?

Hear me pleading for another train, with crossing bells to toll.
Now I'm begging, send another train. My end, those bells will toll.
Use its wretched, burning brightness to obliterate my soul.

XII

First-Mover Advantage
ファースト・ムーバーズ・アドバンテージ

Wednesday, 20 January 2010

184

As David opened his eyes in the dark, it took him a moment to realize his phone was ringing.

"Hello? . . . *Moshi-moshi.*"

"*Sensei,* this is Itō."

"Hi, okay." The fog was thick this morning.

"I break the encryption!"

That cleared it. "You're into the files?"

"Yes! Come fast, *now*! I already call police headquarters. They are waiting. We go together to save Grames-*sensei.*"

Morning was still hours away when David pulled into the university. He found Itō talking with King at the main entrance. Itō's car was running, so David parked. King headed to his car while David trotted over to Itō's. As David buckled his seat belt, Itō punched the accelerator hard. David held on. "Let's get there alive, okay?"

"Alive is good." Itō glanced at David and smiled. "Fast is good too."

"Did King have something to do with this?"

"You did not see him."

"Fine. You were waiting alone. But the police sealed the storage room," said David.

"Police tape is easy to move."

"You know how much trouble you're in?"

"No trouble. They will like my results of work tonight," said Itō.

"You got into the files?"

"Yes. Disk has special encryption software, but King-*sensei*—remember, you did not see him and he did not help—he could guess the password."

"Wait, he's an accomplice?" asked David.

"What is 'accomplice'?"

"Someone who helps with a crime."

Itō accelerated on a long straight stretch. "He helped but did not know the crime. Malik was stupid and mistaked with steganography software, so he asked King to help. King gave him instruction and said, 'Use this password,' and Malik used it!"

"Thank our lucky stars for stupidity. What did you find?"

"AV files, thousands."

"Audio-visual?" asked David.

"Adult video."

"We're risking our lives racing to Nagano with porn?"

"No, students," said Itō.

"What, ours?"

"Woman students are nude in their rooms in the dormitory."

David turned his head and stared at Itō.

Itō glanced over and nodded. "Many thousands of files."

"How?"

"Looks like he hided camera into wireless AP. Many rooms."

"For how long?" asked David.

"Three years. Oldest files are from first year of wireless LAN."

"Serving it right out of the university. You think Ikenami found out?"

Itō braked hard. "I do not know how, but Ikenami-*sensei* suspect something bad. Malik killed him because he is coming too near."

David braced himself as they flew through a series of turns. When the road straightened again, he said, "You realize when you show these to the police, you'll lose your job."

"It is not my fault Malik did sick thing."

"No, but this scandal will end JGU. We all lose our jobs."

"Yes, I thought about that." Itō drove on for a few seconds before he asked with surprise, "We should be quiet?"

"No." David leaned back into the seat. "We should drive faster."

185

WHERE IS DETECTIVE HASEGAWA?" ASKED ITŌ AS HE plugged in the laptop.

"He comes soon," replied the officer who showed them to the room.

David came in carrying a portable video projector and a box. He set them on the table and asked, "What's in here?"

"Enclosure to mount hard disks."

"I thought you copied some files onto your laptop."

"No, I bring all the hard disks. We have all files." As he attached cables, he whispered to David, "I hope Grames-*sensei* did not confess."

Hasegawa appeared and said in Japanese, "He will."

Itō glanced up at him, then returned to connecting cables as he replied in Japanese, "Not when Malik is your killer."

"You have proof?"

Itō turned on the laptop and projector, looked Hasegawa in the eye, and said in Japanese, "Incontrovertible."

David said in English, "It would be appropriate for Will to see this."

Kurimoto, standing behind Hasegawa, translated, and Hasegawa turned to her with a frown. "I'm not bringing the suspect up here."

Before she could translate, Itō said in Japanese, "Excuse me, but I must agree with the professor. Believe me, you'll want his reaction."

Hasegawa looked at Itō, at the bright blue rectangle on the wall, and back at Itō. He told Kurimoto, "Bring him up—in cuffs."

Itō readied the laptop while Hasegawa and David took seats on opposite sides of the table.

Will entered a few minutes later looking haggard. David gave him a thumbs-up. Will didn't respond. He was about to sit next to Hasegawa, but the detective motioned to Kurimoto to seat him on the other side of the table, next to David.

Itō sat by the laptop and, with no introduction, announced, "This is why Malik murdered Ikenami-*sensei*." Itō double-clicked one of the filenames.

Everyone focused on the dorm room projected on the wall. Huong soon entered and locked the door behind herself. She dropped her bag on the desk and flopped on the bed. Nothing much happened for a minute. She merely lay there. When she started singing softly, a few of them chuckled. Soon the singing stopped, and Itō looked over at Hasegawa. He counted off the seconds to himself: one . . . two . . . three . . . and—

Hasegawa's eyes widened, he looked at Will, and Itō realized the detective had seated Will where he could watch him. Will stared at the scene, mouth open. His look of shock soon turned to horror, and by the time the moaning started, he had looked away.

Hasegawa motioned to Itō to kill the video. "How many files?"

"Thousands."

"Like this?"

"I cracked the encryption tonight. I have seen about thirty. Most were women undressing. Two were like this. One was students having sex."

"Malik did this?"

Itō nodded. "Yes. Bring a network specialist with you when you come to the university today and I can show what I know so far about how he set it up."

"How long has he been doing this?"

"I can't say for sure. Your people need to work through the files. It looks like he hid cameras in wireless APs in dorm rooms when we installed that network three years ago."

"When are the latest?" asked Hasegawa.

Itō clicked through the directories. "Five days ago."

"Two nights before the Vietnamese woman was killed. How are the files structured?"

"There is a separate directory for each room, forty-four in all."

"Find the one that goes with the murdered woman."

Itō clicked on directories and opened files for the next few minutes. He watched each video only long enough to identify the woman before he hurried to the next one, but still there were occasional gasps.

Finally, a bathroom door opened, steam came billowing out, and a few seconds later, Trinh stepped out, drying her hair with a towel, naked. Itō immediately closed the file.

Hasegawa nodded toward Will, and an officer stepped over and took off the handcuffs.

"Are there any more recent files?" asked Hasegawa.

"Not on this set of disks. Let me mount another set," said Itō.

Itō mounted disks and searched through the files for ten minutes. "These are newer. The other disks may be processed archive files, and these are raw recorded streams." He worked for another minute. "The latest are from last night."

"Find hers from three days ago, around midnight," said Hasegawa.

The names on the video capture directories matched the archive directories, so Itō didn't need to search. "This is a couple of hours before that." Itō opened the file. Huong was lying on the bed as Trinh stroked her hair. It was obvious Huong had been crying, but she looked peaceful now. After that was video of Huong sleeping on Trinh's bed.

Itō said, "This is Trinh Nguyen's room. You know the young woman on the bed, her friend, Huong Nguyen."

Hasegawa nodded.

Itō opened another directory. "This is from Huong's room."

The room was dark, but they could see a woman lying on the bed, facing the wall. Hasegawa said, "It looks like infrared. His setup was sophisticated."

Itō advanced the file in short increments. There was more of her sleeping. Then a man silently closed the door. He was wearing white gloves. He slipped a nylon stocking over his head. They watched him approach the bed. There was the sound of a mobile phone ringing. As she rolled onto her back and opened her eyes, they could see her face.

"Oh, God, no," moaned Will.

Itō blinked hard as he whispered to Hasegawa, "That is Trinh."

186

DAVID SAT WITH WILL IN A SMALL ROOM WHILE ITŌ CON-ferred with the police. The door to their room was open, and they could see uniformed officers in the larger room across the hall putting the hard disks into evidence bags.

David was glad, especially for Will's sake, that Hasegawa stopped the video when Trinh first awoke and ushered the JGU people out of the room. Kurimoto ran out in tears a couple of minutes later. When Hasegawa came out, eyes red, his rage barely contained, he screamed something in Japanese, and people started running around like a swarm of angry bees. Hasegawa led a group of heavily armed officers and Kurimoto to a convoy of five waiting cars. They screeched away, lights flashing.

Will leaned forward, his face in his hands. "What have I done?"

David put his hand on Will's back. "You've helped solve a murder."

"Or caused one. David, she just glowed."

David put his arm around him. "I know." His voice cracked. "I know."

As Will pulled himself together, David thought it best to get him talking, so he said, "At least they've got Malik."

"We hope. I suspect he's been at things like this a long time."

"He's got a first-mover advantage or something?"

"Not exactly. Besides, researchers have proven that's a myth."

David chuckled. "Always the teacher. I love that about you. Except for one panicked evening, you're amazingly consistent."

"You know, Malik may have planned for this eventuality."

"He is one cold-blooded bastard. It wouldn't surprise me if he's in the wind. I know for a fact that they took his passport, so he won't get far."

"I hope they fry him," said Will.

"Hanging would have to do, but they won't execute a UK citizen."

Itō appeared in the doorway. "We finish here for now. They want to talk to us more at the university, I think."

David gave Will a gentle pat on the back. "Time to go."

Itō shook his head. "No."

Will looked up.

"Peregrine-*sensei* and I go back now. Grames-*sensei* is still arrested."

David stood. "What for? What's the charge?"

"He hided the body," said Itō.

Will straightened.

"Don't worry, Will, we'll get you out of this," said David.

Will stood and looked at David. "Thanks, David, for all you've done and all you will do, but you won't get me out of this."

"Hey, Will, you can't give up hope on me now."

"I haven't. But this isn't going away. I did a terrible thing, and I got caught. Some troubles don't evaporate when the sun comes out; someone has to mop them up. Japan's justice system is giving me the mop."

"I will not see you locked up. It's *much* more likely, if you're convicted, they'll suspend the sentence and deport you."

Will looked down with a wry smile. "Just deportation."

"I can only imagine how that hurts, but assume nothing worse. Your lawyer arrives this morning, a criminal attorney, an excellent one."

Will tried to smile but couldn't pull it off. As David shook his hand, Will drew him close and whispered, "Tell Laurie I'm doing great. Nothing about what we saw. Just 'Will's doing great.'"

David whispered back, "What else would I say?"

187

HASEGAWA CHECKED HIS WATCH: 5:49 A.M. "FASTER."

The officer driving said, "Sir, the other cars are already falling behind."

Hasegawa's voice was deep and angry. "I said faster."

The radio crackled to life.

"Detective Hasegawa, we have an urgent call from Yokohama police headquarters."

"Patch it through."

He turned around to Kurimoto in the back seat. She wore a "what more could there be?" look.

He heard the call connect. "This is Hasegawa."

"My name is Igarashi. Kanagawa Prefectural Police. I'm sorry to tell you we have evidence of a crime in your jurisdiction."

"Go on."

"A fellow faced off against a train in Yokohama yesterday evening. He left a long, rambling suicide note. It said something about him killing a Vietnamese girl, but it was the wrong girl, she wasn't supposed to be there, he didn't mean to kill her, how sorry he is. It seems he was a subscriber to a voyeur service run out of a university up there."

"We're on our way to make an arrest."

"We've recovered messages. He offered a large sum of money to the webmaster of this site for help in raping a woman. We have a message from the webmaster saying no, then yes, then telling him where to pick up a key to her room."

Hasegawa said, "We have the rape and murder on video."

Igarashi didn't immediately answer. "That is the sickest thing I've ever heard. I thought all the psychopaths lived here. Anyway, you're about to arrest someone?"

Hasegawa braced himself as they screamed around a corner. "Five minutes."

188

MALIK STOOD ATOP THE REAR SUPERSTRUCTURE OF THE container ship, his back to the frigid wind, and watched the last lights of the Japanese mainland disappear over the horizon. There was nothing left but water in the growing light of dawn, so he returned to the warmth of his cabin.

Lying down, he felt the gentle sway of the ship, the deep hum of the engine. He drummed his fingers on the side of his berth.

He got up and looked out the small window. If not for the Izu Islands, he would already be in international waters, but that safety was at least six hours away. If he made it that far, they would never get him. It was not a Japanese cargo line, so there was no worry about them turning back at the request of Japanese immigration.

He pulled his passport out of his pocket. When they released him, the police surely notified immigration. Idiots. He imagined them screaming at each other when their mistake dawned on them. They'd make frantic phone calls, scheming for any way to stop him from reaching Singapore eight days from now and Port Klang in Malaysia the next day, all to no avail.

How could they have known how thoroughly outmatched they were in this war of wits? As he chuckled, he ran his thumb over the crest embossed on the red cover: PASPORT MALAYSIA. He opened it and looked at his picture and then at his name: Tengku Malik Bin Muhriz. Royalty. He smiled. Changing his name to Teddy Malik had only been for the UK. It hadn't been a bad name either. It was easier to pronounce and stopped the constant questions about his "last name"— he was Malay, he didn't have one. He decided on the name of Britain's wartime King Edward, but then, on a lark, chose its nickname version, "Teddy." Besides, it was also the last of the Kennedy brothers, as close as you could come to royalty in America. When the immigration officer at the port in Yokohama asked why there was no Japanese entry stamp in his passport, Malik simply acted stupid. After all, immigration's job is keeping people out, not in. Why stop a poor-looking fellow from boarding as a passenger on a cargo ship? As boarding time neared, they waved him through.

He looked again at his tiny cabin. Nine days. No internet. He might as well be in prison.

Malik threw his head back and laughed out loud.

Epilogue:
Double-Entry Bookkeeping
結末：複式簿記

189

WILL HELD A COLD BOTTLE OF WATER TO HIS FACE AND handed one to Laurie. "I thought the northeast was supposed to be cool."

She wiped her forehead with her sleeve. "Wait till winter."

Will smiled. "It'll take that long to unpack. Then, in a year, we'll have to move all over again."

"It could be a two-year visit, right? And somebody's retiring?"

"Yeah, but . . ."

"Will, don't sell yourself short. Do good research with people here and they'll want to keep you. The Japan mess gets forgotten." She took another drink. "Oh, and win a teaching award."

Will laughed. "A permanent position here is a real long shot."

"Just don't carry Japan around like a lead weight."

"I was thinking more of a scarlet letter."

"Oh yeah? I don't see one." She lifted his T-shirt and caressed his chest. "None here either. Should I keep looking?"

"You don't know what letter you're looking for."

"*E.*"

"For what?"

"Employed."

"Not *C* for convicted or *D* for deported?"

Laurie furrowed her brow. "Why do you say things like that?"

Will sat on the floor, leaned against the pile of moving boxes, and stared at his water bottle. "I can't shake feeling . . . tainted."

Laurie sat next to him and took his hand. "There's no *M*, because you didn't murder anybody. No *I*, you weren't incarcerated. And David's prediction was right: once Ikenami's family found out, their grief was for his murder, and their hate was for Malik."

"Trinh might not have—"

"Don't do that. That subscriber killed her. It had nothing to do with Ikenami."

"I know. I get it—in my head—but it doesn't stop what I feel."

Laurie rested her head on his shoulder.

Will said, "It's as if I have a giant red stain that's never coming out."

"Everybody's got some big, nasty mark. The ones that seem fine are better at hiding it, that's all. People get through it. We will. If there's a stain, it's on us both. We'll carry the guilt together."

Will put his arms around her.

They sat for a minute before Will said, "Still . . ."

"What?"

"I wish they hadn't lost Malik."

Laurie kissed him. "I'm just glad I didn't lose you."

190

King slipped out, telling no one. What were the chances that the company's LAN would crash in the twenty minutes he'd be at Starbucks with his new private detective? Work as a system administrator wasn't what King had hoped for when JGU let almost all the faculty go. But you take what you can get—especially when returning to America meant forgetting any chance of recovering a dime from Rumi.

The detective came through the door and saw him. King pointed to two open chairs, took one, and waited, tapping his cup on the table. When the detective joined him, King was direct. "You found something?"

"Yes, someone checks for me. Rumi, your wife, has not left Japan."

"We assumed that. What else?"

"Her sister had trunk room. I think is where your wife keeps things before run away."

"And now?"

The detective frowned. "Everything is gone."

King scowled out the window.

"To locate her maybe takes time. She has no trail."

King didn't move.

"Why find her? Divorce and forget her is simple and cheaper."

King gazed at the detective. "I promised to redecorate her place."

191

A HISTORICAL NOVEL SAT IN SATŌ'S LAP AS HE STARED OUT the window. He kept having to reread, unable to remember who the characters were, and it made him angry.

He was always angry these days, justifiably. What JGU had done to him was unconscionable. Malik was running his business before Satō ever started at the university. Yoshida was the one to blame. He was Malik's immediate supervisor; or the previous president, blind when it all began; or that IT manager, whatever his name was, who let it happen right under his nose. But Satō was president when the police discovered it, and the television news wanted a person's name, not merely the university's. So Satō had to bow and apologize to Ikenami's family. Satō had to grovel when they apologized to the education ministry. Satō even had to own the shame and apologize to the students! So what if some men saw a few of them naked? The girls were almost all foreigners!

Of course, the chairman of JGU's board of trustees, all money and connections, got through it unscathed. His name never appeared in the news. In fact, the same day that police swarmed the campus, they erased any mention of the board from the JGU website. Only Satō paid a price.

He had to endure interminable interrogations for having pushed the police to investigate Yoshida. The worst was Yoshida ending up at a national university, his offer in hand before the scandal ever broke. He claimed he had seen the writing on the wall, but Satō never heard a satisfactory answer as to how the idiot Malik could have done it alone. Yoshida, with his expensive clothes and foreign vacations: the money had to have come from somewhere. While Yoshida had to go along when the senior administrators made their rounds of humiliation, he was just one in the line that bowed behind Satō. Only Satō was named.

Fine. They couldn't shoulder their responsibility? Someone stronger had to carry their load? Let it be me, the one honorable man—

"You! Where's that book I told you to buy for me yesterday?" yelled his wife from the living room.

He gritted his teeth.

"You! Answer, brainless dolt! Or be dead in there, one or the other! Preferably dead!"

Satō studied the cracks in the dirty concrete wall that stood a meter outside his sliver of a window, blocking out all sunlight, his tiny room's permanent eclipse.

He shut his eyes tight. It should have been his own private retirement house. It should have been Lake Biwa.

192

HASEGAWA'S EYES WERE CLOSED AS KURIMOTO DROVE. SHE was pleased that he was so much calmer since he quit smoking. Anyway, she interrupted his reverie. "I saw the final report from immigration on the JGU murders."

"They haven't given up, but they have no way to get him."

"Diplomatic channels are still working on it."

Hasegawa kept his eyes shut. "Malik has money. Someone will always be willing to shelter him."

"We had his passport, sir. There was no reason to believe—"

"There was every reason to believe he was guilty of something. To let him go was the stupidest—"

"Most reversible of mistakes—except that he had a second passport, and immigration let him out of the country. It wasn't even our call," said Kurimoto.

Hasegawa scowled. "You're making excuses for me now?"

"Only for myself, sir."

Hasegawa looked at her with . . . concern? She smiled reassuringly.

193

YAWNING, MALIK CAME BACK FROM THE BATHROOM AND stared at the girl asleep in his bed. Why were they always more alluring the night before? The nights were what mattered, though—unless, like a fool, you fell in love.

He lifted the sheet to give her a sober, daylight appraisal. She was an eight last night, but now . . . a six? Next time, it might be worth it to get one who would still tempt him in the morning.

He stepped over to her few clothes and fished her purse out from underneath. He opened her wallet. No identification, just a bus pass and the two hundred ringgits—about sixty dollars—he'd given her. He'd take fifty ringgits back, but she was sure to double-check before she left. Besides, every girl worked for someone; he did not need that kind of enemy. A city the size of Malacca hardly had an inexhaustible supply of girls. If one unhappy girl told others, he could end up having nothing available but drug addicts and old women.

Should he have settled in Kuala Lumpur? There was certainly more to do. It was only a couple of hours away, though, and Malacca was cheaper. He wasn't short of funds. With his inheritance and all he'd stashed away while in Japan, he need never work again. He was even considering local investments. And Malacca was like home. He had not grown up here, but this was where his father had made his fortune developing tourism properties. So the local government was not hostile, despite repeated police inquiries from Japan's extradition demands. The legal wrangling was a mere irritant. His connections would give ample warning if the case ever gained traction. Then he could disappear.

He was determined to make Malacca the balance point of his life. He was already evening the scales, jettisoning his remorse for having lost, partly by his own carelessness, his richly satisfying life in Japan. Malacca was a beginning, and he wouldn't fall prey to the same mistakes. From now on, less risk, more reward. No one would catch him again.

He looked at the girl. She was so drunk last night she nearly passed out. She was sound asleep now, but he had to hurry; it was afternoon and she would wake soon. He inspected her bag, checking the seams, inside and outside. She must have emergency money or a place to hide what she skimmed off the top. No girl would give everything to her pimp. Malik examined everything: a novel (she could read?), sunglasses in a slip-in case, makeup containers, lotion, tissues, condoms (scads of them), two pairs of panties—and found nothing.

He checked her clothes. He would have guessed her bra as the hiding place, but she didn't have one. Her T-shirt was too thin to hide anything. Her shorts were so small that—

There it was, in the fold of fabric that formed the backing for the zipper. The hole in the seam was small, but he got a finger in. He pulled out a tiny silk bag with four bills: two fifties, a twenty, and a ten. She'd been a busy girl. Never pay full price when you can simply steal it—or part of it, anyway. Malik replaced one fifty with a twenty and pushed the little bag back into place. A discount. That was better.

194

DAVID WAS GAZING OUT HIS OFFICE WINDOW AT THE SUMmer green that swathed the university, when he heard a knock on his open door.

"Getting everything packed up?" asked Anson.

David returned to the box he was filling with books. "I'm supposed to be out day after tomorrow."

"Headed to a law firm in Tokyo, I heard."

"Yup, but they say Japanese legal education is moving toward the western model. I might try for a faculty position at a law school in Tokyo at some point. When do you start looking?"

Anson leisurely put his hands in his pockets. "I'll send my vitae out this fall. It'll be a busy year as the lone finance professor in this skeleton faculty."

"I'm still surprised they didn't shutter the university, but I guess they felt a duty to the first-years to let them finish their degrees."

"Closing would have made more sense, the way the sponsors headed for the hills. Students too. Only half are coming back. JGU was going bankrupt anyway, but it's a ghastly way to end."

"Most of the staff are locals, don't want to leave the area, and are still out of work, but I heard all the faculty found positions, except Watanabe, wherever he is." David closed and taped the box. "I'm especially glad for Will."

"Me too. It worried me."

David started on another box. "Hey, I've been meaning to ask your opinion. A friend gave me a quote from an ancient Buddhist monk named Shinran: 'Even the innocent can gain salvation; how much more so the guilty.' I've asked a few people what they thought it meant, but nobody's had much of an answer."

"It sounds like what Christ said, 'They that are whole have no need of the physician, but they that are sick: I came not to call the righteous, but sinners to repentance.' Heaven's work is salvation more than judgment."

David stopped what he was doing. "That's the best answer yet."

Anson handed David books, and they filled the next box in silence.

Anson spoke without looking at David. "I had to come forward. You know that. I was wrong not to warn you. I just . . . I was too afraid that faced with you and Will asking me not to talk, I wouldn't be able to follow through. When Danny told me about Malik falling into the trap of circumstantial evidence—Danny was so gleeful—but it wasn't enough, wasn't proof, that smoking gun I needed, and I knew I couldn't stay quiet." Anson bowed his head. "When it came out about Malik's website, I was horrified."

"You were in an awful position, Anson. Will and I understood that. You didn't handle it as I did, but I was acting as legal counsel. You were the one person in all this who just straight-up did the proper, lawful thing."

"That may be, but Malik got away, and Will got deported; none of that would've happened if I'd stayed quiet one more day. I've wondered whether I got the answer to that prayer wrong, whether I was selfish, refusing the secret and everything that went with it."

"'Everything' being the legal consequences or the guilt?"

"Both, I guess," said Anson.

"You did what you had to do. You shouldn't have any regrets. I should've counseled Will to come forward at the start—or at least had him anonymously tell where the body was." David sealed the box, put down the tape, and leaned on the bookshelves. "Guilt's weird, isn't it?"

"How do you mean?"

"Doesn't it strike you as an awfully ineffective punishment? I mean, if I were God, I wouldn't be at all satisfied. Look at Will, a good guy—"

"Better than good."

"Indeed," said David. "He gets scared, does a bad thing, and the guilt . . . he was disintegrating. He's back on his feet now, but who knows how long it'll dog him. Yet Malik, who sold those women's most private moments, even got one killed—after murdering Ikenami in cold blood—likely feels nothing."

Anson nodded.

"Isn't it backward? Guilt punishes good people, not bad ones. It's more evidence there's no one up there."

Anson looked into David's eyes and said in an earnest voice, "In the end, God's justice is perfect, the blessings and punishments coming in this life or after. Guilt isn't the punishment; it's a prompting—if we're not past feeling it—to change, to be better, and with that, we're ransomed. Even the worst can be forgiven, just as in your quote, and the guilt disappears."

"So the books balance—by definition—double-entry bookkeeping, debits and credits, neat, internally consistent." David gave Anson a wry smile. "And a total fairy tale."

Anson smiled in return. "Not for me."

"After next year here, then what? You staying in Japan?"

"Not sure. Miho's been saying what an adventure America would be." Anson watched David grab another box and get ready to tape it. "So . . . is Matsuyama-*san* going with you?"

David looked up in surprise.

"Miho sensed it, not me."

David couldn't hide his smile. "I haven't asked her yet, but I'm hoping. I'm not sure she's up for it."

"Ask her."

"You think?"

"I do."

195

Lulled by the hum of the Shinkansen rails, Huong closed her eyes. Did going back to JGU make any sense? A degree from a scandal-ridden defunct university would hardly help her resume; though back home, few would know the school was nothing but ghosts.

She had been in touch with the other JICA students. Most were coming back. It was a free degree, after all. She had even saved money the first year and might save more this year. Still, it wouldn't be what she could have made at a good job in Vietnam.

A cheapened diploma, a meager allowance . . .

Was she doing it for Trinh?

Huong shut her eyes tighter.

I shouldn't be coming back. I was supposed to have died.

Every day since they dug Trinh's body out of the snow, Huong had wished it was her instead.

She searched for the handkerchief in her bag, the sun shining brightly on her lap as lush golden green rice fields flew past the window. Maybe someday she'd be thankful she'd been spared. Whether or not that day came, she would honor Trinh with the life Trinh would have led. The decisions would be her own, but she would live with Trinh's strength and perseverance, with her virtue and charity.

And she would learn to swim. She would learn to swim *fast*.

Huong shut her eyes again and pressed the handkerchief to her face with both hands.

196

THE EQUATORIAL AIR WAS SO THICK, WATANABE FELT AS IF he should be drinking it. Entering the hotel lobby, he stopped, closed his eyes, and savored the miracle of air-conditioning. The gods in heaven loved humanity—the rich ones, anyway.

He opened his eyes and saw the bellhop waiting at the front desk. Watanabe caught up, gave his name, and showed his passport and credit card.

"Welcome to Kuala Lumpur, Doctor Watanabe. We have been expecting you. You are staying with us for two nights?"

"Yes, a brief trip."

The young woman smiled charmingly. "I hope it is a success."

Soon Watanabe was upstairs, and the bellhop was bowing and wishing him a pleasant stay.

Watanabe pulled a Coke out of the mini fridge and popped off the bottle cap. Then he stripped off his shirt and found the air-conditioning vent. From that blessed spot, he looked out at the city in the bright sunshine.

While this trip was, in a way, a vacation, the deeper pleasure was in his dark mission. Stepping out of the cool breeze, Watanabe opened his suitcase, took out his shirts, and picked up the small black bag they protected. He sat on the bed, unzipped the bag, and looked over the contents. Although they seemed to be intact, he took out each insulin vial and syringe for closer examination. Everything was in perfect order.

All he needed now were directions to Malacca.

Song Four: The Reaper's Knife
四曲目：刈り取る者の刃

Spy them afar, through the coming eve,
Faithful while there's light to see,
Gathering armfuls, bound in sheaves, to wait the thresher's floor.
But see their fingers, don't ignore, they take single stalks with care.
Some ripe, but then you cry, too many bare.

And slicing true, the reaper's knife
Cuts short another meager life,
And though it ends that soul's cruel strife, hear him cry that he wants more,
Searching, frantic, for a door to escape the blinding light,
Till forsaking warmth, he flees into the night.

Eternity, a quantum dot,
Remembering every idle thought,
Reliving all in life he'd wrought concurrently as one,
Every wounding lie he'd spun, the innocence he'd torn,
As ghastly stains in blood his skirts adorn.

Each mortal day he'd chosen this,
Full years one breath from black abyss,
Having never offered one true kiss, nor compassed love's pure grace,
Drunk with thrill as he debased, yet more numb with each caress,
Till hands burned raw now weep with his excess.

Full dark, he huddles, sopped in fear,
Wishing he could feel the tears,
Wondering how the light still sears, though he hasn't any eyes.
Will the light betray his lies, or can circumstance be blamed
As he stands, head high, and swears he feels no shame?

Abbreviations

AP: (wireless LAN/Wi-Fi) access point

AWOL: absent without leave

BTW: by the way

CEO: chief executive officer

DNS: Domain Name System

IP: Internet Protocol

ISP: internet service provider

IT: information technology

JGU: Japan Graduate University of International Studies

JICA: Japan International Cooperation Agency

LAN: local area network

MBA: Master of Business Administration

MPA: Master of Public Administration

NGO: nongovernmental organization

NSA: National Security Agency

PC: personal computer

PhD: Doctor of Philosophy

RAID: redundant array of independent disks

UK: United Kingdom

US: United States of America

VLAN: virtual local area network

Japanese Words and Phrases

Novel, Chapter, and Song Titles

Neyuki　根雪　base snow that remains for the entire winter

Zensetsu: kigyō seisa　前説：企業精査　prologue: due diligence

1　*Gentei-gōrisei*　限定合理性　bounded rationality

2　*Moraru hazādo*　モラル・ハザード　moral hazard

3　*Rufu*　流布　word of mouth

4　*Māketingu: shōhisha kachi no sōzō*　マーケティング：消費者価値の創造　marketing: consumer value creation

5　*Seiyaku-tsuki saitekika*　制約付き最適化　constrained optimization

6　*Risutora*　リストラ　restructuring

Ik-kyoku-me: aisatsu　一曲目：挨拶　song one: greeting

7　*Ninchi-teki fukyōwa*　認知的不協和　cognitive dissonance

8　*Hazādo moderu*　ハザード・モデル　hazard model(s)

Ni-kyoku-me: yasuraka ni　二曲目：安らかに　song two: peacefully

9　*Riaru opushon*　リアル・オプション　real option(s)

10　*Tōshi-rieki-ritsu*　投資利益率　rate of return on investment

11　*Jiyūdo*　自由度　degrees of freedom

San-kyoku-me: chi nureta senro no burūsu　三曲目：血濡れた線路のブルース　song three: (railroad) tracks wet with blood blues

12　*Fāsuto mūbāzu adobantēji*　ファースト・ムーバーズ・アドバンテージ　first-mover's advantage

Ketsumatsu: fukushikiboki　結末：複式簿記　epilogue: double-entry bookkeeping

Yon-kyoku-me: kiri-toru mono no ha　四曲目：刈り取る者の刃　song four: reaper's blade

Names of Japanese Characters and JGU

Hasegawa Yūji 長谷川雄二 Police Detective

Hiroyuki 博之 Child who finds Ikenami's phone

Igarashi 五十嵐 Kanagawa Prefectural Police Official

Ikenami Kiyoshi 池波澄 Professor of Accounting

Ikenami Yōko 池波陽子 Wife of Kiyoshi Ikenami

Itō Makoto 伊藤実 Manager, IT Services

Kingu Rumi キング瑠美 Rumi King, Wife of Steve King

Kukku Miho クック美穂 Miho Cook, Wife of Anson Cook

Kurimoto Yoshie 栗本佳江 Police Translator and IT Specialist

Matsuyama Chieko 松山千恵子 Assistant to Dean Yoshida

Ogawa 小川 Police Forensic Specialist

Satō Shinichi 佐藤真一 President, JGU

Watanabe Jirō 渡辺次郎 Assistant Professor of Accounting

Yoshida Junichirō 吉田純一郎 Dean, JGU

Yuriko 由里子 Assistant to President Satō

Nihon Kokusai Daigakuin Daigaku 日本国際大学院大学 Japan
Graduate University of International Studies (JGU)

Words and Phrases

"Ai-ko desho!" 「あいこでしょ!」 called out when playing *janken*
after players have tied by showing the same sign

"A! Nihongo umai desu ne!" 「あっ!日本語上手いですね!」 "Oh!
Your Japanese is excellent!"

dōzo どうぞ please, by all means, come in, go ahead

dōzo o-hairi-kudasai どうぞお入り下さい please come in

fukigen 不機嫌 ill-tempered, cross, sullen

futon 布団 mattress filled with cotton batting, placed on the floor
as a bed

gaijin (*gaikokujin*) 外人 (外国人) foreigner

genkan 玄関 entryway (generally one step below floor level)
where shoes are removed

gomen kudasai　ごめんください　excuse me (called out to alert the residents or employees to one's presence when entering a home or business)

"Hai, nanika go-yō desu ka?"　「はい、何か御用ですか?」　"Yes? May I help you?"

hijōshiki　非常識　absurd, unreasonable, thoughtless, lacking common sense

"Ikken kage ni hoyureba hyakken koe ni hoyu"　「一犬影に吠ゆれば百犬声に吠ゆ」　"When one dog barks, all the dogs bark"

irasshaimase　いらっしゃいませ　welcome (commonly called out by store personnel when a customer enters)

"Iya, sō de mo arimasen"　「いや、そうでもありません」　"No, not really"

janken　じゃんけん　(the game of) rock-paper-scissors

"Jan, ken, pon!"　「じゃん、けん、ぽん!」　called out when playing *janken* as players prepare to show their first signs

kanji　漢字　Chinese characters (about two thousand are commonly used in written Japanese)

karate　空手　karate

ki-muzukashii　気難しい　difficult, ill-tempered, crabby, sullen

"Kōkōsei dorama nanka iya."　「高校生ドラマなんかいや。」　"I hate high school dramas."

konnichi wa　こんにちは　hello, good afternoon

kura (kamakura)　くら　（かまくら）　snow hut

maemuki　前向き　positive, constructive, forward looking, forward facing

mamushi　蝮　（まむし）　viper

mikan　蜜柑　（みかん）　mandarin orange

"Mi ni iku?"　「見に行く?」　"Will you go watch?"

moshi-moshi　もしもし　hello (used only when answering the telephone)

neyuki　根雪　base snow that remains for the entire winter

ohayō　おはよう　good morning (informal)

ohayō gozaimasu　おはようございます　good morning

o-kaeri-nasai　お帰りなさい　welcome back

onsen　温泉　hot spring, spa

-san　さん　polite title, equivalent to Ms., Mr., Mrs., Miss

sensei (-sensei)　先生　professor, doctor, teacher

seppuku　切腹　suicide by ritual disembowelment

Shinkansen　新幹線　high-speed "bullet" train

shōji　障子　sliding door or screen with a wooden lattice covered
　　on one side with *washi,* generally white

suppon　鼈　（すっぽん）　soft-shelled turtle

susuki　薄　Japanese pampas grass

tadaima　ただいま　I'm home

tatami　畳　mat (90x180 centimeters) used for flooring, covered in
　　woven rushes

tōfu　豆腐　bean curd

Toire-no-Hanako　トイレの花子　a common tale of a girl named
　　Hanako who haunts a school restroom

washi　和紙　Japanese paper

yakuza　やくざ　Japanese mafia

yōchien　幼稚園　kindergarten, nursery school

yoroshiku o-negai-shimasu　よろしくお願いします　I look forward to
　　working with you; I appreciate your help; Please think kindly of
　　me; Please treat me kindly

"Zennin naomote ōjō o togu iwan ya akunin o ya."　「善人尚もて往生
　　をとぐいわんや悪人をや。」　"Even a virtuous person can attain
　　salvation; how much more so an evil one."

Acknowledgments

I WISH TO THANK MY WIFE, WHO PROVIDED ENCOURAGEMENT from start to finish. She was my first and last editor throughout the writing process. My children also urged me on through my doubts. Keiko Homma read an early draft, and her help in all things Japanese was invaluable. Chikako Hiura also answered myriad questions. Trung Hong consulted on Vietnamese names. Fran Lebowitz helped me shorten and tighten the manuscript, and Victoria Flickinger copyedited it. More writing and editing followed those edits, so don't blame them if you didn't like the prose. Any remaining errors are all mine. Laura Duffy designed the cover. Marny Parkin did the book design. Friends and family read drafts and gave me wonderfully useful feedback. Adam Brinton was my guide on IT content. He was full of ideas and helped me fix things when they got muddled. Members of Tokyo Writers Workshop provided feedback on early chapters, and members of the Oquirrh Writers chapter of the League of Utah Writers critiqued chapters much more recently.

For more from M. Harmon Wilkinson,
visit www.mharmonwilkinson.com

9 781954 362055